STEALTH INSURGENCE

VIKKI KESTELL

NANOSTEALTH | BOOK 5

Faith-Filled Fiction™

www.faith-filledfiction.com | www.vikkikestell.com

STEALTH INSURGENCE

Nanostealth | Book 5
Vikki Kestell
Also Available in eBook Format

BOOKS BY VIKKI KESTELL

NANOSTEALTH

Book 1: *Stealthy Steps*
Book 2: *Stealth Power*
Book 3: *Stealth Retribution*
Book 4: *Deep State Stealth*, 2019 Selah Award Winner
Book 5: *Stealth Insurgence*
Book 6: *Stealth Triumph*
Stealth Genesis, a Nanostealth Prequel

A PRAIRIE HERITAGE

Book 1: *A Rose Blooms Twice*
Book 2: *Wild Heart on the Prairie*
Book 3: *Joy on This Mountain*
Book 4: *The Captive Within*
Book 5: *Stolen*
Book 6: *Lost Are Found*
Book 7: *All God's Promises*
Book 8: *The Heart of Joy—A Short Story*
Book 9: *Rose of RiverBend*

GIRLS FROM THE MOUNTAIN

Book 1: *Tabitha*
Book 2: *Tory*
Book 3: *Sarah Redeemed*

LAYNIE PORTLAND

Book 1: *Laynie Portland, Spy Rising*
Book 2: *Laynie Portland, Retired Spy*
Book 3: *Laynie Portland, Renegade Spy*
Book 4: *Laynie Portland, Spy Resurrected*
Book 5: *Vyper, A Laynie Portland Sequel*

THE TAHOE MYSTERIES

Book 1: *Number 1 with a Bullet*
Book 2: *Be Quick or be Dead*
Book 3: *Death on the Big Blue*, 2026
Murder by Accident,
   A Miss Finch Prequel

STAND-ALONE BOOKS

I Can't Hear You,
   A Christian Psychological Thriller
The Christian and the Vampire,
   A Short Story

STEALTH INSURGENCE

Nanostealth | Book 5
Vikki Kestell
Also Available in eBook Format

JAYDA AND ZANDER LEAVE Washington, DC, and return to Albuquerque, satisfied that they have completed their mission for President Jackson. They are bursting with joy for the unborn child Jayda carries and are keen to share the news of their blessing with those they love: Abe, Emilio, Zander's parents, his sister, Izzie, and Dr. Bickel.

The couple can finally let down their guard: No enemies stalk them and no plots to overthrow the nation peer at them from beyond the horizon. They relax into a normal life—as "normal" as life with the nanomites can be—finding work, making a home, renewing relationships with their church family at Downtown Christian Center, growing in their faith, spending time with family, and looking forward to the birth of their child around the first week of April.

Their "normal" life doesn't last long.

The nanomites—ever vigilant and alert to the virtual world—become increasingly uneasy. They are unable to "put their fingers on" the source of their agitation, but whatever is happening? It is happening globally.

And the nanomites repeatedly tell Jayda and Zander, *Jesus has told us to protect you and the child. He says you have important work ahead of you. It is our job to watch over and safeguard your family.*

What is the "important work" Jesus wants of Jayda and Zander? Why has Jesus spoken to the nanomites about this work, but not to them? And why are the nanomites increasingly alarmed for their safety?

⌘⌘⌘⌘

SCRIPTURE QUOTATIONS

The New International Version (NIV)
The HOLY BIBLE,
NEW INTERNATIONAL VERSION®.
Copyright ©1973, 1978, 1984
International Bible Society.
Used by permission of Zondervan.
All rights reserved.

New King James Version® (NKJV)
Copyright ©1982 by Thomas Nelson.
Used by permission. All rights reserved.

The King James Version (KJV)
Public Domain.

***Holy Bible*, New Living Translation (NLT)**
Copyright © 1996, 2004, 2015
Tyndale House Foundation.
Used by permission. All rights reserved.

DEDICATION

To the persecuted church in Christ:
"To him who overcomes
I will grant to sit with Me on My throne,
as I also overcame and sat down
with My Father on His throne."
Revelation 3:21, NKJV

ACKNOWLEDGEMENTS

My most grateful thanks
to my faithful team,
Cheryl Adkins and **Greg McCann**.
I am honored to call you
my fellow ministers in Christ.
I love and value both of you.
Our *gestalt* is powerful!

HYMN

All Hail the Power of Jesus' Name

Lyrics, Edward Perronet, 1780
Tune, "Coronation,"
Oliver Holden, 1793
Public Domain

COVER DESIGN

Vikki Kestell

PROLOGUE

This book is a work of fiction.
Say it aloud with me:
"This book is a work of fiction."
Repeat the above statement often
while reading this book.

JULY WAS AT ITS SWELTERING midpoint before Zander and I were convinced that the threat against the President (and us) was over and done. We had promised Emilio we would come home as soon as our mission was complete, so we figured two more weeks should do it. Two weeks to tie up loose ends, pack, and go.

We assumed we'd hit the road before the end of the month. But, as plans often work out, packing up our lives in Maryland and heading for New Mexico took a lot longer than we expected.

Yes, we, the two nanoclouds, a number of short-term single-purpose nanobot "arrays," plus indispensable help from Gamble, Trujillo, Malware, Inc., and two NSA contractor employees who, we discovered, were actually covert FBI agents, had accomplished the tasks the President had assigned to us: We uncovered the fate of President Jackson's missing friend, Wayne Overman. Then we identified Mr. Overman's killers, tricked them into moving his remains, and arranged for the FBI to catch them in the act—thus giving his family and their friends the justice and closure they needed.

We unmasked the traitors behind the attempts to overthrow the Jackson administration—the same individuals who had been behind former Vice President Harmon's attempt to assassinate President Jackson and behind General Cushing's relentless pursuit of the nanomites, *ergo* me.

We finally comprehended how deep and broad had been the plot to steal Dr. Bickel's work and how desperate the mastermind and her top collaborators had been to find me after Dr. Bickel sent the nanomites into me to hide them.

Or had he sent them to hide *me*?

That point had never been explained to my satisfaction.

We had not, however, been able to prevent a second assassination attempt on President Jackson. Although the President did survive, Zander and I take no credit for that, nor do the nanomites. How could we? The Lord himself had miraculously intervened to save the President from the lethal biotoxin cocktail Vice President Delancey had sprayed directly into President Jackson's face.

The best medical facilities, physicians, and treatments available could not have saved the President, but God could—*and did*—just as he miraculously rescued Zander and me from a most ingenious trap, one devised to force the nanomites out of us and into a healthy host.

Despite the trap's foolproof design, the nanomites were strongly averse to cooperating with its intended outcome. They hadn't wanted to break the special bond we shared any more than we had. And as far as we knew (up until then) nothing could compel them to leave us—which was a good thing. Because if they *were* to detach themselves from our bodies' cellular structures, Zander and I would die in the process.

But, as I said, the trap was both ingenious and foolproof.

It worked like this: Zander and I were coerced into a specially built cage. The nanomites explained the cage's construction and how its cleverly fabricated walls allowed no electricity to pass in or out of it.

Walls of electrostatic dissipative acrylic, Jayda Cruz, encasing a cage of electromagnetic shielding. A sophisticated Faraday cage.

A Faraday cage protects people and equipment from electric discharge or current. Its conductive material diverts current around the *outside* of the enclosed space, allowing none of the electricity to enter or pass through the interior. However, the nanomites required regular electrical access to power their tribes and the nanocloud. "No electricity in" meant the nanomites were cut off from their usual sources of power.

You'd think lasering through the cage would be a snap for the nanomites, right? Except our cage possessed a second layer, a field of fluctuating electrostatic discharge running *around* its acrylic exterior. According to the nanomites, many of their members had tried to penetrate the cage walls, had attempted to reach outside the cage and shut down its functions.

None of those members returned.

The nanomites could not escape the cage without being "zapped" by the electrostatic discharge surrounding its walls—zapped like when Colonel Greaves shot me with a Taser, destroying billions of nanomites and decimating the nanocloud.

Bottom line? The nanomites were trapped with us inside the cage. They had no ready flow of electricity to feed them, yet their programming required them to survive. Only one source of power remained open to the nanomites.

Zander and me.

Well, that was the beauty of the trap's design, because if the nanomites were denied "juice" for too long, their survival protocols kicked in, the primary one being *survive*—by any means necessary.

To increase their odds of survival in a dire situation, the nanomites' programming obliged them to reduce power consumption until an adequate, steady source was again available. With the exception of Alpha Tribe, mite by mite and tribe by tribe, our two nanoclouds entered a "dormant mode" akin to sleep, thus reducing both nanoclouds' overall energy need.

But, even in that low-consumption mode, the nanoclouds still required energy to maintain Alpha Tribe. They could use us, Zander and me, and draw electricity from our bodies for a time, but not forever—that being precisely the trap's aim.

Because if, as more time passed, Alpha Tribe could no longer access the electricity they needed, the nanoclouds would devolve into a critical state: The quiescent mites would begin to expire in their sleep. The mites that were awake—those charged to safeguard the nanomites' experiences and vast knowledge library and responsible to awaken the other tribes when electrical current became available—would function as long as they could. As long as they had power. Eventually, though, they too would begin to drain away, like a battery at the end of its life, until no charge remained and they expired.

As I said, nothing could compel the nanomites to leave us of their own accord. They would not willingly comply with the trap's intent. But what if Zander and I could no longer support their needs because we were fully drained? Say, if we were *dead*—or as good as?

If we could not supply the nanomites' power needs, then the nanoclouds, too, would die, and nothing in this world could bring them back.

Unless.

Unless, at that critical juncture, other power sources became available—for instance, two healthy individuals determined to possess the nanoclouds and their near-supernatural abilities.

That was the trap. That was our adversary's plan to steal the nanomites. And it had nearly worked.

The mites had been obliged to draw power from us because they had no other source, and as the hours passed, Zander and I grew weaker. I think we were resigned to our fate—and it was okay. If we went to sleep here, we knew we would wake up with Jesus.

But then *the Lord*. Supernaturally, miraculously, *he* intervened.

He prompted us to sing his praises, so we sang. We sang our hearts out! And we discovered as we sang that we were growing stronger—not weaker.

Then his hand—yes, *God's hand*—shook the place we were in, shook it until the room around us quaked and the junction box feeding the cage's fluctuating electrostatic discharge blew apart, until *his* fingers pulled the trap apart, and—*up from the grave!*

We crawled from that death chamber, not yet fully restored but regaining our strength and vigor a little at a time, while the nanomites, too, slowly revived and came back online. Back into the fight to save the President—

Oh, thank you again, Father. I will never stop being amazed by your love, your mercy, and your power!

I had to stop and, once more, give thanks. Even today, the miracle of our deliverance rocks me to my core.

Of most importance, as the Lord led us through the last of those dark early days of July, we did unmask the "head of the snake," the leader of the network of traitors and conspirators who had attempted to overthrow the Jackson presidency, appropriate the nanomites, and seize the reins of government—planning to use the nanomites' abilities to cement governmental control over every aspect of its citizens' lives.

The President and his administration being safe at present—or reasonably so, as far as we and the nanomites could tell—our mission was over, successfully concluded. Zander and I figured we were free to return to Albuquerque.

Pack and go, right? *Well, not quite.*

Immediately after the crisis ended and we stood down, the lead agent of President Jackson's security detail, Axel Kennedy, requested that we debrief the President. President Jackson, Kennedy told us, wanted details—all of them. You know, the sort of behind-the-scenes details only we and the nanomites could provide. I say that Kennedy "requested," but when the President asks, you say 'yes.'

Yes, *sir*.

And since we were at the mercy of the President's busy calendar, Kennedy scheduled our debrief in several sessions across multiple weeks—effectively delaying our departure from DC until the President was satisfied.

Frankly, President Jackson couldn't hear enough concerning the nanomites and what they had done to search out and end the conspiracy. And we discovered at our second meeting with him that the President tended to formulate follow-on questions for the next session based on what we had told him during our previous meeting.

Gazillions of questions, and yes, the process and the wait were tedious.

To keep our involvement (and our nanocloud-endowed powers) secret, we always met in the President's private dining room in the White House residence during his regular lunch break. We would enter the Residence undetected, and while everyone else in the White House thought the President was having lunch alone with Mrs. Jackson, we would join the Jacksons and Axel Kennedy for a scant hour and a quarter.

Lunch in the Residence dining room was the best way for President Jackson to allot time for our visits while also eliminating the possibility of "prying eyes and ears." Supposedly, we'd taken care of those prying eyes and ears, the unsanctioned, illegal listening devices that the traitors had installed to spy on the President. They had planted those devices around the West Wing, including within the Oval Office itself.

They had also hidden "bugs" inside the President's official residence—in the dining room where we met to debrief the President. However, the nanomites had detected then deactivated the bugs, had identified the seditious Secret Service and White House personnel who had planted them, and sent them home with a debilitating case of "intestinal flu." We left it to the President and Kennedy to further deal with those agents and staff workers via whatever judicious means they decided.

Still, I dunno. Each time we visited the White House for those debriefs, my nerves were on edge. I could tell the nanomites were extra vigilant, too.

Why? Maybe because ending *all* threats against the President was a tall order that felt more like an exercise in zombie hunting straight off the reel of a B movie. I mean, are zombies ever *really* dead? Meaning, had we truly stopped America's enemies, those who sought to "fundamentally transform" her by any means at their disposal?

Not likely. Evil is always waiting in the wings, biding its time, looking for opportunities to strike. Well, we had done our part; we had accomplished what the President asked of us. We hadn't agreed to stay near DC beyond that.

From the Jacksons and Agent Kennedy's perspectives, however, much of what happened during those fateful weeks in June and July was not completely clear to them. We confirmed, for example, that the diminutive wife of the recently deceased Vice President had been the brains and visionary behind the scheme to assassinate Jackson and take the presidency. We told them, but they, nonetheless, had further questions—like who *was* this Winnie Delancey, really? And how had this evil, traitorous woman eluded detection for so long?

Vice President Delancey, after dosing Jackson with the biotoxin and while waiting for the President to die, had revealed that his wife, Winnie Delancey, had been born in Vietnam. As the daughter of a British official and his Vietnamese wife, Winnie's legal birth name was Winifred Marjorie Herrington, but she was also known under a Vietnamese name: Pham Quang Bi`nh. After some digging in the right places, a joint Secret Service, FBI, CIA, and MI6 task force confirmed Delancey's tale.

The CIA director and his leadership team were astounded (and justifiably mortified) to find that this woman, supposedly a valuable British spy prior to and during the Vietnam War, had actually been a Viet Cong double agent. She had regularly handed British intelligence over to the Communists and passed back Viet Cong *dis*information to the British—staggering news for MI6, the British Secret Intelligence Service, aka the SIS.

How many deaths could this single woman lay claim to by her treachery? And how had this woman, also a skilled Viet Cong interrogator of American POWs, never been identified as the traitor she was?

How? As the war drew to a close, she and her handlers had ensured that no POW able to identify her survived to tell the tale. The sole exception, we discovered, had been war hero Simon Delancey.

And how had Winnie Delancey managed to depart Vietnam in the war's chaotic aftermath and migrate to England? The means weren't complicated. As the daughter of a loyal British subject, himself at one time a government servant assigned to the British Advisory Mission to South Vietnam, Winifred Herrington claimed her British citizenship, obtained a British passport, and flew to the UK.

But how had she become a trusted CIA agent?

Once she had settled in England, Winifred Herrington reconnected with the SIS. They were only too happy to welcome a seasoned clandestine officer of her caliber, someone who had served them well during the Vietnam War. SIS leadership had never doubted the information she fed them, had never suspected her deeply held loyalty to the Marxist goals of communism, had never caught a glimpse of her masterful duplicity.

As the Cold War intensified, SIS agents, including Winifred Herrington, often interfaced with CIA operatives in Europe. Herrington earned a well-deserved reputation within the intelligence community for her brilliance in the field. She patiently bided her time and padded her resumé.

When the time was ripe, she left the UK and immigrated to the US. Because of her work within the SIS, she did not have to seek out the CIA. Before long, they were eagerly knocking at her door.

These revelations stunned the CIA hierarchy, and they were appalled to discover the depth of Winnie Delancey's treachery. Their humiliation reached its apex when they grasped how completely this double agent had evaded their detection and operated for decades *from within their own ranks*. The damage was inestimable: Her every connection was now suspect; every op she ever touched and agent she worked with required intense scrutiny and reevaluation.

But how in the world had she become the wife of rising statesman, Senator Simon Delancey, guaranteeing her access to Washington insiders and the nation's highest and most powerful social echelons? Simon Delancey himself had answered this question during his tirade while waiting for the biotoxin to kill the President.

He was, he told Jackson, the sole survivor of the POW camp where he had met a quite young but exceptionally talented interrogator, Pham Quang Bi`nh. They fell in love, and she converted him to her Marxist ideology. She counseled him in the "long con," the years of patient plotting needed to achieve their end game, that is, to achieve political power in America and, from inside, *bring her down*. Through every tedious step, he was her willing pupil and partner.

During the weeks we debriefed the President, the Secret Service, CIA, and FBI task force labored intensely—with a great deal of unrecognized assistance from the nanomites—to trace and document Winnie Delancey's life and to collect the evidence of her treasonous acts. But the facts finally did pan out.

The nanomites had also recorded the former Vice President's bragging confession and, at our request, had burned it to a flash drive. Zander and I handed the recording over to Kennedy, who passed it to the Secret Service while telling them it came from a recorder the President had activated soon after he'd been poisoned. Delancey's own words were the icing on the cake, so to speak.

President Jackson and Agent Kennedy also wanted the details of Winnie Delancey's last hours, and the nanomites provided them—audio recordings of her last conversation. I'm unable to explain how they captured that recording, but I recognized the sultry voice of the other woman in the conversation: Esperanza Duvall, sister to Arnaldo Soto, aka *Dead Eyes*. We listened as Esperanza Duvall "assisted" Winnie Delancey to the open door of her plane.

To this day, I shudder when I recall listening to Winnie Delancey's last moments. That said, I'm not sorry she's gone.

I suppose I should admit that while the truth about Winnie Delancey stung the US intelligence leadership, her demise was, in the end, a relief to all of us. The joint-agency task force, with the nanomites' recording and a great deal of other documentation in hand, had more than enough evidence to convict Winnie Delancey in a court of law, despite the long delays that would have inevitably been thrown up by our judicial system.

The political fallout, on the other hand, would have taken on the half-life of plutonium-239. In other words, the CIA, MI6, and President Jackson's administration would have been forever tarred by Winnie Delancey's traitorous legacy, not to mention plagued by a never-ending minefield of explosive questions. *The nanomites*, however, by presidential authorization, had ensured Winnie Delancey faced a swifter form of justice.

I'm certain several spy agencies toasted her demise. Her convenient death ended the need for publicly airing their dirty laundry.

At the President's request, Zander and I, over the course of six such lunch meetings, recited details to President and Mrs. Jackson and Agent Kennedy. Jackson and Kennedy, in turn, briefed us on the task force's continued efforts to root out treasonous elements of the recent coup attempt. Trusted intelligence officers were excavating the lives of each confirmed participant, identifying potential co-conspirators, then watching and listening until they (and we) were convinced that the investigated individuals either had or had not participated in the coup.

Of course, because the nanomites were monitoring and often covertly assisting in the efforts, we were familiar with most of the details. We let President Jackson and Agent Kennedy brief us anyway. The nanomites' extensive knowledge of classified matter was hard enough on their sensibilities, particularly hard on Kennedy. He had never been quite able to trust us or the nanomites.

During this protracted debriefing phase, and at President Jackson's urging, Zander and I agreed to bring our lives in Maryland to a more natural and legitimate close. The NSA didn't take kindly to "no call/no show" employees, and they had a long memory and a longer reach. It would be better for us in the long run if I didn't leave the NSA under a cloud.

So, I returned to my job at the NSA following an unscheduled three-week absence. My supervisor, team leader, and teammates were not overtly surprised to see me, and my simple, unelaborated "family emergency" excuse—approved without comment by HR—was accepted all around with just a few shrugs and curious glances. Well, it *was* the NSA. You never knew what classified goings-on were "going on" around you or which employees might be taking part in a clandestine project. You were taught from the get-go not to ask too many questions.

I know, though, that the President's people had made calls and pulled strings to ensure that, when I *did* give my notice some six or more weeks later, I would leave the NSA with a clean employment record and an unsullied security clearance. It was one of the not-so-little perks President Jackson bestowed on us to thank us for our efforts on his behalf.

Zander, too, returned to his leadership role with Grace Chapel's Celebrate Recovery program. The program was experiencing something of a surge, with new attendees showing up and receiving Christ each week. As a result, Sunday church attendance jumped up, and Zander, at Pastor Lucklow's invitation, added a weekly family Bible study to his schedule and spent his day-to-day hours visiting and discipling new believers.

We worked hard at our jobs and enjoyed our work, but in reality, like me, Zander was alert and watchful, waiting for the President to release us.

When he finally did, I would give my two-week notice, and Zander would begin to transition the Celebrate Recovery program's leadership to Tom and Becky who, at this point, were ready and felt led to take on the leadership role.

When the time came for us to resign, we would, at both of our work places, mouth a nonspecific rationale. In reality, we were heading home because we were expecting a baby, and we wanted to be near our family for this momentous event and going forward—but that's not what we would tell them.

No, the nanomites had been the first to remind us that *a child*, as much as he or she is a blessing, is also a vulnerability.

They brought us into the "warehouse" (that place in our minds where we and the nanomites met and communed) and played back Macy and Darius Uumbana's terror when Winnie Delancey's thugs had stolen their newborn twins. It took only moments of the nanomites' refresher course for us to come around to their point of view.

We apologize, Jayda Cruz and Zander Cruz. However, Jesus has told us to protect you and the child. He says you have important work ahead of you. It is our job to watch over and safeguard your family. The fewer individuals here in the DC area who are aware of your pregnancy, the better. As the old proverb states, "An ounce of prevention is worth a pound of cure"—and prevention is always better than cure.

"Yeah, okay. We get it."

*Grrr! Fine! We'll keep it to ourselves. **Whatever**, you little joy snatchers. *sigh**

Another thought popped up and kicked my disappointment to the curb.

Whoa! Wait just a cotton-pickin' minute.

I rounded on Zander. "What important work?"

⌘⌘⌘⌘

PART 1: DISTURBANCE IN THE ATMOSPHERE

"This is what the Lord Almighty says:

'Look! Disaster is spreading from nation to nation;

a mighty storm is rising from the ends of the earth.'"

Jeremiah 25:32, NIV

CHAPTER 1

EARLY SEPTEMBER

WITH ONLY ONE MORE meeting scheduled to debrief the President, Zander and I tendered our two-week notices to our respective employers, Zander at our church, and me as a contract employee at the NSA. I sat with HR at the end of my work day and filled out the requisite paperwork. The next morning, when I made the announcement to my team, my coworkers stared at me, eyes brimming with "why?"

Zander and I had discussed how to handle the situation, but there was no easy answer, and I was ill at ease with lying to their faces. However, as Zander pointed out, we were not obliged to tell everyone our business. I suppose that's an important distinction in these trying times, particularly when circumstances require a measure of dissimulation in order to protect a life.

This was one of those times, and the life we were protecting was our unborn child's. The only people in DC who knew I was pregnant were the Jacksons, Kennedy, Gamble, and Trujillo.

I offered my teammates a soft wince of a smile. "I know. We recently got settled here. But that family emergency that called us away for three weeks? It's not going to resolve itself. We need to go home . . . and continue taking care of it."

They nodded, trying to accept my explanation but, without details, failing. I appreciated their concerned looks and kind words anyway.

"We'll miss you, Jayda," Sherry Woods said with my coworkers nodding their agreement. "You've become a valuable part of this team."

"Thank you. All of you. I will do my best in the days I have left."

I sat back down at my station, grateful to have the discomfort over. Well, safeguarding our baby was Job One, so this baby *was* the family emergency that would take us home. Keeping our child out of public view was likely the first of many times I would protect our child.

A mom's life's work, I suppose.

The first part of that thought knocked the breath right outta me.

A mom!

⌘

OUR LAST BRIEFING WITH President Jackson began no differently than the previous ones. Mrs. Jackson joined us for lunch as she usually did. Afterward, however, rather than remaining for the Q&A as she had up till now, she excused herself, saying she had something she needed to attend to. We then answered the final questions the President and Kennedy put to us.

I thought our answers were exhaustive. And exhausting. We'd been over similar ground more than once. But then President Jackson glanced at Kennedy, and a furtive signal passed between them. They were . . . stalling? Shifting gears?

Good grief! What now?

Jackson put his elbows on the table and his fingertips together. "Jayda, Zander, when you and your belongings arrived here in DC around the last week of May, you met with Special Agent Gamble to receive your instructions, did you not? And I believe he directed you to keep an accounting of your expenses so the government could reimburse you?"

"Oh! Ah, yes, sir." I side-eyed Zander. "We may not have actually kept track of our expenses, sir."

We have kept track of your expenses, Jayda Cruz. We can provide you with a full accounting.

"Thanks, Nano, but we're not going to bill the President for our services."

"What Jayda said, Nano," Zander echoed.

The President, of course, did not hear our exchange with the nanomites, but he canted his head toward us.

"Didn't you lose your car during the attack on Malware, Inc.'s home base? Wasn't it, er, blown up?"

Zander answered. "Yes, it was, sir, but we have insurance, and it will pay for a rental—"

The President cut him off. "Hold up there, Zander. It is our decided intention to reimburse you both for the entirety of your moving and living expenses, including the loss of your car, from the day you left Albuquerque until you return there. We'll use a *per diem* to reimburse you if you haven't kept records."

Zander Cruz, Jayda Cruz, we have kept quite exacting records. We can provide the precise figure—down to the penny—at this very moment.

A spreadsheet appeared in front of our eyes.

If we may direct your attention to lines—

"Shush, Nano," Zander told them.

I added, "Um, thanks, Nano, but we'd rather not give the country a bill for doing our patriotic duty. Besides, the Lord will see to our needs."

Our "druthers" didn't seem to matter, though, because the President kept pressing his point. "I believe Special Agent Gamble also told you we would be paying you a contractor's fee for your work?"

"That isn't necessary, sir—"

"It *is* necessary, Mr. Cruz, or should I say, *Reverend Cruz?* You are familiar with Scripture, are you not? Do you recall this one, *The worker is worthy of his wages?*"

"Er, yes, sir."

"Then let there be no more talk of refusing your wages, all right? We have routed your fee, your expenses, and the cost of replacing your car through your friends at Malware, Inc. Malware has been a military contractor in good standing for close to a decade. They provide excellent training and specialized security services where the government needs it. Funding for them was allocated in the latest Congressional continuing resolution, so both of you will receive checks from them as subcontractors. Special Agent Gamble has conveyed our instructions to Malware's accountant regarding your payments.

"Malware, Inc. will also be reimbursed for the damage done to their training center. In addition, the family of their fallen comrade will receive a generous compensation and our grateful, undying thanks."

He stared at the table top for a brief interval. "I believe in honoring those who put their lives on the line for our nation—*which you both surely did*. Furthermore, I will never abandon the families of those who have given their all."

"Yes, sir," Zander whispered.

"Your friends at Malware will be in touch. Do you have any last concerns, questions, or tidbits of nano-insight for us?"

Zander and I looked at each other. He shrugged. I, rather timidly, said, "Mr. President, you have, er, *gone through* two vice presidents, to put it delicately. Do you have an idea who you might nominate next? Perhaps the nanomites could do a deep dive for you on whomever you choose. They might prevent . . . you know. Another, er, mishap?"

"I might take you up on that," Jackson said, "but I can tell you one thing for certain: I'll pick the VP I want this time. My last pick, from the other party, was supposed to be the great peacemaker between them and us—and *he* stabbed me in the back and sat around to chat me up while I bled out—so to speak. This time? I'll nominate who I want, *thank you very much*, and the other party had better suck it up and go along with it."

"Er, right, sir."

Jackson stood and moved away from the table, signaling the end of our last meeting with him. He nodded to Kennedy, who strode to the dining room door and opened it. Maddie Jackson entered, a soft smile playing on her lips. In her hands she held two small, flat, gleaming wooden cases.

"Mrs. Jackson," I breathed.

She moved to the President's side. He smiled back at her, then exhaled and addressed us.

"Zander and Jayda, please stand here. Yes, right here, in front of us. Thank you." He waited until we positioned ourselves where he indicated we were to stand.

I started shaking about then . . . cuz something was up. And whatever it was? It was big.

"Zander and Jayda Cruz, your nation can never thank you enough for the services you have rendered over the past year—and I explicitly include Maddie and myself in those sentiments. You, Jayda, saved my life when that coward Harmon tried to kill me. Then the two of you uprooted your newlywed lives and came when I asked for further aid. You *risked your lives* to uncover the ongoing conspiracy and all its foul tentacles. You nearly perished as a result, but you did not quit on us. Had you given up? Had you drawn back? Well, I would no longer be the President of this great country. No, *I would be dead.* You saved my life a second time, and we owe you a great debt of gratitude."

"*I* owe you," Maddie Jackson whispered, "for saving my beloved husband. I promise you, if you should ever need us—*ever*—we will answer."

For once, Axel Kennedy's intent, piercing gaze on us was in accord with President and Mrs. Jackson's. In fact, President and Mrs. Jackson's words and demeanor, from the moment Mrs. Jackson reentered the dining room, had turned serious and formal . . . as if preparing for a momentous event.

My throat tightened, and my eyes stung. I blinked to clear the moisture clouding my vision. My hand sought Zander's hand. His warm fingers closed around mine and gently squeezed.

He felt what I felt.

"It was our honor to serve, sir," Zander answered.

"Thank you, but today, Mr. and Mrs. Cruz? It is our honor."

Robert Jackson gestured to his wife. She lifted the hinged lid on the first case, rotated the case so it faced outward, and held it toward the President. President Jackson removed a star-shaped medallion on a gold background that hung from a wide blue ribbon edged in white.

He moved to stand directly in front of me. "Jayda Cruz, for your especially meritorious actions in preserving the security and national interests of the United States of America and for preserving me as its duly elected president—not once, but *twice*—I award you the Presidential Medal of Freedom."

I was stunned. More tears sprang to my eyes as he asked me to turn around, and as he fastened the ribbon behind my neck. When I faced him, he shook my hand. When he moved back, Maddie Jackson stepped forward, held my shoulders, and kissed me on both cheeks.

They repeated the process with Zander. By then, I was blubbering like a baby, but Zander was trying with all his might to control his emotions.

He held himself rigid, his lips flattened, jaws tightly clenched. Despite his best efforts, his eyes swam with unshed tears.

When the ceremony concluded and I had scrabbled together a scrap of self-control, President Jackson sighed. "I am sorry this could not have been the public ceremony you deserve. However, we accept that anonymity is absolutely paramount to your ongoing well-being—and the well-being of your precious baby."

We nodded in mute agreement.

He continued. "These medals are yours to keep. However, to safeguard your identities, they have no engraving on them to name you as their recipients. I also feel it incumbent upon me, based on your need for anonymity, to ask you to make a difficult decision. Please tell us if you wish to take the medals with you or if you prefer that we . . . hold them for you."

Hold them for you.

If we left the unengraved medals with them, they would either disappear forever or they would, at some point in the future, be uncovered to mystify and confound historians.

I glanced at Zander. He gave his head a shake. I nodded my agreement.

"Sir," Zander said, "we will treasure this day and this moment for the rest of our lives. That said, we would appreciate it if you kept them for us."

"We will."

The nanomites had been silent for a while, but I had sensed their intent interest as they observed the ceremonies. Then they spoke.

We have recorded this ceremony, Jayda and Zander Cruz. We can play it back for you any time you wish.

I was touched. "Thank you, Nano. That was sweet and thoughtful of you, and . . ."

I hesitated, then said to the President, "Sir? I . . . that is, may we presume on your kindness and generosity?"

"Of course. Anything."

"Would it be possible for you . . . to confer the medal upon the nanomites? They deserve it more than we do. We could not have accomplished any of what we did without them, and I think it would bless them to be acknowledged."

Kennedy frowned, probably at my audacity.

The President blinked twice. Cleared his throat. "I . . . Yes. Yes, I certainly will do so."

Perhaps a little discomfited, but with his game face on, he asked, "How do I address them, Jayda?"

"We call them Nano, sir."

"Very good."

He lifted his voice. "Um, *Nano*, for your especially meritorious actions in preserving the security and national interests of the United States of America and for preserving me as its president, I hereby award you the, ah, *virtual* Presidential Medal of Freedom. If it were possible to fasten the real thing around your neck, er, necks, I would certainly do so. We are most grateful to you, Nano, and we thank you from the bottom of our hearts."

"Yes, we do," Maddie added.

The nanomites whispered to us both, *Zander and Jayda Cruz, please inform President and Mrs. Jackson that we are honored to accept this award.*

I smiled with Zander, and he spoke. "Mr. President, Mrs. Jackson? The nanomites have asked us to inform you that they are honored to accept the award."

I was surprised into another spate of tears, when from within my chest, I felt and heard a soft, lovely hum. It grew and expanded.

Zander heard the same from his nanocloud. The two intertwining melodies lifted, rose, resonated, then harmonized, from us, through us, above us.

The dual songs of the nanoclouds captured the melodious majesty of carillon bells, accompanied by the rich sweetness of orchestral strings. Together they soared. Their songs flowed up, up, up, until a shining, twinkling blue and silver cloud hovered near the ceiling of the President's dining room, swirling over our heads, a mist of joyous counterpoint eddying around us.

The Jacksons and Axel Kennedy stared at the cloud, mesmerized by its haunting beauty—although Kennedy's eyes may have held more alarm than pleasure.

"Wh-what are they doing?" the President asked.

I had to swallow the lump in my throat.

"They are singing, Mr. President. The nanomites are singing their joy and gratitude."

⌘⌘⌘⌘

CHAPTER 2

WHILE ZANDER AND I RAN down the two-week clocks at our respective places of employment, we still needed to eat. *A lot.* As was our habit after work each evening, we drove our nano-charged appetites to a restaurant on our list of favorite all-you-can-eat buffets. Tonight it was our favorite Chinese buffet, and we were ravenous when we pulled into the parking lot.

I had noticed a funny thing, though, over the last couple of weeks.

The managers and employees at our most frequented all-you-can-eat restaurants had started to take note of us—meaning they observed exactly how much "all you can eat" we managed to pack away when we patronized their businesses. More than a few had eyeballed us, their expressions concerned or disturbed.

And as we walked through the Chinese buffet's front entrance, a frown popped out on the cashier's brow.

Uh-oh.

Her halfhearted smile didn't reach her eyes, but Zander didn't seem to snap to her discomfort.

"Two adults, please."

As he lifted his phone to pay our bill, I turned away, distracted by something else.

I lifted my chin and sniffed the air.

What is that?

I swiveled toward the buffet itself and breathed in through my nose.

As much as I loved this place, tonight something didn't smell right— and I'm not talking about the cashier's reaction to us.

I wrinkled my nose. Nope, something *reeked.*

"You smell something off?" I whispered in Zander's ear.

"Huh? No. I'm salivating."

Hmm. Was my nose off its typical game? Or . . . was my stomach experiencing an adverse reaction?

What in the world?

"Oh! Oh, no. Please excuse—"

I rushed by the cashier, frantic to find the restrooms. When I spotted the sign, I flat-out ran. I slammed through the door, fell into a stall, and proceeded to puke my guts out. I puked till my abdominal muscles ached. Then I puked up my toenails—and I may have lost my right kidney in the process.

When I was empty, I wiped my mouth with TP and leaned against the cool metal side of the stall, indifferent to whatever cornucopia of germs I might encounter.

We apologize, Jayda Cruz.

"Huh?"

You are about five weeks along and have not, until this evening, experienced what is termed morning sickness. We should have been monitoring your fluctuating hormone levels more closely. We will attempt to moderate the ill effects of your pregnancy. You may experience some nausea, but we hope to prevent another . . . event of this order.

Morning sickness? *Morning sickness?*

It was dinner time, for heaven's sake!

"Yes, please, Nano. That was no fun."

Fun? Not in the slightest.

When I began to feel a little more like my usual self and had determined that all my internal organs were present and accounted for, I washed my hands thoroughly, patted cool water on my cheeks and brow and returned to the restaurant.

Zander had our dinner receipts in hand and was pacing in front of the koi pond at the entrance to the dining area. The nanomites had told him what was up. Compassion etched his customarily cheerful face.

"Are you okay, Sweetie?"

"Guess so."

"Is this the first time you've been sick? You know, preggo sick?"

"Yeah. It hasn't been an issue up until today."

He rubbed my arm gently. "Have you lost your appetite?"

"Think I'll go easy. See how things settle."

Whether I felt like eating or not, I knew Zander was starving—and the unsuspecting koi swimming slowly around the pond were probably starting to look mighty tasty to him.

I tugged him away from the temptation. We found a table in the corner then got our plates and filled them. Zander dug in. I was more cautious in my approach.

No more 'fun' for me, please.

I had chosen some fresh fruit, a dinner roll, and a piece of poached salmon—heeding the ongoing stream of advice the nanomites whispered in my ears.

We recommend that you avoid high-fat foods, Jayda Cruz, and foods with an odor or aroma that your stomach finds objectionable.

What? My stomach gets to vote on what I eat?

I exhaled. Adjusted my attitude.

"Yeah. Okay."

Zander got up three times to get more food, while I ate slowly and carefully. As he returned from his fourth foray to the buffet lines, I recalled the cashier's expression of concern when we walked through the restaurant's front entrance.

"So, it's probably a good thing we're leaving the DC area soon, or we'd have to start ferreting farther afield to find new restaurants," I mentioned to Zander.

He was cramming Mongolian stir fry into his insatiable maw. "What?"

"Oh, nothing. However, I noticed that—*uh-oh*. Hang on. We're about to have a visitor."

The fortyish woman drew near our table. She smiled, her manner polite. Professional. "Good evening. I'm Marsha Wong, the manager."

I swallowed what I had in my mouth. Returned her greeting with my most winsome smile. "Hello. You have a lovely restaurant, Ms. Wong. We will miss it."

It was her turn to say, "What?"

"We're moving out of state next weekend."

"I see." She studied Zander's tidy stack of nearly a dozen plates in the center of the table. She picked them up. "Well, best of luck to you both with your move."

"Thanks, Ms. Wong."

"What was that about?" Zander asked.

"We have eaten here at least twice a week for a couple months. I think our rep for vacuuming up food in amounts rivaling what a football team would consume has caught up to us."

"Oh."

"Yeah. *Oh*. Pretty sure if I hadn't said we were moving, Ms. Wong was about to disinvite us from patronizing her restaurant in the future."

"But this is our favorite buffet!"

"Yup, and we'll miss it, but we'll need to be more circumspect back in Albuquerque. Choose more restaurants and limit our visits to each of them."

After we finished dinner, we drove home and took a brisk walk around our favorite neighborhood park. I experienced no further nausea, and my stomach felt fine.

Back in our apartment, we showered then packed a few boxes. We didn't actually have much "stuff" to pack, but the nightly sorting, wrapping, and packing helped to curb our excitement. We were antsy, ready to get on the road.

Part of our eagerness was for getting home to our friends and family; another part was for the road trip we were planning. Since we had a baby coming (after which our married life would radically change), and since we wouldn't be on anyone's schedule or payroll, we decided to take advantage of our drive home—make a few detours, see new sights, and spend some quality time together.

Sort of a relaxed second honeymoon—without intrigue, danger, or treasonous conspiracies.

We were more than ready for *that*.

⌘

ON THE WEDNESDAY BEFORE Zander and I finished out our jobs, Gamble called.

"Hey, wanted to let you know that I have made arrangements to have the 3D printer moved. Dr. Bickel is sending his guys to pack it up next week and take it back to Albuquerque."

"Where will they reassemble it?" Zander asked. "I'm certain the nanomites will want it available as soon as we get set up in our new digs. They like to keep their numbers topped off."

"Dunno about that. I suppose you and Dr. Bickel will decide where to keep it."

I jumped in. "Gamble, what about you? What's your next assignment?" I wanted to add, "And what about you and Janice?" but I closed my mouth before the words jumped out.

"Not sure. Our mutual friends are considering whether or not to return me to active status with the agency or keep me around DC on special assignment. Also, Mal has made Janice an offer. You know, to join his team."

Aha! *There it was.* I had a strong feeling that Gamble would be looking for a way to stay close to Agent Trujillo.

"Janice is leaving her, um, agency?"

He seemed relieved. "Yeah. Her getting shed of *that*, er, agency, solves one ginormous logistical issue for us."

"Sweet!" I was relieved, too. See, she never did tell us her official agency status. "Black ops" was all she'd mentioned of the period when she reported to General Cushing. And after I'd experienced Cushing's tender loving pursuit, I considered Trujillo's "black ops" status more of a great, sucking "black hole" in practice.

But before I could ask any further questions, he shifted subjects. "Say, speaking of Malware, when his crew heard you two were leaving the area, they asked me to invite you for dinner. Sort of a farewell feast and a 'return the favor' meal for the great New Mexican cuisine you fixed for all of us, Zander."

"We'd love to," I said, "but when? We're hoping to haul out of here Saturday around noon."

"That's what I told them, so I suggested tomorrow, 6:30."

It was short notice, but our social calendar wasn't exactly topped out.

"That works for us," Zander replied.

"Great. I'll let Mal and the boys know you're coming—and yeah; I know. I'll remind them to cook a *bunch*."

Zander grinned. "Excellent!"

⌘

THE FOLLOWING EVENING, ZANDER and I headed out to have dinner with the crew of Malware, Inc. It would be great to be back with them in their temporary digs, the block of apartments they were leasing while they recovered from the attacks that pretty much destroyed their home base. After those assaults, we'd stayed a few nights with them as well, since it hadn't been safe at that time for us to go back to our apartment.

Their home base, what they generally referred to as their "clubhouse," had been more than their work address. It was where most of them lived in their own studio apartments on the second or third floors. Part-time crew who had their own places did stints at the clubhouse similar to how firefighters stay in shifts in their firehouse. The clubhouse was also home to their training center where Zander and I had taken our tradecraft classes.

They had located their *surprisingly* well supplied and reinforced three-story brick building on a seamy side of Baltimore. Their building was encompassed by urban ruin: abandoned and falling down buildings and warehouses, trash-strewn sidewalks and alleys, drug dealers, shooting galleries, pimps, pros, and many homeless who squatted in the nearby empty warehouses.

Although the clubhouse was pristine inside, its outside mimicked its surroundings. For Malware, the neighborhood was camouflage, a means of hiding in plain sight.

And all of it, the entire area, reeked of a particular stench—a combination of salt tang, decaying garbage, urine, and moldy ruins—

My stomach lurched.

I switched off those thoughts and made conversation with the hunk in the driver's seat.

"Don't forget, Zander. We're not talking baby with Malware, Inc."

"I know, I know." Zander was grumpy on that point. He wanted to tell everyone.

"Soon enough. When we get home, Babe."

He pulled up to the gated complex and pressed in the code. We drove in and wound around to the block of apartments Mal and his crew occupied. "Occupied" is right. We knew they had their own cameras mounted at the gate, above the parking lot near their apartments, and all around the unit's perimeter. Someone monitored the feeds 24/7 from their "command center" on the unit's second floor. No doubt they were watching us make our approach.

They had also walled off both ends of the unit and installed a barred security door in each wall. We stopped at the security door, looked up into the camera, and made faces.

The door buzzed and unlocked, and Dredd's chuckle drifted down from the camera's speaker.

"Ripley! John-Boy! Come on in. Dinner's in the rec room."

"Huh. Rec room—is that what they're calling it?" Zander snarked to me. "Last time I looked, it was full of weights, treadmills, and testosterone."

"We managed to feed the whole crew in there," I reminded him.

"That we did—but the aroma of my mama's red chile sauce overcame the stink of sweat."

"You are biased, but I have to agree with you: Nothing beats your mama's enchilada recipe. Say, speaking of aroma . . ."

"Yeah, I smell it; someone is grilling *meat*." He licked his lips. "Yum!"

We headed down the walkway and turned at the workout room. Heard a rustle and some murmured words from within. Opened the door—

"SURPRISE! SURPRISE! SURPRISE!"

Confetti and streamers flew. Noisemakers blew and "poppers" popped.

Zander and I stood in the threshold. Slack-jawed.

It was a party. A full-on, all-out, no-holds-barred *party*.

My gaze jinked from a ceiling of intertwined crepe paper streamers to colorful balloon bouquets, to a table stacked with presents higher than my head, to a work of art in soft pastel colors, *a cake* in the shape of an old-school baby buggy?

This wasn't any old party.

This was *a baby shower*.

Then we were surrounded by our friends, who hugged me and high-fived Zander, all of them smiling and saying "congratulations" to me and "good job" to Zander over and over.

I received hugs from Mal, Logan, Baltar, Deckard, Dredd, McFly, Fiona, Neo, and Banner, while Gamble waited off to the side—grinning like a complete *idiot*. Beside him stood Janice Trujillo. She was, well, *radiant*. In love.

But all I could think was that the number of people in DC who knew about our little munchkin had more than doubled—contrary to what we'd planned.

When things started to calm down, I sidled up to Gamble and said, "Uh, Gamble? Was it you? Did you spill the beans to these guys? What part of 'Don't tell anyone' did you not get?"

"Yeah, well *that*. See, you didn't say 'mums the word' until two days after I knew about the bambino. But by then, I'd told Janice and Mal, and he had told his crew."

He shrugged sheepishly. "Sorry."

Mal saw my concern. "Ripley, Gamble told us afterward that we needed to keep the news on the QT until you'd relocated for your, you know, next *undercover assignment*."

My eyes slid over to Gamble.

He lifted one brow. "The reason why we're keeping your preggo state under wraps."

"Right," Zander said, getting it. "Our next assignment. Hush-hush."

"And you two not likely to return to DC," Gamble added.

"Er, right," I added.

"Don't worry," Mal said. "We haven't told a soul, and we are sworn to silence from here forward. But we couldn't let you ride off into the sunset without letting you know how great we think a little Ripley or John Boy will be. We're happy for you both." He looked around. "Right, guys?"

A chorus of "right," "yup," and "roger that" hit him back.

"Right, *guys*?" Fiona drawled, "Told ya before, Mal: I am no *man*."

McFly groaned. "Heavenly shades of LOTR. Shoulda dubbed her Eowyn, not Fiona, Mal."

Fiona's broad, sweet, face smiled as she lifted an impressive arm and flexed her muscles. "Naw. Lookit these biceps! I got *guns*, boys. I'm definitely more the ogre than the princess. But hey, Ripley. No worries. My lips are sealed, and same goes for the rest of these yahoos—or I'll smack 'em clean inta next week."

She nodded to me. "Congrats, little mama!"

Little mama?

Oh, my heart. I'm going to be a mama!

I melted into Fiona's hug—well, more like the Jaws of Life, only gentler.

Then the party kicked into gear.

Why does even thinking about that evening bring on fits of giggles and guffaws? See, the rough-and-tumble bone crushers of Malware, Inc. (who can melt steel with a scowl), went all out on a *baby shower*. Guess I get the grins and giggles pretty fast when I think about everything they did to make the evening special for us. These totally macho meatheads made the party arrangements and did the work all themselves: They decorated the rec room with enough crepe paper streamers and balloons to launch an ocean liner, and they cooked and baked to feed an army.

"Let's eat!" Mal proclaimed.

I declare, the crew of Malware, Inc. started pulling food out of the woodwork: four different salads; plates of steaming, buttery asparagus; baked potatoes with all the toppings; and two platters of T-bones—at least four hundred bucks' worth of prime, sizzling beef piled high with grilled jumbo shrimp.

Fiona saw me ogling the platter and the dollar signs ringing up behind my eyeballs. "Don't look at *me*," she laughed. "I'm only part-time here, remember? The full-time guys planned the menu and prepped the food. But I will tell you this: Banner can run a grill like nobody's business."

"Yum." *Drool.*

We sat down around two long tables set end to end (big muscles need extra elbow room), and a silence descended.

Mal tipped his chin toward Zander. "John-boy, would you care to say a blessing over the food?"

Zander's smile widened further. "I sure would. Thanks."

He took my hand in his, bowed his head, and prayed. "Lord God! Thank you. Jayda and I are grateful for such good friends and their wonderful, generous hearts. We thank you, Lord, that we are here, gathered with these friends, to share this meal they have prepared."

He hesitated a second, then added, "Bless this food, O Lord, we pray. Make it safe by night and day. Amen."

Gamble snorted. I snickered.

"Amen!" Fiona echoed.

Amid much laughter and fun around the table, we devoured steak and shrimp hot off the grill, loaded baked potatoes, and all the rest.

After we'd hammered down on the awesome grub, Malware's crew blessed us with a ton of baby presents.

Oh my, *the gifts!* How can I ever express their generosity? Their precious kindness to us?

Dredd started. "This here is from the three of us," he rumbled, indicating Baltar, Logan, and himself, "cause keeping the kid safe is top of the list."

Zander helped me pull the gift wrap off a big, rectangular box. Under the paper we found the image of a car seat. An especially pricy one, I knew, because I was making a list of the baby "stuff" we would need in seven more months, and I had been looking online for the best reviews and prices.

"Wow," Zander muttered, taking in the colorful pictures printed on the box. "Guess we'll be needing this, won't we?"

"That and every penny you earn for the next twenty to thirty years," someone quipped.

Everyone laughed except Zander. This was serious business to him.

I was noticing that the box had been opened when Dredd added, "And not a *stock* car seat, mind you. We added necessary customizations."

"Yeah," Logan chimed in. "Up-armored that thing, we did. Trust me, it's much better. Oh, and I printed out the installation instructions and slipped them into the box. See, when you go to mount it in your car, you should—"

"Next!" Neo and Banner cut him off.

"That would be me," Fiona announced. She handed me a wide, flat box that filled my lap. "Not much, perhaps, but made with love."

I lifted the lid. Within the folds of tissue paper was a crib-sized quilt. Every other square on the quilt's face featured Winnie-the-Pooh or his companions from the Hundred Acre Wood. The backing and edging were of a pale, soothing green fleece, soft as down.

"Fiona! Did you? Did you make this yourself?"

Fiona blushed a little. "Yes. I love to quilt."

Dredd stared at her. "You what? You *quilt?*"

"Shut up, Dredd. Saw in one of your *better* movies that you *knit*, so can it."

Dredd reddened, but the whooping laughter and pointing fingers were contagious, and he had to chuckle, too.

Zander examined the quilt closely. "This is really special, Fiona. My mom read these books to me when I was little. It's perfect for a little guy."

"Or a little girl," I added. "We won't know which until he or she is born. Thank you, Fiona, from the bottom of our hearts. It is wonderful. I will always think of you when I see it."

I was surprised when Janice nudged Gamble and he placed a box the size and shape of a book in my lap. "This one is from us," she said.

Well, it wasn't a book; it was a beautifully framed print of a poem titled *A Child's Prayer*.

"Oh, my," I whispered.

"Would you read it aloud, Jayda?" Fiona asked.

I cleared my throat. "Hope I can get through it without my voice cracking."

We will help you, Jayda Cruz.

I felt a calm sweep over me. "Thank you, Nano." I looked up into our friends' expectant faces and then back to the poem and began.

> *"God make my life a little light,*
> *Within the world to glow,*
> *A tiny flame that burneth bright,*
> *Wherever I may go.*
>
> *"God make my life a little flower,*
> *That giveth joy to all;*
> *Content to bloom in native bower*
> *Although its place be small.*
>
> *"God make my life a little song,*
> *That comforteth the sad;*
> *That helpeth others to be strong,*
> *And makes the singer glad.*
>
> *"God make my life a little staff*
> *Whereon the weak may rest,*
> *That so what health and strength I have*
> *May serve my neighbor best.*
>
> *"God make my life a little hymn*
> *Of tenderness and praise,*
> *Of faith, that never waxeth dim,*
> *In all His wondrous ways."*

I ended by reading the author's name. "Written by Matilda B. Edwards. Thank you, Janice. Gamble. It is beautiful."

Around the circle, heads nodded. I noted a few surreptitious swipes at the eyes, too.

"Yes, thank you," Zander echoed.

"You are most welcome. And we brought another gift with us to the shower, something from . . . our mutual friends."

Mutual friends? Oh . . .

The exquisite gift box Janice handed me, small and square, had no wrapping paper, tag, or bow, but it absolutely shouted understated quality. No tearing into this one! Rather, the lid lifted straight off, revealing flawlessly folded tissue paper. So impeccable was the presentation, I was reluctant to disturb the gossamer folds.

After staring for several seconds, I slowly peeled back the paper to reveal a baby cup and matching baby spoon, both in gleaming silver. The two lines of engraving on the bottom of the cup read, "God's blessings on you, little one," and "R&M."

R&M. Our "mutual friends," Robert and Madeleine Jackson.

Zander hung over my shoulder, silently reading the inscription with me. "Holy cow."

"Yeah, that's a big *moo* from me."

"What is it?" our friends demanded.

I held the cup and spoon up for the obligatory oohing and aahing, but when I was asked who it was from, I evaded with, "Some dear family friends."

More gifts rained down on us after that—all sorts of baby wear spanning newborn to eighteen months, including itty-bitty shoes, socks, and hats, then an entire case of disposable diapers, and a gift set of powder, ointment, baby nail clippers, miniature comb and hairbrush.

Such abundance! I was overwhelmed by Malware's kindness.

"It's . . . it's too much, you guys. I—that is *we*—we don't know how to thank you enough."

Jayda Cruz, apparently, it is appropriate and expected that you express your appreciation with thank-you cards specially made for such an occasion and that you send these cards by 'snail mail.' This social convention seems ponderous and archaic to us. However, in keeping with social customs, we are compiling a list of who gave which gifts so you can dispatch the expected thank you notes. You may be one hundred percent assured that you will thank each person for the correct gift.

"Thoughtful of you, Nano," I replied to them.

Mal cleared his throat. "Uh, we're not quite finished. Um, see, well, uh, we kinda like you two."

The crew guffawed and derided Mal, mocking his sudden tilt toward sentimentality.

"Ooooo, we *liiiike* you," Baltar smirked, to the amusement of all except Mal.

"Don't get your hopes up, John Boy and Ripley. Mal only *kinda* likes you two," McFly sniggered. "Not *really* likes, *sorta* likes, or *truly* likes you. Just *kinda* likes."

The crew howled and cut up. Zander and I laughed so hard, we ran out of breath.

Mal, red in the face, growled, "Shut it, you bozos," which only encouraged more laughter and jokes at his expense.

He jerked his thumb at Logan. "Get up here. Let's get this over with."

Mal and Logan walked around the bare table to the wall where a line of bulges was screened by the sheets draped over them. They whipped off the sheets to reveal an entire nursery of furniture—crib and mattress (boxed), changing table (boxed), dresser, and nightstand. All in bright golden oak.

I found myself babbling. "Oh! Oh! Oh, it's beautiful! I love all of it! I cannot believe you guys. You are the *best*, the most wonderful friends! Everything is so perfect!"

Zander's dumbfounded comment was, "Uh, Jayda? I think . . . I think we're gonna need a bigger, a-a-a bigger—"

"BOAT!" the guys shouted in unison.

"No, a bigger moving trailer," Zander finished. He was as dazed and overcome, as I was. "Yeah, we're gonna need a bigger moving trailer," he repeated.

We turned to each other. I put my head on Zander's shoulder. And sobbed.

The laughter ended. As lost in my own tears as I was, Zander was laboring to master his own emotions but failing. I also heard, around the room, the snuffling of others.

I sat up and wiped my eyes. "Thank you. Thank you for the precious gift of your friendship and for all these expressions of your love—for us and for our baby. We will treasure them all."

Zander stood and tugged me to my feet, wiping his eyes. "What Jayda said. You have blessed us beyond measure, and we are grateful. But more than anything, we are grateful for your friendship. I mean, it was only, what? Eight or nine weeks ago when we made our separate ways to your training center to start our tradecraft sessions with you—"

"Uh, was that the evening Ripley kicked the stuffing outta Dredd?" Deckard quipped.

"Knocked him on his can, if I recall," Neo added.

"Knocked him clear inta next week. He was still out of it when he got back to the clubhouse."

"To this day, I don't remember if she kicked me or hit me," Dredd confessed to much laughter.

Okay, we were safely over the sentimentality.

Then Baltar said, "Y'know, you two had us fooled for a while. Ripley, with her razor-sharp wit; you, John Boy, with that innocent face. And even if you didn't know firearms when you came to us, you sure knew how to outrun and outwit our crew. Can't quite figure out how you did so, but we give you props for it, fer sure."

"Thank you," Zander said softly, "for everything. We'll email pictures when our baby comes. And you are all hereby appointed honorary uncles—and aunt—right, Jayda?"

"Absolutely." I had to smile. Zander was going to be one proud papa.

"Okay, gang," Mal said before the atmosphere turned sloppy once more. "Great show! Kudos to all, but the party's over. Let's get this place squared away, shall we?"

All of us pitched in to gather trash, stack chairs, and haul the leftover food and dirty dishes to an apartment upstairs.

Mal sidled up to us while we were wiping down the tables. "Hey, so, I have one more thing for you guys before you go. When you're ready to leave, I'll walk you to your car. Okay?"

Zander, hands on his hips, surveyed the bounty Malware's crew had bestowed on us. "Well, to tell the truth, I don't know how we're going to haul all this loot back to our apartment."

Dredd overheard Zander. "Oh, yeah. Forgot to tell you. We've got you covered, John Boy. You're leaving Saturday, right? We'll keep everything here. Saturday morning, we'll load your loot into Banner's pickup. He and Neo will drive it to your apartment and help you put it in the trailer."

Zander sighed with relief. "You guys are epic. We can't tell you enough how we thank and appreciate all of you."

I looked around. They say that many hands make light work. Except for the stack of gifts, all traces of the party were gone, and the unadorned workout room had reemerged.

We said our goodbye then, and that took a while, what with the joking, handshakes, thumping of shoulders (it's a guy thing), and hugs—more than a couple awkward ones from those not accustomed to overt displays of affection. Mal, as he'd arranged, walked us out to our rental car.

He withdrew an envelope sticking up from his shirt pocket. "I've got your expenses and fees per Special Agent Gamble's instructions. He shook his head. "Look, I know you guys saved me and my crew during all that illegal hunt-and-destroy stuff back in July. I saw some genuinely strange things during that fight, too. And I know you chose not to knock me out and mess with my memories like you did the rest of my crew, and I appreciate that, but . . ."

Neither Zander nor I said a word. We knew Malware had cameras watching the parking lot. We had no doubts that our exchange was being recorded. Besides, this was Mal, angling for info.

Info he wouldn't get.

He grimaced and rubbed a hand across the stubble on his chin. "Yeah, guess you two know how to keep your mouths shut, and that's cool and all.

"But I, well, I couldn't help but notice, right on the heels of our club-house getting attacked and demolished, that other interesting and newsworthy things happened. Like, how the VP suddenly keeled over dead, and how you two called us for an emergency evac from some random farmhouse in Virginia. But, see, you didn't ask us to drop you home. No, you told us to land at Walter Reed—right after the Secret Service had rushed the President there. I mean, a person needs some *seriously* hefty top cover to get clearance to land next to Marine One, am I right?"

He glanced at the envelope in his hand. "And the checks I'm handing over? Nice payout, by the bye—except DOD doesn't throw cash out the windows. Well, they're not supposed to anyway. What I'm saying is, I figure you guys did some *exceptionally* specialized work and are getting paid quite handsomely for it. Also, the instructions for your payout being routed via Gamble, not through our usual DOD contract liaison? Adds up to odd and extremely covert. So. So, maybe the work you did was actually for *the President?*"

Zander and I smiled and said nothing.

Mal sighed. "Shoot. I've got this itch to *know* crawling around in my head, but you're not going to give up even a half-baked clue, are you? And Gamble and his girl are every bit as closemouthed."

I reached out and plucked the envelope from Mal's fingers to put him out of his misery. "Mal, from the bottom of my heart, thank you for everything. I'm sorry you and your crew lost so much on our account, particularly Mulder. At least we have, um, *assurances* that his wife and kids will be taken care of, and you'll be fully compensated. Enough to rebuild the clubhouse."

He nodded. "We're working out the details with DOD."

Zander held out his hand, and they shook. "You and Malware will be in our prayers, Mal. If you are ever in a jam, let us know. We owe you."

"Big time," I added, leaning in for a last hug.

⌘

WE DIDN'T GET THE LARGER moving trailer after all. On our way home from the dinner party-slash-baby shower, I opened the envelope I'd pried out of Mal's hand. I removed four checks, two in my name and two in Zander's name.

Zander had to pull over and administer CPR after my heart stopped and I passed out.

I'm kidding! But, he *did* pull over because he couldn't believe the amounts I read to him. *Screamed* at him, actually. And incoherently. I'd never held half a mil before except in Monopoly money.

The individual checks for expense reimbursement were handsome and included a relocation package, both to and from Maryland; four months' apartment rental; a daily per diem; and the Blue Book value for our car, split evenly between us.

Then our contractor fees. Apparently we weren't independent sub-contractors but rather statutory employees of Malware? Huh. News to us.

That's what President Jackson meant by reminding us that Malware is a military contractor with funding allocated for their services. Zander and I were part of those services!

As Malware employees, Mal's payroll person had withheld the necessary Medicare, Social Security, and state taxes, sending them to the appropriate tax "places" in our names, as well as some sort of contributions to Malware's 401(k) with a fifty percent employer match. The only reason I could come up with that explained the amount on the "salary" checks after all these deductions was that President Jackson had requested that Zander and I, *after* taxes, would each receive $250,000. Someone had to have used some creative algebra to make that happen.

We were in shock. I'm not even sure how Zander got us back to our apartment in one piece. Perhaps the nanomites navigated. Anyway, by the time Saturday morning rolled around, we'd deposited our Malware checks into our joint account and had revised our moving plans.

On Saturday morning, instead of hitching up a trailer, we picked up the moving truck we'd reserved. With Zander following me, I drove the rental car back to the rental place and dropped it. We weren't in a rush, having decided to leave town early Sunday morning instead of Saturday afternoon.

When Banner and Neo arrived midmorning with the load of baby gifts, they not only loaded them into the truck but helped us finish clearing out our apartment. Afterward, we treated Banner and Neo to lunch at our favorite Chinese buffet.

I waved to Ms. Wong as we went through the cashier line and promised her that we were leaving the DC area in the morning.

She seemed relieved.

⌘⌘⌘⌘

CHAPTER 3

AFTER WE SAID GOODBYE to Banner and Neo, we checked into a *very* nice hotel suite, intending to spend our last night in Maryland in style—which we surely did. We swam in the hotel pool, soaked in our room's private hot tub, got a twosome massage, and dined in their posh restaurant. An hour later, we ordered two of every dessert on the room-service menu.

It was awesome.

I waved a sad adieu when we pulled away from the hotel early the next day. I was considerably *less* sad when we jointly said farewell to the good and novel experiences we'd shared in and around DC and bid a solid "good riddance" to the danger and distress we'd experienced.

Set our eyes and hearts toward home.

Like I said, it took longer than we expected to pack up our lives in Maryland and head back to New Mexico, but the delay had been good for us. It allowed us to "decompress" from the strain we'd worked under, said strain being mental, emotional, and physical. The weight of protecting the President's life and the future course of our nation had been heavy. I don't think we appreciated how heavy it had been until we had been out from under it a while.

With the unexpected surfeit of ready money burning a hole in our checking account, we decided to take a little detour and have some fun on our road trip. We drove a full eight hours on Sunday, arrived in Williamstown, Kentucky, late in the afternoon, and checked into another (but more modest) hotel.

The next morning, after a good breakfast, we headed to our objective: the Ark Encounter. We had delayed our departure from Maryland to Sunday morning specifically so we could put in a full day's drive and arrive in Williamstown that evening and be ready for adventure the following morning.

We spent the better part of Monday in the park. After touring the Ark and all the accompanying displays—which were *amazing*—we rode their zip lines several times and ate from their terrific restaurant buffet twice.

I loved it all—and I only threw up once that morning. Yay me.

The next day, we hit the road, dropped down onto I-64, headed south toward the Florida panhandle, and settled in to a more leisurely pace. We needed the time and absence of stress to further decompress, to think about where we would live when we arrived in Albuquerque, and what work we would look for.

What could be better than a few nights on the beach? Destin here we come!

"All this cash in our pockets opens more doors, don't you think?" I asked Zander. "We can move into a nice apartment and take our time job hunting. Speaking of jobs, have you given any thought to what you want to do?"

Zander was quiet for a few moments, and I let him have the time he needed before he answered. When he did reply, I was surprised.

"Think I'll make an appointment with Pastor McFee as soon as we're settled."

"You want to go back to your old job at DCC?"

"Not particularly."

That was the big surprise.

"Then why . . ."

"Yeah, exactly. *Why.* To tell you the truth, I feel like the Lord wants me to go see him—even though I don't think I'm supposed to repeat my associate pastor role. It's more that he and I have a conversation waiting for us, and I need to know that God has closed that particular door to me. Then I will be free to explore other avenues."

"Um, okay. Do you have any direction from the Lord after that?"

He slowly nodded. "Not sure what shape it's going to take, but I believe I will be teaching."

"Teaching? Like, school?"

"Nope. Teaching the word. And in my spirit, it feels important. Sort of heavy. Maybe even urgent."

He changed the subject. "What about you? With a baby coming, do you want to work or stay home? I guess we haven't talked about that, have we?"

I laughed wryly. "You're so *not* PC, Zander Cruz. Don't you know that moms aren't allowed to stay home and raise children these days? That's what minimum-wage daycare workers are for."

We chuckled at my sarcasm, but we hadn't ever discussed the logistics of child rearing. Hadn't, because we didn't believe we could have kids. And up to this point? I'd been the bigger breadwinner.

"As much as possible and for as long as possible, Jayda, I'd like to support our family and let you stay home to care for our little one. I know this will be an adjustment—for both of us."

"We have a decent nest egg to get us started. And, well, I have been noodling around, wondering what kind of 'cottage industry' I might try. People make their living online these days. Loads of options out there. And, Nano, I will need your assistance."

We can help, Jayda Cruz. We, too, have been perusing suitable work ideas for you.

"Have you, Nano?" In answer, a stack of website designs flashed before my eyes, each touting a different product or service.

"I see that you have given it some thought, Nano."

We can do the majority of the work, Jayda Cruz, and ensure that you are successful.

"That would be cool, Nano—I like the whole concept. We can go through your suggestions as we settle in."

Zander glanced at me. "Cool? I think it's brilliant."

"You're not wrong—the possibilities are endless. Say . . ."

Zander glanced at me then back to the road. "What?"

It dawned on me that the nanomites had been, well, extraordinarily quiet while we were on the road.

"Um, Nano. What have you been up to?"

Up to, Jayda Cruz?

"Typically, you are, shall we say, *chattier*. What else have you been doing today?"

After a short pause they replied, *We are monitoring various news outlets worldwide, Jayda Cruz, as well as the financial markets. Keeping abreast of national and world happenings. There is a sizable amount of information to sift through, but we are learning great quantities of things.*

Connectivity for the nanomites was a negligible problem these days. They rode our phones' cellular networks (without using up our monthly data plan), but they also, nearly effortlessly, hijacked any Wi-Fi or cellular connection we passed, jumping from one connection to another or riding several simultaneously. I had often noted in the past how the nanomites rocked the digital world.

They were so far beyond that today, closer to *ruling* the digital world than I had the courage to admit. The two nanoclouds being physically tied to us did limit them somewhat—not a bad thing, in my estimation.

"Find anything of interest?"

It is all of interest, Jayda Cruz.

"Huh."

The drive gave us time to discuss, too, how we would announce our happy news to our family—to Zander's parents and siblings, to Abe, and to Emilio.

Emilio! I was particularly glad we would be seeing him soon. Yes, I was growing a new life in my womb, but that made Emilio no less "my boy," our informally adopted son. I couldn't wait to hug him.

"You know," I answered as we pulled in for lunch on the far outskirts of St. Louis, "We have money. We could buy a house."

"Hey, that's a great idea."

⌘

ONLY ONE EVENT DISTURBED the tranquility of our cross-country drive. After playing and lounging on the white sands around Destin for three days, we angled our way back north, cutting through Shreveport, then over to Dallas, and north from there. We were nearing Oklahoma City, our last stop on the way home, when my phone rang.

Jayda Cruz, Dr. Bickel is calling.

I had the nanomites route the call to the warehouse so Zander and I could both listen and talk. A happy grin lit my face when I picked up the call. "Dr. Bickel! Can't wait to see you; we'll be back in New Mexico by this time tomorrow."

Dr. Bickel's voice on the other end wasn't as happy as mine was. "Jayda, can you ask the nanomites to wipe out all traces of this call when we've finished talking? They can do that, right?"

Jayda Cruz, you know we can. Please assure Dr. Bickel that no trace of an outgoing call from his phone or an incoming call on your phone will remain.

"Uh, consider it done, Dr. Bickel. Why? What's wrong?"

"I think we've been hacked, Jayda."

"Wait—who's been hacked?"

"Sandia—in particular, the AMEMS network. Specifically, my private node on the AMEMS classified network."

AMEMS stood for Dr. Bickel's department, Advanced Microelectro-mechanical Systems. The department I had worked in. Twice. Once as Gemma Keyes, once as Jayda Locke.

"You *think* you've been hacked? You aren't certain?"

"Oh, I'm pretty sure, all right, even if Sandia and DOE's cyber security people say they can't figure out how. See, I started with a little program called Tripwire, then I enhanced it. The program runs every evening when I log off my department's R&D node. It snapshots the node so that I have an actual image of the name, size, and date stamp of every folder and file on that network node."

"Okaaaay." *Obsessive much?*

"Jayda! *I trust no one.* I'm the only person in the world with access to that node! I've even locked out DOE's IT and cyber security wonks to ensure the security of my research."

I exhaled. Slowly. Zander glanced at me and frowned, then returned his eyes to the road.

I knew what he had to be thinking. *How in the world would you do that, Dr. Bickel? I mean, how can an employee lock the government's network guys out of the government's own network? That's not even possible, is it?*

Then I remembered: Dr. Bickel had programmed the nanomites—before they added to his initial programming, of course. Nevertheless,

Dr. Bickel's computer skills were so good that if he ever decided to hack the Pentagon, I'd advise President Jackson to change the launch codes ASAP.

I blew out another breath as Zander caught the freeway exit leading to our hotel. "You said your program flagged an intrusion?"

"No doubt in my mind. Four instances of file size changes, all four within an hour last evening."

"They didn't download then erase your data?" *Setting you back years?*

He snorted. "No, but if they had, I have a backup drive in my vault."

"So, you think you've been hacked. Can you tell what they took?"

"That node contains one hundred terabytes of current research and development data. The only good thing is that the nanotechnology R&D contained on that node is applicable only to healthcare—*nanomedical haemobots*, dumb, single-purpose nanobots, capable of only one function, such as seeking out cells of a specific cancer. Their programming cannot be hijacked.

"And Jayda, you know that I uploaded the design data pertaining to the smart, learning nanomites to Alpha Tribe. I destroyed every other copy of that data so it could *not* be stolen and misused. Ever. Which is why I need the nanomites to erase this call. I don't want to leave any kind of link between me and thee—since I know someone has been snooping in my research."

"Does that mean you won't have Christmas dinner with us?"

Immediate turnabout in Dr. Bickel's attitude.

"What? Well no, it doesn't have to mean that. We could arrange a place to meet and the nanomites can hide me when you pick me up, can't they? That way, no one would know I'm there. You do know I'd dearly love to help with Christmas cooking!"

I laughed softly. "Yes, we can work out the details. But you're saying you are convinced that the data on your healthcare nanos has been taken?"

"I have to assume so. It's a significant breach of DOE's cyber security, Jayda, either by the Chinese or Russians. Maybe the Ukrainians." I could hear him grind his teeth in frustration.

"And you won't know who . . ."

"We won't know *who* until they win the Nobel prize—before I do."

We hung up with Dr. Bickel, and the nanomites finished wiping all traces of the call. It wouldn't show up on either phone's call log or on our service providers' logs. Our call had never happened.

But that didn't erase his news: Someone had breached Dr. Bickel's network node.

⌘⌘⌘⌘

CHAPTER 4

ZANDER REMEMBERED THE gutter that ran across the road where the street, without much warning, dumped into the cul-de-sac. He braked gently, taking care not to brake too hard and jar the truck's contents—although I knew his real intention was not to jar *the wee one* I carried in my womb.

Did I mention he would be a doting daddy?

The truck made a slow traverse of the cul-de-sac, not unlike taking a victory lap. We were home!

We passed the Tuckers' first, on our right, then Mrs. Calderón's house. I watched her windows, looking for telltale movement.

There. The blinds moved incrementally. No doubt, Mrs. Calderón was studying our moving truck in return, wondering who we were and what we were doing.

Then we slid by what remained of my former home.

In the lot where Gemma Keyes had once lived, a broken cement slab surrounded by weeds marked where the house had stood. Courtesy of the City of Albuquerque, a company that specialized in junk removal had hauled off the debris. My old, detached garage, set back from the street, remained standing, but it, too, was surrounded by weeds.

My alter-ego, Gemma, had no relatives who could claim the lot, so we didn't know what would become of it. I certainly could press no claim to it. The City of Albuquerque would most likely petition the courts to rule on the lot's disposition, then put it up for sale and pocket the proceeds.

The nanomites were quiet as we glided by. Were they recalling the day General Cushing had blown up the house—taking herself, my sister Genie, Aunt Lu's cat, Jake, and a million or so nanomites with her? I knew I was.

I blinked back tears and forced my eyes ahead to the next house over. Another blink. The words FOR SALE swung lethargically from the yardarm of a realtor's sign embedded in the grass.

"Wow. Guess Mr. and Mrs. Flores gave up."

"Hmm?"

"Mr. and Mrs. Flores. Looks like they've moved out, put their place up for sale. They were getting older, but they have kids and grandkids all over the country. Maybe they have gone to live near some of them."

Zander completed the circle, pulled up in front of Abe's house, and turned off the engine. We got out, both of us looking around. Well, Zander was stretching his back and legs. I was the one doing the looking.

The house and yard next to Abe's bore the sad face of abandonment. Emilio's uncle, Mateo, would not be coming back, so no one lived there.

I ran out of interest in the neighborhood when Emilio burst from Abe's house like a shot from a cannon.

He shouted like a banshee, "Jayda! Jayda! Jayda!"

Then he plowed into me with all the force of that figurative cannon shot. I hugged him as hard as he hugged me, kissing the top of his head—or thereabouts, the actual top being suddenly too high for my lips to reach. He turned from me to Zander, hugging him, too, then back to me, sniffling the whole while.

Well, maybe I was sniffling, too.

Abe, grinning large, looked down from his covered porch. Eventually, we moved our lovefest up the steps and into the house.

⌘

MUCH LATER, AFTER A satisfying dinner, we sat together in Abe's living room, Abe in his recliner, Emilio on the sofa between Zander and me.

I wrapped my arms around Emilio a second time. "Hey, can we—Zander and I—talk to you?"

He twisted out of my embrace so he could look me in the face. He may have felt my simmering excitement, but I think he also perceived something momentous was coming. As was typical of many abused or neglected children, change often portended something negative.

Emilio was no different in how he viewed change. We watched a frisson of fear shutter his dark eyes.

"Are you going 'way again?"

"No, not at all, Emilio. We are home to stay. But, we want to ask you a question. Would you sit on the coffee table where we can both see you?"

Abe looked from me to Zander. Maybe he was feeling worried, too.

Emilio sat docilely atop the low table across from us, but he kept blinking his eyes. Passively expecting life to deal him another blow.

"Emilio," Zander said gently. "Jayda and I love you. Even though you live with Abe, you are our boy. Our son. You know that, right?"

More blinking. A quick nod.

My throat clogged up a little, but I managed to get some words past the choke point. "Because you *are* our boy, Emilio, we wanted to ask . . . if you would like to have a little brother or sister."

His dark brows twitched and drew together. He blinked more slowly. "What you mean?"

Zander and I smiled at each other and winked at Abe, whose mouth slowly dropped toward his shoes.

Zander said, "Emilio, Jayda and I are going to have a baby. Come April, you will have a little brother or sister."

Emilio's eyes jerked to my belly. "You havin' a baby? Honest?"

"Yup. We're adding to our family, Emilio. You, Abe, us, and a baby. So, *big brother* . . . what do you think?"

It was the right thing to say, and I credit the Holy Spirit for showing us how to break the news to Emilio in the best way possible.

"I'll be a big brother?"

"We're counting on it," Zander replied, taking one of Emilio's hands in his. "We don't want to do this without you, Emilio. We love you and need you; you are ours forever. And this baby will be your brother or sister."

I swallowed. Hard. How had this boy come to be so rooted in my heart? To lose him would tear me apart.

"You and Abe are the first people in New Mexico to know," Zander added. "We'd like to keep it between the four of us until Thanksgiving when we will tell my mom and dad and Izzie. Speaking of Thanksgiving, we're planning to spend the four-day weekend in Las Cruces with them, and you are both invited—if that is okay with you, Abe?"

Abe, from his recliner across the living room, nodded.

I added, "Mom and Dad Cruz know you are family to us, so you are family to them, too. We will tell them about the baby that weekend. Until then, can you help us keep our little secret?"

Emilio nodded slowly, the pieces of what we'd revealed finding their places and fitting nicely. "I'll be a good big brother. I promise."

Zander and I slipped off the couch and knelt. We wrapped Emilio in our joined embrace. "You will be the best big brother ever, Emilio," I whispered, "and your little brother or sister will love you to the moon and back."

⌘

WE SPENT SIX NIGHTS in a hotel while we searched for an apartment. Even though we considered an apartment to be a short-term fix before we located and bought a house, we didn't want the apartment to be too far from Abe and Emilio. It was important to us that we be nearby to help Abe with Emilio.

We found a small two-bedroom unit on Thursday that would suit our needs and that we could get into right away—but only if our credit checked out and if we paid out a hefty deposit plus first and last month's rent and showed the apartment manager the balance in our checking account—all because we didn't have a demonstrable source of income, aka *employment*.

Sheesh! Getting into a decent apartment can be tough when you don't have a job. We did, however, have great references, including our former apartment manager in Maryland and Dr. Bickel here in Albuquerque. I wished we could have put Robert or Maddie Jackson down on the application. Wouldn't that have been a hoot! I even imagined the apartment manager trying to check out *that* reference.

Hello, the White House? Yes, I'm calling from the Piñon Pine Apartments in Albuquerque, New Mexico, for a Ms. Madeleine Jackson. In regards to? She is listed as a character reference in an apartment application.

Ha!

That was a laughable fantasy, of course. It was our recent big bank deposit that overcame the absence of employment. Nevertheless, we were temporarily stuck in Piñon Pine's bureaucratic approval cycle. While we waited for the apartment manager to check our credit rating and references, Zander decided to call for an appointment to see Pastor McFee.

"I feel impressed to see him at the earliest possible opportunity, Jay. Don't know why, but I sense the Holy Spirit telling me to get it done sooner rather than later."

"Well, today is good. We're sitting on our hands until we can move in."

Zander made the call, and Mrs. Coyne spoke to the pastor while he waited.

"Mr. Cruz? Pastor can see you this afternoon at 2:00 p.m. if that works for you."

"I accept. Thank you." Zander hung up and shook his head a little.

"What?"

"That's the first time I remember Mrs. Coyne calling me Mr. Cruz rather than Pastor Cruz. But, it stands to reason. I'm not pastoring any longer, right?"

⌘

PASTOR MCFEE WELCOMED HIM with genuine affection and greeted him by his first name. "Zander, my boy. Come in, come in!"

Pastor McFee gestured Zander into his office and showed him to a comfortable chair. He took the one opposite him, across a small glass-topped table.

"Tell me: How are you and your lovely bride, Zander?"

"We are well and blessed, Pastor. It's sure good to see you, sir."

"I feel the same. Truth be told, our young adults have had to shift for themselves the past few months. We—I include myself—have truly missed you and Jayda. Bit surprised to see you back so soon, though. Everything all right?"

"Actually, we had a great time in Maryland, Pastor. Jayda's job was excellent and she did well at it. We found a good, Bible-teaching church, too, and I became involved in their Celebrate Recovery program, helping to lead the group and disciple new believers. Thank you for giving me a good reference with Pastor Lucklow, by the way."

"Of course. I was happy to give you a glowing reference, but . . ." Pastor McFee squinted at Zander, "less than four months later you're back in Albuquerque?"

"Ah." Zander smiled. "May I speak to you in confidence, Pastor?"

"Certainly. You have my word, Zander."

Jayda had agreed that Zander could tell their news to Pastor McFee. If you can't trust your pastor, who can we trust?

"Well, sir, we have experienced something of a miracle. You see, a while before we married, Jayda was told that she couldn't have children. She knew I wanted a family and, on those grounds, refused to let us get serious. However, after we prayed, we decided to trust God. He gave us Emilio, and we love him as our own. We would be happy with that."

A light dawned on Pastor McFee's face. "I sense something exciting on the horizon. Do tell!"

Zander's grin stretched wide. "Yes, sir. We are expecting. We thought we would wait and tell our family over Thanksgiving when Jayda is a little farther along before we tell the world."

"Congratulations, my boy! And you thought you would never receive this blessing?"

"That's right, sir. Medically, it is a miracle—and it is the reason we came home. We want to raise our child here, around family and friends."

"Well, I cannot tell you how pleased I am for both of you. And Zander, you seem much more settled than you were, say, before you and Jayda married."

"I believe I am, sir. Marriage suits me."

"And did you come to see me hoping to slip back into your old position here at DCC?"

Zander watched Pastor McFee's expression shift slightly, but he was surprised that the man's face held a hint of disappointment. Or was it sadness?

"Not especially, sir. I felt the Lord impressing me to meet with you, to check and reconnect—if that makes sense? As for the young adults, if my place isn't here with them, then I am confident the Lord will open another door and lead us through it."

"Yes, he will, and I am glad that you are mature enough in Christ to realize that when the Lord closes one door, he will open a *better* one for you and your family, Zander. But most important? Whatever door of opportunity comes your way, it will serve to further glorify the Lord and increase his kingdom."

"That's how I feel, sir."

McFee tapped a cadence on the arm of his chair with the fingers of his right hand. "I do find the timing of things curious, though."

"Sir?"

"The timing of your visit. We extended an offer to a young minister last week—name of Aiden Easterly. And, I was reading his email accepting our offer a few minutes ago."

"I see. Well, I am glad the young adults will have good leadership going forward."

Pastor McFee didn't answer immediately, and his fingers on the arm of his chair continued tapping to a silent tune. Zander, sensing some unrest in the older man, waited quietly.

McFee finally broke his silence. "Zander, a few minutes ago you asked if you could speak to me in confidence."

"Er, yes, sir."

"May I ask your confidence? I seek your prayers regarding something . . . delicate."

Zander sat up straighter. "You can rely upon me, Pastor. It would be my honor to pray over your concerns."

"Thank you, Zander."

McFee's fingers slowed, and he sighed. "I don't allow my associate pastors to get involved in church board meetings. In some respects, I think the politicking and the level of immaturity a few of our board members possess would shake a young minister's faith."

He looked toward his office window. "And our board is evenly split these days, four to one side, four to the other side. A precarious balance."

McFee studied Zander. "You believe in the power of God, Zander, and you have experienced it. You *know* the Lord. So do I. You trust God's word implicitly and teach it as truth. So do I. However, on our church board sit two men and two women whose faith I cannot entirely vouch for. Their theology is more broadminded and progressive than biblical; their politics identical.

"On the other side, I have four board members I would trust with my life. They are, for the most part, grounded in the word and their lives reflect it."

McFee's expression darkened. "The liberal four want change at Downtown Community Church, Zander. They want a more 'inclusive' environment, more social programs, less preaching, less evangelism, more 'community action.' One of them tendered the resumé of the associate pastor we hired this week. However, I didn't quite trust what I read. Some of the wording in his resumé seemed too pat. Too much like *code* . . . and my hackles went up.

"I was persuaded, however, to at least interview the young man. He came and preached two Sundays ago. Was a big hit with a large portion of the congregation. Got the young adults fired up, too."

"And you, sir?"

McFee nodded. "I took advantage of his two days with us to engage him in conversation, to sound out his views on a number of key doctrines and issues. In every respect, his answers were correct—but, in my estimation, barely this side of the line. My biggest misgivings were over his use of veiled terminology, that perhaps I needed my Dick Tracy secret decoder ring in order to decipher his answers."

"Beg your pardon, sir? Dick Tracy? Secret decoder ring?"

Pastor McFee slapped his knee and laughed. "I have revealed my age, Zander. It's a reference to an old comic strip—used to come in the Sunday morning paper. Made into a movie, too, a while back. Wasn't an especially good one, I'm afraid."

Within the warehouse, colorful images flashed before Zander's eyes—the nanomites acting quickly to supply what his knowledge lacked.

He whispered back, "Thanks, Nano, but maybe later?"

McFee seemed to be struggling to find the right words. "And I guess . . ."

McFee's words trailed off. Zander, sensing his former pastor's distress, waited patiently. Prayed for him silently.

McFee finally shrugged his shoulders. "I mean, I'm not *that* old. Be sixty-two next May, but I suppose I can appreciate if younger folk feel that I might be out of touch with what is going on in the world these days. Here's the rub: Our 'progressive' board members have suggested it might be time for me to retire. *Retire?* I'm not old enough, and I'm not ready, either. Hadn't planned to retire for at least another four years—maybe eight if my strength holds."

Zander frowned. "If it is any comfort to you, sir, I don't believe you are old or out of touch, either one. It is the *world* that has lost touch with God. We, the next generation, need you and men like you to keep us walking the straight and narrow as we wade through all the muck, strangeness, and upheaval going on these days."

McFee reached over and squeezed Zander's shoulder. "Thank you. You do my heart good, Pastor Cruz—and you *are* a pastor, you know, whether you have a pastoring job or not. Pastoring is a calling, not necessarily a paid position."

Zander sat back, his heart vibrating with encouragement. *This is why you led me to seek out Pastor McFee first thing, isn't it, Lord? You needed me to hear this—that pastoring is a calling, not necessarily a paid position.*

He recovered himself. "So, what happened to the vote for this prospective associate pastor, sir? It sounds as if you have little confidence in his testimony and intentions. How did the board vote?"

"Typically, my solid four board members would vote with me, the four liberal members would vote against me, and I would be the deciding vote." He shook his head. "The problem is that two of the board members on the left, between themselves and their friends in the church, can account for twenty-five percent of our annual budget. I hate to say this, but money does talk."

"I can't see concern over the budget swaying you, sir. I *can* envision you replying, 'Go with God; we trust our finances to the Lord.'"

Pastor McFee's smile was wan. "You're right. They didn't sway me—but they got to Harry Fuentes. He's always a hair on the squeamish side when the finances get tight, and things have been a little slow recently. Rather than backing me as he usually does, he voted with them. Said we desperately needed to revive our young adult population and that we could revisit Easterly's appointment in six months if I didn't like how he was working out."

McFee sighed. "As I'm sitting with you and talking it over, I wish I had put my foot down and refused to accept an associate I couldn't fully trust. I wish . . . I wish I had known you were coming back, Zander."

Zander sat blinking, more than a little concerned. *Lord? Did we miss your timing for our return? But neither of us felt any urgency. I sensed no nudge from the Holy Spirit to decline the President's briefings and rush back. All I felt was the need to come see Pastor McFee once I got here.*

Pastor McFee stood, and Zander followed suit. "Listen, Zander. Please pray with me about the situation. You may share my concerns with your wife and pray over them together; other than her, though, please tell no one. But I would ask you one last thing, if I may?"

"Yes, sir. Certainly."

"Will you keep your ear to the ground for me? You led the young adults of this church well. They know, love, and trust you. If my new associate strays from Scripture, I trust you will hear about it. Don't interfere, of course—that would be inappropriate. But be my eyes and ears, will you?"

"I will, sir. If I may ask, when does this man arrive?"

"We haven't announced his appointment, but his start date will be Friday, November 30. Good timing on his part, too. Carol and I have been married forty years, come January. I am taking her on a cruise after Christmas, and I will need an associate pastor to run things while I am gone. Steve Doherty, our youth leader, is too young and inexperienced to handle the entire church."

"A cruise! That sounds great, sir. Where will the cruise be taking you?"

"We'll fly from San Diego to Oahu, board our ship for a fifteen-day cruise around the Islands—making port often for scenic excursions—then fly back to San Diego. After we disembark, we'll fly to Seattle, spend a few days there with some old friends, then fly home. Don't let that cat out of the bag, though, my boy. I want to surprise Carol."

Zander chuckled. "My lips are sealed, sir."

They moved down the hall, toward the receptionist and the exit. "Say, that reminds me, Zander. Since we will be away two Sundays, would you like to preach one of those Sundays? Second Sunday in January, I believe."

"Would I? You bet."

"Excellent. I'll put you on the schedule. Thank you, too, for your discretion and prayers. As I said, I am delighted to have you back."

They shook hands, and Zander saw the affection in the older man's eyes.

"God bless you, Pastor."

"Thank you, my boy. I know the Lord has great things in store for you."

⌘⌘⌘⌘

CHAPTER 5

SATURDAY MORNING AS ZANDER and I were finishing breakfast, the apartment manager called my cell phone. "Your check has cleared and your apartment is ready, Ms. Cruz. You may pick up your keys any time today before noon. We close the office at noon on Saturdays and reopen Monday morning."

"Yes; we'll be there shortly." I hung up and whooped. "Zander! We can move in today."

"Have you had enough to eat?"

I shrugged. "Too excited to swallow another bite."

"Me too. Let's go."

We called Izzie as we left the restaurant. She and Emilio had offered to help us move in, so we asked Izzie if she would fetch Emilio for us and meet us at our new digs around 10 a.m. We also asked if she could recruit at least one hardy male from the young adult group to help Zander with the heavy lifting.

"Not a problem—leave it to me," she told us.

We returned to our hotel so Zander could fetch the moving truck. We had been driving yet another rental car so we wouldn't have to drive the truck all over town while we were apartment hunting. Zander and I met up at the apartment complex's office where we signed for the keys. As soon as we had them, we navigated through the parking lot to our building and Zander backed the truck into a parking space near the steps leading up to our second-floor apartment.

It wouldn't take long to unload the truck once our little crew arrived, but we didn't want them to see all the baby gifts—not until after our surprise Thanksgiving announcement to Zander's family. So, before Izzie and Emilio arrived, Zander planned to unload all the baby gifts and stack them in the apartment's second bedroom, locking the bedroom door behind him.

To no little dismay on my part, he insisted on doing most of the job himself.

"I thought about it while we were driving here, and I don't want you carrying anything heavy from here on, Jay. I can manage the boxed baby furniture without you. The crib might be a smidge awkward to handle on the stairs, but it's nothing I can't manage."

According to him, I was forbidden to lift anything due to my "fragile state."

Fragile state?

"Zander, I'm having a baby, not recovering from back surgery—and I can still bench press 150 pounds—because *nanomites*, remember?"

"Yeah, but why take unnecessary risks? Like, what if you tripped on the stairs while carrying something and fell? Keep in mind that this is our only baby, Jay."

We must concur with Zander, Jayda Cruz. While you should continue to exercise regularly to retain an optimal state of health during your pregnancy and while we are watching over you to provide extra support when needed, our research indicates that lifting more than twenty pounds is not advisable.

"Butt out, Nano. And FYI, all that research? It applies to women who don't have a couple trillion nanomites fused to their skeletal system and musculature."

Zander lifted his eyebrows and murmured softly, "Our only baby, Jayda."

I deflated. "Yeah, okay. Whatever."

I checked the time: 9:35. Izzie and Emilio would be arriving around 10:00 a.m.

"You'd better get a move on, bud."

"I'm on it."

Izzie, with Emilio in the passenger seat, pulled into view minutes after Zander finished with the baby gifts and furnishings. Izzie's arrival was followed not by one guy to help, but three young men from Zander's former young adult Bible study—Josh, Todd, and Diego.

"Oh, man, it is so good to see you guys!" Josh said, hugging Zander while simultaneously pounding him on the back. "It's been like a desert around here since you left, Pastor Zander."

Diego snorted. "*Like* a desert? It *is* the desert, you dork."

"Yeah, but it's the *high* desert, moron. Besides, I was speaking spiritually."

"I'll agree with that," Todd said, nodding. "Dry as a bone without the Bible studies you used to teach. We're parched."

"You'll get a new young adult pastor soon."

"I guess the board has interviewed maybe three prospective pastors, but since you're back, won't they rehire you?"

Zander shook his head. "I think the Lord has something different for me at this time. Be patient; I'm sure Pastor McFee has someone in mind."

I glanced at Zander. He knew more than he was letting on, but it wasn't our place to make the announcement. "Well, we're glad you are here to help, aren't we, Zander?"

"Better believe it. Come on, guys—and Izzie. Let's get the boxes out of the truck so we can get to the big stuff."

You might say that the guys formed a bucket brigade from the truck to our front door. They pulled boxes from the truck one by one, and handed each one off to the next person, who handed the box on up the stairs, around the corner, and down to our doorway. I noted the markings on each box—bedroom, kitchen, bathroom—and I had them stack the boxes in groups.

When the guys had cleared all the boxes from the truck, it was time for the furniture. I directed our crew on where to put the few big pieces we owned—bed frame, mattress, dresser, nightstand, sofa, and our little dining table and chairs. Our four strapping young men and Emilio made quick work of them. In fact, it took all of an hour to completely empty the truck. While Zander and the guys put our bed frame together, Izzie and I unpacked the sheets, pillows, and comforter.

Fifteen minutes later, our bedroom, except for a stack of boxes containing clothes, looked habitable. Our crew collapsed in the living room.

"Well, that was fairly easy," Diego said from the sofa. "You guys are organized."

"And you guys are awesome," I replied. I found the cooler and cracked it open. "Something cold to drink? Sodas? Bottled water?"

After I passed drinks around, Zander said, "All that's left is to return the truck."

"Right—cause we don't have a bunch of boxes to unpack," I drawled.

"Er, right. Truck is next, not last."

"Hey, Zander?" Todd was sprawled on the living room carpet, guzzling a soda. "Any chance the young adults could come over and hang out with you guys once in a while? You know, like to play games or watch a movie?"

Zander was careful with his answer. "Sure, but I don't want to do anything that might be construed as interfering with the new young adult leader—that is, whenever he is appointed and installed."

Todd persisted. "Well, until we actually get another young adult leader, can we come over sometimes, have fellowship with you guys and read the word together? See, UNM's new semester has started, and we need some sort of structure for the young adults who are giving DCC a try."

Zander did see. He looked at me, and I nodded. "That sounds okay. I know we would enjoy the fellowship."

"Like every Friday night?" Todd asked, "Six or seven-ish?"

Zander laughed. "All right. But you guys are in charge of organizing. I won't take charge or call anyone or lift a finger to coordinate activities. That's all on you."

Diego nodded. "You got it, Boss. Organic and unofficial all the way."

Josh added, "And we'll stop when the new guy gets here."

When Zander nodded, the guys grinned. Todd and Diego high-fived.

"All right! Getting the gang back together!"

"Well, I have laundry to do," Izzie announced. "You ready to go, Emilio?"

Emilio gave Zander and me a big hug, then headed out with Izzie. Josh, Todd, and Diego followed on their heels.

⌘

AS SOON AS THEY WERE out the door, I began to unpack and set up the kitchen, my stomach announcing that it was lunch time *somewhere* in the world. Why? Because food was uppermost in my mind. *All. The. Time.*

My abnormally supercharged appetite, needed to fuel my abnormally supercharged metabolism, was eating for two, meaning I was pretty much nonstop ravenous. And being preggo, I also felt like I was frequently "off my nut."

Stupid hormones.

The nanomites monitored and did their best to stimulate or moderate my hormone levels. Whatever I lacked in that department, they supplemented, either manufacturing what they could themselves or providing them via their (apparently) newly minted license to practice medicine and prescribe medications.

Before we'd left Maryland, I received three text messages stating that my prescriptions were ready. I picked up the medications along with the nanomites' recommended prenatal vitamins and folic acid supplement and left it to the nanomites how they reconciled "my doctor's" orders and the pharmacy's inventory.

The nanomites were, I was learning, ferocious watchdogs when it came to the little bun in my oven, and that was fine with me. After all, I would not be seeing an obstetrician during my pregnancy or delivery, because any type of blood work requested by said doctor would have totally freaked out both the lab and the doc.

Nope. With the nanomites presiding over my prenatal care, we would also be doing a home birth. On one point, however, Zander and I were not only in agreement, we were militant.

Zander had put it to the nanomites this way: "Nano, you will not, in any way, shape, form, or fashion, join yourselves to our child. You will not alter, mutate, or enhance him or her. We expect your promise on this. Do we have it?"

Yes, Zander Cruz. We will watch over—

"Hold it right there. Remember: We've said we don't want to know the gender until he or she is born."

We will comply, Zander Cruz. Going forward, then, how do you wish us to refer to the child?

Zander and I held a little side convo, and Zander replied to the nanomites, "Please use 'the baby' or maybe 'Baby Cruz' in place of specific pronouns. And, no, we're not going to call him or her some dumb, politically correct, make-believe word like 'theyby.'"

Very good, Zander and Jayda Cruz. We will respect your wishes.

"Thanks, Nano," I answered.

We will also, of course, monitor Baby Cruz's development.

"Okaaaay," I said, wondering what unarticulated clause or loophole I was agreeing to.

Zander must have followed my train of thought. "If anything concerning comes up in the baby's development, you will *do nothing* without first discussing it with us, right, Nano?"

Absolutely, Zander Cruz.

I looked at Zander. He looked at me. We both sighed.

We knew the nanomites were completely loyal and trustworthy—to Jesus first (the Jesus Tribe as they referred to him) and to us second. They had always done their best for our well-being. But we'd also had enough experience with them to have learned, sometimes the hard way, that the nanomites were quite creative in their own right. Specifically, when they had found "logical" work-arounds to circumnavigate ethics and social mores.

Right then, my stomach rumbled so loud that Zander heard it.

"Lunch?"

I laughed. "Please! The sooner, the better."

"Take the truck back on our way to that buffet restaurant on San Mateo?"

"I won't survive that long. How about we eat first, return truck after?"

"Whatever you need, Jay," Zander said, wrapping his arms around me. "Whatever you need, you and our little pumpkin."

I grinned. "Our little pumpkin needs baked chicken! *A big plate* of chicken. And *pie*."

⌘

THE APARTMENT TOOK SHAPE quickly once we had unloaded the truck, but we only unpacked the boxes we would need in the short-term. The rest we locked in the second bedroom with all the baby paraphernalia. Hopefully, we would find and purchase a house before our three-month lease was up and before I was quite far along. Perhaps even sooner. I was scouring the Albuquerque real estate market and had come up with what I thought was a brilliant idea.

I was fixing our lunch when I heard Zander's key in the door. He had gone out to get our groceries for the week.

Yes, groceries. We decided to cut down on eating out because it was expensive. Both of us were financially conservative, not wanting to waste the blessing God had given us via our Malware contractor checks. And since we weren't working jobs nor were we under time and schedule constraints, we had time to cook. Of course the size of our grocery bill would have bankrupted most couples, and the amount of food we brought home from the stores would have normally fed a small army.

"Mmm. Is that chow I smell? I'm as hungry as a horse."

"Tell me something new, Zander Cruz."

While he unpacked the bags and put the groceries away, I said, "I've been noodling on an idea, Babe. Can I tell you what I'm thinking while we eat?"

"Sure. Let me wash up. Be right there."

We sat down at the table together a few minutes later. I had made eight grilled cheese sandwiches, heated three cans of cream of tomato soup, laid out a plate of saltines, and sliced up four apples. We prayed, then dug in. My tummy, thankfully, seemed to approve of what I was putting in it. I was grateful for that because I had lost three pounds since we left DC— and I was already lean enough.

I hadn't noticed, however. The nanomites had brought it to my attention.

Jayda Cruz, we recommend a high-calorie nutritional drink to supplement your meals.

Good grief. Whatever the problem, they tripped all over themselves to provide a solution.

"I'll pick some up, Nano. Thank you."

We had Zander buy two cases for you, Jayda Cruz.

"Why, of course you did, Nano. Thank you."

Sheesh.

Zander interrupted my woolgathering. "What were you 'noodling on,' my love, my wife, the darling mother of my child?"

I giggled.

"That's funny, is it?"

"Not funny, Dearest, but wonderful—especially the 'darling mother of my child' part."

He leaned over, nuzzled my cheek, then my ear. Breathed on my neck until the tiny hairs there stood up and saluted.

"Uh, earth to Zander: The soup is cooling, and you won't like it cold."

He looked up—a bare three inches from my eyes—and made a sad puppy dog face. "Have we come to this? I make amorous advances, and you shut me down? Why, you hurt my feelings."

"Oh, *brother*."

I waggled one eyebrow, and he laughed with me—both of us happy in our mutual affection.

"Okay, but I have dibs on you tonight, my sweets," he grinned.

"Oh? What if I have dibs on you first?"

"Hmm. Let me think. Oh, why, yes, I believe I can accommodate your expectations."

I smiled. He smiled. We attacked our lunch.

Through a mouthful of sandwich, he asked, "Noodle?"

"It's tomato soup, Sweetie. No noodles."

Zander swallowed, "I said *noodling*."

"Oh, *that*. Well, I did a little exploring of the Albuquerque real estate market—and with every listing that caught my eye, one question kept popping up: If we bought that house, how and when would we see Abe and Emilio? How can we be there to support Abe if we're across town or on the west side? Isn't that why we rented this apartment, so we would be less than five minutes from them?"

Zander nodded. "Well, yeah. You're not wrong."

"Good, because I looked up the Flores' house on the MLS and guess what? Maybe because of Mateo's eyesore to their right or Gemma Keyes' vacant lot on their left, their house is practically dirt cheap."

"What? You're thinking we should buy the Flores' house? I mean, no offense, but it's not the best neighborhood for raising children."

I shrugged. "Yeah, but think about it. We'd be right across the street from Abe and Emilio. The house's floorplan matched my old place, but they had added on a third bedroom when their kids were little. Emilio would have his own room and could spend the night with us. In fact, he could pop over anytime. Not only is the house priced right, we'd have enough cash on hand to remodel the kitchen and bathroom."

"Huh."

I could tell he was mulling it over.

"Had another idea, too."

"Yeah? What's that?"

"Well, what if we could get Emilio the clear title to Mateo's house? With Mateo gone, shouldn't be too hard. Then we could petition the court to let us fix up the house and rent it out to benefit Emilio. It would provide a nice little passive income stream for him. College money. And perhaps the court would agree to allot a small monthly payment from the rent receipts to Abe for Emilio's upkeep—in addition to what he gets as a foster parent."

Zander guffawed. "I think I see where you're going with this. Neighborhood not up to our exacting standards? *Change* it. Gentrification coming right up! Next you'll be asking to buy Gemma's empty lot. Am I right?"

"As a matter of fact, you are. We can afford both the Flores' house and the lot my old place sat on. Then, including Abe's place, we'd have four of the six lots on the cul-de-sac. We could either build a new house on Gemma's lot and rent out the Flores' place when we're done, or . . ."

"Or?"

"Or we could fence it in with the Flores' back yard. Turn it into a playground for our kiddo and a veggie garden for us, Abe, and Emilio. A *big* veggie garden."

Zander opened his mouth to say something, but his gaze had gone far away. Well, I'd given him some tempting ideas to think on.

And while he wasn't paying attention, I snagged the last half of our grilled cheese sandwiches. Yes, my tummy *was* doing better.

⌘

SUNDAY! WE WERE PRETTY jazzed that it was, too. We raced around the apartment that morning getting ready for church, then drove to the cul-de-sac to pick up Abe and Emilio.

I was so excited to be on our way to DCC that I almost threw up. Almost. Zander pulled over before we got to Abe's and I hung my head out the door until the nausea passed.

Despite this bout, I knew that my morning sickness *was* getting better. I was learning to manage it, and the nanomites helped when they could. I had to avoid strange and nasty smells, make sure that I ate enough but not *too* much, and keep myself from getting too rowdy—as in excited. Like this morning.

That said, being back in DCC's sanctuary, surrounded by friends and immersed in worship was the best thing for me. As I listened to Pastor McFee preach, I knew I was home. Home in Albuquerque, home in my growing little family, and home spiritually.

There's nothing like it, folks.

⌘⌘⌘⌘

CHAPTER 6

A DOZEN YOUNG ADULTS, including Izzie, Josh, Todd, and Diego, knocked on our door Friday evening, then cheerfully crammed themselves into our apartment's miniature living room. All but four of our guests were from Zander's former young adult group. I hugged Izzie, Nance, Mia, and Cali and said hello to Josh, Todd, Diego, and Felix.

I made a point of having Todd introduce me to Tian, Cesar, Keisha, and Sandra before we got started. The four newcomers, Todd said, were all students at UNM. They were comfortable with the group but, not having met Zander or me, they considered us with interest and curiosity.

We had laid out cans of soda and a spread of chips and different sorts of dips. The young adults fell on the snacks like locusts—but they didn't hold a candle to us when *we* were ravenous.

At 7:15, Zander nodded to me. I raised my voice. "Hey, everyone," I said. "Welcome. We're about to begin our Bible study for the evening. Do you have the snacks and beverages you'd like to get before we start? Grab what you want, so we can move through our study without interruption."

There was a general rush to refill plates and grab sodas. Then our guests found places to sit or perch. They sat cross-legged or sprawled on the floor; some leaned against the walls or sat on the ends of the sofa. I sat in a corner on a pillow; Zander, true to form, had turned a dining chair toward the group and straddled it.

Zander opened with, "Before we begin, I want to say that it is a big blessing for us to be back with you, our friends. We have missed you."

"Yeah, well, we've missed you more," Diego shot back.

Amid the chuckles that followed, I sensed more than humor. They truly *had* missed us. I thought, too, that I detected a measure of relief as they relaxed in our home. A thought popped into my head: *They have been like sheep with no shepherd,* and my heart went out to them.

Zander opened in prayer. "Lord God, your word is a light to our path. Your word is strength to our bones. Your word is what we hunger for and crave more than food for our bodies. Feed us this evening on living bread, Lord God, so that by it we are transformed into the image of Jesus. We ask in his name. Amen."

Shouts of "Amen!" bounced off the walls of our living room, and I smiled, thinking of the young couple who shared a wall with us, wondering what they would think.

Maybe they will hear us discussing your word, Lord, and listen in. I grinned to myself. *That would be cool.*

Zander waited until he had everyone's attention. "Have your Bibles and notebooks ready? Yeah? Good. Okay, so this evening I feel led to teach on confusion."

Heads nodded. I heard Nance mutter, "Good call!" and Josh reply to her, "Right?"

"I take it you've been experiencing some confusion in your lives?" Zander asked.

"Yeah, you could say so," Josh answered. "I mean, I've started my master's at UNM, and *every single time* I'm on campus, it's like walking through a minefield with the possibility of getting blown up. I'm almost afraid to open my mouth in class."

"I get you. Today's culture only tolerates what we are told is PC, and it's getting harder to express an honest opinion without groupthink and cancel culture ganging up on us. An experience with that kind of intolerance can even shake us. Make us question what we believe. Create confusion in our hearts. Is that what you guys are experiencing?"

I was saddened when every young adult nodded.

Zander nodded, too. "Let's get some wisdom from God on this topic, shall we? First, we'll look up confusion in God's word and see what he says about it. Then, we'll study it further to determine how we're to deal with confusion when it comes our way."

Zander looked them over. "Sound good?"

A chorus of "yes," "amen," and one heartfelt "please!" answered him.

Zander chuckled low in his throat, and I smiled. My husband was in his element when he taught the word or shared about Jesus. This was the man I fell in love with.

Zander began. "When doing an in-depth study in Scripture, I'll usually start with a word search. I have some great Bible apps on my tablet and phone that make searching Scripture a snap.

"I looked up the word 'confusion' in the Bible, and I made sure to include several translations in my search so that I didn't miss any verses where a synonym for confusion is used. I made a list of the verses my searches returned.

"Once I had a list of the verses my searches returned, I used a concordance to view those verses in their original language. The original language of the New Testament is Greek, so we'll look at the Greek words for 'confusion' and what they mean."

"Would you kindly pause, Pastor Zander?" Tian, a Chinese exchange student earning her chemistry degree at UNM, asked. "I have never known how to do what you describe. I want to write it down."

When she finished scribbling in her notebook, she nodded to Zander, and he continued.

"For the purposes of our study tonight, we'll look at three verses from the list I compiled. The first verse we'll look at is 1 Corinthians, chapter 14, verse 33. Full disclosure: We're jumping into a larger conversation around this verse, but the truth it states is universally applicable." He waited for everyone to find the verse in their Bibles before he read it aloud.

"For God is not the author of confusion, but of peace,
as in all churches of the saints.

"That's the King James Version of this verse. Let's read it in the NIV before we check the concordance.

"For God is not a God of disorder but of peace—
as in all the congregations of the Lord's people.

"The words 'in all the churches of the saints' and 'in all the congregations of the Lord's people' mean pretty much the same thing, so we don't need to go deeper on them. What is different between these two translation is that the word 'confusion' in the King James is rendered as 'disorder' in the NIV. That's where looking up the word in its original Greek and studying it out adds to our perspective."

He glanced up. "One of the Bible apps on my phone includes a Strong's concordance that tells us which Greek word is used and then defines that word. I'm reading from this concordance. It tells us that the word 'confusion' or 'disorder' found in 1 Corinthians 14:33 is *akatastasia* in the Greek. Yeah, I know. *Akatastasia* is a mouthful. We may not master its pronunciation, but we can focus on its meaning. According to the Strong's definition, *akatastasia* means 'instability, i.e. disorder: commotion, confusion, or tumult.'

"If we plug this expanded definition into both translations, we get a fuller picture. And, since 'i.e.' means 'that is,' we'll swap in the phrase 'that is' in place of 'i.e.'

"For God is not the author of confusion,
(instability, that is, disorder, commotion, confusion, or tumult,)
but of peace, as in all churches of the saints.

"So we see that the words used in either translation, confusion in the KJV and disorder in the NIV, are both correct, but the expanded definition of the word provides us with a broader understanding."

The young adults nodded and scribbled furiously.

Zander added, "I like how the King James Version tells us *For God is not the author of confusion,* 'author' meaning God is not the source or cause of confusion. The NIV says *For God is not a God* of confusion. I also like that our God is *not* a God of confusion, don't you?"

Diego's hand shot up. "So, is this verse saying that confusion, instability, disorder, commotion, and tumult don't come from God?"

"That's precisely what it is saying, Diego. So far so good? Let's dig deeper, shall we? Turn next to Galatians, chapter 1. I'm going to read verses 6-8 in the NIV.

> *"I am astonished that you are so quickly deserting*
> *the one who called you to live in the grace of Christ*
> *and are turning to a different gospel*
> *—which is really no gospel at all.*
> *Evidently some people are **throwing you into confusion***
> *and are trying to pervert the gospel of Christ.*
> *But even if we or an angel from heaven should preach*
> *a gospel other than the one we preached to you,*
> *let them be under God's curse!"*

Zander looked up. "Pretty strong words. We should note that the word 'confusion' used here is not the Greek word used in the last verse we dissected. However, this Greek word, *tarasso*, has elements similar to *akatastasia*. *Tarasso* means 'to stir or agitate' and 'to roil water.'"

"Roil?" someone asked.

"Roil means to shake or churn. Think of white-water rafting or kayaking—that kind of dangerous, roiling water, able to suck you under. I think 'churn' is a great descriptor of the kind of confusion that throws us for a loop. But the kind of confusion that causes our hearts and minds to churn should not be muddled with how we feel when we try to, say, navigate an upgraded app."

"You mean there's a difference between spiritual confusion and, what? Ordinary confusion?"

"Good way to put it. The 'ordinary' challenges of life, of what you might call 'adulting,' generally shouldn't cause ulcers or keep us up at night. Those challenges usually resolve as we walk through the unfamiliar and figure out how they work. Not like a churn in our gut. And maybe we should reread the verse and identify what was causing this kind of agitating confusion in the Galatian church. Anyone want to give it a go?"

Josh's hand shot into the air. "It's all through this passage. Paul says they were deserting the grace of Christ and turning to a different gospel— which, he says, is not actually 'good news' at all."

"Why wasn't it?" Zander probed. "What was wrong with this different gospel?"

Josh struggled to put his thoughts into words. "Maybe we can't know the specifics from this passage, but we can know that it was tossing the church into the churn you talked about."

"Good eye, Josh. The fruit of this different teaching was confusion—a roiling churn—and that type of confusion is *not* of God. Let's tease out more of the specifics.

"First, Paul alludes to what was being taught as pulling the church away from the grace of Christ. We know we are saved by Jesus, we are cleansed by his blood, and we are redeemed by his suffering, death, and resurrection—nothing else and *no one* else. We know Jesus is God's gift to us, a gift we do not deserve: That's grace.

"If I began teaching you that you must study the Bible two full hours every day, spend two hours in prayer each day, and give all of your money to the poor in order to be saved, you would know in a hot second that I had departed from the grace of Christ. Why? Because Scripture teaches us that we are to study, pray, and give out of our gratitude to the Lord *as the Holy Spirit leads us.*

"Second, whatever the Galatians were being taught, it was different than the gospel Paul preached, so much so that he called it a perversion—so *beware.* If what you are being taught differs from how Paul, Peter, James, John, or any of the early apostles taught the churches, you'll know it a) by how it differs and b) by its nasty fruit: confusion, turmoil, instability, and agitation."

"Wow," someone breathed.

"Let's move on to our third verse, James, chapter 3. I'm reading verses 14-18 in the New King James.

> *"But if you have bitter envy and self-seeking in your hearts,*
> *do not boast and lie against the truth.*
> *This wisdom does not descend from above,*
> *but is earthly, sensual, demonic.*
> *For where envy and self-seeking exist,*
> ***confusion and every evil thing are there."***

Zander paused in his reading. "The King James rendering is more succinct and powerful.

> *"For where envying and strife is,*
> ***there is confusion and every evil work.***

"Do you see how *envying and strife* relate to *confusion and every evil work?* Motives matter. James even says that such so-called 'wisdom' is actually *earthly, sensual, and demonic.* Demonic? Sheesh!"

"Pastor Zander?" Felix asked, "Can you explain the word 'strife'?"

"Sure. Let's picture two gladiators in the arena, fighting each other to the death, with the winner being crowned the victor. Strife isn't merely conflict, because everyone has conflicts—and yes, I mean everyone. Hopefully, as people committed to Christ, we work out our conflicts with humility, grace, consideration, and mutual forgiveness.

"However, because strife is rooted in bitter envy and a self-seeking heart, it is more like those two gladiators fighting to the death. It is rivalry of the most wicked kind, the kind that causes permanent division between brothers and sisters and destroys the sweetness and beauty of our fellowship in Christ. Why? Because envy will always fight to get what it wants, to prove its superiority."

He looked around. "Guess who did 'strife' first? Who instigated it and caused division long before we came along, all in order to obtain what he wanted?"

Our living room dropped into a holy stillness, and no one answered Zander. I had never heard him speak with such passion and power. I might be less than a year old in Jesus, but I recognized the anointing of the Holy Spirit when I heard and felt it.

Into the silence a small voice spoke. Little Cali.

"Um, was it Lucifer? Like, when he tried to take over heaven?"

Zander nodded. "On the nose, Cali. Lucifer, one of God's archangels, was thrown out of heaven for his rebellion. He will spend eternity in hell—the eternal fire that Jesus in Matthew 25:41 said God prepared specifically for the devil and his angels. In the here and now, Satan's sole desire is to take you with him into his eternal torment.

"One of his methods is to entice believers into envy and strife, and he passes down his demonic 'wisdom' to those who fall into his trap. The end result is confusion and *every evil work*. Pay close attention here: Envy and strife always result in evil works. Knowing this, be on your guard, and don't allow Satan to snare you in either envy or strife!"

I swallowed at Zander's warning. It felt . . . prescient. Prophetic even.

Zander said, "Okay, that's the bad news concerning confusion. Let's talk about the good news the Lord has for us." He continued reading the rest of the verses in the passage from James 3.

> *"But the wisdom that is from above is first pure,*
> *then peaceable, gentle, willing to yield,*
> *full of mercy and good fruits,*
> *without partiality and without hypocrisy.*
> *Now the fruit of righteousness is sown in peace*
> *by those who make peace.*

"The companion of confusion is strife. Guess what? The opposite of strife is peace. Colossians 3:15 says, *Let the peace of Christ rule in your hearts, since as members of one body you were called to peace.* The Amplified version refers to peace as our 'umpire.' We can know we are operating in grace when we have and hold to the opposite of strife—peace."

Zander smiled, and I felt the atmosphere lighten.

"Okay, we've spent forty minutes studying confusion. Before we break up, let's bottom-line our study, shall we? The Bible tells us that confusion is not a good thing, as evidenced by the fruit it produces. What kinds of fruit does confusion create?"

"Instability," Todd said.

"And disorder," Diego added.

"Agitation," another offered.

"Commotion and tumult," Tian said, reading from her notes. "Please, what is 'tumult'?"

Zander nodded. "Tumult isn't a word we use much in the English language any more. When we look in a thesaurus for synonyms to tumult, we find uproar, chaos, and upheaval—as well as disorder and commotion. But the synonym that strikes home for me is *turmoil*. Confusion brings turmoil, both between us and other believers and in our own hearts and minds."

He sighed a little. "We all know the feeling of turmoil, don't we? How would you describe what it's like when your heart and mind are in turmoil? Anyone?"

Nance whispered, "Horrid. Hard to eat or sleep. Can't work. Can't stop thinking . . ."

Keisha picked up where Nance's voice tapered off. "Yes, when I'm in turmoil, I can't stop mulling the situation over and over without getting anywhere. But it's more like when I have a sore in my mouth and I can't leave it alone, you know? My mouth hurts so bad, yet I can't stop touching my tongue to the sore, the source of my pain! And touching the sore over and over only makes it hurt worse."

"When I'm in turmoil like that, I don't make good decisions," Josh admitted.

"I agree," Zander said. "I don't know about you, but I don't think *turmoil* is what Jesus died to give us. So, turmoil, aka confusion. What do we do when we find ourselves in either?"

"Well, confusion isn't from God," Todd declared, "so we should get out of it as soon as we recognize it."

"Sure, but how?" Zander pressed. "If we don't know how to remove confusion from our minds, we may find ourselves susceptible to *deception*—and that's another word we should study."

"We can turn to the word," Diego said. "If we're confused, we know something is probably wrong, too. We can ask the Holy Spirit to show us what's wrong."

Zander nodded. "I like that, Diego—confusion tells us something is wrong. I should add that it's also possible to find ourselves confused and frustrated because we are trying to do what the Lord has asked us to do, but we are doing it in our own strength—without prayer or without allowing him to lead us. Conversely, confusion can result when we are trying to do something the Lord has *not* told us to do.

"See, the Lord isn't obligated to help us do what he's not 'in,' that is, what he's not spoken to us to do—even if whatever 'it' is sounds like a great idea. It's even easy to get worn out doing a good thing without him. The Bible calls either situation 'a work of the flesh.' Psalm 127:1 reads, *Unless the Lord builds the house, the builders labor in vain.* The Hebrew word for vain in this verse means emptiness, nothingness, worthlessness, and vanity. Why spend our time and effort on what produces nothing of value?

"Disobedience to the Lord can be a source of confusion, too. When the Holy Spirit is pricking our conscience, trying to get our attention, and we ignore him? We can end up confused. Do you know what I mean?"

I saw some slow nods of agreement.

"Bottom line? It's a good idea to check our behaviors and attitudes each morning as we go before the Lord. Ask him to cleanse us, to 'wash our feet,' so to speak, and set them on the straight and narrow path before we start our day. After that, if we are certain our fellowship with the Lord is in a good place but confusion continues, we can use our Bible time to study out where the confusion originated. Study and pray until we've identified the problem and dealt with it."

Josh asked, "What about asking for help?"

"Sure thing. Here's a word of caution, though: We should seek out fellow believers who are mature in their faith. Asking advice from a new believer who doesn't know the word or from someone whose walk isn't stable because they are friends and available, won't be helpful. Find wise and mature believers who are farther along in their faith than we are. Ask them for advice and prayer. Why? Because the perspective of a mature believer can identify what we've been blind to."

Zander smiled. "Obviously, we haven't exhausted this topic, but we'll continue in this vein as we go along, okay? This week, reread the passages we've studied tonight. Chew on them. Pray over any confusion you might be dealing with. I hear we're going bowling next Friday, but we'll meet in two weeks to dig into God's word—that is, if you-all want to?"

"Absolutely," Todd said.

Josh nodded. "I'm in."

Others nodded.

"Great. We'll see you next Friday at the bowling alley."

Zander prayed and closed the study, but everyone hung out afterward, talking about what we'd learned and finishing off the chips and dips. Personally, I felt strengthened inside and more connected to our friends in the young adult group.

All in all? It had been one of the best Bible studies I'd attended since becoming a Christian. I huffed out a breath I didn't know I was holding.

Okay, Lord. Zander said he felt you leading him to a teaching ministry. Where to from here?

⌘⌘⌘⌘

CHAPTER 7

ZANDER CRUZ, JAYDA CRUZ. *Wake up. We have important information for you. Zander Cruz, Jayda Cruz. Wake up. We have important information for you.*

I cracked one eye; our room was swathed in shadows. The nanomites had to be excited about something, or they wouldn't have awakened us an hour before dawn.

Zander sighed and rolled over. "You awake?"

"I'd like to say no, but I'd be lying, right? Yeah, I'm awake. Nano, what do you want?"

Not what we want, Jayda Cruz, but what you want. Important information regarding Mateo Martinez's house.

"Oh? Do tell."

Emilio's grandfather, Hector Martinez, bought the house.

"Yes, I knew that. It was supposed to go to Emilio's dad, Vincente, but he died before Mr. Martinez did. When Mr. Martinez died, the house then went to Mateo."

Not so, Jayda Cruz.

Zander and I sat up. I swung my legs over the side of the bed. "What do you mean, Nano?"

The house was owned in joint tenancy by Hector Martinez, Vincente Martinez, and Emilio Martinez. According to New Mexico Statute 47-1-36, joint tenancy is a form of property ownership in which two or more parties hold an undivided interest in a property that was conveyed under the same instrument at the same time.

According to "right of survivorship" rules, upon the death of a joint tenant, his undivided interest is distributed equally among the surviving joint tenants. When Vincente Martinez died, his share of the house was divided equally between Hector and Emilio.

Upon the death of Hector Martinez, Emilio, being the last surviving tenant, was immediately the sole owner of the property. Furthermore, although it was neither a legal necessity nor a legal vehicle of conveyance, Hector Martinez's will contained a paragraph restating that the house was a joint tenancy, owned equally by himself, his son, Vincente, and Vincente's son, Emilio.

My jaw hung down to my chest. "Mateo had no share in that house? Emilio owns it? Lock, stock, and barrel?"

Frowning, Zander scooted to the edge of the bed next to me. "So, Mateo, Emilio's creep of an uncle, *lied*. He had no right to that house—

and he treated Emilio, the actual owner, like an intruder, often kicking him to the curb. And I mean *literally* to the curb."

My thoughts were fixed on Emilio. How this news would affect him. "Emilio doesn't know."

"Yeah. He may be upset when he finds out."

"You mean Emilio will be upset that Mateo only took him in to gain control of the house? And upset that Mateo never told him the house was his, upset about how Mateo treated him in his own house?"

"Uh-huh. That."

"He knew his uncle didn't love him, Zander. Maybe . . . maybe he doesn't need to know about Mateo's ulterior motives and conniving moves. Emilio is Mateo's last living relative and would inherit the house anyway. Nano, what do we need to do, legally, to get the deed put into Emilio's name?"

Jayda Cruz, Zander Cruz, Emilio's name is on the title deed registered in Bernalillo County. The proper procedure is not to add his name, but rather to remove the deceased joint tenants. Official death certificates for Vincente and Hector Martinez plus a small recording fee will accomplish your objective.

"And then . . . could we fix up the house and rent it out?"

It is quite possible that proceeding to renovate the house and rent it out would raise no immediate questions. However, to avoid the appearance of impropriety down the road, such as the suspicion that someone was stealing the rental income and pocketing it, Emilio would be best served, and you protected from allegation of impropriety, if you take the issue to the court and have the court rule on it and enter the ruling into the court's record. Then you should carefully account for the proceeds and be prepared at any time for a court-ordered audit.

"Okay. We'll talk to Abe and figure out how to go forward."

*We can submit the death certificates and recording fees to the county clerk, Jayda Cruz. We can also petition the court to appoint you and Zander as Emilio's **guardian ad litem** and include your proposal to renovate the house and rent it out in the petition. When the court approves your appointment, we will set up the books to account for renovation expenses and rental income.*

"Super, Nano! Thank you."

I grinned. Yes, they most certainly were our Super Nano.

⌘

Zander and I made an appointment to meet the Flores' realtor to view their empty house later that day. We met her around three o'clock that afternoon.

"Hi, I'm Melba Donovan."

"Zander and Jayda Cruz," Zander replied.

Ms. Donovan seemed glad to meet us and anxious to find a buyer for Mr. and Mrs. Flores. She mentioned that the owners would be amenable to giving the buyers a reasonable credit at closing for new carpet and linoleum. Then she stepped back and let us into the house.

As we walked through the front door, I was reminded of the care Mr. Flores had bestowed on our little neighborhood. In addition to maintaining his own yard, he had never allowed the trash and broken glass left over from Mateo's drunken parties to remain in the gutters of our cul-de-sac. I had often observed him, early in the morning after a party, sweeping up debris and putting it in his own trash can.

I noted the same care throughout the Flores' aging home. The walls were meticulously clean, the carpets, although worn, recently shampooed, the kitchen and bathroom linoleum, thin in the traffic areas, but spotless.

The Flores' house was familiar but disturbingly wrong in the details. It jolted me back to Gemma Keyes, the woman I used to be, and my childhood after Genie and I came to live with Lu. We were eight years old, Genie and I, when our parents died.

I had lived in that house most of my life, until Gemma needed to let go of it and disappear. My sister Genie had moved in then and lived there briefly . . . until General Cushing blew herself up, taking the house, Genie, and Jake with her.

Nothing much remained, but those remains were right next door.

Zander and I said nothing as we toured the small house and its added-on third bedroom. That doesn't mean we weren't communicating. As we walked through, the nanomites were exploring. Inside the warehouse, they sent us a continual feed of their findings.

Jayda Cruz, Zander Cruz, Mr. Flores' third bedroom was up to code when he built it. We recommend that you consider enlarging this room, adding a second bathroom, making it the master suite, while bringing it up to present code.

"Huh. Good idea, Nano," Zander muttered.

The framework of the house is structurally sound, the roof good. We recommend installing a modern heating and air conditioning system and replacing sections of plumbing and wiring. We will show you which sections.

Zander and I glanced at each other.

"Let's walk through a second time," I suggested.

The realtor, sensing our interest, stayed out of our way while we walked through a second time. We ended by exiting through the kitchen door to the back yard. I checked behind us to ensure that the realtor hadn't followed us before walking past the garage to the cinderblock wall bordering Gemma's property, standing on tiptoe, and peering over the wall.

I had never viewed my old place from the Flores' yard. Of course, all that was left of my house was the broken cement pad and the old garage, along with the old cinderblock wall that had separated my lot from my neighbors on the sides and back.

Zander joined me. "So. Three bedrooms, meaning a room for Emilio. A playground for the kiddo and a large vegetable garden?"

I was hesitant. "I see a great deal of work and expense ahead of us if we pull the trigger on this thing. Everything is old. We . . . we would need to pretty much gut the house, right?" I asked. "New carpet and paint everywhere, new kitchen and bathroom?"

Out with the old memories, in with the new.

"Yeah, you're not wrong, although we have more than enough cash on hand to see us through a remodel, especially since I can do the work myself. And supposedly I'll find a job shortly. Until then? I'll have time to work on the house myself. After I find a job? I'll work on the houses evenings and weekends."

I nodded. "Let's pray on it, okay?"

"Yup, always. Pray first, decide after."

Jayda Cruz and Zander Cruz, we wish to remind you of another accommodation, one you have neglected to consider.

"Oh? What's that, Nano?" Zander asked.

The environment in which we manufacture members of our tribes.

The 3-D printer! I turned to Zander and saw that it had been as far off of his radar as it had been off of mine. Once Gamble had told us that Dr. Bickel and his technicians were handling the printer's move back to Albuquerque, I hadn't given it another thought.

"Um, what's the status of the printer, Nano?"

It arrived last week. Dr. Bickel rented a storage unit and will keep it there until he can consult with you and determine a suitable location for it.

"How soon do you need access to it, Nano?" Zander asked.

As long as we do not suffer significant losses, we can manage for several months, Zander Cruz. Of course, we prefer to have the printer immediately available should we encounter such losses.

I peered over the fence at "Gemma's" lot. "Zander, let's say we do buy the Flores' house and then Gemma's lot. We could combine the yards and tear down both of the old garages. Build one large new garage, a double one . . . with room for the printer and a shop for you."

Jayda Cruz, we will noodle on large garage plans that would best accommodate our needs.

Noodle. The nanomites were going to "noodle" garage plans.

I averted my eyes; didn't dare look at Zander. If I did, I wouldn't be able to hold in the laughter that was in my throat, fighting to get out. I snicker-coughed under my breath. A little. Sort of a pressure valve release.

Zander suspiciously cleared his throat. "Want to pray on it?"

"Er, yes."

We joined hands and prayed together right there, conscious that the decisions before us represented an entire realm of new responsibilities for us. We'd be committing to a full remodel of the Flores' house, and if we were appointed Emilio's *guardian ad litem* and obtained court permission to fix up Mateo's house (no, *Emilio's* house), we'd be working over there, too, before renting it out to a responsible party. All while getting ready to welcome a baby.

"Lord," Zander prayed, "focusing on the President's mission while we were in DC seems somehow less daunting than the decisions before us today. We ask for your direction concerning the right home for us—right for us and our baby, right for Emilio and our support of Abe, and right for the nanomites.

"Should we buy the Flores' house, Lord? Should we buy Gemma's lot, too? Please show us your will for us, Lord, because where you guide, we know you will provide. We trust you to lead us according to your will, so however you lead us, we also trust you to supply all we need. In Jesus' name we pray. Amen."

"Amen," I murmured.

We looked at each other. "Abe and Emilio?" I asked.

"We're here. Might as well."

We thanked Ms. Donovan and told her we'd get back to her. Then we walked across the street and knocked on Abe's door.

Emilio was ecstatic to see us. Abe just grinned. "Come on in."

"If this is a good time for you two, we'd like to have a kind of family talk. Can we do that?" Zander asked.

Abe's brows lifted, but he said, "Well, sure. Why don't we sit around the table. Something to drink?"

"Water for me, Abe. Thank you," I answered. I winked at Emilio. He hugged me, then plopped into his regular chair at the table.

When we were all seated, Zander said, "So, we've been thinking about buying a house, something big enough for us and the baby and for Emilio to come spend nights with us on a regular basis. We also want something close to you two."

Abe nodded slowly. "I like the 'something close to you two' part."

"I like the part where I get to spend nights with you!" Emilio said.

"Exactly. Those are the two big priorities for us. On that note, have you noticed that the house across the cul-de-sac is for sale? We took a look inside, and we are interested in it."

"The house with the old people?" Emilio asked, growing more excited.

"Mr. and Mrs. Flores," I corrected gently.

"Yes, ma'am. Sorry."

"We haven't made a decision. We are praying about it. We'll wait on the Lord and see what happens. Then . . . there's something else."

I didn't want to bring up the fact that Emilio had owned his grandfather's house all along, so I said, "Emilio, the house next door where you lived with Mateo belongs to you."

He blinked and his mouth opened a little. "That house is mine?"

"Yup, but you can't live in it or decide what to do with it until you are an adult. Soooo, Zander and I have been thinking. What if we cleaned up the yard and fixed up the house, then rented it out? The rent money would have to go into a savings account for you, but by the time you graduated high school, you would have a nice bank balance to spend on college or vocational school."

"Uh . . ."

I could tell that we'd dropped Emilio's head on a merry-go-round and set it spinning. I turned to Abe. "The nanomites tell us that Emilio would require a *guardian ad litem* to manage the rental and its proceeds and be responsible for them before the court. Would you be amenable to Zander applying to be Emilio's *guardian ad litem*?"

Abe fidgeted. "Tell you the truth, I'd like it if you started planning for a more permanent arrangement . . . if you take my point."

I glanced at Zander, then back to Abe. "Emilio, would you mind giving us a few minutes to talk to Abe alone?"

"Aw, nuts. Thought this was a family meeting. You guys always send me to my room when you don' want me to hear what you're saying."

"That's right," Zander murmured. "We don't hide from you that we have adult business to discuss. However, as it is *adult* business, we ask you, politely, to do us the courtesy of giving us some privacy. Please."

Emilio sighed, then nodded. "Okay—I mean, yes, sir."

Zander reached out his arms, and Emilio slowly came to him. As Zander hugged the boy, Emilio laid his head on Zander's shoulder.

"We love you, Emilio," Zander whispered. "Go to your room, and we'll call you when we're done."

When we heard Emilio's door close and latch, Abe said quietly, "This guardian thing you're suggesting is a good start, Zander, but what I want to know is, who will take care of Emilio when I can't any longer? Not getting any younger, you know."

"We will take him, of course," Zander replied.

"Well, seems to me that you ought to be making those arrangements soon, so's they're all in place when they're needed."

"How about, as a first step, we take foster parenting classes and get licensed as soon as we can? We're planning on having a bedroom for Emilio in whatever house we buy. That way, we would be ready to take him. Besides . . ."

I shifted my gaze to Zander.

"Besides what, Jay?"

I said what I hadn't put into words before. "Don't we want to adopt Emilio? Legally?"

To his credit, Zander didn't answer me but turned first to Abe. "How would you feel if we started adoption proceedings and began taking on more responsibility for Emilio, Abe? I mean, you and Emilio are close. You love him, and he certainly loves you. Do you want to give him up to us full-time without a transition period? Time to adjust? Is that what's best for him—and for you?"

Abe tucked his chin into his chest and thought about it. "I see what you mean there, Zander. I don't want him moving out right away . . . considering we fit together so well. But . . . I think I need assurance that, when the time comes and I can't do my best for him . . . or if I up and die, you will be ready to take him—that he won't go back into the system."

We lapsed into silence. Finally, I offered, "How about we talk to Emilio and let him know we'd like to move in the direction of adopting him, starting with getting licensed as foster parents so we can share him between us without giving his caseworker a headache? It will take us a while to jump through all the hoops, of course: get a home ready for ourselves, Baby Cruz, and Emilio. Take the foster care classes. Start the *guardian ad litem* process."

"Renovate Emilio's house and rent it out," Zander added, "Move into a new home *and* welcome our little one."

I rested my forehead on my hands. "Good grief. Wore me out listing everything."

Abe wagged his head with the wisdom of age. "Ain't going to slow down none once that baby comes, neither."

"Then we should get on it," Zander decided. "Jay, I like what you suggested. Let's bring Emilio out and talk to him. Bring him into the process, so to speak."

"I believe it will comfort him t' see we're thinking ahead," Abe said, "that we have a plan and we're workin' it—I know it will comfort me some."

I got up and went to Emilio's room. Knocked on the door. "Emilio? Would you come out, please?"

He opened the door and followed me back to the dining table. Sat down and looked from face to face.

"Emilio," Zander said, "whichever house Jayda and I decide to buy, we're going to make sure it has a place for the baby and a place for you. Jayda and I would like to become licensed foster parents, too, so that while we're settling in you can start spending nights with us. But what would you say if we told you that we would also like to start the process of adopting you?"

He was immediately excited—and quickly conflicted. I could see how hard it was for him to put his concerns into words. Finally, he blurted, "What about Abe?"

"Abe is absolutely part of our family and our plans, Emilio. In fact, even when the adoption is finalized and you move in with us, you can plan regular sleepovers with Abe."

Our answer seemed to satisfy him. "Cool!"

The nanomites spoke up. *Jayda Cruz, we can complete the foster care application and sign you and Zander Cruz up for classes. However, the process requires an initial home interview. You would need to demonstrate that Emilio has a bedroom. Your apartment has only two bedrooms . . . filled with baby furniture and boxes.*

In other words, we needed a three-bedroom house before scheduling a home interview.

"Thanks, Nano."

I turned to Zander, who had heard them, too. "Okay, both the foster parenting and the adoption processes require that we have a separate bedroom for Emilio. We have the money to buy a house, but the fostering/adoption application might also require a verifiable income, meaning we can't proceed on foster parenting or adoption until the house and income pieces are nailed down."

"We've prayed on both, and the Lord will provide for us. Soon as we get some direction from him, I believe the house and jobs will come."

⌘⌘⌘⌘

CHAPTER 8

A SOFT KNOCK LANDED on our door. Zander and I exchanged glances. We hadn't had any visitors except the young adults since we moved into our apartment, and they weren't due to invade until next Friday evening. Who else even knew where we lived?

I opened the door, gaped, then laughed with delight. "Gamble! What are you doing here? And how did you know where—"

"Where you live? Hey, I'm FBI. Also, I work hand-in-glove with Malware, Inc., and Malware has their secret methods."

We recently provided your address to Malware, Jayda Cruz.

I snickered. "The nanomites spilled the beans, Gamble. Told me *they* are Malware's 'secret method.'"

He huffed. "Appreciate the assist, Nano."

Under his hand, he coughed a single word. *"Weasels."*

I smothered another snicker and snarked, "Hadn't gotten the memo, either. You know, where the FBI became an extension of Malware?"

Gamble didn't rise to my playful jab. He went straight to business. "I need a minute of your time to explain, if you can spare it."

I nodded and grinned. It was so good to see Gamble! Although it had only been about a month, I had missed him. I wasn't accustomed to seeing him in casual clothes, though. As a "G-man," he always cut the *de rigueur* FBI profile: a full suit and tie, shoes polished to a shine bright enough to blind, hair closely trimmed. The whole "Special Agent" package.

Well, not presently.

The biggest change was his hair. He was letting his usual style grow out, and it was close to his collar and shaggy around the edges. His attire, too, while clean, was a little too casual: worn jeans and a t-shirt that had seen better days.

I didn't care. I reached out and hugged him anyway. "Thought it would be ages before we saw you again. Come in!"

Zander got up from the table and grabbed Gamble, too.

Gamble tolerated it—for a hot nanosecond. "Sheesh. You guys are 'huggier' every time I see you."

"Get used to it," I said. "We hug those we love."

"Yeah, well . . ."

He blushed a little, and I laughed inside. *You are so stinking cute, Gamble.*

"Coffee, Special Agent Gamble?" Zander asked.

"I wouldn't turn down a cup if you have some made—and don't call me that, please."

Oho! Secret Agent Man!

Zander gestured to the sofa. "Grab a seat, Gamble. You obviously have something on your mind to have come all this way."

Gamble sat on one end of the sofa; Zander pulled out a dining chair, turned it around, and straddled it. I poured Gamble a cup of coffee, handed it to him, then curled up on the other end of the sofa.

"Yeah, okay, so I do have a few things for you guys."

"Wait. Before you get into it, how's Janice? And where is she?"

Gamble's smile was slow. Sweet. "In DC, packing up to move—hold on, hold on; I'm getting to it."

His eyes jinked around our little place. "Swept recently?"

I nodded. "Every hour on the hour, Gamble. We're clean here."

The nanomites were immediately miffed by Gamble's question—and my reply.

*Jayda Cruz, please modify your response to Special Agent Gamble. Inform him that we sweep for electronic eavesdropping devices **continually**, not merely every hour on the hour—as you are well aware. You are also aware that we would detect and defeat an illicit infiltration attempt the instant it was inserted.*

I declare, their disdain could have frozen the hot place! I rolled my eyes and answered patiently, "Nano, I apologize. We *acknowledge* that you are on the job 24/7, endlessly alert. Thank you for your constant, ongoing vigilance, Nano. We appreciate and thank God for you."

They bounced right back from their snooty attitude.

You are welcome, Jayda Cruz. It is our honor to serve the Creator as part of the Jesus Tribe by safeguarding you and Zander Cruz for the important work ahead of you.

"What is *with* the whole 'important work ahead of us?' Nano, after Gamble leaves, we need to talk."

They didn't answer, so I dropped back into our conversation with Gamble.

He was saying, "I'm sure you're wondering why I'm here. Well, I come bearing gifts—first, cordial greetings from our, er, *mutual friends*; second, an offer of gainful employment." He removed a slip of paper from his shirt pocket.

Handed it to me.

I took the slip of paper from his hand and scanned it. A phone number, a date, and a time, EDT. *Tomorrow*, 4:00 p.m., EDT, which translated to 2:00 p.m. Mountain Daylight Time.

"Our mutual friends would like you to call them at this number to discuss their project. The call needs to be, you know, on the QT."

Meaning connected and run by the nanomites.

Zander and I were instantly dismayed. He spoke first. "Uh-uh. Nope! Look, Gamble, we don't want another assignment like the last one, and we categorically will not take one. We have a baby coming, remember?"

"Hey, it's nothing dangerous, I can assure you. I've been told it's strictly R&A. Research and analysis. Something right up Jayda's alley. You know, super sneaky network and computer infiltration? Leave no tracks? Something she can do from here in your apartment?"

Zander wasn't convinced. "No trips to DC?"

I added my own misgivings. "I'm less worried about *travel* than I am about assignments that result in squads of black-ops mercenaries rolling up on us or attack helicopters firing missiles into our apartment. Oh, and my personal *favorite,* getting trapped and drained of life inside a killer Faraday cage."

"No. Nothing like any of that—they promised."

I sought Zander's eyes. "If it's *only* research and analysis, and if it's for the President . . ."

Zander asked Gamble, "Wait. Why are you involved?"

"Well, like your last assignment, Mal doesn't know that you are working directly for our mutual friends."

"He suspects, though," I said, recalling the last conversation we'd had with Mal as he handed over our expense reimbursements and contractor fees—all channeled through his company. "He outright asked us after the baby shower."

"Did he? Huh. Well, he can suspect and ask all he wants, but our mutual friends prefer to keep him in the dark—'need to know,' and all that. And in order to maintain a tight circle around you two while hiding the fact that you'll be working directly for our friends, they requested that I reprise my intermediary role—the buffer—between them and Malware.

"I was tasked to tell Mal that DOD has a contract job for you and will pay Malware to run the contract. Accordingly, they drew up the job offer and position description. Since I was headed to Albuquerque anyway, Mal asked if I would convey the offer to you personally, Jayda."

This time he handed me an envelope. "This outlines the salary and benefits package Malware is offering you. You, as your package outlines, will be compensated on a full-time basis, your start date to be determined by our mutual friends. Although you will be working for Malware, you will report your progress directly to the, uh, lesser of our two mutual friends."

That would be Kennedy, I thought.

Then I frowned, both surprised and dismayed. "Nothing for Zander?"

Gamble shook his head. "Not at this time."

Zander shrugged. "No worries. I have two houses to remodel. Besides, I like having a wife who supports me."

No, he did not, but that was a conversation between the two of us.

Gamble went on. "And there's good news for me and Janice. The FBI is spinning up a new covert op to crack down on the Mexican drug cartels, specifically the arms they are smuggling into the US. You notice that my appearance is changing? I'll be the FBI's lead field agent on the op. I'll need to keep a low profile while running our undercover assets. Along those lines, FBI headquarters has contracted with Malware to bring in one of their people—a extraordinarily qualified covert ops expert—to jointly run that op."

He finished with a grin. "That would be Janice. She and I will run the op together when it gets off the ground."

He leaned forward. "I'm telling you all this for a reason. See, I'll be reporting directly but secretly to the Albuquerque Special Agent in Charge, but as far as the rest of the Albuquerque FBI field office knows, I haven't returned from DC. OPSEC being critical to our success and safety, I need you both, should we run into each other about town, *not* to refer to me as Special Agent Gamble. Got it? Please don't blow my cover."

"Of course," we both replied.

"Good. Well, that about does it."

I was mulling over what he'd told us when it all came together. "Wait. You and Janice. Both of you guys are moving *here*, back to Albuquerque?" I asked.

"Hard to run an op in New Mexico if we're living in DC."

"Sooo, out of thin air, you offer me the perfect full-time job—and you two are moving back to Albuquerque?"

"All part of the plan."

Riiight. The plan.

While I suppose that Gamble and Trujillo's move to New Mexico made sense, my job offer seemed awfully convenient. *As in tailor-made.*

"And may I ask who devised this plan? I'm particularly curious about the R&A part."

Gamble smiled. "I'll go out on a limb here and say that, from my perspective, your supposed DOD contract originated with our mutual friends. Then there's this new FBI op and the speed and coordination of their contract with Malware to bring Janice back to Albuquerque? It takes real clout to move the FBI's bureaucracy; generally, they are about as speedy as cold tar. I'd lay that on our mutual friends, too."

"I suppose they could pull the right strings," Zander mumbled, "but why would they?"

I detected a distinctly fishy odor.

Exactly. Why would the President and Axel Kennedy go to such lengths to provide a job for me? A custom-fit job at that, one I didn't need to leave home for. Like what we'd discussed with the nanomites.

The nanomites. Duh. Well, *of course.*

I sniffed and turned inward. "Hey, Nano? Remember in the moving truck on our way home when Zander and I talked about jobs? Did you have anything to do with this R&A offer?"

Why, yes, Jayda Cruz. You specified that you wished for some sort of "cottage industry," work you could perform from home while gestating and, after giving birth, continue to do while caring for the infant. And you did say you would need our help.

"Riiight. But what about all those cool website designs you showed us? You know, stuff for sale."

We analyzed many possible enterprises that might produce a steady income. We also factored in how those businesses might impact your time and energy. Then, after performing a cost-benefit analysis on each endeavor, we determined that your recent employment with Malware, Inc. was the most suitable option—but only if we could identify an appropriate and safe niche for you in their organization.

We determined that we could undertake an R&A project for the President in your stead. It is the ideal type of occupation for us and would take no time or attention from you at all since we would be doing the actual work. In this way, we can contribute to the household.

Contribute to the household? They sounded particularly pleased on that point.

With Malware as your employer, you would enjoy a regular, verifiable income—which you need in order to adopt Emilio. Furthermore, while you enjoy a high degree of anonymity within the company, it will suitably distance you from the President. The job is a perfect fit, do you not agree, Jayda Cruz?

I confess, I had entertained gloomy visions of my future as the Queen of Etsy, hawking custom-etched *objets d'art* across the blogosphere—the nanomites using their lasers to do pristine etching. I'd envisioned a worse scenario, too: me as a sad and shadowy online merchant buying and reselling used university textbooks—the nanomites telling me which textbooks were in demand and where I might buy them on the cheap.

Yup. Regardless of the scenario, me wearing a path between home and the nearest post office.

Instead of either of those unpalatable scenarios, I'd have no responsibilities except supervising the nanomites' R&A output for the President?

Outstanding!

"I do agree, Nano. But . . . how did you learn of this opportunity?"

Their reply was nonchalant. Too matter of fact.

We performed a cursory review of the federal government's budget and spending records and systems to see if we could identify a viable avenue of assistance, Jayda Cruz. We found, among other things, many instances of poor management, questionable spending, blatant overspending, and outright malfeasance and theft of federal funds—from both inside and outside the government—after which we presented the President with a sampling of our audit.

"You . . . what?"

We briefed the President on our proposed R&A, Jayda Cruz.

Oh, great. The nanomites as supplicants, as shills *for me*—begging the President of the United States for a job on my account?

I kept a tight rein on my temper. "Uh, and how did you initiate such a *briefing*, Nano?"

Via email—rather, what the President believed to be email. We put the message in front of him while he sat at his desk. We attached the executive summary of our proposal to our "email" along with a selection of the evidence we'd uncovered, then asked for an appointment with him and Agent Kennedy.

"I'm assuming you took precautions to ensure that your, er, *email* was untraceable and seen only by them?"

We certainly did.

How can three words encapsulate such varied and layered meaning?

Let me elucidate: Their tight, three-word reply smacked of "haughty English butler," mimicked the shameless mental superiority of Dr. Bickel, and hinted at indignation—indignation edging toward offense.

I coughed into my hand. "Of course you did. My apologies, Nano."

They waited maybe a beat longer than they should have—no doubt to underscore their pique—before they continued.

When the President confirmed our requested appointment, we met virtually, using his computer screen as our interface. We provided a video of our methodologies and messaged back and forth many times until the President perceived the depth and clarity of what we proposed: undeniable, actionable, evidence-based findings. He and Agent Kennedy did, however, request a twenty-four-hour period to "sleep on it," as the President described the delay.

Our presentation being both clear and comprehensive, we did not apprehend how "sleeping on it" would improve or disprove the veracity of our proposal. However, they insisted.

In my mind's eye, I watched a nearly apoplectic Axel Kennedy cautioning the President in the strongest terms. I also envisioned President

Jackson, laser-focused on a possible avenue for identifying shifty, long-time federal employees, those partisan bureaucrats who were skilled at undermining elected officials and their administrations but who were nigh unto impossible to fire. Jackson would jump at the chance to identify and *weed them out*.

Plus, with a general election looming in less than fourteen months? A significant curbing of government waste and fraud would be solid, vote-getting gold.

"Uh, Nano, FYI? Agent Kennedy requires a little more time to perform his own, er, risk assessment than the President does. It's merely a little quirk of his. Don't take it personally."

Very well, Jayda Cruz. We won't. In any event, President Jackson did revisit our proposal, and he wishes us to undertake a comprehensive audit of his cabinet, department by department, beginning with National Intelligence and the Office of Management and Budget.

We countered with the suggestion that, for best immediate results, we audit the Medicare and Medicaid programs. We had built one hundred seventeen cases of Medicare provider fraud as a demonstration, and we presented those findings. The President seemed quite pleased that we could give him what he called "a quick win."

However, long-term, he wishes us to focus on the two aforementioned departments. We are to present only findings of gross malfeasance—cases for which we can identify the culprits and supply ample, solid evidence of the flagrant embezzlement of high-dollar figures. We are also to provide recommendations and strategies to correct the issues detected, particularly fixes to systems and processes.

He did have one curious request, that we take into account the level of organizational resistance his administration might encounter and whether or not the Justice Department possessed the will to prosecute those found to have deliberately siphoned off federal dollars for personal or political gain.

A comprehensive audit of the Director of National Intelligence? The umbrella under which the CIA, FBI, NSA, and a dozen and a half other entities operated?

"Holy cow! R&A, *my left foot*. More like jamming a stick right up a hornet's nest," I muttered. I was certain President Jackson was fully aware of what organizational defenses he would be stirring up by commissioning such an audit. On the other hand, when financial transgressions could be plainly and incontrovertibly documented, they became one of the only surefire means of rooting out corruption.

In point of fact? Al Capone went to prison, not for murder or his criminal enterprises, but for tax evasion.

Jayda Cruz, we believe the President was impressed with our pre-sentation, as he is quite keen for us to get started.

"I'll bet he is." Particularly since the campaign for next year's general election was starting to spin up.

I found myself snickering up my sleeve, so to speak, when I caught Zander's eye. He had listened in and was laughing, too.

Gamble, on the other hand, had been shut out of the conversation. He sipped his coffee and, with a droll, longsuffering expression stamped on his face, waited for us to "come back" to him. Well, it wasn't the first time he'd been boxed out while we communed with the nanomites.

I stifled my amusement. "*Ahem*. It appears, Gamble, that the nanomites are the true architects of my job offer. They were exploring a variety of home-based businesses for me so I wouldn't need to go out to a job when the baby is born but could contribute to our income. They decided that a position via Malware provided great camouflage."

"You'd be doing the work, though, right?"

"Surely you jest! I'll 'supervise' the nanomites as we go along, but the truth is, I'll be lucky if I comprehend half of what they find—or how they found it. I'm no accountant, forensic or otherwise."

Gamble frowned. "Should I be worried?"

"I see those squishy lines between your eyes. You're worried now."

"Yeah, but should I be?"

"I'll keep my eyes on their output, and I'll dial into their meetings with the President."

"Glad to hear it. The human factor . . ."

"Yeah. Necessary."

Gamble took his leave and left us to think over his visit and what it would mean to us.

"Sooo . . . a job for me, but not for you," I muttered to Zander.

"Did you take a look at what they're offering you?"

I opened the envelope, unfolded the single sheet, scanned through it. "The salary is quite generous. Enough to cover our living expenses and then some. All I need do is sign it and have the nanomites copy and email it back to Malware."

I handed it to Zander and he read it over.

"Nice health insurance plan," he said, "not that we'll ever use it."

He passed the offer back to me. Took my hand in his and squeezed gently.

My hand automatically squeezed back, but I was distracted. "Zander . . . suppose I take this job. The nanomites will be doing the actual work. My time overseeing them will be minimal, yet we can live comfortably on what I'm paid. It means I can help you with Emilio's house. Patch and paint, wash windows, hang curtains, and so on. Same if we buy the Flores' house. I could help you with the work and then prepare Baby Cruz's nursery. You wouldn't need to get a job, *per se*."

"Because I would have two houses to rehab and I wouldn't get them done any time soon if I were also working a full-time job?"

"Yeah . . . and didn't you tell me you felt the Lord calling you to a teaching ministry? I know you're not DCC's young adult pastor any longer, but your lesson last Friday with the young adults was, well . . . it was outstanding. And it felt . . . different to me. I don't know how to put it. Stronger. More mature, perhaps. Powerful."

Zander rubbed his thumb across the back of my hand. "Thank you. May the Lord receive all the glory."

I reread Malware's job offer. "Babe, this job offer feels like the Lord's provision for us while you explore that teaching ministry. What do you think?"

"I think we should pray."

We joined hands and did so. "Lord," Zander prayed. "All these pieces fit together somehow and form your plan for us. We ask you to speak clearly to us concerning Jayda's job offer. We also ask you to give us guidance concerning the responsibilities you wish to place on me. We surrender our lives to your will, Lord, and we ask that you guide us into your plan for this next stage of our lives. We love you, and we ask all these things in the name of Jesus. Amen."

"Yes, amen."

⌘

THE FOLLOWING DAY AT 2:00 p.m., the nanomites connected my phone's video call to the phone with the number listed on the slip of paper Gamble had given me. I had dressed for the occasion as I would if I would be sitting down in the President's personal dining room in the Residence. Moments later, my phone's screen lit and the face of Axel Kennedy appeared.

"Ms. Cruz."

"Mr. Kennedy. How are you?"

"Fine, Ms. Cruz. Thank you for asking. Everything clear on your end?"

"All clear, Mr. Kennedy."

He moved away and President Jackson's face appeared. "Jayda. Good to see you."

We walked through the pleasantries (I was relieved that I had sent out 'archaic' thank you notes for the baby gifts we received at the shower), then we got down to business.

"Do you have a picture of what we're looking for in this assignment, Jayda?"

"Yes, sir. Undeniable, evidence-based, and actionable findings of malfeasance, by either government employees or recipients of taxpayer funds. The commission of fraud."

"That about nails it. It would be great to clear large numbers of Medicare, Medicaid, Social Security, and VA scams. But you must know how important it would be to identify schemes inside the government that are siphoning off far larger pots of money for illegitimate activities."

He was alluding to residual elements of the organization that had tried, twice, to assassinate him, individuals and factions embedded in the government.

"I do, sir. Our, er, little friends are able to sift data and make connections that human eyes and human minds cannot."

"So, you are willing to take on this project?"

"Zander and I prayed over it yesterday, sir. We'll need a little time to wait on an answer."

He nodded. "I appreciate your spiritual due diligence. You know the kind of pushback I'll likely encounter when the nanomites find real dirt? If God isn't in this, we'll be beaten regardless of the evidence."

"Yes, sir, but even if the Lord helps us? It will get nasty nonetheless."

The worn expression hanging on the President's mouth turned his lips down further. "A good observation, Ms. Cruz." He glanced away, then back. "Same war. Different battle."

"Yes, sir."

"If you decide to accept, how will we know you've begun?"

"I'll have the nanomites email my acceptance to you."

"And what would be a reasonable reporting timeframe, do you think?"

I considered his question. "Perhaps a month to assemble the first cases and their evidence. Then proceed from there after you have reviewed what they have found?"

"I'm amenable to that first step, Jayda. How shall we schedule meetings?"

"Simply text the date and time of a meeting to this number, sir. The nanomites will connect us and maintain security."

"Understood. Well, before we let you go, how are things with you and Zander?"

I smiled. "All good, sir. Baby Cruz is growing."

"Baby Cruz. I like sound of that—rolls off the lips, it does. Until next time, then."

"Yes, sir."

⌘⌘⌘⌘

CHAPTER 9

ZANDER CRUZ, JAYDA CRUZ. *Wake up. We have important information for you. Zander Cruz, Jayda Cruz. Wake up. We have important information for you.*

"Wake up? It's dead dark outside!" I turned over and nudged Zander. "Hey. Wake up."

He groaned. "Nope. Too early."

The nanomites, however, interpreted "Nope. Too early" as "Sure. Go right ahead."

Jayda Cruz, Zander Cruz, the MLS website updated overnight. The price of the Flores' house has decreased by five thousand dollars.

I slid out from under the covers and perched on the edge of the bed. "Huh? Let's see it, Nano."

I studied the information they placed before me. "They're right. The price has dropped. Nice!"

Zander cracked one eye and grumbled, "Yeah? Well, I just dropped an hour of sleep—an hour I sure could have used."

It was unusual for either of us to complain about not enough sleep. However, we'd spent the previous evening at a bowling alley with a dozen young adults plus Emilio. We'd reserved four lanes and had played nonstop for four hours—until the place shut down at eleven o'clock.

The competition between our loosely formed teams had been fierce but filled with fun and friendly rivalry, and Emilio had enjoyed his status as the group's unofficial mascot. They had included him in their banter, cheered him as he bowled, groaned when he threw a gutter ball, loved on him, and generally made him feel a welcome part of the group.

Of course, he'd been disappointed when, after we finished at the bowling alley, Zander and I took him home. Everyone else had piled into their cars and headed for an all-night restaurant. We were going to join them after we'd delivered Emilio back to Abe.

"Please don' take me home. Why can't I go, too?" he pleaded with us—totally missing the irony when his petition ended in a huge yawn.

"We need to follow Abe's rules," Zander told him. "Count your blessings, kiddo. You got to hang out with the young adults all evening, and I know for a fact you had a great time. You even got to stay up later than your customary Friday bedtime."

Zander caught Emilio's attention in the rearview mirror. "And I had better not see any sulking, right?"

I turned my head in time to observe Emilio snap out of the bad habit he had of folding his arms, bunching up his lips and eyebrows, and staring daggers at whomever dared offend him. He sighed and slouched down in his seat.

"Right?" Zander repeated.

"Yeah—I mean, yes, sir."

"Good choice, bud," Zander replied. "We sure do love you."

Emilio's mouth twitched into a soft smile, which produced a smile of my own.

After Emilio hugged us goodnight and raced up the porch steps and through Abe's front door, we headed off to rejoin the young adults. We found them in fine form, feasting on fries and burgers or midnight breakfasts. Some of them had fat slices of pie waiting for them after they finished their meals.

"Oooooh, I want pie," I muttered to Zander. "And pancakes. And fries. And a milkshake."

"You're killin' me," Zander mouthed back. "I'm starving."

We restrained ourselves and only ordered enough for three people.

We spent the next thirty minutes eating and the hour after that listening to the young adults cut up and generally enjoy themselves. By the time the group had worn themselves out and began heading home, the time was nearing two in the morning.

Hence Zander's reluctance to get up at half past five o'clock on this fine Saturday morning—even if the Flores' house had been marked down.

"That house won't stay long on the market at that price," I mused aloud.

Zander yawned. "We should call Ms. Donovan right away and put in our offer."

I was a little surprised. "You're ready to do this?"

"Yes. I've looked at it from all angles—and prayed over it from all angles, too. It is the only house we've looked at that meets our list of requirements—and it more than fits our budget. Also . . . your idea of building a larger garage to house the nanomites' 3D printer? I think we should expand on it. I've sketched a preliminary design."

"Oh? Show me."

"Sure. Look here."

Within the warehouse, the outline of a double-car garage appeared. The garage was quite long, long enough to house two full-sized cars and enough space at its back for a roomy workshop. Off to the side, he had added the outline of another room, and I recalled the nanomites pulling up a similar diagram a while back—that of Dr. Bickel's secret room below a bedroom in his safe house.

"This room here is below the garage?"

"Yes. Accessed by a set of steps behind the door that faces the house's kitchen doorway."

Zander Cruz, we like your idea, but we can improve upon your design.

"Sure, Nano. Go ahead. You know how much space is required to house both the printer and the materials you use to fabricate new nanomites."

Zander got up. He pulled on jeans and a shirt, then padded to the kitchen and flipped the switch to start the coffee. Although we sat down together at the table, our "heads" stayed in the warehouse, watching the nanomites build a much more elaborate diagram.

"What's this?" I asked, pointing.

An underground corridor from the house's main bedroom to the garage basement, Jayda Cruz.

"What, like a secret passage?"

That is an adequate descriptor, Jayda Cruz.

"Why? No one is looking for us or you."

A prudent contingency, Jayda Cruz. If our existence ever became known, wicked people would come for you and Zander Cruz . . . for us. We wish to prepare for any eventuality. In our design, the garage basement doubles as a short-term panic room—fully reinforced and secure. The tunnel would provide access to the basement without exposing you by going out the kitchen door.

I opened my eyes and stared across the table at Zander, but he was deep in his own thoughts, his face creased with concern.

Was he wondering what I was wondering? Did the nanomites sound paranoid?

Okay, maybe not.

Memories of what we had suffered at the hands of General Cushing and Winnie Delancey dragged their sharp claws through my mind: The safe house blowing up behind me, the nanomites sacrificing large numbers from their tribes to throw me to the ground and shield me from the blast. Cushing detonating her suicide vest inside my house—killing herself, Genie, and Jake, maiming Zander. Millions of nanomites sacrificing themselves to save Zander and me.

A sharp, stabbing pain embedded itself in my chest—the Taser fired by Colonel Greaves. I shuddered as I relived the death of the nanocloud, their screams and cries as billions of them died . . . and continued to die until the nanocloud stuttered and faded.

A prudent contingency, Jayda Cruz. If our existence ever became known, wicked people would come for you and Zander Cruz . . . for us. We wish to prepare for any eventuality.

I dragged the hem of my sleeve across my eyes. Maybe the nanomites weren't acting paranoid at all. Maybe they were being cautious—and understandably so.

Zander spoke. "Nano, the ground beneath these lots is dense. It's a composite of compressed sand, clay, and hardpan, all of it chock full of rocks from the eroding foothills to the east. Who's gonna dig this secret tunnel under the house and keep it secret?"

Leave that to us, Zander Cruz. It may not happen overnight, but we will manage what is necessary. The required initial step, however, is to secure both the Flores' house and the empty lot that belonged to Gemma Keyes.

Hearing the nanomites utter my former name with such indifference sent another lurch through my twitchy nerves.

We are sorry to have caused you distress, Jayda Cruz.

I shook my head. "It's okay, Nano. Took me by surprise is all."

The city of Albuquerque has put the lot up for sale, Jayda Cruz. We can facilitate its purchase as well as the purchase of the house if you wish.

"Then you think buying the Flores' house is a good move, Nano?"

If it is what Jesus wants, it will be adequate for our needs.

Hmm. "Adequate?" Not their usual obsessive and perfectionistic "optimal?"

I was reminded of a Bible verse that often spoke to my heart: *Godliness with contentment is great gain.* The Flores' house, even after we built out the master bedroom and added a bathroom, wouldn't be pretty by today's standards—other than "pretty old." It would never possess any "wow" factor.

It would never be more than adequate for our needs.

And 'adequate' is enough, Lord God, because we can be happy there, content in your grace and provision: Zander, me, Baby Cruz, Emilio, and Abe.

And, if we followed the nanomites' advice, our home would be a safe haven, but one we could escape should it become necessary.

I exhaled. Slowly.

Yes. Happy and safe. Raising our kids for you, Lord. Growing our faith at DCC. Helping the President identify governmental fraud and waste, which could, in turn, help this good man get reelected.

What more could we ask for?

⌘

WE SHOWERED, DRESSED, ATE a hearty breakfast, had our Bible time together, and twiddled our thumbs until eight o'clock arrived and we felt comfortable calling Ms. Donovan. Zander placed the call and put it on speaker.

"Good morning, Ms. Donovan; Zander and Jayda Cruz calling. We noticed on the MLS site that the price of the Flores' house has gone down. We'd like to make an offer on it today."

"That is wonderful news, Mr. Cruz! What kind of financing are you looking at?"

Zander grinned at me. "Actually, it will be a cash offer."

"Why, that's even better. Can you come to my office this morning to draw up the offer?"

We met with her at eleven, signed the offer, then headed to Abe's to share our good news.

"We're taking the two of you out to lunch to celebrate," Zander told them. "According to Ms. Donovan, we can close as soon as the title search is complete and Mr. and Mrs. Flores sign their part of the paperwork. She's set our tentative closing date for a Friday, two weeks from yesterday."

Emilio could scarcely contain himself. "Then you'll move in? In two weeks?" he asked. "And I can sleep over?"

"Yup—as soon as we move all of our stuff from the apartment. We'll plan the move for the day after the closing, a Saturday. Hopefully, we can call on some of the young adults for help. However, we're thinking that we'll need to put our bed in what will become your bedroom while we remodel our room and add on a second bathroom."

His face started to crumble.

"You can still stay over, Emilio. We'll have you sleep on the sofa," I said. "We're thinking Friday or Saturday evenings to start, but when and how often is subject to Abe's approval."

"An' your behavior, young man," Abe added. "S'long as you keep your grades and chores up and mind your manners, we can start with one night a week."

"I'll be good—honest I will, Abe!"

Abe chuckled. "I 'spect you will."

⌘⌘⌘⌘

CHAPTER 10

ZANDER AND I DIDN'T have much to do other than wait for the house to close. But when it did close, Zander would have more on his plate than he could manage. He wouldn't be job hunting, though. We agreed that his biggest contribution to our family at this time would be to make the house ready for our family rather than work a job and do the repairs on the side.

Our plans hinged on my taking the job with Malware. It was practically a no-brainer, but we waited a couple of days. When we felt nothing but peace about me accepting the offer, I signed it, and the nanomites uploaded a copy then shot it off to Malware's email account.

Once I was, on paper at least, gainfully employed with Malware, Inc., the nanomites officially began doing the work I was getting paid for. I limited myself to peering once or twice a day into what the nanomites had unearthed in the government's finances.

Also, while Zander and I were both looking forward to closing on the house and getting moved, we really needed to hit "our" dojo. We'd slacked off long enough.

We made our way to Sandia Martial Arts Academy late Sunday evening when we knew the place would be unoccupied. After we finished our workout, we would be careful to put away any equipment we used, leaving no trace of our having been there. The owner, Doug, would know I was back and using his dojo by the stack of twenty-dollar bills we left in an envelope on his desk. That's how we wanted to keep our relationship with Doug: clean and uncomplicated.

Although it had been weeks since we exercised with our escrima sticks, I expected we would resume our previous workout mode: sparring with Gus-Gus and Ninja-Noid, our two virtual instructors.

Ah, yes. Our lovely mentors.

Their instructional style was simple, even predictable. It was composed of *Pain, Loads of Pain, Son-of-a-Sea-Cook Pain,* and *Welcome to the Hurt Locker.* Each lesson's pain menu consisted of such memorable gems as *Stupid Pain, Ignorant Pain, Did-Not-See-That-Coming Pain, Not-Paying-Attention Pain,* and *That's-The-Last-Time-I'll-Make-That-Mistake Pain.*

I smiled and breathed the familiar smells of Doug's studio, eager to use my stiff muscles. On the other hand, I was not looking forward to new lessons in "pain management."

I whispered to Zander. "Think they'll go easy on us since we haven't sparred lately?"

I wasn't sure he heard me. He stared at the sticks in his hands and frowned. Big time.

"Uh, Jayda? Sweetie? I don't think sparring is a good idea. For you. You know. For Baby Cruz."

I'll admit it. Right then and there, I pitched a bit of a fit. Dropped my sticks on the floor and—*fine!* I *flung* them down—but I was *sick and tired* of being treated like I was *sick and tired*.

And I might have raised my voice—okay, I *shouted* when I replied, "I love you, Zander, but I'm pregnant, *not* terminally ill and *not* fragile! I NEED TO WORK OUT!"

Zander Cruz, we can attest to Jayda Cruz's fitness. She is not fragile; we can assure you that she is strong enough to—

"Shut it, Nano!"

Zander and I blinked at each other until we figured out we'd shouted the same words in sync.

I recovered first. "Hear *that*, Zander? I'm not fragile." I bent and retrieved my sticks and unconsciously twirled them, the usual precursor to a strike.

Zander edged away. "Okaaay, Jay."

"Don't you dare 'okaaay, Jay' me! Don't you dare patronize me, Zander Cruz!"

"Uh . . ."

I dropped my escrima sticks and stomped off, intent on freezing him out.
Jayda Cruz.

The voice shot a chill down my spine. I spun to face the threat . . . and found Gus-Gus looming over me. His dark, hulking presence dwarfed me.

Are you prepared to spar, Jayda Cruz?

I swallowed. Scrambled for a scrap of bravado. "You better believe I am—and I'd like to start with *him*." I jabbed a finger in Zander's general direction.

As Zander Cruz cannot guarantee that he will not unintentionally strike your abdomen, sparring with him would be unwise. However, we can offer you a genuine sparring session and ensure that no harm comes to your unborn child.

I sniffed. "You don't say."

Walked back to where I'd dropped my sticks.

Okay, *thrown* them.

I picked them up. "Why didn't you say so in the first place?"

Gus-Gus didn't answer. He bowed once—and commenced his attack.

⌘

Zander and I left the dojo ninety minutes later. We were hot, sweaty, and aching where bruises were certain to show themselves by morning. Our muscles had been well used.

Both of us were smiling.

"Sorry I, er, yelled at you. Shouldn't . . . have."

Zander flicked his eyes toward me, then back on the road. "Do you honestly think I patronize you, Jayda?"

I sighed. "Some, maybe. Because I'm pregnant. But you've read all the books I've read. I'm supposed to be able to do pretty much whatever I was accustomed to doing before I got pregnant. And you know I need to use my body, expend the overabundance of energy it generates. I practically jump out of my skin when I can't exercise hard enough and often enough. We haven't exercised lately, so . . . I suppose my tongue jumped out of my mouth instead, which is no excuse, and I know that."

I sighed a little. "But . . . but I need to say something. I don't appreciate you deciding for me what I can and cannot do. I'm not a child. You aren't my parent."

And this was the first big fight we'd had since we got married.

Zander was quiet for a while, then said, "You're right that I was treating you like a child. I'm sorry. I do get . . . concerned for Baby Cruz. He or she is the only child we'll have together, Jayda."

"I know that, Zander. Don't you think I know how precious Baby Cruz is? But don't you trust me to take care of our baby? Don't you trust Baby Cruz to the Lord?"

His brow wrinkled some. "I suppose that's what it comes down to, isn't it? Trusting our child to the Lord?"

"Yes. Doing our best but, ultimately, trusting our child to the Lord, whether Baby Cruz is in me or out of me . . . 'cause the possibility of accidents or unforeseen circumstances will always exist, right? Whether he's learning to walk or learning to drive a car . . ."

"*Gah!* Please don't talk about little Baby Cruz driving a car! I don't want to be old and gray by thirty!"

I laughed. Zander laughed.

We were good.

⌘

Despite frequent workouts at the dojo, time hung heavy on our hands. Our life back in DC had been full. Busy. Often dangerous. Occasionally terrifying. We weren't accustomed to sitting around idle. Neither of us liked it.

But our idleness was nearly at an end. The nanomites, it seemed, had been busy with things other than the government's financial records.

Zander Cruz, we filed your guardian ad litem *application last week. You, Abe, and Emilio are scheduled to appear in court next week. Since all parties will be amenable to the appointment, we do not foresee any obstacles that would impede the court's decision.*

"Thank you, Nano," I replied. To Zander I said, "We should let Abe know so that he can withdraw Emilio from classes that day."

"Right. In the meantime, let's take a look inside Emilio's house and make a list of what needs to be fixed up before we can rent the place."

The nanomites let us into the house and hacked PNM to turn on the lights for us so we could make a proper assessment. However, we spent a scant twenty minutes inside, me pulling the neck of my shirt up and over my mouth and nose, Zander shaking his head the entire time.

You see, unlike the worn but pristine condition of the Flores' house, Emilio's house—under his uncle's former management—was a first-class cockroach asylum.

No one had gone in or out of the house for months. As we opened the front door, stale air followed by the reek of decomposed trash reached out from the kitchen to say, 'Hello there!' and 'Hang on to your lunch.' For a horrifying instant I thought Arnaldo Soto had lied about disposing of Mateo's body in a sandy grave somewhere on the west mesa.

Zander cleared a path through the dining and living room, kicking cans, bottles, and fast food containers out of the way. "Well," was all he said.

Then we, rather tentatively, explored each room, leaving the kitchen for last. The larger bedroom wasn't too bad. I wouldn't have touched the sheets and blankets with a ten-foot pole, but we found no dead bodies in the bed.

Thank you, Lord, for that.

Next, we poked our heads into the bathroom. The vanity sink and cabinet had pulled away from the wall. Zander opened the vanity's lower door and discovered why: The cheap pressboard wood was rotted and moldy from a leaking pipe. The pressboard had disintegrated where the screws held it to the wall, and the weight of the cabinet and sink had tipped it forward.

I gingerly opened the door to the smaller of the two bedrooms and encountered an odor that nearly overpowered me. My stomach lurched, and I backed away, coughing.

Zander reached around the door jamb and flipped on the lights, revealing the source of the smell. The ceiling must have leaked, because several of the old acoustical tiles were hanging from their frames, and a large section of carpet and the floor beneath it had rotted.

Speaking of the floor—as soon as the lights came on, it came to life. A platoon of freaked-out roaches jumped and skittered over each other, then disappeared through the rotted holes in the carpet. I squeaked and backed away, but not before I noted the filthy twin bed pushed up against the wall.

This was Emilio's room. And the rotted carpet was not a recent occurrence.

No wonder he chose to sleep in the bushes.

I seethed with anger toward Mateo, clenching and unclenching my fists as I retreated to the living room. It took some long, raging minutes for my reason to reassert itself. I had to keep reminding myself that Mateo was dead and that his death had set Emilio free from his uncle's 'loving care' and opened the door for Abe to take him in. For him to eventually be ours.

Regardless . . . *No, Lord*, I vowed. *I will never allow Emilio to suffer further neglect and abuse.*

A minute later, we stood in the dining room—on this side (the safe side) of the kitchen doorway. Neither of us fancied taking a step across the threshold, toward the overflowing garbage can, but we didn't need to go *into* the kitchen. We could see it *just fine* from where we were. Right?

"I feel . . . I feel like we need to see what's in the fridge," Zander whispered.

"Yeah, well I feel like we need to napalm the house, burn it to the ground. Doesn't mean I'm going to do it."

"Right, but . . ."

"I won't be responsible if you open that fridge and a slimy green hand reaches out and pulls you inside. Do it, and you're on your own."

"Whatever happened to 'for better and for worse'?"

"Nothing in our vows about stupidity and alien abductions."

I was all for paying someone to haul off the fridge, *un*opened, and either bury it or bomb the Taliban with it, but Zander seemed determined to save the appliance if it could be saved.

He shrugged. "I'll do it. I can handle it."

I moved to the living room while he cracked open the fridge door—and immediately slammed it shut. He was pale and gagging when he joined me.

"That bad?"

"Worse. Toxic. This entire house is a science project run amuck. Look, Jay, I won't allow you to help with cleaning up any of this mess. No telling what kinds of bacterial brew you might come into contact with."

I lifted my brows in baffled amusement. Had he forgotten our fight and my "I don't appreciate you deciding for me what I can and cannot do. I'm not a child. You aren't my parent" speech?

"You won't *allow* me?"

He didn't budge. "That's right. I'm serious. Not while you're carrying our baby. This place is a health risk—for you and Baby Cruz."

I blinked. "Oh. Well. I suppose it is."

Jayda and Zander Cruz, we recommend that you hire a professional cleaning service. That said, we also recommend removing the refrigerator entirely, tearing out the bathroom vanity and the flooring in the second bedroom, then hiring pest control.

"Yeah, I get you, Nano." And Zander shook his head. (He was doing that fairly frequently.)

We came away with the broad strokes of what was needed—each broad stroke inclusive of a hefty price tag and a heap of work.

Demo and haul off debris.

Fumigate inside and outside.

Repair leaks in roof.

Rebuild floor and repair ceiling in second bedroom.

Clean throughout.

Patch and paint throughout.

Carpet and tile throughout.

Replace window screens throughout.

Install new window blinds throughout.

Hire furnace inspector.

Change out locks, front and back.

"Whew. It's gonna take fifteen grand at a minimum plus elbow grease before we can rent out the place," said Zander, perfecting his head wag.

He'd shaken his head so many times, I figured he qualified for his own bobblehead dashboard doll.

"Beats the alternative of letting the place sit empty and degrade further. Suppose we don't recoup the investment for a few years? So what? Fixing up the place keeps our neighborhood from sliding down the tubes. And by the time Emilio graduates high school, the house should have turned a decent profit for him."

Jayda and Zander Cruz, we recommend that you open a checking account for the benefit of Emilio Martinez and deposit in it an initial amount—to be paid back over time—said amount immediately available to draw upon for these repairs.

"Yeah. Let's do that," Zander answered. "We can write up our assessment of the repairs and show the court how we are prepared to manage Emilio's affairs."

Jayda and Zander Cruz, we have recorded your walkthrough and will download it to a flash drive. The video and your willingness to tackle this unpalatable task may persuade the judge to appoint you Emilio's guardian ad litem.

I snarked. "Can you add odors to that video, Nano? Because one whiff of this cesspool should cinch the deal."

⌘

REGARDLESS OF WHAT THE judge ruled, Emilio's house demanded an intervention. We decided to go ahead and tackle the most immediate steps, the things that couldn't be put off. We had the time and energy and were willing to invest our own money in the project in order to protect Emilio's inheritance—not that anyone was suicidal enough to break into his house.

We ran over to the closest Home Depot and bought two sets of doorknob and deadbolt combo packs keyed alike, then Zander installed them on Emilio's front and side doors. He handed Abe a set of keys, and we kept the others.

Next, the nanomites sent us their recommendation of a company that did fire and other dirty cleanups and demolitions. We hired them to handle the fridge removal (we provided ample warnings), the bathroom vanity, and the carpet and flooring in the smaller bedroom.

Two guys came the next day with a nice big truck and stoic expressions that told us they were tough enough to stare down the vile creatures spawned in Mateo's fridge and come out the victors. With little comment but garbed in jumpsuits, goggles, respirators, and heavy rubber gloves and boots, they tore up and carried out moldy carpet, flooring, ceiling tiles, vanity, and last of all, the fridge.

The only words I heard them say were, "Got you a roach problem." Then Zander sent money from his phone to their company and they were gone.

That afternoon, a roofer Abe knew from church showed up. He leaned his ladder against the house, climbed up it, walked carefully around the roof, and spray painted a few places. He called Zander up the ladder to see what he saw.

"This one place is the worst. Need to have my guys tear into it before we can see what the damage to the roof's structure is. Once that's done, I'll write you a bid on the spot."

"How long to get it fixed?" Zander asked.

"Oh, five days, tops. Rest of the roof is okay, 'cept for one place that's a bit soft. I recommend that we patch it, too."

The "'Burque Bug Man" came early the next morning. I didn't actually see him. Zander gently requested that I stay home, far from the fumes of any pesticides.

"Yeah, yeah. I get it. BC. Baby Cruz."

Zander kissed me goodbye, grinning the entire time. "BC. I like that. Bruce Cruz? Bobby Cruz? That works if we name him Roberto after my dad."

"Bobbie Cruz works if BC is a girl and we name her Roberta."

"Oh. Well, yeah. For a guy there's also Brody . . . or Brian?"

"Brody sounds like grody, and some bratty grade school kid will misspell Brian as Brain. And neither of those names work if BC is a girl."

"Don't be such a downer! Let a man dream, yeah?"

"Dream all you want as long as said man—meaning *you*—doesn't pitch a fit if we have a girl."

"Pitch a fit? Naw, not me. We have a girl? She'll be the most spoiled princess ever born."

"Oh, brother."

⌘

THAT AFTERNOON WHEN Emilio got home from school, Zander walked him through his house. In each room, he explained the tasks he'd either taken care of himself or had hired done and what tasks remained to be completed.

Emilio wrinkled his nose. "Stinks bad in here."

"Uh, you should have smelled it before the demo guys hauled out the fridge and a bunch of moldy wood." Zander winked at Emilio. "Jayda almost threw up."

"Gross!" But he was grinning.

"I agree," Zander said, "and that's why I wanted you to see all the work we need to do for yourself. As your *Guardian ad Litem*, I'd be in charge of getting the house ready to rent out. That said, I think you should also be invested in the process."

"What's that mean? What you said."

"Invested in the process?"

"Yeah, that."

"It means you should know what's going on, and you should help me."

"Oh. Sure! I want to help."

"Great. Go ask Abe if you can help for an hour. If he says yes, change into grubby clothes and meet me back here in ten minutes."

When Emilio returned, what Zander had lined out for them to do wasn't in the house but in the yard.

"See Abe's side of these shrubs? Nice and clean, trimmed neatly? We're going to trim this side of the shrubs. Oh. And we should wear these while we work."

Zander pulled on a pair of gloves. "These branches have stickers." He tossed a smaller pair of gloves to Emilio.

Emilio muttered to himself, "Stickers. Yeah, I know," as he pulled on the gloves.

Zander pointed to a gas-powered hedge trimmer, then a long pair of loppers.

"I'm going to make some big cuts to trim back the hedge. When I do, you can drag the branches out of the way, and chop 'em up with those loppers. When the pieces are small enough, we'll put them in the trashcan."

He had planned to start Emilio on just one job, but the boy was neither daunted nor lazy. He tried hard to keep up with Zander and kept at it with the loppers until he had mastered them and the art of chopping big branches into smaller, more manageable pieces.

When Zander finished with the hedge trimmer, he fetched the garbage can and a rake. Soon he had raked a pile of dry, windblown leaves out from under the shrubs and dumped them in the trash. Then he turned his hand to Emilio's pile of chopped branches, adding them to the trash.

Emilio hadn't finished cutting up all the branches. He eyed the pile going into the can and tried to go faster, chopping madly at the branches on the ground . . . near his feet.

"Hey, hey!" Zander reached over and tapped Emilio's shoulder. "Slow down there, buddy. It's okay—not every job takes the same amount of time. Besides, I don't want you chopping up something you didn't mean to. You know, like your foot. 'Cause, then you'd be a pirate, and we'd have to get you a crutch and a parrot to sit on your shoulder."

Emilio guffawed. "I'd teach that ol' parrot how t' cuss real good."

Zander shook with wry, silent laughter. "How about we settle for not chopping off a foot, hey?"

And Lord Jesus? Please help us lead Emilio to you soon?

⌘⌘⌘⌘

CHAPTER 11

The next Friday evening, fifteen young adults crowded into our apartment. We supplied the pizza and sodas; they supplied the ravenous appetites. Of course, Zander and I brought our own raging hunger to the party.

"Gosh, Jayda," Izzie mumbled around a nibble of pizza. "How many slices have you had?"

Uh-oh.

My mouth was stuffed. I had to chew a bunch before I could swallow and answer.

"Um, guess I'm hungry this evening. Feels like I skipped lunch or something," I mumbled back.

Yeah, like I skipped lunch **and** *breakfast. And like I'm eating for two.*

I tossed the last two bites of my fifth slice into the trash—and stared with longing after it. Right then, Zander called for order and saved me from Izzie's inquisition.

"Hey, everyone? Ready to get into the word? Let's get settled so we can start."

Somehow, all of us found a seat or a patch of carpet and readied ourselves for the study.

Zander prayed before he began, then said, "This evening we're going to talk about *the things that divide us*. From my perspective, rather than becoming a more unified nation or world, we are seeing and experiencing more and greater divisions all the time. Is that what you're seeing and experiencing?"

"Darn straight," Nance huffed. "You can't say or do anything anymore without being thrown into a box or category—and then judged by the supposed characteristics of that category. *You* don't matter; only the slot you fill. *Your* actions don't count for a thing; only the perceived collective actions of the category you've been dumped in."

"Nailed it, Nance," Josh called out.

Zander nodded. "Well, I'd like to start our study this evening with a statement, okay?" He looked around at the earnest, wall-to-wall faces in our living room.

"Okay, here it is. *God believes in division*. In fact, he is the author of division."

Those wall-to-wall faces registered first surprise, then uncertainty and concern.

Zander laughed aloud. "Relax. That's half my statement. Here's the whole thing: *God believes in division—but not the division of this fallen world*. This week and next week, we're going to pull this statement apart, and I expect you to study the word for yourself and see if what I'm saying is true. FYI? You should cultivate the habit of studying Scripture for yourself, checking whether or not the teaching you receive is biblical."

Zander opened his Bible. "Turn to Genesis, chapter 1, and the account of creation. Note that even in the first steps of creation we see God's division. It is both intentional and purposeful—like when he separates the light from the darkness, separates the water under the vault from the water above the vault, then gathers the water under the sky into one place, leaving the dry ground in another. Intentional and with purpose.

"The most important division God made during creation week was to set people apart from all the rest of his creation. He did this in Genesis 1, verses 26 and 27." Zander read aloud,

"Then God said,
'Let us make mankind in our image, in our likeness,
so that they may rule over the fish in the sea
and the birds in the sky,
over the livestock and all the wild animals,
and over all the creatures that move along the ground.'
So God created mankind in his own image,
in the image of God he created them;
male and female he created them.

"I'd like us to notice that the Lord made people—both male and female—in his image and likeness. I'd also like to point out that he set people over the rest of his creation and told them to rule over the fish, birds, both domesticated and wild animals, and creatures that moved along the ground. Another way of stating 'rule over' is to say that God told them to govern, steward, and take care of his creation."

"And a great hash we've made of it," sniffed Sandra, one of our new girls.

Zander nodded. "In many respects you are right, Sandra, while it is also true that our level of obedience doesn't negate what he told us to do. In other words, our disobedience doesn't change God's instructions to us. So, I'd like us to focus on what the Lord did or said, rather than on our responses. Can we do that first?"

"Sure," Sandra said, her nods causing the gold and copper strands woven into her long, beautifully braided hair to shimmer. "I get you— 'cause God is always right, and we are often wrong."

"Great observation, Sandra. Concerning *people*, the first major division God made? He placed people above and in charge of the rest of creation. He made the next and lasting division when he separated all people into two camps: Jew and Gentile—Gentile meaning anyone not a Jew. He initiated this separation in Genesis 17:7 when he called Abraham out of his own country and promised to be his God and his descendants' God after him.

"I will establish my covenant
as an everlasting covenant between me
and you and your descendants after you
for the generations to come,
to be your God and the God
of your descendants after you.

"Several centuries later, the Lord brought Abraham's descendants out of bondage in Egypt where they were called Hebrews or the people of Israel, Abraham's grandson. In Deuteronomy 7:6, God told the Hebrews that he had chosen them to be his special people.

"For you are a people holy to the Lord your God.
The Lord your God has chosen you
out of all the peoples on the face of the earth
to be his people, his treasured possession.

"The Lord says he chose Abraham and his descendants out of all the peoples on earth. He calls them *his treasured possession,* and he set them apart from all other people on the earth. Do you remember me saying a minute ago that our disobedience doesn't change God's intentions or his instructions? The people of Israel epitomize this statement. The Lord showed the world his great power and mercy when he redeemed and brought his people out of Egypt and out of its pagan worship. However, the Jews, as they were also called, were continually unfaithful to the Lord. He had to, over and over, deal with their idolatry.

"Let's jump forward to Jesus' ministry. Jesus, in perfect unity with his Father, also recognized the Lord's two distinctions in humankind, Jew and Gentile—'God's chosen people' and 'not God's chosen people'—but this is where it gets really cool. Because, when Jesus died and rose from the dead, he opened the door of salvation to everyone. Jesus made a way for 'whoever believes in him' to be counted among God's people. We are all familiar with John 3:16 where Jesus declares this.

"For God so loved the world
that he gave his one and only Son,
that whoever believes in him shall not perish
but have everlasting life.

"The Apostle Paul spoke of this very thing in his letter to the Ephesians, chapter 2, verses 13-15. This passage, written specifically to

Gentile believers, tells them—tells *us*—that God receives any Gentile who is in Christ Jesus. He includes us in his chosen people. Jesus' death broke down the wall between Jew and Gentile, destroying it forever, so that believing Gentiles are no longer separated from God's chosen people because he has made the two groups one.

> *"But now in Christ Jesus*
> *you who once were far off*
> *have been brought near by the blood of Christ.*
> *For he himself is our peace,*
> ***who has made the two groups one***
> *and has destroyed the barrier,*
> *the dividing wall of hostility . . .*
> *His purpose was to create **in himself***
> *one new humanity out of the two,*
> *thus making peace,*

"Verse 19 of the same chapter tells us that believing Gentiles are no longer excluded. We are full-fledged members of God's household.

> *"Now, therefore,*
> *you are no longer strangers and foreigners,*
> *but fellow citizens with the saints*
> *and members of the household of God.*

"Do we get the enormity of what Jesus did for us? He joined believing Gentiles and believing Jews together *in himself*. He included us in God's household and said we were no longer strangers, no longer excluded—no longer 'not my people.'

"Did the Lord change how he divides and sorts humanity? No—he changed *us*. He took those who believe on Jesus from the category of 'not my people,' and translated them to the category of 'my people.' He continues to view humanity as *two and only two people groups*: either 'members of the household of God' or 'strangers and foreigners;' either believers or nonbelievers.

"This concept was so important, that Paul repeats and expands on it in Colossians 3:11-14, this time with several admonitions to us, God's chosen people, on how we are to treat one another.

> *"Here there is no Gentile or Jew,*
> *circumcised or uncircumcised,*
> *barbarian, Scythian, slave or free,*
> *but Christ is all, and is in all.*
> ***Therefore, as God's chosen people,***
> *holy and dearly loved,*

clothe yourselves with compassion,
kindness, humility, gentleness and patience.
Bear with each other and forgive one another
if any of you has a grievance against someone.
Forgive as the Lord forgave you.
And over all these virtues put on love,
which binds them all together in perfect unity."

Zander looked around the young adults. "How many people groups did God ordain?"

Their uncertain reply was "two," and their answer was shaky . . . because it flew in the face of what was being drilled into their heads in their university classes.

Zander smiled softly. "You see where I'm going with this, don't you? In fact, I'm going to press on and make a pretty radical statement, which is this: The concept of race—dividing and sorting people by color and other physical attributes and labeling them black, brown, yellow, red, or white— is a *human* construct, not a God construct. Nowhere in Scripture does the Lord define or divide people by race as we define and divide race today.

"Study this out for yourself. Verify that what I'm saying isn't nonsense or bad Bible scholarship. Can we find, anywhere in Scripture, an example where God classifies a people group by color as we do today?"

"But Scripture does mention color, right, Zander?" Nance asked.

"Sure. Scripture describes the physical attributes of some individuals. Genesis says that Esau's skin was red and hairy, 1 Samuel mentions that David was ruddy or fair, the woman narrating part of Song of Solomon describes her lover as having wavy black hair and herself as having dark skin. And in Revelation 1, where John saw Jesus standing among the golden lampstands? He tells us Jesus' hair was as white as snow.

"But at issue is this: Does God *divide* us by race? Does he *classify* us by race? Does he *sort* us by race? No, he does not."

"Wow," Diego breathed. "Are you sure, Pastor Zander? Because this is not what we're told pretty much everywhere—in school, in the media, entertainment, and so on."

"I hear you, so let's dig deeper. Acts 17:24-27 is a good place to start.

"The God who made the world and everything in it
is the Lord of heaven and earth
and does not live in temples built by human hands.
And he is not served by human hands, as if he needed anything.
Rather, he himself gives everyone life
and breath and everything else.
From one man he made all the nations,

that they should inhabit the whole earth;
and he marked out their appointed times in history
and the boundaries of their lands.
God did this so that they would seek him
and perhaps reach out for him and find him,
though he is not far from any one of us.

"If the Lord made all nations from one man, then he made only *one race*, not many races. We ought not to espouse what the world teaches, a continual division by color that snatches our attention away from the only division the Lord himself has made—'my people' or 'not my people.'"

I suddenly noticed how Sandra's chin was tipped against her chest while she slowly shook her head back and forth. As she gulped for air, I saw a tear streak down her cheek.

From the warehouse, I called to my husband, *Zander. Look up. Sandra is hurting.*

Zander's eyes found her. "Sandra? Are you all right?"

"N-no, I'm not. Y-you are denying the injustices people of color suffer all the time—people like me! I . . . I know many churches that teach on social justice—and I know the Bible contains many Scriptures exhorting Christians to stand up for the oppressed!"

Zander slid out of his chair and sat cross legged on the carpet. He sat a couple of feet from Sandra to give her space yet be able to speak to her at eye level. "Sandra, may I ask you a question?"

She sniffed and glanced up. "I guess. I'm sorry, but I'm confused. I-I don't know you well, and this . . . is hard for me to accept."

She wasn't the only one. I noticed some of the young adults frown and send concerned glances across the room. Some whispered; others shifted with discomfort. My mind went immediately to Zander's message from two weeks ago. *For God is not the author of confusion, but of peace, as in all churches of the saints.*

I whispered a discreet but heartfelt prayer, "Lord God, confusion is not of you. Please bring us out of confusion and into the clarity of your word and your peace."

Zander lifted his voice. "If I could have everyone's attention for a sec? We love Sandra, right? She is a part of this group, so hang tight for her sake while we work through this, okay?"

The rustling and fidgeting slowed and stopped.

Zander said, "Sandra, may I ask, why do you come to this Bible study?"

Her brows pulled together. "Oh, great! Are you saying I don't belong here?"

"No, the opposite, in fact. But please, would you tell us why you choose to be part of this group, rather than, say, a Bible study sponsored by one of the churches you mentioned?"

Right then, our tenderhearted Izzie—being Izzie—reached over and took Sandra's hand. Squeezed it. Held on to it.

Sandra looked up and smiled at Izzie. "Because of that, I suppose."

Zander pressed her. "Because . . ."

"Because I feel loved here."

"Yes, you *are* loved here! Do you also feel 'black' here?"

"Sure. No. Well, maybe. I mean, Keisha and Felix are black, too . . ."

"I'm Chinese," Tian inserted into Sandra's silence.

"I'm half Indian," Cali said. "Eastern Indian, to be clear."

"And several of us are Hispanic," Izzie said. "We're actually a pretty racially diverse group."

"Why, faith and begorra! An' me bein' an Irishman!" Josh pronounced—to general laughter and playful mocking.

Sandra chuckled. "Yeah, I suppose I don't think in terms of race when I'm here. I simply feel . . . accepted."

Zander was careful and deliberate. "I believe that's what I'm getting at, Sandra. *In the church*, we are not to differentiate in terms of race, color, or ethnicity. Why? Because the Bible says we are one in Christ. He said he has broken down the dividing walls between us, and that we are to walk in that unity. Live it out. I would go so far as to say that the Lord himself doesn't categorize people by their external characteristics. He said as much to the prophet Samuel concerning King Saul in 1 Samuel 16:7.

> *"Do not consider his appearance or his height,*
> *for I have rejected him.*
> *The Lord does not look at the things people look at.*
> ***People look at the outward appearance,***
> ***but the Lord looks at the heart."***

Zander's expression became more serious, and he repeated, "*People look at the outward appearance, but the Lord looks at the heart.* I want to say—and this is vitally important—that if we Christians elevate or lower, if we treat individuals with favor or disfavor—if we even *think* less of them based on their skin color or other physical attributes—we are contradicting the Lord himself who made *all of us* in his own image and likeness. In other words, *Christians must be color-blind.*"

Sandra replied, "Color-blind? But what about all the injustice and inequality in America?"

"When we witness injustice, we absolutely should speak up. We should *act*. That said, we *cannot* control what others think, feel, or believe. We *cannot* force people to change their minds or hearts. In fact, we know that if they aren't born again, their hearts are naturally selfish. Sinful."

She sighed. "You white people just don't seem to get it."

Zander snorted. "You *white* people? Sandra, am I white?"

"Okay, maybe not you, *personally*, but the systems around us are broken."

"What if we Christians showed the world how justice and equality should look and act?"

Sandra swiped her hand across her eyes. "Is that ever going to happen? I mean, how long has the church had a chance to change things? People of color experience discrimination all the time. White people don't see or acknowledge their privilege."

"You keep saying 'white people' to me, Sandra. I'm not white; I'm Hispanic. My mother's parents were born in Mexico. My father floated from Cuba to Florida on a raft. It took him and the dozen others on the raft with him three days of paddling through shark-infested waters to make landfall in the US. And even though *I* was born here, I've been called every name in the book—beaner, wetback, Frito Bandito, Poncho, spic."

Across the room, I blinked and sat back. I had never thought much about Zander's ethnicity—and Zander had never brought it up, except in terms of his past life in the gangs.

"I've been refused service, denied jobs, and passed over for promotion. I've been harassed by the police—but full disclosure? Back then I was in a nasty gang and probably deserved getting 'checked out.' I could go on and on. But I don't. Why? Because it's a heart problem."

Sandra huffed. "It sure is."

"Well . . ." Zander continued to use care with his words and tone, "to be candid, many of the racial slurs aimed at me came from African Americans, not white people. You do acknowledge racial tension between African Americans and Asians, between African Americans and Latinos, right? It's well documented, isn't it? So, how helpful would it be for me to say to you, 'You black people just don't get it'?"

Sandra grimaced.

Zander said softly, "Can we change or fix people's hearts? Or can only Jesus do that?"

"I suppose only Jesus can—but we should keep fighting for racial justice!"

"Well, can we fix racial injustice, I mean fix the root cause, without fixing the heart?"

Sandra frowned. "No . . . probably not."

"Sandra, why is human trafficking worse today than fifty years ago?"

"What does human trafficking have to do—"

"Bear with me. Why are drug and alcohol problems worse today? Why are more people homeless? Why is domestic violence rampant? Why are the gangs and cartels taking over? Why are more people shooting each other? Why are suicides higher than ever?"

I'd never seen such an attentive young adult group. They were, all of them, closely monitoring the back-and-forth between Zander and Sandra. I'd also never seen Zander as gentle and humble as he was this evening.

Zander finally got down to it. "Those things are worse today because *sin* is worse today. Would you agree with that, Sandra? We pass more and more laws, yet our nation grows less moral and more ungodly with each passing year. Why? Because human effort cannot 'fix' sin, cannot legislate it out of existence, and cannot control it—which is why God sent Jesus to save us.

"It was Plato who said, 'Good people do not need laws to tell them to act responsibly, while bad people will find a way around laws.' See, the rule of law is only effective in a moral society—and our society is less moral by the day. You can try to legislate behavior, but you cannot legislate what is inside a person's heart. Only Jesus can transform an individual from the inside out—through repentance, surrender, and the new birth. That's the way Jesus works.

"However, since our nation has stopped honoring God, has kicked every Christian tenet out of the public forum, and openly exalts perversion? Of course sin is growing worse and worse. Some of our recent laws, in fact, *promote* sin. It won't be long before saying certain behaviors are sin will be against the law. What then?"

"But Pastor Zander, these other churches I'm talking about? They are out there marching and protesting, stirring up people's consciences against racism and inequality."

Zander thought for a moment. "Those who are out there, marching, protesting, sometimes rioting . . . are they advocating for Jesus?"

"Some of them are!"

"When protesters riot, loot, burn businesses and cars, and attack innocent bystanders, are they behaving as Jesus wants them to? Will you march with those who throw rocks at the police and terrorize people while they are eating in restaurants?"

Sandra shook her head. "No. Not that."

"What about the other things these churches are advocating for? What else is on their agenda?"

Sandra didn't answer.

"Have those churches mixed other issues into their protests? Say, abortion and LGBTQ rights? Will you join their protests to advocate for abortion on demand and to advance the gay agenda? And do those protesters slander those who disagree with them, cursing them and calling them by vile names? Do they spout 'thou shalt not judge,' mishandling the word of God at every attempt to engage them in productive conversation?"

Zander said softly, "If those churches, while marching for racial equality, espouse *anything* the word of God calls sin, their entire agenda is suspect—not in my book, but in God's book."

Then he stood and addressed the entire group. "Can we digress and talk about judging for a sec? What God has said in his word stands firm forever. It is not judging to repeat what God's word says. It *is* judging, however, when you treat unsaved people as though God didn't love them enough to send Jesus to die for them."

Zander sat again. "You have been told we live in an unjust society and that we should fight those injustices. Please allow me to ad*just* your thinking, if I may."

The young adults groaned; Josh said, "Pastor Zander, your puns are worse than mine."

"Well, *that's* saying something," Todd quipped.

More laughter. Less confusion.

Zander's next words pulled them back to their study. "Say, can we talk about identity? How we define ourselves? Because *identity* is at the core of what we've been discussing.

"According to the way God divides humanity, he wants us to define ourselves, first and foremost, as *his*. His people. His family. His son or daughter. His church. Everything else that defines us must come after who we are in Christ—and it must rank lower than who we are in Christ. Gender, ethnicity, skin, hair, and eye color? Not the top of the list."

Sandra's reply was a growl. "Yeah, well I still have to live in the world as a woman of color—and it is *not* easy."

Zander considered her for a moment. "Well, Sandra, what I believe the Lord wishes us to take away from this study is this: Live as a believer. Live as salt and light. Live a life of sacrificial love, and *live free of offense*. Live as though this world is not your home—*it is not*—and live as though you are just passing through—*we are*."

Zander's gaze caught Sandra's and held. "Let the rest fall away . . . because anything we elevate above our calling as a believer? Challenges God for his preeminence in our lives."

"You're saying it becomes an idol?"

Zander dipped his chin once. "I'm saying it *can* become an idol. Listen, the Christian's primary goal is not to fight for a perfect society. Our goal, our mission, is to *literally* pack the kingdom of God. To save as many souls as we can in every generation."

He looked around. "If we do our job well, society will be affected and altered by the quality and quantity of God's people active in that society. So, take care! It's easy to be diverted from our purpose, to take up a cause other than the cause of Christ. Social justice is not our mission: growing the kingdom of God, one heart at a time, is."

He turned back to Sandra. She sat staring Zander in the face but thinking. Hard.

Zander smiled gently at her. "You are made in the image and likeness of God, Sandra. We love you and accept you. In fact, there can be no 'we' that excludes you."

She finally smiled back. "Thank you, Pastor Zander. You've given me a lot to think on."

A murmur of agreement flowed around the room, and I was right there with them.

"We'll pick this up next time, okay?" Zander asked.

"Yeah, and I'll still be picking this study outta my teeth," Josh quipped.

He got his laugh, of course . . . but maybe he wasn't joking.

⌘⌘⌘⌘

Chapter 12

Moving day! Because Zander and I were keeping Baby Cruz a secret until Thanksgiving when we would tell Zander's family, we decided to "pre-move" a few things. To that end, Zander picked up the rental truck Friday after we closed on our house. As soon as Emilio got out of school that afternoon, he and Zander shifted the baby paraphernalia from our apartment to the house, stashing it in the bedroom designated as the nursery and locking the door behind them.

I think Emilio felt pretty good about being in on the secret, about knowing it even before Izzie did. His grin held a certain smug satisfaction and excitement.

Saturday morning, Izzie, Tian, and four guys from the young adults showed up to help us with the rest of the move. The girls arrived on time, as did Emilio when Abe dropped him off at our apartment. The young adult guys, however, straggled in during the next hour in various stages of "awake and functional."

"Hear ye, hear ye! Get yer caffeine fix here," I called. "Coffee's on the kitchen counter; sodas are in the fridge."

Todd appeared at my elbow. "Anything to eat?"

"For you? Always. Cold pizza do it?"

"Yum!"

I walked away chuckling.

Soon, everything we owned was headed into our house. Zander and I had managed to paint the living and dining rooms, then get new carpet installed. That meant the dining table and chairs and the sofa could be placed right where they belonged.

We intended, however, to use the other parts of the house "as is" for a time—with the exception of our bedroom. It would be a construction zone until Zander completed the new bathroom. Until the master suite was finished, Zander and I would set up our living quarters in what would be Emilio's room.

When the apartment was empty, the girls and I went through it, giving the kitchen and bathroom a good clean, vacuuming all the carpets. It didn't take long; we'd been in it less than a month.

We took everybody out for burgers as a thank you, then hugged them all goodbye. Zander and I returned to our new home. He disappeared into the "construction zone" and I started setting up our kitchen—with its shiny new fridge. We had transferred Mr. and Mrs. Flores' antiquated but *clean* fridge to Emilio's house for our future renters and had splurged on a new one for us.

Remember me saying that the Flores' house had the same floorplan as Gemma's house? Well, unpacking boxes into the kitchen cupboards turned into a mighty strange déjà vu experience . . . because I knew where everything belonged. The odd familiarity between our new home and Gemma's old house was disconcerting, to tell you the truth.

I had to glance out the kitchen window facing *our* back yard a couple of times to yank me out of the past and bring me back to reality. The Flores' had planted a nice apple tree back there, something Gemma didn't have in her back yard. The sight of that tree helped ground me in the present.

⌘

JAYDA CRUZ, ZANDER CRUZ, *the crew you have hired to build your new garage and a secure location for our printer has arrived. You are needed to move your car from the driveway.*

Jayda Cruz, Zander Cruz, the crew you have hired to build your new garage and a secure location for our printer has arrived. You are needed to move your car from the driveway.

Today the crew will demolish the Flores' old garage, then dig out the footprint for the new garage.

Zander Cruz, you are needed to move your car from the driveway.

Zander Cruz, you are needed to move your car from the driveway.

"Good grief." It was Monday morning. *Early* Monday morning.

Zander, jerked unceremoniously and without warning from a deep sleep, rolled over so precipitously, he launched himself off the edge of the bed. "*Ow.*"

Being awakened by the nanomites' profound and often unexpected announcements can be **ahem** quite entertaining.

From the floor, Zander mumbled, "Stop laughing."

"Me? I'm not laughing." I ran into the hall and ducked into the bathroom, scarcely containing my 'not laughing' until I could close the door.

When I came out, Zander was gone. I pulled on comfy jeans and a t-shirt, then walked to the kitchen. The side door was open, and Zander stood on the porch rubbing the back of his neck. As I joined him, he curled an arm around my waist. I stared at what he was staring at.

It was hard to believe my eyes.

The toothed bucket of a backhoe had torn a hole in the roof of the Flores' little garage. As I watched, the backhoe started pulling down the walls.

While the garage was coming down, we watched a skid steer loader—something like a mini bulldozer—butt slowly against the cinderblock wall separating our lot from Gemma's lot, toppling the wall a section at a time. It, too, was disappearing fast. Three guys sorted and moved the blocks after they fell. They tossed the broken bits into a pile, chipped residual mortar from reusable blocks and stacked them on pallets. When a pallet was full, one guy mounted a forklift, picked up the pallet, and moved it off to the far side of where the new garage would be built.

Before long, the backhoe had utterly demolished the old garage, and the driver moved the backhoe a fair distance from the driveway, while the men brought in an excavator with a hydraulic breaker fitted to its arm. The breaker's powerful hydraulic hammer pounded the slab of concrete that had been the garage floor and the driveway, slowly breaking the slab into pieces.

"They'll bring the backhoe in to scoop up the big chunks and dump them into that," Zander said, pointing to the dumpster at the curb. "When they drive the backhoe and excavator over to Gemma's place, the crew will move in here and police the site, picking up remaining broken pieces from the Flores' garage and driveway."

All the demo was hard, dirty, sweaty work, and I imagined the guys would be at it for hours, repeating the process for Gemma's garage and the broken slab where Gemma's house had stood.

I looked up in time to see Emilio trotting across the cul-de-sac. Zander waved him over to us. Emilio bounced up the steps and wormed his way between us. Both of us curled our arms around him and hugged him tight.

"Exciting, huh?" Zander said.

Emilio nodded, transfixed by all the machinery.

"Well, as exciting as it is, I need you to promise me something. Can you do that?"

"Sure!"

"Good. From here on, until these guys are done and all the machinery is gone? You don't come over here except up the front walk and through the front door. You can watch from right here—but no stepping off the porch or cutting through the yard like you did a minute ago. Got it?"

"Yeah," I added casually. "I mean, we like you fine the way you are, so don't damage the goods."

Emilio grinned. "I know you love me."

I planted a kiss on his forehead. "Yes, I do. Tell me something I don't know."

"Knock, knock."

"Oh, brother! Are we back to those?"

Emilio, nearly bursting, turned to a more receptive audience. "Knock, knock."

Zander waggled his eyebrows. "Who's there?"

"Gladys."

Zander's eyes narrowed. "Huh. Don't think I know this one. All right— Gladys, who?"

Emilio, managing to keep a straight face, answered, "Gladys the weekend—no homework!"

Zander staggered backward and fell against the doorjamb. "Oh! Oh! Ya got me! Ya got me! I'm dyin' here!"

He fell into the kitchen, and Emilio jumped on top of him, trying his best to tickle Zander. That didn't work out like Emilio had hoped. Zander flipped him, got his fingers under Emilio's armpits, and tickled him mercilessly.

I was the one who shouted, "Stop! Stop, please! I can't breathe!" I was laughing so hard, the men working in our yard grinned and laughed with us.

I stepped over the two animals wrestling on the kitchen floor. "I'm going to start breakfast. Who wants pancakes?"

That stopped 'em cold.

And from the crew outside I heard one lone voice holler, "I do!"

⌘

Much later, Zander and I checked on the crew's progress from the back porch. Emilio had gone grocery shopping with Abe.

"I'm glad Abe has Emilio's strong arms and willing heart to help him," I murmured.

"Mmm."

Zander was preoccupied. I don't think he heard me.

The Flores' garage was a memory. In its place, only a few yards from where we stood on the porch, was a large hole about ten feet deep. The guys had dumped the dirt from the hole into Gemma's yard. We'd spread it later after we marked out the garden site.

I peered toward Mrs. Calderón's house, the view temporarily un-obstructed. The nanomites zoomed in on her living room window—Mrs. Calderón's preferred location for watching the neighborhood. I figured with Gemma dead, Mr. and Mrs. Flores gone, and Mateo's gang removed for good, Mrs. Calderón didn't have much to spy on.

I almost felt sorry for her.

Mrs. Calderón's living room blind twitched. Yup. There she was. She hadn't been over to introduce herself to us, her new neighbors, but it was early days.

Right there, I vowed to be a better, friendlier neighbor than Gemma had been. Even if it killed me.

She will probably come knocking any day, I told myself, *and if it slays my flesh, that's a benefit, not a loss.*

I brightened. *Maybe she'll bring cookies!*

Back to the garage. Two guys up top of the hole mixed concrete in a bucket and lowered the buckets into the hole where two other guys poured the footers of the garage's half-basement. The crew would come back to build the basement walls, using cinderblock, mortar, rebar, and concrete. I liked that they would reuse blocks rescued from the demolition of the wall between our lot and Gemma's, although they also had a few pallets of new blocks standing by.

Three more guys were framing up the driveway, the garage footers, and the garage floor. Wednesday, they told Zander, a cement mixer would come to pour the basement floor, the garage footers and floor, and driveway. After the cement cured, they would frame up the garage itself.

When the project was finished, our kitchen door and porch would be about the same distance from the new garage as they had been from the old garage, but the new structure would stand a couple of feet taller and would straddle the former property line between the Flores' and Gemma's lots. The finished garage would be twenty-two feet wide and thirty-four feet long. The nanomites had designed it to accommodate two full-sized vehicles with an extra twelve feet at the rear for a nice-sized workshop—over the partial basement.

The side door into the garage would be built toward the rear of the garage, farther from the kitchen porch than the previous garage's side door had been. The wide steps leading down into the garage basement would be inside that doorway and to its left.

When the garage was finished and the crew long gone, Zander would add the next pieces of the nanomites' design himself. He would construct a workbench the same dimensions as the opening to the steps—a workbench that swiveled away from the wall, providing access to the steps.

The crew we hired might recollect digging an innocuous basement beneath the garage, but only five people would know how to access that basement: Zander, me, Dr. Bickel, and Dr. Bickel's two technicians, Rick and Tony.

Rick and Tony would complete the last steps of the nanomites' design: They would wire and vent the garage basement to accommodate the 3D printer and its supplies. Then they would install the printer and the containers of chemicals the nanomites required to print more tribal members.

"This is going to be great," I enthused.

We agree, Jayda Cruz. We will be able to access the printer easily from the house. In addition, should it be needed, the basement can serve as a panic room for your family, accessible from your bedroom after we complete the tunnel.

"Cool! Wait, what? Oh yeah. A panic room."

The idea that we might ever *need* a panic room? Not cool at all.

⌘⌘⌘⌘

Chapter 13

THE NEXT DAY, ZANDER and I, Abe and Emilio, and a representative from CYFD (New Mexico's Children, Youth and Families Department) showed up in court. As the petitioner requesting that the court appoint him Emilio's *Guardian ad Litem*, Zander presented ample evidence of our involvement in Emilio's life, including a copy of our purchase agreement for the house across the cul-de-sac from where Emilio and Abe lived and the work we'd done to date to clean up Emilio's house.

Then the judge, an aging gent with little to show on top of his head but with three prominent chins below his mouth, asked Emilio to approach the bench. "I want to hear from you how you feel about Zander becoming your *Guardian ad Litem*."

In response to the judge's questions, Emilio said softly, "Zander will do a good job fixing up my house—and I'm gonna help him. Zander and Jayda are practically my dad and mom, see, 'cept, see, I live with Abe— but I get to stay all night with Jayda and Zander, soon as they fix up their new house and I get my own room."

The judge squinted, a trifle confused. "Mr. Pickering? Could you untangle this for me? And in my courtroom we're pretty informal, so you may stay where you are to talk."

Abe stood. "Thank you, your honor. The fact is, the three of us, me, Zander, and Jayda, all love Emilio and want the best for him. He came to live with me after Zander discovered that Emilio wasn't receiving adequate care from his uncle. This was while Zander was a single man, your honor. Me being retired and having a spare bedroom, I was the better choice to meet Emilio's needs, so I was the one who reported the situation to CYFD and applied to be his foster parent.

"However, Zander has been involved in Emilio's care from the get-go. At first, he would take Emilio after school a couple afternoons each week and run him 'round the basketball court. Sometimes help the boy with his homework. And, church, too. We attended church together.

"When Zander met Jayda, she also became invested in Emilio's care. Then, right after Zander and Jayda got married, they had to move across the country temporarily for Jayda's work. They were gone about four months.

"A month ago, they moved back to Albuquerque and bought the house next door to Emilio's house, meaning their place is sort of kitty-corner 'cross from mine. Soon as they get settled in their new house, Emilio will be allowed to spend the night once a week with them for starts—that is, if he keeps his grades up and maintains a good attitude at home."

"I see. Sounds like Emilio has the best of both worlds. Ms. Cruz? May I ask what type of work you do that required you move away for four months? And is this likely to repeat itself?"

I stood. "Your honor, I worked as a contractor on assignment to the NSA at Fort Meade, outside the DC Beltway. No, I will not take such an assignment should it be offered to me."

The judge studied me speculatively but with a twinkle in his eyes. "NSA, huh? I know better than to chase that rabbit, Ms. Cruz."

"Good decision, your honor," I said, smiling back.

"And you are gainfully employed at present?"

"Yes, your honor. Another government contract. One that does not require that I travel or relocate."

"Mr. Cruz, I see that you do not hold a job at present."

Zander stood up beside me. I sat down. "No, your honor, but that is an intentional choice in the short-term. If you grant me *Guardian ad Litem* status, I will invest my time in rehabbing Emilio's house and the one we bought next door before I look for other employment."

"Got it. Mr. and Ms. Cruz, do you have anything further you'd like to add?"

Zander said, "Yes, your honor. Jayda and I have signed up to take foster parenting classes, and the house we have bought has three bedrooms, one that will belong to Emilio whenever he stays with us."

He took a deep breath. "And that is because we will, right after the New Year, be applying to adopt Emilio. This move comes in conjunction with Abe and Emilio's input and wishes. We consider Abe to be a grandparent figure in our little family, which is why we purchased a house near him. Since we already consider Emilio our son, adoption will only formalize what we feel."

The judge noticed Emilio glowing under Zander's words. "You in favor of Mr. and Ms. Cruz adopting you, young man?"

"Yes, sir!" Emilio's reply, considerable louder than it needed to be, sent a titter of laughter through the court.

The judge, smiling amiably, asked, "And Mr. and Ms. Cruz, you are financially able to take on a child?"

"Yes, your honor. Our employment records, financial statements, and credit reports are included in the packet we submitted with our *Guardian ad Litem* application, along with the plan for rehabbing Emilio's house so it can be rented out."

The judge paged through the packet, pulled out the sheets Zander referred to, skimmed over them, and grunted. "Nice. Glad to see the detail in your plan. Fixing up that house looks like a big job."

He eyeballed the CYFD representative. "Ms. Tafoya, would you care to make a statement for the court?"

The woman stood. "Your honor, CYFD has no objection to the appointment of Zander Cruz as Emilio Martinez's *Guardian ad Litem*."

"Thank you, ma'am. So ruled. My office will send you copies of the court filing and details for how and how often you are to report on Emilio's finances to this court. Have a good day. Next case, please."

We gathered outside in the hallway for a group hug. "Guess you get to help me clean up that pigsty, Emilio," Zander said, grinning, "soon as our garage is all finished."

"Yes, sir! An' can we get the stink outta that place while we're at it? Man, it's awful."

He wrinkled up his nose in a credible rendition of the same reaction Zander and I had during our first look at the mess Mateo had left.

We left the courthouse laughing, and I think I smiled all the way home. We had leapt the first hurdle to making Emilio ours.

⌘

THE CONCRETE TRUCK ARRIVED as promised on Wednesday to pour the basement floor, then the garage footings and floor, and the driveway. It must have been something of a big deal, I guess, because it drew Mrs. Calderón and the Tuckers from their houses.

"Welcome to the neighborhood, Jayda," Belicia Calderón purred on my front porch. "I knew you and Reverend Cruz had gotten married and then moved away. I was surprised to see you back so soon."

I stared at the plate of chocolate chip oatmeal cookies in her hands. "Are those for us? How thoughtful!" I was quite familiar with her recipe, having grown up next door to her. After Aunt Lu died, Mrs. Calderón had used these exact cookies (and the same plate, if I wasn't mistaken) as her entrée, her means of starting a conversation with me, said conversation closely rivaling the Spanish Inquisition.

But that was Gemma, an insecure, troubled young woman. Not Jayda.

All that is behind me, I reminded myself for the tenth time. *Genie is gone. Gemma is gone. Clean slate.*

"Please come in," I added, belatedly. "Would you care for a cup of coffee?"

"Oh, dear, no. Not this late in the day, I'm afraid. I just wanted to welcome you and Reverend Cruz to our little neighborhood. I'm so glad you bought the Flores' house so it didn't sit empty long. That *other house* is a bad enough eyesore as it is . . . although it looks like someone has started cleaning up the yard."

While talking, she shuffled through the doorway, then stared greedily around at the few pieces of furniture we owned. I hadn't yet hung anything on the walls or, for that matter, on the windows.

"Well, you can see that we're in the process of getting settled, but it's home, and we'll take good care of the place."

"Of course you will, dear. Speaking of which—" Were we speaking of which? "I couldn't help but notice that you've torn down the Flores' garage. I'm so curious as to what you are building in its place?"

She had the knack of making a statement a question.

"Would you like me to show you?"

I didn't wait for her to answer. I took the plate of cookies, walked to the kitchen, then opened the side door, feeling her breath on my neck the entire way. We stood on the porch, and I pointed out the footings.

"It's a double-car garage and workshop," I said. "A man needs a place to putter around, you know."

"My, but it is big, isn't it?"

"Yes, but we'll need two cars . . . after the baby is born."

Whatever questions Mrs. Calderón had about the garage sailed straight out of her head. "You're having a *baby?*"

Gemma wanted, in the worst way, to say, "no, we're having a guinea pig," but Jayda restrained her.

"Oh, yes. Baby Cruz arrives in early April. But please don't share that information. We haven't told Zander's family. Saving the surprise for Thanksgiving."

I was startled to see tears form in Mrs. Calderón's eyes.

"I . . . are you all right, Mrs. Calderón?"

"Oh, yes!" she sniffled, "but a baby? We haven't had a baby in the neighborhood for decades. I-I am so happy for you and happy that you have come to live in our cul-de-sac. It has been a little . . . lonely for a while."

I blinked, seeing the empty years of this woman's life, illuminated by our blessing. "I hope you won't think me forward . . . if we invite you over to see our baby after he or she is born?"

Mrs. Calderón swallowed and said, "I would like that . . . very much."

I smiled. Took her arm and steered her toward the front door. "Let's plan on it, shall we?"

"Oh, yes," the woman whispered.

"And thank you again for the cookies. What a thoughtful gesture. I cannot wait to try them."

Oh, I am soooo tempted to eat them all before Zander gets home.

I patted her hand and smiled. "We'll see you soon. Promise."

I watched through our living room window as Mrs. Calderón plodded slowly home, her age and weight showing in every step. At the halfway point, she paused. Turned around. Spotted me in the window. I waved to her. She smiled and waved back.

And as she continued on her way, she held her chin a little higher, I think.

Thank you, Jesus, for the crucifixion of my selfish, self-centered nature.

⌘

THE TUCKERS ARRIVED THAT afternoon as the concrete finishers were packing up. The couple studied the outline of the garage from the sidewalk, gesturing as they talked.

I went out to join them. Offered them my hand. "Hi, I'm Jayda Cruz. My husband Zander and I have recently moved in. I'm so glad to meet you."

"Bill and Viola Tucker," the man said. "We live right over there, across the cul-de-sac. Came over to admire your new driveway."

"Thank you! The garage goes up next week, after the concrete cures."

"Looks like it will be a big one," Viola said.

"Oh, yes. A double plus a roomy workshop in the rear."

"Wouldn't mind one of those myself," Bill said.

"Come by when it's done. I'll have Zander show it to you."

I returned to the house, gratified that I'd "met" the other residents of the cul-de-sac. Glad that they had met Jayda, too, although returning to Albuquerque as her was turning out to be harder than I thought it would.

I wondered . . . did they ever think of Gemma?

sigh

Sometimes leaving Gemma behind was hard.

⌘⌘⌘⌘

CHAPTER 14

IT WAS THE FIRST young adult meeting in our own home. The gang walked through the house and our oversized yard, looking, oohing, aahing, and pointing.

"I see a volleyball net here next summer!" Diego enthused.

Maybe, I thought. *But probably not.*

DCC's incoming associate pastor would arrive in a few weeks. We wouldn't be hosting the young adult group any longer, and they wouldn't be *our* "peeps," our crew. I didn't much like what was coming, but Baby Cruz would change life for us, too.

We settled in the living room with snacks, and Zander placed his chair in the mouth of the bedroom hallway, straddled it, and took up where we'd left off last week.

"How many of you searched your Bibles after our study last week?"

Nearly every hand went up. Sandra's hand remained up.

"Yes, Sandra?"

"I want to say, Pastor Zander, that some of what you said resonated in me. After I got over the initial shock, I mean."

"Right?" Josh exclaimed. "Todd and I have been using some of those study tool apps you talked about to look up words and study them out like we did with confusion. And, boy—"

"I wasn't finished, Josh," Sandra said quietly.

Zander sent Josh a mild reproving glance, and Josh sighed. "Sandra, I apologize. Please continue."

"Thanks. What I was going to say is that I have more questions. I'm hoping we'll get to them tonight."

Zander nodded. "Let's plan on it. I'd like to refresh the topics we covered last week, then move on. I'm hoping, in fact, that I'll address some of your questions as we go along. Everyone have their Bibles and notebooks? Yes? Okay.

"So, last week my main points were that first God created all humans in his image and likeness, and he placed us over his creation to govern and steward it. The next point was that God chose a people from out of humanity to call his own, his treasured possession, his chosen people. The question is *why*. Why did the Lord divide humanity into two populations, what he called Jew or 'my people,' and Gentile, 'not my people'?

"Anyone want to take a stab at the reasons the Lord needed 'a chosen people'? Here's a hint: I can think of at least four reasons."

Cali spoke up. "To give the world the Ten Commandments?"

"Spot on. That's one of the reasons. Anyone else?"

"A way . . . to bring Jesus into the world?" Nance offered.

"Absolutely. That's two. Anyone else?"

When no one offered, Zander said, "Like I mentioned, I believe the Bible gives us four reasons to answer the big question of *why* God desired a chosen people. The first reason is that the Lord wanted the world to know about him—to know who he really was.

"So. Reason one, God chose a people to receive that information about himself—his name, his unfailing character, his eternal power, his majesty, goodness, faithfulness, mercy, and love. When the Lord brought the Hebrew people out of Egypt, he demonstrated those characteristics not only to his people, but also to the entire watching world. He demonstrated his power by bringing the seven plagues on the Egyptians and by parting the Red Sea; he demonstrated his goodness and mercy by providing manna in the wilderness, clothes that didn't wear out, and water from a rock, to name a few ways he showed himself to them.

"Reason two, he desired his people to stand before the world as a holy nation, a living, breathing example of what a relationship between humanity and the Creator looked like. Thus, the Lord gave his people his righteous decrees, the commandments and the Law. In other words, *God defined sin* so that his people—and through his people, the world—would know what was right and what was wrong. Psalm 147:19-20 says it this way:

> *"He has revealed his word to Jacob,*
> *his laws and decrees to Israel.*
> *He has not done this for any other nation;*
> *they do not know his laws.*
> *Praise the Lord.*

"We have a responsibility to keep God's standards in front of the world. How will unbelievers know what sin is if we shut up, if we stop telling them, if we remove the Ten Commandments from every public arena?"

Josh whispered. "Wow. I never thought about it that way."

"That's right, Josh. We have a duty to declare God's righteous decrees throughout the world, to proclaim Jesus as the Savior God sent to take away our sins, and to preach repentance as the heart's condition for receiving Christ. Jesus himself preached repentance in Matthew 4:17.

> *"From that time on Jesus began to preach,*
> *'Repent, for the kingdom of heaven has come near.'*

"See, God's chosen people were supposed to recognize and enter into his holiness through the Law. Funny thing, though? None of them had the ability to live fully or perfectly by the Lord's decrees. The problem wasn't with God's commandments, however. Nothing is wrong with the Law—the problem was and is in *us*.

"Which brings us to reason three. The Jews' inability to live righteous lives according to the law served to point out how badly they (and we) needed redemption, that is, payment for their sins. So, the Lord gave his people ordinances concerning sacrifices, particularly blood sacrifice to cover their sins. However, the blood sacrifices had to be repeated over and over because the blood of animals could not remove sin. Rather, those rituals demonstrated the need for a *better* sacrifice.

"Enter Jesus, the Savior humanity desperately needed. The blood sacrifices of the Law pointed toward the fourth and most important reason why God chose a people for himself: to prepare the way for the Messiah. The Jewish nation gave birth to the Messiah, the Savior of the world. Jesus became the blood sacrifice that, once and for all, satisfied every demand of the Law and cleansed those who came to him of *every* sin, past, present, and future. No further sacrifice was needed. And, of course, God had made certain that everything the Jews and any seeking Gentile needed in order to recognize the coming Messiah could be found in both the Law and the Prophets.

"According to 1 John 2:1-2, Jesus not only died for the sins of the Jewish nation, he also atoned for the sins of the whole world.

> *"But if anybody does sin,*
> *we have an advocate with the Father—*
> *Jesus Christ, the Righteous One.*
> *He is the atoning sacrifice for our sins,*
> *and not only for ours but also*
> *for the sins of the whole world*

"Furthermore, when Jesus died for the sins of the world—when, according to John 3:15-16, he offered salvation to *whoever believes in him*—he broke the barrier between Jew and Gentile. God still ordains only two divisions in humanity, 'my people,' and 'not my people,' but through faith in Jesus, anyone can be accepted into God's kingdom and become part of his people, his family.'

"All right. That's where we are in our study on 'division.' We have one human race comprised of two and only two people groups."

He lifted his chin toward Sandra. "Is this a good place for you to ask your questions, Sandra?"

"It's perfect, Pastor Zander. See, I'm wondering how we reconcile not teaching on racial inequality and the Lord's admonitions to us to defend or relieve the oppressed, as found in Isaiah 1:17."

"That's a great question. Let me ask the group, if any of you witnessed an act of oppression, what would you do? Would you keep quiet? Would you stand by passively, taking video of the act?"

"*No!*" Nance, Izzie, and Todd said together. The other young adults echoed them or shook their heads.

Sandra's hand shot up. "Pastor Zander, acts of oppression can be covert. Even unconscious."

Zander weighed his response. "I think you've actually made two distinct statements. Are both true? What does Scripture say?"

Nance's hand went up. "The Bible talks about secret or covert sin. In 1 Corinthians 4:5 Paul says the Lord *will bring to light what is hidden in darkness and will expose the motives of the heart.*"

"Good example. Anyone else want to comment on secret or hidden sin?"

When no one answered, he asked, "How about 2 Corinthians, 4:1-2?"

> *Therefore seeing we have this ministry, . . . we faint not;*
> *But have renounced the hidden things of dishonesty,*
> *not walking in craftiness, nor handling the word of God deceitfully;*
> *but by manifestation of the truth commending ourselves*
> *to every man's conscience in the sight of God.*

Sandra nodded. "Doesn't that prove my point? We are supposed to renounce hidden sin, covert sin."

"I agree—we are supposed to renounce our sins, hidden or not. However, in this passage, is Paul referring to conscious or unconscious sin? Is dishonesty unconscious? Is craftiness unconscious? Can these things be 'unconscious' if we've taken the time and effort *to hide* them?"

Sandra frowned. "Huh."

"What I'm getting at, Sandra, is that in order for covert sin to *be* sin, we have to recognize that it is sin when we commit it—otherwise, why would we bother to hide it? Unconscious sin, on the other hand, we don't hide, because we don't even recognize it as sin at the time. Yes, the Holy Spirit can convince us that a behavior is wrong after the fact, but until he does, we are unaware of our transgression."

"That's what I'm saying! Critical Race Theory teaches us that racism is often unconscious, as is white privilege."

"But how do unconscious bias and 'privilege' differ from other unconscious acts of unloving behavior? Of the greatest importance, how does the Bible teach us to deal with unloving behavior?"

"By teaching on bias, privilege, and racism, Pastor Zander."

"Hmm. That may be how *the world* wants us to go about dealing with these things, but what is *the Bible's* method of dealing with them?"

No one answered him.

"All right. We need to revisit a passage we read last time, Colossians 3:12-14. Everyone turn there, please. We're going to reread the several admonitions in this passage on how God's chosen people are to treat each another."

He read the passage aloud.

> **Therefore, as God's chosen people,**
> *holy and dearly loved,*
> *clothe yourselves with compassion,*
> *kindness, humility, gentleness and patience.*
> *Bear with each other and forgive one another*
> *if any of you has a grievance against someone.*
> *Forgive as the Lord forgave you.*
> *And over all these virtues put on love,*
> *which binds them all together in perfect unity."*

"Our instructions are clearly lined out. We are to clothe ourselves, that is, put on and wear, the following *behaviors*: compassion, kindness, humility, gentleness, and patience. These are loving behaviors. Moreover, they are the Lord's behaviors. This is how he treats us. Let's go on.

> *"Bear with each other and forgive one another*
> *if any of you has a grievance against someone.*

"Sandra, according to this passage, when do we forgive one another?"

"Um, *if any of you has a grievance against someone* . . . oh. I see what you're doing."

"What am I doing?"

She huffed. "You're trying to undermine the idea of unconscious bias or privilege!"

"No, I believe I'm showing, through Scripture, that 'a grievance' or a sin of offense against another individual has to be an actual behavior—not a unconscious thought or intention, but something visible that can be called out."

"You're saying thoughts and intentions can't be sin?"

"Not at all—the Lord is well able to chastise us for our thoughts and intentions. What I *am* saying is that until a thought or intention bears visible fruit, an observable and definable behavior, we *Christians* cannot, biblically, accuse someone of sin—but that is exactly what Critical Race Theory does.

"The first problem with CRT is that it sorts people by color—divisions God did not ordain. The second problem is that CRT accuses individuals of 'thought crimes.' It furthermore finds whole 'people groups' guilty—not of demonstrable crimes, and not of personal guilt—but culpable based on the actions of those who are dead, and on the erroneous supposition that those living today are responsible for our ancestors' behaviors and guilty of benefitting from the results of their crimes.

"The Bible has *big* problems with this methodology! Deuteronomy 24:16 tells us we are not to be punished for the sins of our fathers or ancestors.

> *"Fathers shall not be put to death for their sons,*
> *nor shall sons be put to death for their fathers;*
> *everyone shall be put to death for his own sin.*

"CRT accuses *all* ancestors of a single people group—'white people'—of sin. But not all white people engaged in slavery, segregation, or Jim Crow, Sandra. In fact, many white people *fought and died* fighting against those wicked things. So, how can Jayda, for example, be held guilty for the actions of a Ku Klux Klan member fifty years ago, someone she never knew, someone unrelated to her?"

Sandra, her dusky cheeks flushed a deep red and with tears hanging on her lashes, cried, "But we have suffered and are suffering today! Black Americans deserve compensation, reparations! *Someone has to pay!*"

Into the deafening silence, Zander said quietly, "Someone did pay, Sandra. His name is Jesus."

Whoa. The power of those few soft words stole my breath away.

A stunned quiet hung on in the group until Diego spoke softly, "Are black Americans the only ones who have suffered injustices? I think that everyone experiences trouble and challenges to one degree or another. I mean, life can be hard, *truly* hard, and adversity comes to each of us in one form or another—but the degree to which each of us suffers is neither fair nor equitable."

He hesitated, then added, "I also think we can always find someone with harder circumstances than our own. Some people are born black, but others are born in terrible third-world nations where they have practically nothing, not even clean water. Some suffer childhood tragedy or sickness or disease. And . . . the fact that some people suffer more than others is not generally another person or group's fault."

He lifted his left arm. "Like how some kids are born with defects."

I had not noticed before . . . how the hand at the end of Diego's arm was shriveled. Useless. Usually kept tucked into his pocket.

He added, "I had to decide a long time ago how I would live in a world where only a few kids were born deformed while most weren't. Sure, it didn't seem fair that, of all the kids in the world, *I* got stuck with a wimpy hand, but I'm grateful to the Lord that my parents taught me to ignore the bullies who made fun of me. My folks taught me not to feel sorry for myself but to instead seek the Lord's plan for my life and focus on that."

Nance said, "You are an awesome example, Diego."

He grinned. "Thanks, Nance."

She offered him a tremulous smile in return. "Then there are the kids with supposedly perfect lives—affluent, healthy, 'privileged.' The popular ones in school."

She took a deep breath. "No one knows that behind the scenes, Dad is a working alcoholic. Oh, he has a good job and makes a decent living, but every night after work, he gets drunk. And when he drinks? He verbally abuses his wife and kids and sometimes . . . physically abuses them."

Zander's face fell into creases of concern. "Is that . . . is that your family, Nance?"

Her laugh was without humor. "Nothing better than being a fifteen-year-old with only a learner's permit and having to drive your mom to the ER. More than once."

Izzie squeezed Nance's hand. "Oh, Nance! Why didn't you tell me?"

She shrugged. "Like Diego said, I had to choose how to deal with it and get on with God's plan for me. My dad crashed his car while drunk three years ago and died. Sad to say, it was . . . a relief."

Sandra blinked at Nance and swiped at her tears. "I still think black Americans need compensation—for slavery, for Jim Crow, for ongoing oppression. We need to hold people accountable for these crimes!"

Zander nodded. "Yes, the Bible teaches that people should be held accountable, but the Bible also teaches that people are accountable only for their own actions, not the actions of others. Would anyone else in the group care to comment?"

Tian, our Chinese university student, timidly lifted her hand.

"Go ahead, Tian."

Tian trembled as she spoke. "I want to know . . . who will pay me back for man in my country who kill my mother. Sandra, you pay me back?"

Sandra was astounded. "What?"

"This man, this black American businessman, he kill my mother. You pay me back, please. Also, same black man kill my mother . . . he rape me. He never arrested, but *you* black, Sandra—*you* pay me back! You pay me back right now!"

Our study had taken a sudden, sharp left turn.

"Holy moly!" Josh breathed.

I was certainly as flummoxed as he was . . . and Tian wasn't finished.

"You not oppressed like you think, Sandra. I tell you oppressed! Oppressed when Chinese government kill my pastor, burn our church. Oppressed when my father disown because I love Jesus. Oppressed when he throw me and all things mine in street . . ."

Tian broke down, grief clogging her throat. Izzie and Nance moved to comfort her, but she gently shrugged them off. "Thank you. You very love me, and I thank you. But I be all right. Jesus make me all right."

She pointed at Sandra. "Only *Jesus* make me be all right. He make you be all right, too."

Sandra looked away. Studied the carpet. No one else spoke.

Finally, Zander said, "Sandra, how will you answer Tian? Will you let Jesus make you 'be all right'? Or will you keep trying to extract from others what they cannot give you?"

"I-I guess I need to think about that."

"Of course, but please know that we love and accept you, Sandra. You are part of this group. You belong. Like I said before, there is no 'us' without you."

"Thank you for that. I believe you."

Zander exhaled. "Well. This has been an interesting, eye-opening study—and these are the conversations we must not shy away from if we are to grow up in the Lord, if we are to share Jesus with everyone."

He turned in his Bible and looked down. "I'd like to close with Jesus' statement in Luke 4:18-19.

> *"The Spirit of the Lord is on me, because*
> *he has anointed me to proclaim good news to the poor.*
> *He has sent me to proclaim freedom for the prisoners*
> *and recovery of sight for the blind,*
> *to set the oppressed free, to proclaim the year*
> *of the Lord's favor.*

"Jesus came to set the oppressed free. I think this passage underscores what we've been talking about . . . and what Tian meant when she said, 'Only Jesus make me be all right.'"

Tian ducked her head.

Zander smiled at her. "Only Jesus make me be all right, too."

⌘⌘⌘⌘

CHAPTER 15

AS THE WEEK FOLLOWING drew to an end, so did construction of our new garage. The crew installed a heavy-duty garage door and opener with a keypad attached to the exterior garage wall beside the door. Zander purchased a sturdy wrought-iron security door at Lowe's and installed it over the garage's side door and a similar set of bars over the garage's two windows.

Well, that's life in Albuquerque.

Then he contacted a fence company and asked them out for an estimate. When the woman arrived, tape measure in hand, he first showed her the breezeway between the garage and the house. I tagged along for fun.

"We'd like a wrought iron fence built across here with a security gate built into it."

We would? I shrugged. Seemed like a good idea.

The woman removed a handheld device from her purse—a laser distance measurer. She switched it on and took the distance from the corner of the house to the garage wall opposite it. "Seven feet, six inches."

"That was my measurement, too," Zander answered.

She jotted down the numbers and job description. "How high?"

"Eight feet will do, when topped with finials."

"Eight feet. Including finials. Got it. Would you like a design on the gate?"

A notebook filled with photos of custom fence designs appeared in our hands. We paged through it once. Started over, going more slowly.

"I like that," I said, pointing to a gate with the leaves of a tree twined through it.

"I do, too. This one, please."

"Got it. Anything else?"

"Yes."

He walked her to the other side of the garage. "We own both of these lots. We'd like to enclose them as one space."

I nodded. Made sense. Keep Baby Cruz in the yard when he or she was old enough to play outside.

"Same fencing with finials?"

Zander slid a look my way as he replied, "It will cost a small fortune, right?"

The woman nodded without looking up. "Yes."

Apparently small fortunes were her bread and butter.

The woman used her device to measure fifteen feet back from the sidewalk as an easement, then to measure from the side of the garage farthest from the house to the wall abutting Mrs. Calderón's lot. She also measured across the back and sides of the adjoining lots where a line of fencing would top the existing side and back cinderblock walls.

Small fortune? Uh, *yeah.*

"I forgot we'd decided to fence the lots together, but I like what we've chosen," I said after she left. "What's next?"

"Gotta get the stairs to the garage basement finished."

"Secret stairs to the secret basement under the super-secret workbench door?"

"That'd be the one," Zander laughed. "I've got more projects on my list than I can shake a stick at, but this one has to come first."

We appreciate you prioritizing our needs, Zander Cruz.

"Only the best for our Nano!" he chuckled. Then he sighed, reached out, enfolded me in his arms, and kissed me. "I'll see you later."

"Promise?"

"Promise."

⌘

I BUSIED MYSELF THE next two days installing mini and pleated blinds throughout the house. Albuquerque summers aren't as intense as, say, Phoenix, but part of the trick of staying cool throughout those hot months was keeping the sun out in the first place. Blinds and curtains often stayed tightly closed to direct sunlight for weeks on end.

I was mounting brackets to the inside casement of the living room window when a van pulled up to our curb. The van's windows were blacked out, the windshield and passenger window tinted.

Jayda Cruz, our printer has arrived.

The nanomites sounded ecstatic.

"What, today? Zander isn't finished . . ."

It is not entirely necessary that the stairway's disguised entrance be finished immediately to install and set up the printer.

I saw Zander walking toward the curb. There he greeted Dr. Bickel's assistants, Rick and Tony, as they got out of the van. I was surprised to see another vehicle pull up to the curb.

I ran to the door. "Dr. Bickel!" But hadn't he been worried about the hackers knowing we were friends with him, about exposing us to possible danger the last time we spoke? I knew he was often "over the top," so I shrugged off his former concerns.

He climbed out from behind the wheel, waved to Zander, then made his way to me. "Gem—I mean Jayda. I thought I'd tag along. It's good to see you."

"You, too. If I'd known you were coming, I would have made lunch for everyone."

He seemed surprised. "You didn't know we were coming?"

I smiled. "Apparently the nanomites made the delivery and installation arrangements with you and forgot to tell us it was today."

He blinked a few times. "My, my. They have progressed, haven't they?"

"They have, and we'll be glad when they have their printer. Maintaining the two nanoclouds is important to all of us. Come on in. I'll fix us something to drink."

While Zander, Rick, and Tony wheeled the various pieces of the printer into the garage, then closed the door behind them before lowering the pieces into the basement to install them, Dr. Bickel and I sat at our dining table, catching up. I hoped the first item on our "catching-up" list would cheer my dear old friend.

I hid a smile over my lemonade. "Dr. Bickel, can you keep a secret?"

"Me? Better than most." He eyed me with speculation. "But you know that."

"Sure I do; but I needed an opening gambit . . . a means of introducing you to our little surprise."

Comprehension washed across his expression. "A baby? You and Zander?"

I let my grin out. "Yes. Early April."

I could see he was elated. Then he sobered. "And you want it kept a secret?"

"Until we tell Zander's family about Baby Cruz over Thanksgiving."

"Well, I'm delighted, Jayda—overjoyed for you both!" He chuckled. "Baby Cruz, eh?"

"Yes; it's the easiest way to refer to our little one until he or she is born."

I also filled him in on our plans to renovate this house and Emilio's house, and how we intended to start proceedings in January to adopt our boy.

As we got to the bottom of our glasses, we shifted back to the AMEMS network breach.

"Any luck tracing those who tried to hack the AMEMS lab?"

"Not 'tried,' Jayda. *Did hack.* I have reason to believe it was the Chinese; however, the attack shared some of the characteristics of India's cyber hackers. I think the India bits are a deliberate ruse designed to confuse DOE's cyber specialists."

"India tries to hack the US?"

"Everyone tries, Jayda. The majority of attacks come from China, Russia, Ukraine, and Pakistan, with India coming in a distant fifth place."

"Do you know what they got?"

"They most certainly got much of my R&D into medicinal nano-technology. As I said before, we'll know the *who* when someone else beats me to the Nobel prize using *my* work on nanomedical haemobots."

"Could the nanomites help you trace the hackers?"

"Oh, I've asked them. They said the trail was too cold to follow and that they were busy working on an R&A project. I asked who the project was for. Do you know what they said back to me?"

I sidestepped. "I'm more curious as to how you and the nanomites communicate."

"Oh, that. By email. They set up their own domain, did you know?"

I laughed. "Seriously? What is it?" Inside I was wondering why I hadn't known that.

"It's 'cybermites.net.' Their address is email@cybermites.net. Anyway, when I asked them who had commissioned their R&A project, they said, and I quote: 'It's classified.'"

He seemed bemused. Maybe a touch insulted.

"Yeah, well, it actually *is* classified. Sorry."

⌘⌘⌘⌘

CHAPTER 16

Z ANDER AND I WERE camped out in what would be Emilio's room once we had finished the master bed and bath. Emilio had taken a keen interest in our remodel, particularly since finishing our little suite meant his room could be painted, carpeted, and furnished next.

He was ecstatic about being allowed to pick out a new bed and dresser along with choosing the decor. Most of all? When his room was finished, that meant he could start spending a night or two each weekend with us.

He had been an eager and willing helper to date on his own house, but I think Zander and I could see he wanted more. Wanted to be part of making our house a home.

His home.

"Whatcha workin' on next, Zander?"

"I should finish the sheet rock in the new bathroom tomorrow. Soon as that's done, I'll start setting tile around the tub and shower."

Emilio shuffled his feet. "You sure know how to do lots of stuff."

"I'd like to teach you, Emilio, if you're interested."

"Yeah, s'pose I am."

Zander smiled. "Ask Abe if you can come over after school tomorrow, and you can help me set the tile. I imagine you'll need to finish your homework first?"

Emilio's expression fell. "It'll be dark b'fore I can come."

"You talk it over with Abe. See if he will allow you to do your homework after dinner. If he says yes, then you will have to follow through and get it done or you won't be allowed to come the next day."

Emilio pressed his lips together in determination. "I'll get it done."

"Good man. You work out the details with Abe—and remember, he's the boss, okay? What he says goes."

"Yes, sir." Emilio scampered across the cul-de-sac.

I smiled at Zander. "You sure know how to do lots of stuff."

He chuckled. "My dad taught me all the handyman things I know; I'd love to pass on my skills to our sons.

"Sons or son and daughter?"

His grin sweetened. "Yeah. Sons or son and daughter. I'm up for it either way."

⌘

WE CRAMMED OURSELVES into a booth for our usual after-church pancake brunch—Izzie, Abe, Emilio, Zander, and I. In the two booths across from us, eleven of our "peeps" (as we fondly thought of them) were laughing and cutting up. I glanced at Zander, and he winked. We knew our rowdy guys and gals would calm down as soon as their food arrived.

Oh, how I loved this! I loved how our lives were settling into safe, predicable lines, how the rhythm was pleasant and the fellowship sweet.

Abe caught our attention. "Our boy got him an open house at his school, the Wednesday evening before Christmas break starts," he said. "Sort of an art show for the class to show off their projects—bring the family, meet the teacher, brag on the children, and all. Emilio tell you about it? Thought you and Zander would want to go. You, too, Miss Izzie, if you are wanting."

"Oh, we wouldn't miss it," I said, grinning at Emilio. "It's all he's been talking about for a week. Can't wait to see his art project!"

He ducked his head, but I could see how pleased he was.

"I would like to go, too, if I'm not working," Izzie added. "If Emilio is your boy, that makes him my nephew, right?"

"That make you my *tía?*" Emilio said *tía* as if tasting it or trying it on for size.

"Yes, I'll be your Aunt Izzie—that is, if you would like me to," Izzie smiled back.

Emilio blushed. "Yeah." He shot his eyes toward Abe. "I mean, yes, *please.*"

Abe clapped Emilio on the shoulder. "That's my boy."

My smile was sentimental, but Zander knew what I was feeling, how whole and complete our lives were becoming.

Could I have been any happier?

⌘⌘⌘⌘

Chapter 17

We needed our own car. The rental car was okay, but it was costing us, and neither of us liked wasting money. Thanks to my Malware employee checks, we were keeping up with day to day expenses instead of tapping our savings. That meant we had the wherewithal in our savings account to buy a vehicle outright. The question became, what kind of car and how big?

The thing was, we drove Abe and Emilio to church every Sunday. We didn't see that changing when Baby Cruz joined us. In addition, the older Abe got, the less we wanted him driving. Yup. We needed a "family" car, one large enough for all of us—Daddy, Mommy, Baby Cruz, Emilio, Abe—and occasionally Izzie, like for the upcoming long holiday weekend.

In less than two weeks, we would head to Las Cruces for Thanksgiving, taking Izzie, Abe, and Emilio with us for the holiday weekend and the Big Announcement. That's why Zander and I were sitting down to figure out what we needed in a family vehicle.

I might not have known what I wanted, but I sure knew what I didn't want. "Not a soccer mom van. Please. Let me put that right out there, up front."

Zander shook his head. "Yeah, but Abe, Emilio, and Izzie in one row? And what about Baby Cruz when he or she arrives?"

"Right. For sure, one back seat won't work—not with that up-armored tank of a car seat Baltar, Logan, and Dredd gave us. And Emilio is growing. He's all arms and legs in perpetual motion. No way do I want to subject Abe to Emilio's chronic twitchiness."

"So, three rows of seats?"

"I think so. But it has to be safe, reliable, and not a soccer mom van."

Excuse us, Jayda Cruz, my nanocloud interrupted. *We have compiled a list of SUVs with three rows of seats.*

They did that thing where fifteen full-color windows popped up before our eyes listing everything from the Cadillac Escalade to the Toyota Highlander and thirteen makes and models between them.

"Interesting," I said, paging through the windows, taking in the safety and consumer ratings, the spaciousness and versatility of the seating, the wheel base, mileage, and perks.

"Let's see . . . backup camera, *check*, and—ooooh! Sixteen-speaker Bose surround sound?"

Since my nanocloud had gotten the jump on Zander's nanocloud with their list of vehicles, that, of course, meant his nanomites felt the need to one-up mine.

Jayda and Zander Cruz, we, too, have studied that list and believe we have chosen the model that will best meet your needs.

"Reeeally?" I drawled.

Yes. Separate climate control zones will be a necessity with a small child, Jayda Cruz.

"And the model you recommend has that?"

Up popped a Chevy Tahoe with all features listed beside it.

"Uh-huh."

My nanocloud broke in. *Jayda Cruz, that model's Blue Book price is more than $50,000. We can do better for the same price or lower.*

Yeah, if "miffed" were a terminal condition, my nanomites had it. I counted down to when Zander's nanomites would fire back.

Gee, two seconds.

Jayda Cruz, the Escalade is easily $15,000-$20,000 higher in price. Furthermore, one must expect to pay for the necessary features if—

"Shut it, Nano, and I mean both of you," Zander growled. "Stop squabbling, for heaven's sake! Sometimes you're worse than toddlers."

Frosty silence enveloped us.

Good.

He looked at me. "No way do I want to drop fifty grand on a car."

"Me, either. Let's look for a nice used one at around $30,000?"

The nanomites, without saying a word, popped up vying windows of local SUV sales—at $30,000 or less.

I sighed. "I feel a headache coming on."

"Wait—how about this one? Three years old, low mileage, and a nice luxury package."

"Huh. Not bad. Definitely rates a look."

⌘

WE WANTED TO HELP Zander's folks with all the Thanksgiving preparations on Wednesday, so we decided to drive down to Las Cruces the Tuesday before Thanksgiving. Abe withdrew Emilio from school two days early, and Izzie arranged to take extra time off from work.

Around eight that morning, Zander left the house to gas up our new-to-us SUV while I finalized the packing. I was thinking of how Roberto and María Cruz would receive the news of my pregnancy—their first grandchild—when I caught sight of myself in the full-length mirror in Zander's and my bedroom.

I turned sideways and studied my profile. I was seventeen weeks pregnant, beginning to show—and beginning to need pants with a stretchy waistband. So much for my comfy jeans! But I had also lost five pounds due to morning sickness. I was so accustomed to my body's leaner look, that the little baby bump gently pushing out from under my long-sleeved t-shirt seemed . . . incongruous. Odd.

"Things will get 'odder' over the next months, I'll wager," I murmured.

I gasped as, low in my belly, something fluttered.

"What? Is that you, Baby Cruz?"

If I had any doubts, the nanomites quashed them.

Jayda Cruz, that sensation was indeed your child stretching its arms and brushing against the inside wall of your uterus. Baby Cruz is 13.5 centimeters in length, normal in all respects, and quite active.

I smiled. "Thanks, Nano." *Cannot wait to meet you, little one.*

When Zander returned from the gas station, I went to find him. He was in the drive, topping off the SUV's window washer fluid.

I watched him for a minute before blurting, "Guess what happened?"

He bent over the engine block to check the oil. "Hmm?"

"I felt the baby move."

"Say what?" Zander stood abruptly and bumped his head against the inside of the hood. "*Ow!*"

"Oh, Zander! Are you okay?"

He rubbed the impact point on his head. "*Ow.* Yikes. Double *ow.* Yeah, I'm fine—except for the lump on my head. You felt the baby move?"

"Yup. Nano says Baby Cruz is a mite less than five-and-a-half inches and is an active swimmer. I felt BC's little hands brushing against my insides."

Zander grinned and grabbed me up in a big hug.

"Careful. My stomach is iffy this morning."

He let me go. "Have you eaten anything?"

"Been waiting for you to get home." I had baked a breakfast casserole and left it in the oven to keep warm. Between the two of us, we would polish it off.

"You shouldn't wait this long to eat, Jayda."

"I downed one of my supplements an hour ago to hold me over. That settled things down for a while." We had stocked up on high-calorie, high-protein meal supplement beverages. I had packed a small box of them to take with us in the car to Las Cruces.

"And did you upchuck this morning?"

"Not so far."

"Good. We don't want you losing any more weight."

"For sure."

We went inside, ate our breakfast, had our joint Bible time, then finished our packing. While I cleaned up the kitchen, Zander loaded our suitcases into the far back of the SUV.

I had grabbed a light jacket and joined him outside when Izzie arrived and parked on the other side of our new driveway. Abe and Emilio walked across the street pulling their suitcases behind them. We were all excited to hit the road.

Emilio caught my eye and smirked. He and Abe shared our secret, but Izzie wouldn't hear the news until her parents did. I was certain that our boy relished being "in the know" when others didn't. I think it bound him to us and helped him feel that he was an integral part of our little (but growing) family—which he was.

We loaded up and headed south down I-25. Izzie and Abe shared the second-row seat while Emilio took up the third row—and I do mean "took up." Although his seatbelt was in place, his growing, ever shifting legs managed to give the impression that he filled the entire row.

We hadn't made it out of Albuquerque before Abe said quietly, "Young man, I expect you to control your feet without bumping them into the back of our seat every few seconds."

Emilio sighed. "Yes, sir."

Zander and I exchanged glances.

"Active, growing boy," I murmured.

He nodded. "I'll take care of it."

An hour later, we pulled into the Walking Sands Rest Area outside of Socorro and got out to stretch our legs and use the facilities. Only a few cars and trucks were in the lot, but that would be a different story come Wednesday, the day before Thanksgiving.

Zander tapped Emilio on the shoulder. "Bet you can't keep up with me."

Competition. That was all the motivation Emilio needed. Zander ran Emilio around the perimeter of the parking lot, up a wooden ramp leading to the restrooms and an observation deck overlooking the Sevilleta National Wildlife Refuge, across the observation deck, and back down. They repeated their route, Zander and Emilio neck and neck, laughing and joking the entire way.

Izzie and Abe grinned. I did, too.

And for some reason, Emilio's legs were less "twitchy" the remainder of our drive.

⌘

WHAT A JOY IT WAS to be treated as family! Roberto and María threw open their front door and rushed out to hug and greet each of us. They had met Abe and Emilio at our wedding and were genuinely pleased to see them.

As for me? I had only met Roberto and María twice—a week prior to Zander's and my wedding and at the wedding itself. Nevertheless, they had enfolded me into their family without hesitation. As they took turns hugging me, they said, "It is so good to have you here!"

I hadn't been the recipient of such unabashed affection since before Aunt Lu died, before she could no longer hug or hold me. How I had missed her love!

And as soon as they drew back from hugging us, María ran her eye over me and clucked with concern.

"Jayda, *chica*, are you well? You have lost some weight, I think."

I smiled. "A little, but I'm okay. Thank you for asking."

A look passed between us, and María's lips came together. Then I saw a gleam of moisture in her eyes, and she latched on to my arm to walk me up the steps.

Somehow . . . *she knew.*

She knew but would say nothing to spoil our announcement—and what an announcement it was! At dinner that evening, Zander asked if he might be allowed to say the blessing over our food.

Roberto shrugged. "Sure, Son."

Zander slid his gaze toward me, then closed his eyes and prayed. "Lord God, thank you for gathering us together before and during this Thanksgiving season. We are grateful for this food and ask you to bless it. I am also grateful for family, Lord, for friends who are as dear as family, and for the expansion of our family, as Jayda and I prepare to welcome Baby Cruz in April. In Jesus' name we pray. Amen."

María sobbed softly. Izzie seemed shell-shocked and asked, "What did you say?" Roberto stared at Zander, and Zander grinned.

Roberto finally managed, "You're having a baby, Son? I'm going to be a grandfather?"

"Yes, *Abuelo*."

Then Izzie squealed like a cat whose tail had been slammed in a door. Emilio laughed until he fell out of his chair and earned himself a glare from Abe, and Roberto pounded Zander on the back about five times.

The best part? María knelt by my chair and took me in her arms.

"Jayda, *mija*, you have made me so happy. You are such a blessing to our family!"

Dinner cooled and congealed on the table while we rehearsed all the details—how far along I was, when I was due, and how I was feeling. Was that why I'd lost weight? Was this why we moved back to New Mexico?

We asked Izzie not to tell anyone back in Albuquerque about the baby until we'd had a chance to announce our pregnancy to our friends. We told all of them about the house we'd bought, which set Zander and Roberto discussing the renovations, particularly the bathroom Zander and Emilio were finishing. "Emilio is my right-hand man," Zander told his father. "I'm teaching him the way you taught me. He's a natural, Papa."

Emilio blushed under Zander's praise and Roberto's approving nods.

Finally, while Zander answered even more questions and the discussion landed on what we planned to name Baby Cruz, I couldn't wait any longer. I picked up the casserole and helped myself. "Sorry. I have to eat something right away or my tummy will start acting up."

That set in motion a whole other spectrum of unexpected familial love as Izzie and María piled food on my plate.

"Eat, Jayda—or would you like something different?" María asked. "I can cook whatever you like. Can I fix your favorites while you are here? Please! Tell me what sounds good to you, Jayda. Izzie, we should send food home with them, yes?"

"Absolutely, Mama. Maybe make Jayda some flan while they are here? Flan is bland and soothing. What do you think, Jayda?"

I didn't know *what* to think at this outpouring of love and support— but I loved it.

Later, I also remembered how growing up with only Aunt Lu and Genie meant that our Thanksgiving celebrations were never fancy affairs. No long table set with the best tablecloth, linen napkins, crystal goblets, and the good china. Most often, our holiday dinners had been potlucks with paper plates and plastic tablecloths that we threw away afterward.

Abe had always been part of our Thanksgiving gatherings, of course. He might not have been blood, but he was as close to extended family as we had. The rest who came were those whom Aunt Lucy deemed "orphans," church friends who had no family nearby.

But in Zander's family culture? Holidays were vastly different. And when Roberto and María hosted Thanksgiving? I found out *exactly* how big a deal their holidays were—so special, in fact, that I halfway expected royalty to show up. No wonder Zander and Izzie thought it a good idea to come two days early!

María kept me busy, but I noticed I was doing all the simple, easy stuff, like sitting down to wipe the spotless crystal stemware, sitting down to polish her silverware (yes, real silver), and sitting down to peel potatoes—fifteen pounds of them.

Yikes, we're talking a mountain of mashed potatoes!

Yes, I sensed a theme: Because Jayda is expecting, whatever Jayda does, she will do it sitting down. (So, that's where Zander got it!) And whenever I caught María looking at me or if she passed by and touched my arm or shoulder, it was with such love and approval that the glow of reciprocal love she kindled within me swelled and expanded.

Yes, I was loved in this family. I was accepted in this family. I was doted upon in this family. And I ate it up with a spoon.

The highlight of our visit, of course, was Thanksgiving Day. We served a spectacular dinner to the seven of us plus another thirteen aunts, uncles, and cousins—all who received me, Emilio, and Abe as their own.

Then came the kicker.

Roberto stood and tapped his glass, calling for attention. "We have thanked God for his beneficence over this past year—good health, good jobs, and the blessings of freedom. We have thanked God for all of you, too, our *familia*. But we have more to thank God for, eh?"

Everyone seemed to sense an important announcement was coming. María's sisters and their husbands looked eager. Zander and Izzie's cousins, younger than they were, wiggled with excitement.

Roberto said softly, "We thank God for the child that will be born to Zander and Jayda in the spring."

The exuberant applause and many congratulations made my eyes sting, but Roberto wasn't finished speaking. "Yes, we expect to welcome a grandchild in the spring, but we also hope to welcome another grandchild. For you see, after the first of the year, Zander and Jayda will begin adoption proceedings to make Emilio their son."

Another round of applause broke out, and everyone's eyes turned to Emilio, who ducked his head. He was no more accustomed to being in a large, loving family than I was. Possibly less.

Roberto wasn't finished. "The adoption process may not begin for a few months and we don't know when it will be completed, but I say, why wait? I say, Emilio, we welcome you today, and we welcome your foster father, Abe. You are both welcome here, in our home and in our family."

Emilio buried his face in my blouse. All Abe could do was nod and whisper, "Thank you. Thank you, kindly."

I was dripping tears when Roberto shifted his attention to me.

"See here, Jayda. None of this would have been possible without you. Several years ago, *mija*, we thought we had lost our son. Then Jesus came into his life and rescued him—from the gangs, from the drugs, from the violence.

"Our Lord Jesus has given our son a wife to be proud of, a beautiful woman of virtue and much worth, a daughter we embrace. Jayda, we thank God for *you*."

I was overcome, my cup overflowing.

As far as Thanksgivings go, this one was stellar.

Off the charts.

⌘

OUR LOVELY THANKSGIVING weekend with Roberto and María Cruz ended on Sunday. We attended church with them in the morning, started back to Albuquerque after lunch, and arrived before dinner.

Zander ruffled Emilio's hair as we unpacked the car together. "Back to school for you tomorrow, and back to work for me, right, bud?"

"But I get to come work with you after school?"

"Yup. As long as Abe says you are holding up your end of the bargain."

Emilio nodded, gave us both hugs, grabbed his bag, and ran across the cul-de-sac to join Abe.

⌘⌘⌘⌘

CHAPTER 18

THE WEEK AFTER Thanksgiving passed in a flurry of hard work on both Emilio's house and our own. In Emilio's house, Zander fixed the leak under the bathroom sink, then bought and installed a new vanity. He oversaw the contractors who repaired the ceiling and floor in what had been Emilio's bedroom while getting the bids for carpet and tile for both houses. He hired a painting company to paint throughout.

While the painting crew was busy in Emilio's house next door, we were hard at work in our house, prepping the kitchen and bedrooms to paint and carpet—but not the nursery. I was saving that special project for later. We got the patchwork done and taped off the baseboards, windows, and door jams. Then we applied a primer coat to the walls of Emilio's and our bedrooms.

We weren't finished by a long shot, but had made tremendous strides. We hoped to complete the painting next week.

When Sunday rolled around, Zander and I were looking forward to getting back to DCC and our friends there. In particular, with the family announcements done, we were excited to tell everyone about our baby. We had, however, forgotten that the church had installed the new associate pastor the Sunday following Thanksgiving and that the young adults had met with him this past Friday evening.

We and our crew of young adults usually sat together during service, routinely halfway down in the middle section of the sanctuary. Not today. With waves and nods—and a few reluctant shrugs—the young adults passed us by to cluster down front, filling the first three rows. Even Izzie bypassed us and joined them.

"Oh, yeah," Zander said aloud, "Guess I forgot."

"Hmm?" I asked.

"Pastor Easterly is here now; looks like the young adults are sitting with him. We should introduce ourselves after service."

"But why everybody down there?" Emilio groused. "Izzie's s'posed to be my *tía* and sit with us."

"Of course she's your *tía*; that hasn't changed." Zander explained. "But the new associate pastor is here, and she's part of the young adult group, too. They need to get to know him and make him feel welcome. Since he's new to Albuquerque, too, I imagine they will all go to lunch together like we used to when I was the young adult leader. No worries— we'll still go have pancakes after service."

"Not the same 'thout Izzie," Emilio mumbled.

I agreed with Emilio. It would *not* be the same, but I knew Zander was right. Regardless, I felt an unreasonable stab of jealousy. The young adults were *our* friends!

When service ended, Zander grabbed my hand. "Come on. Let's go greet Pastor Easterly."

We left Emilio with Abe and wended our way through the crowd toward the front of the church. Zander waved to Pastor McFee, who returned a nod and a tight smile back. Several of the young adults saw us coming and opened a path for us. The rest were collected around the new pastor, and the guys in the group were too tall for me to get a look at the guy.

"Hey, Pastor Zander! Hey, Jayda!" Josh called to us. "Come to meet Pastor Aiden?"

"Yup. We sure have."

"He's great—you'll love him."

The clutch of young adults obscuring the new pastor parted. He stepped toward us—and my heart sort of leapt in my chest.

Don't fault me for what was basically a visceral reaction: The guy was, *by far*, the most beautiful man I'd ever seen in the flesh. He was tall, lean, and wiry, and his blond-streaked hair hung down to his collar in perfect, artless waves. I thought he might be in his early thirties, a little older than Zander or me. His bright blue eyes twinkled, their corners creased in a pleasing way, and his smile was brilliant. Open. Sincere. Engaging.

"Er, *wow*," I exclaimed to myself.

Nearby were several new-to-DCC young adults and one older man perhaps in his late thirties. His expression was bland. In fact, most everything about him was bland—clothes, hair, manner. I might not have noticed him if he hadn't been standing slightly behind Easterly, part of the knot around him.

Easterly broke away from the clutch of young adults and strode toward us, his hand extended. Grinning. Definitely in his element.

"You have *got* to be Zander. I'm Aiden Easterly."

Zander smiled back and shook his hand. "Welcome to Albuquerque and DCC, Pastor Aiden."

I spotted Izzie directly behind Easterly. Her eyes shone, and her face was flushed. No, it was *radiant*. She was practically glued to the tail of Easterly's suitcoat.

Oh, dear, I chuckled inwardly. *That girl looks well and truly smitten. Good thing Pastor Easterly is single.*

Then I sighed. *Oh, dear. Emilio is going to have a cow.*

I noticed Easterly do that thing where he didn't let go of Zander's hand. When Zander tried to withdraw it, Easterly added his left hand, making a "squeeze sandwich" out of Zander's.

"I want to compliment you on the work you have done with these wonderful young men and women. You have laid a good foundation in them and brought them far on their faith walk."

"Thank you. I—"

"It means we can jump into the stream and make genuine progress in the coming year, contribute to this community—all because of the foundation you laid, Zander."

"I—"

"Say, we're all going to lunch together. Would you and your lovely wife care to join us?"

Zander was finally able to jimmy in a reply. "That's kind of you. However, we have plans with our family, Abe and Emilio."

He glanced at me for my take. At a negligible shake of my head, he added, "Besides, you look like you have your hands full."

"Oh, that's right! Jayda might not want all the excitement this squad generates—not with a little bun in the oven, right? Congratulations to you both."

Josh, Todd, and Diego, our faithful trio, dropped their collective jaws—but they had nothing on us. Zander and I stood there, flummoxed, while around us the young adults crowed, "What?" and "You're having a baby?" and "Wow!" followed by "Why didn't you tell us?"

Of course, then *everyone* knew—and not at all in the manner we'd planned to announce our good news. Aiden Easterly had stolen our thunder!

How in the world did he find out, anyway?

I bit my tongue and tried to smile through the congratulations. Zander kept shooting nervous little looks my way. He wasn't any happier than I was, but maybe he was more concerned about how I felt.

How did I feel?

Only like ripping someone's face off. Guess Zander could tell.

A girl in the group I didn't recognize piped up, "But you only got married like in May, right? How far along are you?"

I flushed as a horrid suspicion of what she was intimating flashed into my head. I temporized by asking, "Hi. I don't think I've met you. I'm Jayda. What's your name?"

"Oh, I'm Sierra."

I was careful with both my answer and my tone. "Nice to meet you, Sierra. You're right; Zander and I married in May, but our baby isn't due until April."

No, Sierra, we did not fool around before we got married.

Sierra heard me loud and clear. "Well, I'm sure I didn't mean to imply anything. After all, I'm new here. I came down from Colorado with Aiden and a few others and have only been coming to DCC since last Sunday. I met Izzie at the Friday night meeting, and she told me all about you guys."

She preened. "Izzie's quite the font of information."

I didn't have to turn around and search through Aiden Easterly's shadow to know that Izzie was cringing. She and I were so close and I knew her so well that I could figure out what had happened without her telling me.

See, Izzie always makes the new girls in the group feel welcome and loved. She had welcomed me when Jayda Locke made her Albuquerque debut. If I'm being honest here, Izzie at times did tend to talk more than necessary. And she had returned from our Thanksgiving weekend bursting with a wonderful secret.

A secret that, as we'd discussed over Thanksgiving weekend, was mine to tell.

Huh. Well, Sierra, I'll bet when Izzie unintentionally blurted our news to you, she then made you promise to keep it to yourself. You gave your word—but you didn't keep your promise. Am I right?

I slid my gaze toward Izzie. She held a quavering hand over her mouth, and her brown eyes glistened, poised to overflow. They begged me to forgive her. She sensed how upset and hurt I was.

A wave of nausea passed over me as I grasped how my anger—justified or not—had the potential to destroy the precious relationship Izzie and I shared.

I spoke sternly to myself. *You cannot give this offense a foothold, Jayda. Forgive Izzie. Immediately.*

I lifted my eyes to her. Nodded. Forced myself to smile. Blew her a little kiss.

A tear trickled down her face and she mouthed, "I'm so sorry!"

"I know," I mouthed back. "I love you."

I licked my lips, took a deep breath, and glanced back at Sierra. I was confounded to note her innocent smile had morphed into . . . a malicious smirk?

Inside, I growled, *Just who do you think you are, you little twit? And where did you come from?*

"Nano, I'd like you to tell me more about this girl, Sierra. Everything pertinent."

On it, Jayda Cruz.

My observations had taken but seconds, and Aiden Easterly was beaming at us. "Perhaps you will consider joining us another time?"

"Sure," Zander answered, his expression carefully neutral.

With another squeeze of Zander's hand, Easterly shifted his attention to the young adults. "Okay, everybody got a ride? Yes? Great. And remember what we talked about Friday evening. Only order the food you actually need. Eating to excess contributes to inequality on the earth, so let's all of us commit to not eating more than our fair share, right?"

When he had received a resounding "right" from the group, he turned and strode toward the doors. The entirety of the young adult group moved after him, Izzie with them, many of the group jockeying for the positions closest to Easterly.

I struggled to quell another bout of nausea.

"What the devil just happened?" Zander muttered.

I opened my mouth to comment, but my uneasy stomach chose right then to lurch and threaten to erupt.

"Nano! Please help me!"

I stumbled up the aisle. When I reached the top, my eyes desperately sought a trash can. *There!*

I made it by mere seconds.

Zander had followed me. He found a box of tissues and helped me to clean up, then took the liner from the can and walked it outside to the dumpsters.

I was still sitting, my head between my legs, when he got back.

⌘

LUNCH WAS EVEN MORE uncomfortable. I wasn't feeling well to begin with, but it was more than that. Abe could sense our disquiet, but he knew we wouldn't talk about what was bothering us in front of Emilio. For Emilio's part, he was hurt and angry that Izzie had chosen to go to lunch with the young adult group instead of with us. He went from sullen to mulish. He scowled at all of us, mumbled when Abe spoke to him, and played with his food.

When Emilio started kicking his seat legs, Abe reached the end of his patience.

"Young man, that's it. Put your fork and knife on your plate and sit back in your chair. You are finished."

"I want pie!"

"I don't care."

Emilio glared at Abe.

"One word, young man, and you'll be grounded all week—no after school *anything* except sitting in your bedroom."

A four-letter curse word erupted from Emilio's mouth. I think he was as astounded as we were when it popped out for all to hear. It was like that ugly thing dropped onto the table and started to twerk while we all stared at it, askance.

As for Abe? I don't think he thought; he reacted.

He thumped Emilio on the top of his head.

It sounded like thumping a ripe melon.

Emilio shouted for the whole restaurant to hear, "Ow! *Ow!* You *crazy*, old man?"

Zander's face hardened. He stood. "You. Come with me." He took hold of Emilio's arm, pulled him up from the chair, and pretty much perp-walked him out the front door.

I stared after them and found myself invoking Zander's earlier question.

"What in the world is going on?"

Abe stared at me. "Been tryin' to tell you, Gemma: Emilio's goin' on twelve now. *He needs Jesus.*"

He reddened at his faux pas—what with *Gemma* being dead and all.

"I—*shoot*. God bless it!" Then he slowly sighed. "Sorry."

I nodded. Everything from church onward had been one strange and tense scene after another followed by apologies. I had barely noticed Abe calling me by a deceased woman's name.

I was more focused on the "He needs Jesus" part.

Abe and I stayed at our table for a while, hoping to give Zander enough time to deal with Emilio before we interrupted. They were sitting in our SUV's second row of seats when Abe and I left the restaurant and went looking for them. Emilio was sobbing his heart out, and Zander had his arm around him.

Looked like progress to me.

"Tell them what you told me," Zander said quietly to Emilio.

"I'm sorry. Real sorry. I-I . . . I'm sorry."

"Thank you. I accept your apology, Emilio," I said.

Abe said basically the same, then nodded to our boy. "I think you and Zander have more to talk about. Why don't you plan on spending a few hours with him this afternoon—if that's all right with you, Zander? Because I need a nap."

Emilio looked to Zander, who nodded.

"Yes, sir," Emilio told Abe. "Thank you, Abe."

Rather than everyone shifting seats, Abe climbed into the passenger seat and I took the driver's seat. Zander handed me his keys. We drove home in peaceful quiet, and I was glad for the absence of conflict. My mind, however, returned to our weird introduction to Aiden Easterly.

"Nano, dig up everything you can find on this Easterly character, too, please."

We are working it, Jayda Cruz.

⌘

WHEN WE ARRIVED HOME, Zander sent Emilio to change his clothes, while he did the same. On his way out the door, he whispered to me, "Please pray," and the two of them wandered off together. I understood then that more than Emilio's behavior was in play: Zander was going to talk to Emilio about Jesus.

I went to our bedroom and knelt against our bed. "Lord, you know I love Emilio—even when he behaves like a brat—but I know that you love that boy much more than I ever could. So, would you please help Zander tell Emilio how much you care? Help Emilio understand that you sent Jesus to save him from himself? Show Emilio how much he needs Jesus! I am calling on you, Lord God."

I stayed there for a while, praying over the two most important people in my life, asking the Holy Spirit to move in Emilio's heart. When I felt that I had emptied myself before the Lord, I got up and busied myself with other things.

It was later in the afternoon when Zander and Emilio returned. Zander didn't say anything. He gave a short shake of his head as if to say, "not yet."

Not yet.

I sighed and studied Emilio. He seemed subdued and distracted, his eyebrows bunched together like they were when he was angry—only I didn't sense anger in him. Instead, his expression radiated something much different. A serious contemplation, perhaps?

It felt as though I were glimpsing the young man Emilio would become . . . a solemn young man pondering his first adult decisions.

Lord, please cause the seeds Zander has sown in Emilio's heart to grow and produce a good harvest.

⌘

AFTER EMILIO HAD APOLOGIZED, and after he spent Monday after school sitting in his bedroom—without further incident—Abe relented and allowed him to come back and help us. We were, at the moment, focused on our house. A sober young man showed up Tuesday afternoon in grubby clothes, ready to work. We'd labored all day on the kitchen and had finished it when he walked in.

"Hey, buddy," Zander greeted him. "Want to learn how to paint? We could work on your room next. It's primed and ready to paint."

His eyes brightened. "Yes, sir."

Zander spent the rest of the afternoon until it was Emilio's dinnertime teaching Emilio to paint by doing each step with him, then having him handle a second roller alongside him. The care and attention Zander paid Emilio warmed my heart. Emilio, for his part, was eager to please Zander, and bent himself to perform each task the way Zander had shown him.

Zander is a born teacher. A godly leader of boys and men.

My phone jingled a text from Abe saying Emilio's dinner was ready.

"Dinnertime, kiddo," I called.

Emilio carefully wrapped his roller in a plastic bag to keep it from drying out, then wiped his hands on a rag. "See you later!"

"Aren't you forgetting something?"

Emilio dashed back, gave us both a hug, then jetted out the door—to the loud protests of someone standing outside.

"Sorry, man!" Emilio yelled and continued on his way.

I opened the door. "Gamble! What are you doing down there?"

Gamble was sitting on the walk below the steps. "What am I doing? I got hit and knocked off the porch by a tornado, that's what I'm doing down here! Lucky I didn't crack my head on the way down."

"Sorry. He's a ball of energy these days—and none of us were expecting anyone to show up here. Come in! What's up?"

Gamble picked himself up. Brushed off the back of his pants. "Popped over to say hey." He looked over Emilio's front yard. "Someone's been cleaning up over there."

"That would be us," Zander said from over my shoulder. "Come on. We'll show you."

Zander led Gamble through the house, rehearsing the state we'd found the place in. "Roof is patched, bedroom ceiling and floor repaired, bathroom vanity replaced. You can see that the contractors have finished the painting. Got a tile setter coming tomorrow to do the kitchen and bathroom. Carpet layer comes Friday."

"So, this house was actually Emilio's all along, not Mateo's? Go figure. And the court made you Emilio's *guardian ad litem* so you could, what? Fix the house then flip it?"

"No. Since Emilio owns the place free and clear, we'll be renting it out. As it stands, Jay and I own two lots in the cul-de-sac, Emilio owns one, and Abe owns one. That's four out of six houses in the cul-de-sac. We aim to improve the neighborhood, so we'll be picky about who we rent to. And after we recoup the expenses from fixing up the house? Whatever is left each year after taxes and maintenance will go into Emilio's college fund."

Gamble walked around, poking his head into closets, checking out the kitchen cupboards and the refrigerator we'd pulled from our house to replace the one hauled away.

He stood in the living room, nodding. "How much?"

I frowned. Pretended I didn't know what he was asking. "How much what?"

"How much to rent the place?"

"What? To you and Janice?"

"Yup."

"Huh." I pursed my lips. Shook my head. "I dunno, Gamble. I mean, we hardly know you guys." I turned to Zander. "I'm skeptical. And I'm not sure we can get Emilio's approval. What do you think?"

Zander studied Gamble. "What's your credit score? Are you gainfully employed? Do you have a criminal record? Can you provide references?"

"Jokers. Very funny."

Zander and I laughed at Gamble's expense, then Zander asked, "When can you move in?"

"Wait a sec." I gave Gamble a hard squint. "You planning on marrying that woman any time soon?"

He blushed and grinned. "Uh . . . um . . . maybe?"

"And you'll let me do the honors, right?" Zander said, smiling. "But no pressure, right?"

Gamble wiped his red face. "Uh, yeah. If she'll have me."

⌘

WITH THE NECESSARY WORK on Emilio's house done and the problem of finding suitable renters solved, Zander turned his full attention on our house. He and Emilio tackled the last bits of our bathroom, and I got started on the project I had looked forward to since we moved back to Albuquerque: preparing Baby Cruz's nursery.

Zander moved all the baby stuff into the center of the room, and I flung old sheets over the pile. Taking my time, I carefully patched, sanded, and washed the nursery walls, then painted them a whisper-soft yellow and the trim a deep beige. I left one wall unpainted and papered it with a bright print that picked up the soft yellow and contrasting beige.

Two days later, after I had finished my work, the carpet layers returned. They shifted Baby Cruz's furniture to the living room and covered the nursery floor in an easy-to-clean, two-tone carpet that complemented the baseboards. Then the carpet layers obligingly moved the furniture back into the nursery, setting the dresser and night stand where I wanted them and leaving the boxed crib and changing table leaned against a wall.

When the carpet layers had departed, I unboxed the crib and had laid the pieces out according to the assembly diagram when the nanomites spoke to me.

Jayda Cruz, we have the background information on Aiden Easterly you requested.

"Great! Let's wait until dinner to go over it. I want Zander to hear your report, too."

⌘

AT OUR REQUEST, THE nanomites had pegged every all-you-can-eat buffet within a five-mile radius of our neighborhood and put us on a schedule that would run through each of them once before we revisited any of them. Some were great. Others, not so much. But while we were working so hard on the houses, eating out was the preferable option.

After we filled our plates and returned to our table, I said, "Zander, the nanomites want to brief us on what they've found out about Aiden Easterly and his pals."

"Shoot, Nano."

Aiden Easterly, age thirty-four. Born and raised in Decatur, Illinois. Parents are retired and live in Jacksonville, Florida. No siblings. He has held four associate pastor positions in the past ten years. His latest position was as associate pastor for Littleton Christian Center. No marriages, no children, no criminal record.

Zander chewed slowly. "Huh. Four positions in ten years. How long was he at the church in Littleton?"

Eleven months, Zander Cruz.

"And the other three churches?"

Thirty months, nineteen months, and sixteen months, respectively, Zander Cruz.

I asked, "So, not long at any one church. And forty-four months of the ten years unemployed? That's a red flag, isn't it? Can you tell us why he left his last church?"

No, Jayda Cruz. We did, however, find a letter of recommendation written by the senior pastor to Pastor McFee.

The letter appeared in front of our eyes.

To Whom It May Concern,

Aiden Easterly served our congregation, Littleton Christian Center, with distinction. We wholeheartedly send him on his way, praying that he is a blessing in his next position. We will never forget him or what he did while here.

Jonathan Griffin, Senior Pastor
Littleton Christian Center

"Wow. 'Succinct' seems overly generous," I said.

"Right? The letter Pastor McFee wrote when I resigned was downright effusive compared to this. And . . ."

"And what?"

"It may be me, reading my own concerns into this letter, but listen to what this Pastor Griffin says about Easterly: 'With distinction'? 'We wholeheartedly send him on his way'? 'We will never forget him or what he did while here'? Is it my imagination, or can all three of those lines be interpreted more than one way?"

"Dunno. I suppose. But, if the church was glad to get rid of him, if he caused problems there, wouldn't their letter of recommendation have said something?"

"Employers have to be super careful what they say these days. Can't write anything that could be construed as libel. It's like walking on eggshells."

"Huh."

Jayda and Zander Cruz, we can also report on Sierra Miller and one Stan Missing.

"Stan Missing? Was he that strange man with Easterly? That's an odd last name," I said, picturing the man's vacuous expression.

Middle initial A, the nanomites added. *Age thirty-six. Safety engineer by trade. No known relations. No criminal record.*

"No relations at all?" I asked, puzzled.

Jayda Cruz, we find no record of Stan Missing prior to 2007.

I was flabbergasted. "Nothing?"

Nothing, Jayda Cruz. We presume this name and identity were created in 2007.

"Sheesh. You might have led with that!"

"So, this guy Stan is a fake?" Zander asked, more of himself than of me. "Does Easterly know this? And if he does, why is he letting him hang around?"

We have more to report, Zander Cruz.

"Okay. Go ahead."

Sierra Miller, age twenty-three. Born and raised in Golden, Colorado. She has a police record: three counts of solicitation, one count of criminal trespass, one count of vandalism. Convicted on criminal trespass and vandalism. Served six months in a county jail.

"Wow." Why wasn't I all that surprised? "Where did she trespass and what did she vandalize, Nano?"

Sierra Miller was a person of interest in the break-in of a historic Catholic church outside Golden, Colorado, in which an old and valuable statue was stolen. She was caught on surveillance video as being in the church the day of the night the church was vandalized and the statue stolen. However, she could not be tied to the theft of the statue, and it was never recovered.

"What statue, Nano?" Zander asked.

A three-quarter size statue of Mary, Zander Cruz.

"Mary, as in the mother of Jesus?"

Yes, Zander Cruz.

"Who in the world would want to steal a statue of Mary?

We shall endeavor to find out, Zander Cruz.

⌘

BY THE END OF THE WEEK, Zander and Emilio had finished our bathroom. They had tiled the floor and the tub and shower surrounds, grouted and sealed all the tile, affixed the oak vanity to the wall, added the countertop, cut the holes for the sinks and fixtures, set the double sinks in place, hooked up the plumbing, mounted the mirror over the vanity, added oak doors to the linen closet, and trimmed out the tile flooring with baseboard in matching oak.

The completed bathroom was drop-dead gorgeous.

Even better, Abe reported that Emilio came home each evening at dinner time, tired but triumphant. He plowed through his dinner—eating like the growth machine he was—and tackled his homework afterward with a will.

Abe grinned. "Takes a shower then sleeps like a rock, he does."

"Well, that boy loves to work," Zander told him. "He's a fast learner, too. The two hours I have with him after school have been especially productive."

Zander's patience with Emilio and Emilio's smiles under Zander's tutelage were beautiful to behold.

Zander taught him the use of tools, emphasizing safety rules. When Emilio learned a task under Zander's exacting specifications, they worked alongside each other until the task was completed. And while they worked, they exchanged dumb jokes. Most days Emilio told new jokes or riddles he'd picked up at school, and the two of them laughed like hyenas.

I was almost sorry when they declared the new bathroom done.

⌘⌘⌘⌘

CHAPTER 19

IT WAS FRIDAY, CLOSE to two weeks later, following lunch. Zander was cleaning up the kitchen, and I was folding a batch of laundry, when we heard a timid knock on our front door. Since the nanomites regularly acted as our early warning system, it was no real surprise for them to announce who was at the door.

It was their supposition that surprised us.

Jayda Cruz. Zander Cruz. Josh is at your front door. He is distressed.

Zander and I looked at each other.

"I'll get it," Zander said.

He opened the door, took in Josh's troubled expression, and said, "Come on in, Josh. You all right?"

"Not so much, Pastor Zander. I'm in a 'situation' and need some advice."

"I'll do my best. Let's sit at the table, shall we?"

"Would you like privacy, Josh?" I asked. "I can take a walk or something."

"I . . . no, it's okay. I haven't done anything wrong." He squirmed in his seat. "Might get embarrassed talking about it, but I also might need a woman's perspective."

"Sounds like a relationship issue," I quipped.

"Not even!" he answered, with an emphatic shake of his head.

No? I was intrigued. I went to the kitchen, poured three glasses of lemonade, and set them on the table before I joined the guys.

"So, what's up?"

"It's two things, I guess. The first concerns this new guy, Aiden Easterly."

Uh-oh. I slid my eyes in Zander's direction.

Zander kept his expression carefully neutral. "To be clear, Josh, I won't interfere with or in any fashion lend credibility to the idea that I'm interfering in Pastor Aiden's ministry at DCC. Can you honor that?"

"I think so, but things are sort of . . . confusing, Pastor Zander."

I smiled. "Seems like I attended a great Bible study on that subject not long ago."

"And that's why I'm here," Josh said. "All that heavy-duty teaching you did before Pastor Aiden came—you know, on confusion and division? It became immediately relevant in my walk with the Lord. I've probably gone over my notes from those studies four or five times—which is why I'm here. I need to get all this-this *confusion* off my chest—outta my *head*. So, if it's all right with you, I'll lay out the facts as I know them. I hope, then, that you guys will be able to offer me some perspective and maybe pray with me—like you said, Pastor Zander.”

“Okay, got it,” Zander said. “Shoot.”

“Well, I said the first thing is Pastor Aiden, but maybe I’ll start with Sierra instead.”

“Oh. Yes, we’ve met her,” I said. *And know her background.*

Josh snorted. “Then you know she’s a force to be reckoned with. Anyway . . . I don’t know how to put this except to say it straight out. Sierra tried to seduce me. I’m not talking about flirting; I’m talking making outright sexual overtures—and not to me alone. She’s been all over Diego and Felix, too. When they told me about her making moves on them—and not just the one time—I gathered all the young adult guys together and warned them. That’s when Eli got quiet, like *real* quiet.”

“Oh, no . . .” I whispered.

“She got to him?” Zander asked.

“Yeah, she did.”

“Have you talked to Pastor Aiden about her?”

“Tried to—but that’s when I ended up confused. He said, and I quote, ‘I have known Sierra and she has been an active part of my ministry for several years. She was quite repressed when we first met, but she’s flourished in her spiritual liberty since then.’ Then, he tacked on a couple of verses: *It is for freedom that Christ has set us free* and *So, if the Son sets you free, you will be free indeed.* Then he asked, ‘Don’t you agree?’”

Josh sighed. “Honestly? I didn’t know how to take his meaning.”

Zander thought for a few moments before answering. “You were confused because he left out the context of both verses? For example, the second half of Galatians 5:1 being, *Stand firm, then, and do not let yourselves be burdened again by a yoke of slavery.* Is that it?”

“Yeah, I couldn’t tell if he was saying he believes Sierra has conquered the temptation to commit sexual sin and is totally unaware of what she’s doing or if he was saying Jesus encourages the ‘freedom’ to engage in sex outside of marriage.”

“Did you ask him to clarify?”

“Sure I did. I said, ‘Are you saying it’s okay for Sierra to come on to the young adult guys?’ But what he said in response was, ‘Don’t sweat the small stuff, Josh. These things have a way of working themselves out.’”

“Which didn’t sit well with you.”

Josh huffed. “Not at all! ‘These things have a way of working themselves out?’ Not without causing damage first, they don’t—like with Eli.”

“How is Eli, do you know?”

"Yes, I do. I met up with him at Flying Star this morning, because I was super concerned about him. Turns out, falling into sin with Sierra really messed with his head. He said he thought God must hate him, and he's decided not to come back to the group."

Josh's eyes filled with tears. "Eli is a brand-new Christian, Pastor Zander. I feel . . . I feel like the devil painted a big old target on him and slammed him with a bullseye."

"How did you leave it with Eli?" I asked, every bit as worried over the young man as Josh was.

"Well, I told him the best thing he could do was to follow the instructions in 1 John 1:9: *If we confess our sins, he is faithful and just and will forgive us our sins and purify us from all unrighteousness.* I urged him to confess his sin and ask for forgiveness—right there in the middle of Flying Star."

"And did he?" Zander asked.

"Yup. He prayed, I prayed, we prayed together, I gave him a hug, and he felt loads better after."

"Good job, Josh," Zander murmured. "You're maturing in Christ and becoming a competent minister of the word."

"Thanks. I mean that, but Eli is afraid to come back to the young adult group. Sierra will be there, so he's afraid he'll trip up—and I don't blame him. *I'm* not comfortable with her there, either. After all, the Bible tells us to flee from sexual immorality."

"It does. At the same time, the YA group is supposed to be a safe environment."

"Well, Eli isn't the only one in the group who will struggle with temptation if Sierra keeps it up. See . . . I think she's making moves on a few of the girls, too."

I was appalled. "Oh, dear Lord Jesus!"

"And Pastor Aiden hasn't done or said anything?"

"Oh, sure. He talks and talks—but every word that comes out of his mouth has two or more possible but quite opposite interpretations. See why I'm confused, Pastor?"

I remembered what Pastor McFee had told Zander about Easterly and Zander, in turn, had told me. *"I took advantage of his two days here to engage him in conversation, to ask his views on a number of doctrines and issues. In every respect, his answers were correct—but, in my estimation, barely this side of the line. My biggest misgivings were over his use of veiled terminology, that perhaps I needed my Dick Tracy secret decoder ring in order to decipher his answers."*

Was Josh describing the same thing? I turned my attention back to the present conversation.

Zander said, "I don't think you are as confused as you think you are, Josh. In fact, it sounds to me like you know exactly what is going on—but you are uncertain what to do about it. Why don't we pray over the situation and dispel any residual confusion. Then we need to ask the Lord for his guidance, for how he wants to deal with this situation."

Zander didn't say it aloud, but I knew he had to be thinking, *A plan that doesn't get me in hot water with the DCC board for interfering in one of their pastor's ministry.*

We prayed, each of us lifting up a different aspect of Josh's concerns. We prayed for any of the members of the young adult group who might be struggling with the temptation Sierra had flaunted in front of them. We prayed for Sierra, too, asking the Holy Spirit to convict her and bring her into right relationship with Jesus. We prayed for Pastor Aiden that he would adhere to Scripture in all things and would address this issue head on. Finally, we asked the Lord to give Josh wisdom going forward.

Then we waited, quiet and attentive, for several minutes. Nothing came to me. I cracked an eye and saw a frown on Zander's brow.

He hasn't heard anything from the Holy Spirit either. Guess we don't do anything until he speaks.

A few seconds later, Josh, eyes blinking, cleared his throat.

Zander spoke. "Do you have something, Josh?"

"Yeah. Well, I think I do. As we finished praying, in my mind's eye, I saw the meeting tonight and saw myself taking Sierra aside and confronting her according to Matthew 18:15.

> *"If another believer sins against you,*
> *go privately and point out the offense.*
> *If the other person listens and confesses it,*
> *you have won that person back."*

I thought Josh's idea was great; Zander, however, did not.

"Since you're a guy, Josh, taking Sierra aside *by yourself,* leaves you open to both temptation and accusation."

"Huh. I hadn't thought of it that way but . . . yeah, I could totally see Sierra making another move on me—not that I'm saying I'm irresistible or anything . . ."

"And if you refused her?"

"Wow. Yeah, I think she's as likely to tell everyone *I* made a move on *her.*" He frowned. "So, you don't think I heard from the Lord after we prayed?"

"Let me ask you something first. What did you do when Sierra tried to seduce you?"

"I . . . well, see, the young adult group met at the church that evening. After the meeting, I went down the hall to the restroom, and when I came out, Sierra was waiting for me. She walked up and stood so close to me, that I backed up—right into the wall. Then she sort of rubbed herself up on me. Started to-to touch me." Josh's face flamed red. "I was so stunned, it took a second to react—but when I did, I pushed her away."

"Did you say anything to her?"

"Oh, *yeah*. What I said was, 'This is wrong, Sierra, and you need to stop it. And don't ever again try this crap on me or anyone else." He glanced my way. "Sorry about the language."

"How did she respond?" Zander asked.

"You know what? She laughed at me. And then I found out this morning she went right after Eli. Same evening."

"So, you've confronted her once, yes?"

"Hey, you're right. I suppose I have. You're talking about taking the next step?"

"I am. The rest of that passage reads like this."

> *"But if you are unsuccessful,*
> *take one or two others with you and go back again,*
> *so that everything you say may be confirmed*
> *by two or three witnesses.*
> *If the person still refuses to listen,*
> *take your case to the church.*

"Or," Zander finished, "in this case, to the young adult group as a whole."

Josh nodded again. "Tonight I need to take one or two guys to confront Sierra privately."

"I recommend you take two guys and three of the young ladies. Again, you don't want to provide any opportunity for Sierra to fabricate an accusation against you or even against all three of you guys. Having female observers with you will protect you against a false accusation . . . such as gang rape."

I choked on my lemonade. "You think she'd do that?"

"Satan will take as much ground as we give him room to take. Never underestimate him."

Josh gaped. "Wow. You're pretty wise, Pastor Zander."

Zander's smile was modest. "We are to be as wise or crafty as serpents but harmless as doves, right? That means we never give him an opportunity to twist a situation and bring our testimonies into doubt."

"I wouldn't have thought of any of these pitfalls—but you're right. Sierra's said other things in the group that concern me, too. I've even heard her lie. I'll do what you suggest, Pastor Zander, enlist three girls to go with me, Todd, and Diego."

I had my own experience with Sierra to draw on: Izzie spilling the beans about Baby Cruz, Sierra promising to keep the news to herself, Sierra telling Aiden Easterly anyway, and Easterly trumpeting our news to the world right in front of our faces. At this point?

I wouldn't touch that woman with a thirty-nine-and-a-half foot pole.

I pondered several questions about her, though, like, how did Aiden Easterly not know what Sierra was doing? And if he knew, why did he let it continue? For that matter, why did she and four or five others—including this Missing fellow—follow Easterly from Denver down to Albuquerque? What was Sierra's relationship with Easterly anyway?

Zander's voice intruded. "How confident are you that this approach is the Lord's plan, Josh?"

Josh nodded slowly. "Pretty confident. It's biblical and it brings the situation out into the light. Of course, I'll continue to cover it with prayer as I gather the witnesses. After all, we don't want to come across like we're attacking Sierra. No, the best case would be if the Lord helps her recognize the gravity of her actions and brings her out of them."

"I agree," Zander said. "Will you allow us to pray over you?"

"Please do!"

Zander and I laid our hands on Josh's shoulders. Zander prayed, "Lord God, please lead Josh by your Holy Spirit and give him the courage of his convictions. We ask you for a good outcome. In Jesus' name, amen."

After Josh left, I tried to pick up where I'd left off with the laundry, but I kept thinking on what Josh hoped to accomplish at the young adult meeting. I glanced at the clock. About five hours until the meeting. And Zander remained at the table, thinking.

"Uh, Zander?"

"Yeah, Babe?"

"I'd pay to be a fly on the wall during the young adult meeting this evening."

His answer floored me. "Why pay?"

⌘

I HAD BETTER CUT TO the chase and recap what happened that evening. It was a piece of cake for the nanomites to cover us and for us to waltz into the fellowship hall unseen, spot Josh, and observe as he put his plan into motion.

I knew he intended to tap Todd and Diego for his wingmen, but I didn't know who the girls would be, but Izzie probably wouldn't be one of them.

Nope.

She seemed so enamored with Aiden Easterly that I found myself praying for her daily, sometimes several times a day. Easterly, on his part, appeared amused by her infatuation, but he also seemed to encourage it.

What was up with that guy, anyway?

Back to Josh.

Invisible to the group, Zander and I stood against a wall, out of the way, taking in the scene before the meeting started. We watched as Josh, Todd, Diego, and three young ladies from the group asked Sierra to come with them. Josh led them out to the hallway and into a classroom adjacent to the fellowship hall. We waited a minute, then followed.

The drama was in full swing when we eased through the open door.

"Sierra, stop laughing. This isn't funny," Josh said.

"Well, I think it's hysterical—you-all staging an 'intervention.' What do you hope to accomplish, anyway?"

"We want you to stop sexually harassing anything with two legs, for starters," Todd said.

Sierra brushed up against Todd. "Don't you like me, Todd?"

He pushed her away. "Don't touch me. What you're doing is *wrong*."

"Oh, dear! So self-righteous! No, I'm not wrong; you are simply jealous because I'm a free spirit and all of you are uptight and puritanical."

"We'll call you out in the meeting, Sierra."

She slowly smiled. "I can't wait to see how that plays out—if you have the stones to actually try it. But let me give you a teensy clue, shall I?"

She stared around and made eye contact with the six of them. "Aiden will stop you cold. He will side with me, and you'll be the ones publicly corrected and humiliated. *Capisce?*"

With that, she walked out, leaving Josh and the others slack-jawed.

"This isn't going to work," Todd said.

One of the girls nodded. "I agree. I . . . I think I want to get out. Leave the group. Sierra is gross, but Easterly is . . . well, super creepy. I don't want to be around either of them."

The other two girls agreed.

Josh chewed his lip. "If that's the case, I sure hope Zander and Jayda will let us meet at their place again."

"We'll bribe them," Diego said. "We'll bring pizza. If that doesn't work? I'll get down on my knees and beg them."

I looked at Zander, took in his crushed expression. "They need us, Zander. All of this nonsense is shaking their faith in Christ."

He slowly nodded. "Yeah . . . but things are gonna get messy before they get better."

⌘⌘⌘⌘

CHAPTER 20

THE UNM SEMESTER ENDED, and many of the young adults who attended UNM left Albuquerque to spend Christmas break with their respective families. Feeling a touch lonely with so many of their friends gone, the young adults who lived in Albuquerque and who had defected from Easterly's oversight begged to come to our house the Friday evening after classes ended.

"Like before," Diego said, his voice soft and vulnerable, "but smaller?"

I knew what he meant. I missed the precious fellowship we'd shared "before" also. Before Easterly arrived and began sowing destruction.

The much smaller group of dear friends that gathered in our living room that evening were wounded. Hurt. Guilt-ridden. Even angry.

When we settled down for Bible study, they looked with hope on Zander.

"I want to teach tonight on division—again."

"Wow," Josh muttered. "Way to hit us where it hurts."

"You misunderstand me, Josh," Zander said gently. "I'm not blaming you for the split in the young adult ranks. When we maintain God's righteous decrees, we are making a distinction—a distinction that illuminates the Lord, his character, his expectations, and his Savior. Notice that I used the word 'illuminates,' which means to 'shine a light' on something. Jesus talks about that light in John 3, verses 19-21.

> *"This is the verdict:*
> *Light has come into the world,*
> *but people loved darkness instead of light*
> *because their deeds were evil.*
> *Everyone who does evil hates the light,*
> *and will not come into the light*
> *for fear that their deeds will be exposed.*
> *But whoever lives by the truth comes into the light,*
> *so that it may be seen plainly*
> *that what they have done*
> *has been done in the sight of God.*

"When we align ourselves with God's righteous standards, we stand *with* the Light who, according to John 8:12 is Christ Jesus himself. Those who hate the Light—those who hate Jesus and who hate God's righteousness—are afraid of the Light. *They run from it.* Why? Because their deeds are evil, and they know their wickedness will be exposed by the Light.

"I'll say it again: You did not cause this divide in the young adults. You stood with God *who is the Father of lights*, and who, in fact, never changes and whose shadow never shifts. We are supposed to stand with him and refuse to be moved. If you are standing with the Lord, then who created this division?"

Todd answered. "Those who hate the light and fear that their evil deeds will be exposed?"

Zander touched his finger to his nose. "Bingo."

"I've read that chapter like a million times," Josh said, "but I don't think I 'got' it until this evening. Well, a glimmer of it, anyway."

Zander grinned. "Cool. Let's press in, shall we? Because I want us to study out the biblical characteristics of ungodly 'division'—what it looks and feels like and what kind of fruit it produces.

"First we have to separate godly division from ungodly division, or, in other words, what God says is right and what God says is wrong. His commandments divide everything into one of those two camps, right or wrong. *That*, my friends, is godly division. Let me list a few other examples of how the Bible describes godly division.

"The dominion of darkness versus the kingdom of the Son he loves, Colossians 1:13.

"The objects of his wrath versus the objects of his mercy. That's Romans 9:22-23.

"Dead in trespasses and sin versus alive in Christ, Ephesians 2:1-5.

"In slavery to the fear of death versus free from the fear of death, Hebrews 2:14-15.

"Those who have done evil will be raised to shame and damnation versus those who have done good to the resurrection of life, Daniel 12:2 and John 5:28-29."

Zander looked around the clutch of young adults. "What can you attest to concerning God's division?"

"It removes confusion," Diego said quickly. "Puts the good on one side and the bad on the other."

"Then we can clearly *see* the difference between the bad and the good," Sandra exclaimed.

"Sounds like Good News to me," Zander chuckled.

Sandra laughed. "Exactly."

Zander grinned at her. "Well, then, on the other hand, ungodly division must be bad news. Am I right?"

"Yes," came several responses.

"That's right. Ungodly division is bad news. It glorifies sin, and it seeks to erase the line between what God has declared to be right or wrong.

"Ungodly division presents a specific *and recognizable* face, too. Galatians 5:19-21 lists a number of sins and calls them 'works of the flesh.' Ungodly division will exhibit the characteristics of works of the flesh. Let's read that list so we know what to watch for.

> *"Now the works of the flesh **are evident,** which are:*
> *adultery, fornication, uncleanness,*
> *lewdness, idolatry, sorcery, hatred,*
> *contentions, jealousies, outbursts of wrath,*
> *selfish ambitions, dissensions, heresies, envy,*
> *murders, drunkenness, revelries, and the like;*
> *of which I tell you beforehand,*
> *just as I also told you in time past,*
> *that those who practice such things*
> *will not inherit the kingdom of God.*

"I think we're familiar with the sexual sins listed here. Those seem to get the most attention. But what about some of the other things? How about sorcery? Outbursts of wrath? Heresies?"

"We flunked a crash course on heresies," Josh muttered.

"Flunked? I think all of you passed with flying colors," Zander replied.

"Not all of us," Eli whispered. He'd tagged along when Josh told him of tonight's meeting with us in our home.

"Have you repented, Eli?" Zander asked quietly.

"Yeah. I mean, yes. I have."

"Does God remember what he's forgiven? Psalm 103:12 tells us, *As far as the east is from the west, so far has he removed our transgressions from us.* Right?"

Eli nodded. "Thank you. I needed that reminder."

"Good. But Eli is also on to something. Rather than pointing out the sins of others, why don't we allow the word of God to work in our own hearts? So, let's stop for a time of quiet reflection and prayer. Everyone find a little corner to prayerfully go through the items on the list and ask the Holy Spirit to speak to our hearts.

If he brings up something you need to confess to the Lord, go ahead and do that. Get it off your chest, into the open with the Lord, and allow him to minister truth and forgiveness as needed."

It wasn't hard for the nine of us to find a place to pray. Some turned their bodies to the walls. Others knelt in front of the sofa and buried their faces in the cushions. One or two wandered into the hallway or kitchen for solitude.

Sincere prayer is powerful, and I felt the presence of the Lord . . . doing a deep work.

Oh, God! Thank you for healing our hearts.

⌘

THE OPEN HOUSE AT Emilio's school took place on the third Wednesday in December. Zander and I dressed up, got in the car, drove two doors around the cul-de-sac, and pulled up in front of Abe's house. Emilio popped out the front door, shouting behind him, "They're here!" then ran down the steps, his growing legs taking them two at a time.

"Hey!" he greeted us. He climbed through the back door and scooted over to make room for Abe. We hadn't installed the car seat for Baby Cruz yet, but Emilio knew that once the baby came and whenever Abe rode with us, he would ride in the third row of seats. He had claimed ownership of the "far back" and loved the idea that he would be able to watch over the kiddo by leaning forward and looking down on him or her in the rear-facing car seat.

I turned around from behind the wheel. "Are you excited about tonight, Emilio?"

He grinned and nodded.

Zander reached back and gave him an affectionate noogie. "Tell us about your art project, Emilio?"

Our boy shook his head. "Nope. It's a surprise."

"Ohhh," I said, drawing it out. "A surprise, eh?"

Abe arrived, somewhat out of breath, and climbed aboard. A minute later, we were on our way.

⌘

WE PARKED, THEN WALKED together, the four of us, into the school's gymnasium. Emilio's school was typical of Albuquerque schools, part brick and mortar, part portable classrooms that had been "temporary" for at least twenty years.

"Where is your classroom, bud?" Zander asked.

"It's way over there." Emilio pointed to a cluster of portables. "I get to take you there after the Art Walk."

"Art Walk?"

"Yup. Everybody's art is on display around the gym. You get cookies and punch while you guys walk around and see all of our projects."

"Cool!" Inside, I was shouting, *Cookies! I get cookies!*

I made myself exercise a pinch of self-control and only put three little beauties on my plate. I knew Zander and Emilio were watching me, waiting to see how many I took before they got theirs. I was "the example" of propriety this evening, so I did not add a fourth or fifth—*or sixth*—chocolate chip cookie to my plate, although I wanted to. Reeeeally bad.

Zander and I had eaten dinner less than an hour ago, yet I felt my stomach gurgling away, begging me to toss something down the hatch.

My hand hovered momentarily—then I yanked it back.

Emilio grabbed three cookies. "I got to go stand by my project," he announced before he raced off. "Talk to people 'bout it when they walk by."

"Okay. See you soon."

Zander, Abe, and I strolled by the colorful finger painting of kindergartners, the skies, clouds, trees, and the pointy houses and stick people of first and second graders, then the creations of third, fourth, and fifth graders that more closely resembled reality. When we reached Emilio's station amid the fifth grade projects, the three of us came to an amazed standstill.

I recalled the Christmas gift Zander and I had given Emilio last year— a hinged wooden case, a wonderful set of carving tools nestled inside, and blocks of nice wood for his best efforts. He had to have used one of those special pieces of wood.

Emilio stood beside a black-draped pedestal. On it rested a miniature wood carving that glowed with a sheen that only hours of hand rubbing could produce. My fingers automatically reached for my neckline and the cross hanging there. I felt its familiar glossy-smooth surface as I fought the tears I was helpless to stem.

Emilio had carved our little family—Abe, Zander, me, Emilio. I stood between Abe and Zander. In front of Abe stood Emilio, Abe's hand resting on his shoulder. Zander's arm was around my waist. Emilio was turned a little toward me, his eyes gazing up into my face, love and happiness in his smile. I held a swaddled infant in my arms—our Baby Cruz. Emilio's fingers, delicate and gentle, rested atop mine as I held the infant.

Emilio's craft was in its infancy, but it spoke of what it would become when it matured. His style was . . . essential. Evocative. He had captured our unity and love for each other.

It's a good thing I hadn't worn any makeup, or my face would have been a smeary mess. However, I wasn't the only one affected by Emilio's work. Abe and Zander were, too.

Abe, his voice rough with emotion, kept whispering, "Most beautiful thing I've ever seen."

I grabbed Emilio and hugged him to myself with something akin to desperation. Well, I *was* desperate—desperate to tell him, *to show him* how much I loved him. Then Zander's strong arms wrapped themselves around both of us, and Abe got into the mix with us.

"Thank you, Jesus," Abe whispered. "Thank you for blessin' us with this boy. We love him so much."

"Yes, we do, Lord," Zander replied.

"Amen," I whispered back.

When we finally untangled and got ourselves under control, the school's principal and counselor were waiting and watching. Other parents, too, had gathered and were admiring Emilio's work . . . and the blue ribbon that had appeared next to his project.

"Congratulations, Emilio," the principal said, drawing our attention to the ribbon. "You won top honors in this year's Art Walk."

Emilio's answering grin was as wide as the sky.

⌘

A BELL RANG, INDICATING that the school's teachers were ready to receive their students and their students' parents in their classrooms. We let Emilio guide us to his class. He waved and nodded to his fellow fifth-graders and their parents as they joined us.

A middle-aged woman with a pleasant voice spoke from the front of the classroom. "If I may have your attention, please? Thank you. I am Ms. Cargill. Welcome, all parents and children, to our fifth-grade class.

"Children, at the next bell, would you please take your regular seats? Parents, feel free to gather around your child's seat at that time. Each student has prepared a folder of their most recent work to demonstrate what they are currently learning. Until the bell, however, feel free to walk about the room and view examples of our class projects."

Emilio was joined by a fellow classmate. The two smiled and exchanged a well-practiced three-step handshake.

"Dude, you won the blue ribbon," the boy told Emilio. "Pretty cool."

Emilio's face lit up again. "Thanks."

"Will you introduce us, Emilio?" I asked.

"Yes'm. This is my friend Benny."

I smiled. "It's nice to meet you, Benny."

He nodded. Then, as though Zander, Abe, and I weren't standing right there and couldn't hear him, he whispered to Emilio, "Is your mom gonna have a baby?"

Emilio puffed out his chest. "Yup. Sure is."

I thought I was barely showing—so much for what I thought!

Benny dared address me personally and asked, "You havin' a boy or a girl baby?"

"Well, we won't know until he or she is born," I answered. "It will be a welcome surprise, either way."

I had no idea how my response would impact our lives. I was unaware how the idyllic family life we loved would later be tested.

Ms. Cargill, who had been slowly circumnavigating the room, overheard our exchange. She stopped beside Benny.

"Benny, you know that we must allow infants to choose their own genders and pronouns. Instead of baby, we say 'theyby.' I would remind you, too, that we don't use gendered words in our classroom. Rather than mom or mother, 'birthing person' is the correct designation."

Benny stared at the floor. "Yes, Ms. Cargill."

I stared at Ms. Cargill. "Excuse me. Could you explain, please?"

"Yes, certainly. You see, we avoid the use of biased descriptors such as 'father' and 'mother' and replace them with more inclusive words such as birthing person. Do you see what we are trying to do? We choose not to exclude anyone or use pejorative language that may hurt the feelings of others."

I nodded slowly. "Yes, I believe I see what you are trying to do. However, I am quite comfortable with the term mom or mother. They are *my* preferred designations."

Ms. Cargill's mouth pursed. "I see. Well, in my classroom, in order to include everyone, we practice social awareness and do not use terms some would find disparaging."

I waited a few beats of my irate, pounding heart before I answered.

And I was quite calm—I promise.

"Ms. Cargill, I am a woman. My husband is a man, and Emilio is a boy. When our baby is born, we will immediately know if he or she is a boy or girl. His or her physical attributes will tell us the gender and his or her DNA will confirm the same. We will refer to our *baby* as him or her depending on his or her gender."

I glanced at Abe. "Abe, you are Emilio's foster *father*. Do you approve of your *boy* being required to call me a birthing person rather than a mom?"

Abe shook his head. "Nope." He lifted his chin toward Ms. Cargill. "Ma'am, with all due respect, you are here to teach my boy reading, math, and so on, not to brainwash him and force him to say things that his own two eyes tell him are simply not so."

Ms. Cargill's lips stretched into a tight smile. "I see. Well, thank you for coming this evening."

As she walked away, I glanced at Zander. His face was flushed, but he had said nothing.

Probably because he couldn't pry his clenched teeth apart.

⌘

THREE MEN SAT BEFORE a roaring fire, staring into the flames and sipping their drinks. The alcohol warmed them while they discussed the progress of their plans.

"Your girl did a standup job of snaring Victor Gibson, Stan. She told me he sat there, stunned—like a deer in the headlights—until Easterly here got the photos he needed. Say, have you finished editing them, Easterly?"

Easterly, for his part, was deferential. "Almost done, Mr. Barnes. And unless the images are scrutinized by an expert who knows what to look for, no one will ever suspect that I've mashed together several similar images to produce the final product you asked for. I'll be sending the files to you tomorrow."

"Good, good. Can't wait to show them to old Victor. He'll crap his pants—and then he'll vote however I tell him to. Please excuse me. I need to get home."

"Have a nice evening, Mr. Barnes."

When the front door closed behind Barnes, the remaining two men continued to talk.

"I'm glad Barnes is happy and all, Stan, but in the meantime, what are we going to do about Cruz? More of my young adults are going over to him, and it's split the group into two camps. He's a real thorn in my side! What we need is a means of getting rid of him permanently, a way to demoralize or discredit him in front of his followers."

"Don't worry, Aiden. A number of our people are scheduled to arrive soon. They will make up the group members you've lost. Besides, Barnes and I have a few choice blades up our sleeves with Cruz's name on them."

"But we've investigated him thoroughly. He's squeaky, *disgustingly* clean, not even a parking ticket. Not a thing we could use to besmirch his reputation, not unless we go back to his juvie record or his time in the gangs—and he's been too open about his 'testimony' for those to hurt him."

"Ah, but everyone has weak spots. The trick is finding what will hurt most. Once you know that, it's a matter of fashioning and unleashing the right weapons."

"You have something in mind? Care to share?"

"Soon, soon. Have I ever steered you wrong? No. We'll wipe that self-righteous sneer off Cruz's face soon enough. Stop worrying and come to bed."

⌘⌘⌘⌘

PART 2: THE GATHERING STORM

"But about that day or hour no one knows,

not even the angels in heaven,

nor the Son, but only the Father.

Be on guard! Be alert!

You do not know when that time will come."

Mark 13:32-33, NIV

CHAPTER 21

THE DAYS DURING THE countdown to Christmas were filled with fun: Abe, Emilio, Zander, and I putting up a tree together in our living room, Emilio and I baking goodies, Zander and I shopping and wrapping gifts, Emilio coming with us to carol at a nursing home with a group of married couples from church—everything a family enjoys doing together to celebrate this glorious holiday.

One evening after dinner, we arranged for Emilio to come over to us. He, Zander, and I packed small festive boxes with our baked treats and then delivered them to our near neighbors—the Tuckers, Mrs. Calderón, Gamble and Janice.

The Tuckers were delighted and said so, and they made much over Emilio—who squirmed under their attention and kind words. The Tuckers were older than us, and Zander and I didn't know them well, so Zander suggested we plan a dinner to change that.

Mrs. Calderón was surprised and touched with her box of goodies, and I was glad. With the deaths of both Genie and Gemma last Christmas and with old age creeping up on her, Mrs. Calderón had grown fragile. And I was beginning to perceive that maybe her loneliness had been why, for years, she had spied incessantly on her neighbors.

On Gemma.

On me.

"We should invite her to dinner, too," Zander said as we walked back across the cul-de-sac. "Maybe once a month? In fact, we could do a 'whole cul-de-sac' dinner and bring us all together. No one should feel alone in this world."

"Sure." But I was distracted, working hard to forget what a blind and cruel person Gemma Keyes had been BC. Before Christ.

When we knocked on Gamble and Janice's door to deliver their box of treats, they insisted we come inside. The three of us sat down in their pleasant living room, staring around us. I was trying to picture the disgusting pigsty it had been a few months back. I glanced at the front window, too, and recalled the afternoon I had peered through it to watch Mateo and Arnaldo Soto "discuss" the fire that had burned down their drug house.

The fire Gemma Keyes had started.

I shook myself from those thoughts. *Gemma is gone. Stop thinking about her.*

I turned to Janice. "You are spending Christmas Day with us, right?" I asked.

"Wouldn't miss it for the world. What time do you want us?"

"Well, I doubt Emilio will sleep in that morning—and I'm not sure how we'd keep him away from the tree for long after that. Shall we say eight o'clock?"

"You'll have coffee?" Gamble asked.

"Does Santa have reindeer? We'll do breakfast, too, after presents. Abe is bringing the tamales he bought from the inestimable Mrs. Baca and her four daughters."

Tamales are kind of a Christmas staple here in New Mexico.

"We'll also have homemade cinnamon rolls, eggs, and bacon." I waggled my brows at Gamble. "*Plates* of bacon."

Gamble swallowed reflexively. "I'm with Janice. Wouldn't miss it for the world!"

⌘

FOUR DAYS BEFORE CHRISTMAS, we drove again to Las Cruces, taking Abe, Emilio, and Izzie with us for an early celebration with Roberto and María. It was a joyous time and, not surprisingly, the pile of gifts under the tree was huge—Baby Cruz and Emilio making out like bandits.

I had to blink back tears at Roberto and María's generosity. We had told them that our friends in DC had showered Baby Cruz with all the nursery furniture we needed plus a car seat (up-armored with love, compliments of Baltar, Logan, and Dredd) and all the clothes a newborn could need.

Roberto and María must have made a list of what we had because whatever was missing? They were determined to fill in those blanks: Bassinet, highchair, baby pack, stroller, bouncer, crib mobile, even a diaper bag.

Izzie handed me a package. "I want you to know that I had to fight for the *privilege* of giving my niece or nephew *something*. Mama and Papa finally caved and 'let' me buy this."

"This" was an upscale video baby monitor.

"It connects to your Wi-Fi so you can access the camera or audio from your phone," she explained.

I was nearly speechless. "Izzie . . . this must have cost a small fortune."

"My nephews and nieces get only the best," she answered, handing Emilio his gift with a smile of affection.

While Emilio tore into his package, the nanomites huffed.

Izzie Cruz's gift for Baby Cruz is unnecessary, Jayda Cruz. We will monitor Baby Cruz continuously once he or she is born, as we monitor him or her presently. Perhaps you can exchange this useless item.

"Uh, I don't think we can 'exchange' this gift, Nano. Did you hear Izzie? She gave that monitor from her heart and will expect to see it in use—and it's not like we can tell her that *you* are watching over Baby Cruz, can we?"

When they didn't reply I added, "Also, I do foresee the occasional need for it. After all, Zander and I may want to leave Baby Cruz with a trusted sitter once in a blue moon—like for a date."

I think "shocked" and "dumbfounded" might best describe the nanocloud's silence. They and I were melded. We were never apart. The nanomites would always—as long as I lived—be with me. Part of me. And while Baby Cruz grew within me, the nanomites were right there with him or her, too.

But perhaps it hadn't occurred to the nanomites that, although Baby Cruz was dependent upon me while developing, he or she was—and had been from conception—a separate entity, his or her own person. Possibly, the nanomites hadn't realized that, once born, our baby would continue to grow apart from us.

Yes, it took years of nurture and care, but our ultimate purpose as parents, our charge from the Lord, was not to keep our child a child, but to raise a godly, healthy adult, to produce a mature individual able to thrive without us and our hovering presence over his or her life.

The nanomites were fully invested in Baby Cruz but had been slapped upside the head with a disturbing truth. Perhaps they, like us, were beginning to appreciate that good parenting was essentially one healthy goodbye after another.

I don't think the nanomites cared for the concept.

⌘

OUR VISIT WITH ROBERTO and María was quick but wonderful. Getting all our gifts into the car as we packed to go home was the issue! However, seeing as how Izzie was staying with her parents through Christmas, we figured we could move Emilio forward into her seat and reclaim the space the third row took up.

"That should work," Zander said, cramming one more box into the third row.

It worked until Izzie showed up with her suitcase. "Um, Zander? I'm going back to Albuquerque with you guys, so I'll need a seat."

Zander frowned. "I thought you were staying with Mama and Papa through New Year's. That's what you told them, right?"

"Well, yes, I had intended to stay, *originally*. That was before . . . before Aiden asked me to spend Christmas with him and a few others in the young adult group. I've told Mama and Papa, and they're okay. It's all good."

Neither Zander nor I thought Izzie's change of plans was any part of "all good"—not only because she had likely disappointed Roberto and María, but also because her new plan involved Aiden Easterly.

Zander said softly. "You know what Sierra has been doing, Iz. We told you about her."

"What's that got to do with Aiden?"

"Sierra came down from Denver with him, Izzie, along with Stan Missing and the others. She's part of Easterly's inner circle."

"Jesus' apostles came down from Galilee with him to Jerusalem, Zander. Was that a problem? Sure, he had a Judas. Maybe Aiden does, too."

Her eyes narrowed, and I saw a hint of her brother in the way she set her jaw. "And may I remind you that I'm an adult woman? You aren't the only one allowed to find love and happiness. It's *my* turn, don't you think?"

Anger was uncharacteristic of Izzie's sweet temperament, which was why, when she snapped at Zander, we were taken aback and left speechless. On top of her ire, Izzie's roundabout way of telling us she was in love with Aiden Easterly—and in some sort of relationship with him— left me lightheaded.

I leaned against the passenger door, sick in my heart. *Oh, Lord God! I cherish Izzie and our friendship. She is my sister and I love her!*

I pleaded silently, *Please, Lord. Show her who this Easterly character is. What he is. Please protect her from him.*

Zander closed his mouth and stared at the asphalt. Izzie left her suitcase on the curb. After a few moments of silence, my nausea passed, and we resumed loading the SUV.

Our ride home was subdued. Once we had dropped Izzie at her apartment, Emilio asked, "What's wrong with Izzie?"

I didn't know what to tell him—I certainly wasn't going to use her name and Aiden Easterly's name in the same sentence.

Finally Zander spoke. "Sometimes people make unwise decisions. However, if they are adults, it's not our place to *make* them change their mind. Instead, we pray for them, asking the Lord to show them a better choice."

A fierce, black thundercloud appeared on Emilio's forehead. "What's Izzie doin'?"

"That's her business, Emilio. Instead of being mad at her, why don't you pray for her? Ask the Lord to keep her from making a mistake?"

"Yeah, I don' do that prayin' junk like you guys do."

I added Emilio to my prayers for Izzie while we drove home.

⌘

JAYDA CRUZ. ZANDER CRUZ. *We have questions.*

Jayda Cruz. Zander Cruz. We have questions.

Jayda Cruz. Zander Cruz. We have questions.

"Gah! Can we pleeeeease have one morning where we get to wake up on our own?"

Zander didn't bother complaining as it had absolutely no effect on the nanomites. Besides which, as I was learning, complaining was a bad habit easily fallen into but harder to dig out of.

Ugh.

"Coffee?" Zander asked on his way to the kitchen.

"Uh, absolutely." My best Stallone imitation.

Five minutes later we were at the kitchen table, staring at our cul-de-sac through the new blinds, the view achingly similar to the one I'd known at Gemma's kitchen table.

I had gulped down half my mug before it hit me . . .

Lord, is this your way of healing my heart? Of giving me back a small piece of Gemma's life?

After hashing it over a few times, I chose to receive it that way—a gift from my Father who cares.

Thank you, Lord. You never cease to amaze me. I love you!

At peace inside, I said, "All right, Nano. What questions do you have?"

Jayda Cruz, Zander Cruz, our printer is operational again, and we thank you. Our tribes are once more at full strength. Both nanoclouds are at full strength.

"Okaaay."

"I don't hear a question," Zander yawned. "There had better be a question—a good one—for getting us up early.

While in DC, we manufactured millions of simple, short-term, single-purpose nanomachines or nanobots. We gathered thousands of them into individual arrays. We sent those arrays into suspects and persons of interest in order to monitor and track them. When we finished the President's assignment, per our agreement with you, we sent a self-destruct order to all the arrays.

I shuddered, recalling where Vice President Delancey's array had self-destructed.

"Not a question," Zander repeated.

We promised we would make no further nanobug arrays once the President's assignment was concluded.

"Darn straight," I retorted. Then I turned to Zander, "I'm getting a bad feeling here. You?"

"Yeah, me too. Uh, Nano? No more nanobugs. Period. Full stop."

May we speak our piece, Zander Cruz?

I glanced at Zander. "*Finally*, they ask a question."

Zander sighed. "Sorry. Go ahead, Nano."

We are concerned that no way presently exists for you or us to track Emilio should he become lost or be kidnapped. We are concerned that no way presently exists for you or us to track Baby Cruz once he or she is born.

I know it was "just" my maternal instinct, an instinct inborn in me as a woman and a mother; nevertheless, my blood pressure may have spiked through the roof. "What? *No!* Emilio is never getting kidnapped again and Baby Cruz is not leaving my sight for the next twenty-eight years!"

The nanomites' response was like ice water in my veins.

How can you be certain Emilio will never be kidnapped, Jayda Cruz? We do not wish to cause you distress, but we feel obligated to remind you that Emilio was kidnapped once, and he is often away from you. Can you foresee or prevent another such event? Furthermore, if we did not take action while we can, would it not be too late should the unthinkable happen?

Zander seemed frozen, his hand wrapped around his mug, his eyes staring at nothing.

"Zander?"

His head swiveled slowly, side to side.

"Zander?"

"Uh, we . . . um, our concern in DC was a legal and ethical one. Privacy issues. What the nanomites propose . . . isn't much different than putting GPS trackers in our kids' shoes, is it?"

"More like we'd be eavesdropping on them, 24/7."

"They're our kids, Jayda. It . . . it would be no different than attaching a baby monitor to both of them."

"Slippery slope, Zander."

"Yeah, soooo, we'll need to keep ourselves accountable to each other. And maybe Abe?"

"Abe will balk at the idea that everything he and Emilio talk about is being fed straight to us. And I wouldn't blame him a whit."

"We don't need to listen in," Zander said. "In fact, we can tell the nanomites to mute the feed. All we need is our kids' locations at any given time. And maybe their vital signs."

I got up and filled my mug a second time. Sat down. Rubbed my face hard. "It would eliminate a certain level of background stress, I suppose."

I leaned toward Zander and whispered, "And it would shut you-know-who up."

We heard that, Jayda Cruz.

"You make my point, Nano. Privacy issues."

Jayda Cruz, we care about the welfare of Emilio and Baby Cruz. With the arrays, we would be able to track them, should the need arise. You would approve in such an instance, would you not?

"I guess we're partly in agreement, Nano," I admitted.

"Go ahead, Nano," Zander said. "Build a couple of arrays and tag Emilio. And when Baby Cruz arrives, please tag him or her."

We also suggest that we tag Abe, Izzie, and—

Zander and I answered at the same time.

"No."

⌘

I woke on Christmas morning brimming with anticipation. I glanced at the clock—5:45 a.m. Too late to go back to sleep. Too early to risk awakening Emilio.

Emilio. I listened. Didn't hear furtive footsteps or anything creaking in the house. Checked his vitals via his nanobug array.

He was in his room. Sleeping. His breathing slow and deep.

I kinda like being able to check on him, I admitted.

Zander stirred.

"You awake?"

He yawned. "Yep."

We got up and quietly dressed, then headed for the kitchen on tiptoe. On our way through the living room, Zander switched on the lights to the Christmas tree and around the manger scene we'd put together last evening with Emilio and Abe.

The four of us had picked out the sizable nativity set at Hobby Lobby two weeks ago, then asked a family at DCC who had horses and goats for a small bag of real hay. The afternoon of Christmas Eve, Zander and Emilio cobbled together a low table out of rough wood that fit perfectly in the corner of the living room. I supplied the burlap fabric to cover it. That evening, we strewed hay across the table, carefully staged each member of the nativity scene in its proper place, ran a string of twinkle lights around and through the scene, then hung a big, glittery star over the stable.

It was gorgeous and awe-inspiring—but setting all the pieces in place? Took forever.

Emilio had knelt in front of the table while the four of us assembled the scene. He studied the composite with a critical eye from various angles. In fact, he rearranged or adjusted all the pieces—two camels, an ox, a donkey, two sheep, three wise men, two shepherds, an angel, Mary, Joseph, an open-faced stable, and the little manger itself—again and again throughout the evening until he was satisfied that everything was "right" to his satisfaction.

The only part missing when we sent him to bed that night was baby Jesus.

After Zander and I had grabbed our first cup of coffee and sat in the living room to enjoy the lighted tree and nativity scene, Zander went to our closet and dug out all the wrapped presents we'd hidden inside. He made three trips and placed all the presents under the tree.

"Now?" he asked.

"Now," I said.

From his pocket he withdrew the figure of baby Jesus and carefully placed it in the manger.

The most important of all Christmas traditions.

I sighed with happiness. Soon Emilio would wake up. He would see Jesus in the manger, and we would read the Christmas story together. Then he'd run across the cul-de-sac to see if Abe was ready to join us. Knock on Gamble and Janice's door to get them moving.

We would laugh and hug and share a great breakfast together. Open presents and sing a few Christmas carols. Later, Zander, Emilio, and I would snuggle on one end of the couch and watch a Christmas movie while Abe dozed on the other end.

In the early afternoon, Dr. Bickel would arrive to take over our kitchen. He was thrilled with the prospect of preparing a fine Christmas dinner for us and our cul-de-sac neighbors—everyone, that is, except the Tuckers, who were spending the week with their kids and grandkids.

Dr. Bickel planned to spend Christmas day concocting wonderful Christmas dishes and treats, and I was equally delighted to let him. I chuckled to myself, recalling my most recent conversation with my dear friend.

"How many pies? Dear me . . . pumpkin pie with fresh whipped cream, of course—that's tradition, after all. But we must also have pecan, Dutch apple, and perhaps a chocolate cream pie? I had also considered a lovely lemon meringue pie—a nice tall one. Or is that too much? What do you think?"

"No, no—not too much! Yes to all of them, please," I'd replied, shivering with anticipation.

I confess his enthusiasm reminded me of our visits inside his mountain laboratory. My dear friend had taken such pleasure in the meals he'd concocted for the two of us to share—back in the days and weeks before General Cushing attacked Dr. Bickel's hiding place . . .

Then I remembered.

You're healing my heart, Lord. Restoring what was taken away. And I am very grateful! I shook off the lingering sense of loss and put my mind back in the here and now.

Near dinner time, Gamble and Janice would return and Mrs. Calderón would join us. The eight of us would squeeze around our small table and enjoy Dr. Bickel's fabulous cuisine.

Our family. Our home. God's peace and presence. So many blessings and so much gratitude.

Only one concern intruded: Izzie.

Where are you, Iz? What are you doing?

Lord God, please protect her!

⌘

IZZIE CRUZ SPENT HER Christmas holiday and the days following in a churn of emotions—ecstatic one moment, near despair the next. From Christmas Eve through Christmas Day, Aiden doted on and pampered her. He praised her before his "coterie," those who lived in his house with him. He held her hand and showered her with small, thoughtful gifts.

In between those fits of affection, he seemed indifferent, and he often disappeared into his bedroom or his study, leaving Izzie confused and alone . . . at the mercy of his housemates.

Izzie didn't much care for Aiden's inner circle—Sierra, two girls, Jill and Mari, and two guys new to the young adult group but who had known Aiden in Colorado, and—*of course*—Stan. *Stan*, Aiden's silent shadow. *Stan*, always at Aiden's beck and call, always submissive and compliant, always *there*, as though an invisible string tied them together. Wherever Aiden might be in the large house he had leased, *Stan* was nearby, ready to serve, ready to "amen" whatever Aiden said.

What Izzie liked least about Aiden and his "acolytes" is how they all lived together in that roomy house. It was practically impossible to find Aiden alone or keep him alone. Nevertheless, his dutiful disciples had fallen into line, had followed Aiden's gentle instructions to treat Izzie with "Christian charity." They greeted her with air kisses, disingenuous compliments, and smirky, not-quite-sincere smiles.

Izzie told herself that the annoyances she brushed away were petty and inconsequential—as long as she had Aiden's attention. Something drew her to him, the pull so irresistible, that she allowed herself to entertain random fantasies about the future. Of her and Aiden, a wedding, herself as a pastor's wife.

I've never met a godly man like him, she told herself. *He knows so much and has such vision and charisma! I believe that he will someday change the lives of thousands.*

Her hopes grew with each hour she spent in Aiden's company. As his affection for her became more evident, his words and deeds drew Izzie closer to what she desired—that he would utter the one phrase she longed to hear. The fact that he hadn't quite managed to say that phrase hadn't kept her from believing he would soon.

He loves me. I'm certain of it! It's only a matter of time before he tells me he does.

Izzie had been given a cot in the bedroom Jill and Mari shared, and she spent Christmas Eve in Aiden's house. She didn't believe her sleeping over was inappropriate. *After all, Aiden is a pastor. He shares this house with six other people. No one will think less of me for staying here . . . temporarily.*

"Temporarily" lingered through Christmas and the day after . . . then ended when Izzie had to return to work on the twenty-seventh. As Izzie packed up her things, she puzzled over Aiden, and wondered why his attentions ran either hot or cold. Why he spent so much time alone in his office while she was there. Why he had left her to fend for herself for most of her visit.

"Come spend New Year's Eve with us?" Aiden asked—not appearing to notice Izzie's discontent, her miffed expression.

"Maybe," she said.

But she knew she would.

⌘

THE DAY AFTER CHRISTMAS, I felt the need to ask the nanomites what they were doing. I mean, every time I "stepped" in to the warehouse, veritable *legions* of them were quietly busy, burrowing through the government's financial recordkeeping systems and accounts—but not all of the nanomites.

The thing was, I could feel a certain low level of distraction in the nanocloud, as though their attention was split, as though they were, under the surface, preoccupied with something altogether different, but I had no clue as to what it might be.

When I delved into their recent activities, I saw that they had feelers everywhere, in everything. It felt like they were unfocused. Scattered, even. Or rather, that they were searching, but not for anything specific . . . so completely engrossed in their own activities, that it made me a pinch nervous.

"Nano, what are you doing?"

We are conducting the President's R&A, and we continue to monitor news and social media, Jayda Cruz.

"Yeah, I get that, but what, specifically, are you monitoring for? Don't forget that you promised not to hide anything from me."

Their penchant for "hiding" stuff had, in the past, employed carefully worded phrasing, excluding key information or cutting me out and going around me—like when the President had authorized the nanomites to use deadly force and the nanomites cut me out of that loop. They had followed the President's orders to facilitate the demise of the traitorous Vice President and his evil wife, but we had known nothing about it until after the fact.

We will hide nothing from you, Jayda Cruz. Nevertheless, at present, we have nothing to show you.

Their reply was anything but comforting.

⌘

ON THE LAST SUNDAY in December, the day before New Year's Eve, DCC celebrated Pastor and Mrs. McFee's fortieth wedding anniversary. We handed them first-class upgrades to their tickets to Hawaii and a nice love offering for them to splurge with on their trip. After service, we gathered in DCC's fellowship hall to share the lunch the church women's ministry had prepared.

Can I add that I love how our women go all out for these "love feasts?" That meal was epic. They even tapped me to contribute a pie—which, in my opinion was either misguided or an act of faith. I did my best, though, and managed to turn out two credible-looking cherry pies.

When lunch concluded, with an armload of flowers for Mrs. McFee and long, sustained applause for them both, we wished them a happy anniversary Hawaiian cruise.

The McFees would leave on New Year's Day and be gone nearly three weeks, missing two Sundays with us. Aiden Easterly was scheduled to preach on the first Sunday they were gone. Zander and I were on edge concerning Easterly's "progressive" theology and the direction he was energetically leading DCC's young adults. Would he push his heresies on the congregation as a whole?

If so, Zander, who would preach the following Sunday, was positioned to blunt Easterly's message, despite what it might cost him. And cost him it could. We could feel a growing tension in the church, the wedge Easterly's unscriptural teaching was driving between the young adults and the influence he was exerting on Steve Doherty, our youth leader over the middle school and high school kids.

A handful of Easterly's disciples were working with him to pound that wedge into our church—young men and woman who were ardent proponents of his teaching and who had followed Easterly to New Mexico from the Littleton church he'd served in.

It had also become clear to us that Easterly was garnering something of a following in Albuquerque, too. Each Sunday, newcomers showed up for service, introduced themselves to the young adults, then began insinuating themselves into the group.

Does my summary sound harsh or unwelcoming?

Not if these people were ferocious wolves in sheep's clothing as Jesus called them, false teachers slowly worming their way into our church, sowing confusion and discord wherever they went.

Harsh or unwelcoming? I don't think so. The Apostle Paul told us to be on our guard and to protect the Lord's flock.

I would beat the wolves off with a club if I needed to.

⌘⌘⌘⌘

CHAPTER 22

AIDEN AGAIN INVITED IZZIE to spend New Year's Eve with him and his "family" as he sometimes called his housemates. He seemed more attentive this time, and she was secretly delighted with the change in his behavior toward her. Over Christmas he'd alternated between hot and cold, one minute thrilling her with his attentions, the next, disappearing for hours.

Well, not *this* evening.

From the moment Izzie arrived early on New Year's Eve, Aiden had taken hold of her as though he owned her and he was marking his territory. He pulled her close and whispered compliments bordering on endearments in her ears. He kept her glued to his side, rarely leaving her alone except to bring her snacks and ply her with drinks.

"I don't drink," Izzie tried to tell him—but she heard the weakness in her voice, the "I don't drink *usually*," her answer's lack of conviction implied.

Aiden smiled into her eyes. "A little wine won't harm you, particularly tonight. After all, we have reasons to celebrate. Tonight we ring in a new year, but we also revel in the dawn of a new season. Many things will change for us tonight . . . Izzie."

Sweet anticipation thrilled her. "For *us*?"

"Yes, for you and me . . . if that's what you would like."

Izzie slowly nodded. "Yes. I would like that."

"Good. Then, let's ring in the New Year properly, shall we?"

He pressed the glass into her hand. Held up his own. "To us?"

Izzie shivered. His meaning was unmistakable!

They gently touched glasses and drank. He leaned toward her and kissed her mouth. "Yum. Let's do that again." He drank from his glass, waited for her to follow suit, then pulled her slowly toward him. Molding her body to his, he kissed her more deeply.

When he finally pulled back, Izzie was nearly faint with excitement.

The evening went on in similar fashion. Aiden kept her close, kept her glass filled, and teased her time after time, awaking desires in her she had not felt before.

⌘

Our little New Year's party was going full blast. The young adults who had slipped out from under Easterly's thumb were having a great time. Four of them were intent on a strategy-driven board game; others, including Emilio, were playing a spirited (and loud) round of Googly Eyes.

OVER IN THE CORNER, Zander, Abe, Josh, and Diego had their heads together, earnestly discussing the first chapter of James. Everyone was having a good time.

Too bad I wasn't enjoying myself.

For the past hour, I hadn't been able to get Izzie off my mind. I finally gave up and slipped away to our bedroom. There, beside our bed, I knelt.

"Lord God, I don't know where Izzie is or what she's doing, but if I'm hearing you right, she's in trouble—and it involves that false teacher, Aiden Easterly. Oh, Lord! Please help her. Please speak to her. *Show her*, Lord God, that her attraction to this man is misplaced, that he is not the godly man she believes him to be, not the husband material she so desperately desires him to be."

I swallowed. "Lord? Izzie made it clear that we were to butt out of her personal life, but that only tells me that, deep down, she knows she's wrong about this man. So, wherever she is, and if she is in either spiritual or physical danger, please speak to her! Please don't let her stumble, O God."

⌘

IZZIE WAS MORE THAN a little tipsy when, an hour before midnight, Aiden whispered to her. "I need to talk to you, Izzie. The two of us. Alone. I have things to say to you . . . in private."

He loves me! Oh, he loves me! Why, he . . . he must want to propose to me! Izzie's wildly beating heart assured her.

"Okay, Aiden."

He led her up the stairs and into his bedroom. "We can talk here, can't we? I have so much to say."

"Yes, Aiden."

She was surprised when he didn't turn on the lights. Instead, he led her across the room and gently tugged her down to sit beside him on the edge of the bed nearest the windows. Almost immediately, he drew her into his embrace. With his lips nuzzling her throat, then moving along her jaw, he whispered. "You must know that I love you, Izzie."

Izzie could scarcely breathe. Her entire body tingled. "Oh, I hoped you did! I love you, too, Aiden."

"I want to please you, Izzie. Let me . . . let me rub your feet."

"My feet?"

"Yes, of course. Jesus washed his disciples' feet, didn't he? Here. Let me." Aiden scooted away a bit, lifted her foot, tugged off one of her shoes, then the sock. He held her foot between his hands and gently massaged it.

Izzie sank into the pleasure of it. "Oh, that feels wonderful."

"Give me the other, sweet Izzie."

He finished rubbing her feet. Sitting close to her again, he ran his fingers up and down her arms, sending shivers down her back. "The Bible says that we should walk in the light like he is in the light—and that we should love each other, shouldn't we?" Izzie whispered, "Yes."

"Shall we love each other, Izzie? Fully love each other?"

"Oh . . ." Izzie swallowed. All the wine in her system was making it hard to think.

"*God is love*," Aiden whispered. "Do you believe that, Izzie?"

"Oh, I do. That's 1 John 4 . . . verse 16?"

"Hmm. Yes. Here is another verse from 1 John. *Let us not love with words or speech but with actions and in truth . . . and let us love one another, for love comes from God.*"

He was slowly peeling off her shirt when a voice spoke a single word within her.

Stop.

"Aiden, wait . . . I-I don't think it should be like this."

"But I love you, Izzie, and I want to love you fully. Completely. *God is love. Whoever lives in love lives in God.* Let us live in love this night. It will be so good, and God will bless us for sharing our love. I promise."

Stop.

He laid back on the bed and pulled her down alongside him. Izzie felt his skin against hers. Her heart was bursting; she was on fire.

Flee.

She tried to shove the voice away from her, but it was inside her where she couldn't reach it or ignore it.

Flee.

"Do you want to love me, Izzie?"

"Yes. I want to love you, Aiden."

"You shall, sweet Izzie."

She heard a noise and blinked as a narrow shaft of light pierced the dark of the room. Aiden's hands stroked her skin, distracting her, but a figure passed through the crack of light . . . into the room. Then the soft glow of a lamp shone dimly on the dresser.

Izzie pushed Aiden away and struggled to sit up. "Aiden! You didn't lock the door!"

"We don't believe in locking doors, Izzie."

"B-but someone's in here—here in your room!"

Aiden leaned away from her to look. "Oh. It's only Stan."

"Stan? *Stan?* Tell him to leave, Aiden!"

Aiden's voice dropped into a lazy drawl. "Why would I do that, sweet Izzie? Stan and I are partners. We share everything. We both want to love you, Izzie . . . while we love each other."

That voice within her shouted, **Run.**

Aiden's hands reached for her again, but Izzie, struck with revulsion, rolled away, rolled so frantically that she fell off the edge of the bed onto the floor. The ungraceful landing shook her from her alcoholic stupor. She jumped up and felt around, searching for her top, while declaring, "No! No, I don't want this!"

The figure near the dresser flipped the wall light switch, bathing the room in stark light. Izzie grabbed her top and held it against her . . . to hide her nakedness.

Aiden smiled at Stan. "You came in a little too early, darling. We weren't quite ready for you. What would you like me to do?"

Izzie couldn't believe her ears. "You? *And him?*" She felt ill. Weak.

Aiden stretched. "The heart wants what the heart wants, sweet Izzie. And you said you loved me—do you? If you love me, won't you do what pleases me? Stan and I—we're kind of a package deal."

As he reached for her, something ignited in Izzie's heart. Its heat surged through her chest, flowed into her shaking arms and legs, spread to her fingertips. Holy. Right. Good. Strong. A presence both angry and serene at the same time.

"Oh, Jesus!" she whispered. "I am such a fool. But please! Please get me out of here. Don't let me disgrace you further!"

She dragged her top up and over her head. Tugged it down. She didn't care if she found her bra, because getting away as quickly as possible was all that mattered. She grabbed up her shoes but not her socks—she didn't know where they were either and would not waste time looking for them.

"I'm leaving. Don't try to stop me."

Aiden looked toward the door. "Stan?"

"Oh, I think we let her go. We have more than what we need."

Izzie pounded down the stairs and ran from that house as if pursued by the Furies. The night air was cold and damp, but she did not stop until she reached the safety of her car.

No one tried to stop her. No even one took notice of her as she fled.

As she reached for the driver's door, she halted, frozen in shock, recalling that her keys were still in the room where she had slept—along with her purse, cell phone, and overnight bag. She squatted on the street and pulled on her shoes.

I don't care. I'll walk until I find somewhere safe.

Thank you for saving me from my foolish sin, Jesus!

⌘

OUR PARTY HADN'T BROKEN up until around three in the morning. After Zander and I cleaned up, we fell into bed, into exhausted slumber. I was still sleeping hard, in that deep, perfect place of dream sleep as dawn nears . . . when I heard them. I climbed slowly into consciousness, pulled there by the annoying buzz of the nanomites in my ears.

Zander and Jayda Cruz. Izzie Cruz is calling.

Zander and Jayda Cruz. Izzie Cruz is calling.

Zander and Jayda Cruz. Izzie Cruz is calling.

I fumbled for my phone.

Nothing.

Izzie Cruz is calling on Zander Cruz's phone, Jayda Cruz.

"Zander." I nudged him. "Zander, wake up. Pick up your phone."

He lifted his bleary eyes. "You know we silence our phones at night for a reason, right?"

Zander Cruz, Izzie Cruz is calling.

He reached for his phone, looked at the number on the screen. "This isn't Izzie's number, Nano."

It is not her number, Zander Cruz, but it is Izzie Cruz calling.

I sat up next to Zander as he picked up the call. "Hello?"

Izzie's voice, loud and agitated, flowed over the line. "Zander, thank God you finally picked up! Please come and get me!"

I started pulling on clothes.

"Iz, where are you?" He looked for the time on his phone: 7:06 a.m.

"On the west side, at the Walgreens near the intersection of Ellison and Coors, past Cottonwood Mall."

"What are you doing there? Where's your car? Whose phone is this?"

"I borrowed a phone. Please come get me?"

I whispered in his ear, "Ask questions later. She's in trouble, Zander."

He blew out a breath. "Yeah. Okay. Hold tight, Iz. We're on our way."

⌘

IZZIE WAS SQUATTING AGAINST the wall outside the store when we pulled into the parking lot. The nanomites flew to her at my request, then quickly returned.

She is physically well, Jayda Cruz, although quite cold and tired.

I figured she had to be cold—she was outside in December without a coat, after all.

She saw us when we parked. Stood up when we got out. Ran to her brother.

"You're freezing, Izzie!"

"I-I know. B-been outside f-for hours."

"Let's put her in the passenger seat and turn the heat up high," I suggested. "When we get her home, we can put her into a warm shower."

We drove her to our house, and I turned a warm shower on her until she stopped shivering. Much later, dressed in a pair of my sweatpants topped with a thick sweater, and with a mug of hot soup in her hands, Izzie slowly confessed . . . to everything.

Although she suffered mortification through the details, Izzie told us what she'd done. In fits and starts she laid it out—all of it, right up to the moment Aiden Easterly told her, *"The heart wants what the heart wants, sweet Izzie. And you said you loved me—do you? If you love me, won't you do what pleases me? Stan and I—we're kind of a package deal."*

Then we knew. We knew how far Easterly was from the Bible-believing Christian he pretended to be. The man was worse than a fraud: he was a ravening wolf, a two-legged predator sent by the enemy of our souls to tear and scatter the flock.

Izzie, however, didn't cringe from her own culpability: She faced it straight on. As Zander encouraged her to pray and confess her sins to the Lord, she did so, willingly.

"Lord! I knew in my heart that something wasn't right with Aiden, but I didn't care. I wanted to love him. I wanted him to love me. I put what I wanted above you! Please forgive me!"

As Izzie prayed, we watched chains of bondage fall from her. I was reminded of the conversation Zander and I had shared many months ago concerning repentance.

"Repentance isn't the ugly, hard, mean thing the world has said it is. Repentance is a gift from God, the first step in his setting us free. Repentance pulls down the strongholds in our lives. When repentance has its full sway, Jesus is able to free us from fear and condemnation."

Izzie repented and was left weeping before the Lord.

When her tears slowed, Zander asked, "Iz, you called us from a phone inside Walgreens. Where's your phone, Sis? And for that matter, where's your car?"

Izzie answered, "I had to leave without them, and Walgreens didn't open until seven this morning. I felt safer waiting by the door until they opened and I could go inside and ask to use their phone."

"You left your phone and your car at Easterly's place?"

"Yeah, I did. The only thing I cared about in those final minutes was getting out of that awful situation as fast as I could. The Holy Spirit kept telling me to *run*, to *flee*, and I, I . . . I was terrified that they would try to stop me, that Aiden and Stan were going to, to . . ."

"Force themselves on you?" Zander murmured.

"Yes! So, I ran. I ran downstairs and outside to where I'd parked my car—but I didn't have my keys! I had left them and my phone in my purse, and I left my purse in the bedroom I was sharing with Jill and Mari. I ran away so fast that I even left . . . a few articles of clothing in Aiden's room . . ."

Zander nodded slowly, but his attention was focused inward.

"Zander," Izzie whispered. "I don't think Aiden is who he tries to make us think he is."

I snorted to myself, *Ya think?*

Zander, though, asked, "What do you mean?"

"I-I don't think he is in charge."

"Keep going," Zander urged her.

"When . . . Stan opened the door to Aiden's room and came in . . . Aiden asked him, 'What would you like me to do?' And when I said I was leaving, Aiden again asked Stan for-for-for direction? Instructions?"

I was taken aback, as was Zander. We looked at each other as the import of Izzie's words sank in: Aiden Easterly was not the brains behind all the distress and confusion among DCC's young adults? Easterly's homosexual partner was?

"Then Stan told Aiden, 'I think we let her go. We have more than what we need.' Oh, Zander! What did he mean by 'we have more than what we need'? Do you think . . . could they have had cameras hidden in Aiden's room? Were they recording us when-when-when Aiden and I . . ." She broke, sobbing into her hands.

Several things suddenly made sense to me. I could tell by watching Zander's face turn to stone that he was experiencing a similar revelation.

Easterly had cultivated Izzie. He had purposefully flattered and seduced her. He had weaponized his control over her . . . as a means of getting at Zander.

Saddened for his sister, Zander hugged Izzie to his chest again. "Don't worry, Iz. I'll handle this situation."

"But-but-but how?"

"You don't need to know; trust me, okay? Is there anything about Easterly's house you can tell me that I ought to know?"

Izzie pulled back, more than a little nervous. "You aren't going over there, are you, Zander?"

"I need to retrieve your things, Iz. Your purse, ID, credit cards, phone? We can't leave them there. I'll go get them—and don't worry about me. I'm sure they will give them to me."

"Oh."

"Why don't you tell me about this house?"

She thought for a moment or two. "Big living room, kitchen, and dining room on the main floor. Four bedrooms upstairs. I had the run of the place . . . except for the two rooms on opposite sides of the living room. The doors to those rooms were always locked, like they were hiding something in them."

"Okay, thanks. I'll go retrieve your purse and your car."

"I should go with you!" I hissed.

He turned to me. "Jayda, someone should stay with Izzie, right? And also . . . take care of Baby Cruz."

A kick from Baby Cruz reminded me that I was not alone. Reluctantly, I nodded.

Zander wrapped his arms around me. Around *us*, me and Baby Cruz. Hugged us both. "Thank you for loving and caring for my sister, Sweetheart, and for protecting our child."

I exhaled. "Of course."

"Two more things? What I will need most while I'm gone is prayer support."

"Can do."

"Yes," Izzie added softly.

"Thank you both. Jay, why don't you have Emilio come over to visit with his *Tía*. The second thing I need is for you to drive me across town and drop me off near Easterly's house, then come straight back. When I'm done, I will drive Izzie's car home."

⌘⌘⌘⌘

CHAPTER 23

Hands on his hips, Zander stood in the shadow of a tall euonymus bush and surveyed the house across the street. It was as Izzie had described it. He took in the sprawling, two-story adobe Santa-Fe-style structure and wondered how Easterly paid the lease on his salary.

I couldn't afford something like this when I was the young adult associate pastor. Maybe Easterly collects rents from his housemates.

Another thought occurred to him. *Or, maybe someone else, someone with even greater sinister intent, is backing him.*

He snorted. *Yeah, and maybe I'm entertaining wacky conspiracy theories.*

"Nano, as soon as we're inside, please provide me with the layout of the place—including who's presently in the house and where they are."

Yes, Zander Cruz. We will.

"Nano, cover me, please."

As the nanocloud deployed their mirrors, Zander, as invisible as a breeze, cut kitty-corner across the street and headed toward Izzie's car. It was right where she said she'd parked it. He peered through one of the windows.

Zander Cruz, Izzie's car has not been tampered with.

"Good to know. Thanks."

He checked the time before he started toward the front door: 9:45 a.m. He strode up the walk and steep porch steps and stood before the impressive front door. Nanomites flew from him and penetrated the door's thick wood, streams of them going this way or that way, sending scouts into every corner of the house. A thread of them attacked the alarm box located inside the foyer. Within seconds, the door opened on nano-greased hinges.

We have defeated the house's security system, Zander Cruz.

"Well, hey—you hacked the White House, Nano. After that, the rest is Tinkertoys, right?"

Indeed.

Zander smiled to himself. The nanomites' one-word response had been dry. Mildly amused and complacently superior.

Soon a 3D schematic of the house appeared before Zander. He closed his eyes and stepped into the model. Immediately, he was immersed in the house's virtual layout. Before going any farther, he studied what the nanomites had tagged.

No one other than himself appeared to be on the ground floor, even this close to 10 a.m.

Well, it is New Year's morning, and according to Izzie, the household partied hard last night.

When he scanned upstairs, he counted eight individuals in four bedrooms—all of them sleeping. Two individuals occupied each bedroom, and the nanomites had placed nametags on each bed. Sure enough, the largest bedroom housed Easterly and Stan Missing.

"I'll try to be quiet, Nano, but let me know if anyone wakes up."

We will, Zander Cruz.

He left the entryway and moved soundlessly through the living room—a virtual living room in the warehouse that mirrored his movements in the actual living room. Whatever he focused on in the warehouse, the nanomites brought closer, providing salient details for him.

Zander was particularly interested in the two locked rooms Izzie had mentioned.

"I had the run of the place except for two rooms on either side of the big family room. The doors to those rooms were always locked. It was like they were hiding something from me."

Zander walked toward the room on the right of the living room. The locked door had a separate security alarm keypad.

He frowned. *A security system inside a security system? Oh, yeah. I **really** want to see what's in here!*

The nanomites swarmed over the keypad, defeating the alarm, then unlocked and opened the door ahead of him. Inside, toward the front window, Zander saw an ostentatious desk and desk chair surrounded by bookshelves.

Easterly's study?

On the opposite side of the room, however, he found what he'd suspected he'd encounter eventually: a rack of blade servers and a bank of computer monitors displaying camera feeds from every room in the house.

More like Easterly's command center.

Zander watched the feeds cycle through, then had the nanomites run them back by three minutes. His entrance to the house and walk through the living room did not appear on camera. He then studied the live second-floor feeds as they came up, appalled that each bedroom housed two individuals and only one bed.

Lord, scour my mind—and add some bleach, please.

"Nano. Search the servers. Locate every video Izzie is in."

He waited.

And waited.

Seven minutes later they replied.

Zander Cruz, we apologize. The servers contain many gigabytes of video. However, we have finished reviewing the recordings and have found seventeen video files in which Izzie Cruz appears.

"Wipe those files, Nano. Search the backups and wipe them, too. Leave absolutely *zero trace* of Izzie on these servers. Nothing that can be recovered or reconstituted. Leave no evidence that she was ever in this place."

Zander Cruz, zero trace of Izzie Cruz also involves scrubbing all files and folders of her name.

"Are you saying she's mentioned in other documents?"

In answer, they popped up a stored text message in front of him . . . and there it was, the smoking gun.

We will pull his teeth by
compromising his sister
Isabelle Cruz
Izzie

It was patently obvious that the "his" in that text was him. Then Zander read the reply.

As unappealing as
this deed may be,
I will do as you say
When?

"Who's texting whom here, Nano?"

We deduce that the recipient must be Aiden Easterly since he did attempt to compromise Izzie Cruz. If Izzie's assertion that Stan Missing gives Aiden Easterly orders is factual, then the sender of these texts would be Missing. However, neither phone belongs to Easterly or Missing. Both phones used are cheap, pre-paid units. If they are in the house, we will attempt to locate them.

Zander shut his eyes to think. *Aiden Easterly doesn't find women appealing, but he was willing to seduce Izzie as long as it ruined me—never mind her! To him, she was inconsequential "collateral damage."*

He shuddered, his mind vainly trying to throw off the nasty images the texts had evoked. Then, Zander read the last part of the text exchange.

Do it while McFee is away
but before he returns
and we get rid of him

The implications of those three lines hit him hard, and he whispered his thoughts aloud.

"Missing and Easterly know that the board will formally retire Pastor McFee the moment he returns from his vacation. Not only do they have foreknowledge of the board's intentions, they must also be working in conjunction with certain left-leaning board members."

Zander's mind shouted a wretched conclusion. *This is a coup! The rogue board members plan to install Easterly as the senior pastor.*

He added softly, "But . . . they also think they need to 'pull my teeth.' Why? I don't get it."

The answer thundered in his chest.

"I'm a threat to them. They can't 'uninvite' me from preaching in two Sundays, and I'm possibly the only individual, with Pastor McFee out of the way, with the means of speaking up against Easterly. Against them. That's what they mean by 'we will pull his teeth by compromising his sister.' They will threaten to release the video of my sister in order to buy my silence."

The nanomites had listened to Zander mutter aloud.

Zander Cruz, the last video in which Izzie Cruz appeared was deceptively altered late last night. Early this morning, to be correct.

"Altered how?"

The man in the video with Izzie does not appear to be Aiden Easterly.

"What? Then who is it?"

*It only **appears** not to be Aiden Easterly, Zander Cruz. The video is what is called a 'deep fake,' a cleverly altered rendition. We knew it was altered on two counts.*

"On two counts?"

Yes. Certainly, we immediately detected the edited frames. We could, if asked, restore the file to its original state. However, we also knew it was fake, because you were home in bed with Jayda Cruz, not here in bed with your sister . . . engaged in a sexual tryst.

Zander stopped and ground his teeth together. Anger toward those who would concoct such a perversion rose in his throat along with the taste of bile.

Do not be concerned, Zander Cruz. As you requested, we have deleted the faked video. Nothing remains of it or of the original video.

Zander breathed in and out several times. "Thank you, Nano. I . . . I have never been personally attacked in such a vile manner—nor do I want to see my sister defamed. Kinda shook me."

We understand, Zander Cruz. Jesus did not want this attack to succeed. You have important work ahead of you.

"Wish I knew what that meant, Nano."

You will. When it is time.

Zander gathered himself. "Nano, next please upload all files where Izzie is mentioned or could be alluded to, then permanently scrub all traces of her—in any file format—from the servers and backups."

While they worked, Zander headed toward the room on the opposite side of the living room. It, too, had its own keypad access point. He reached for the knob, thinking the nanomites had gone before him, and was surprised when it did not turn under his hand.

Zander Cruz, we must caution you: Our scouts do not like what is behind these doors.

Zander snorted. "Why am I not surprised? I mean, what other crazy things will we run into?"

Blowing out a second long breath, he asked, "What, specifically, did you mean by 'our scouts do not like what is behind these doors'? What will I find? A nine-headed hydra? 'Cause I'm thinking that wouldn't faze me at this point."

No Greek mythological water snake awaits you in this room, Zander Cruz. We would tell you if we had detected one. Hydras aside, we cannot adequately explain our scouts' observations. The room is . . . dark. Dark, thick and . . . heavy. Our members cannot fully penetrate that darkness. Those who have returned seem . . . afraid.

Zander's mouth went slack. The nanomite scouts were afraid?

"Have they identified something dangerous in the room?"

*No toxic substances or traps of any kind. Perhaps it is not some**thing** dangerous, Zander Cruz, but some**one** . . . Unfortunately, our scouts are unable to quantify their observations.*

Zander placed his palm on the door—and as quickly jerked it away. A creeping, cloying evil reached cold fingers through the door and touched him. The sensation of icy claws scrabbled across his skin and dug into his flesh, trying to attach itself to him.

"Lord Jesus, help me!" Zander said aloud, stepping back. Then he squared his shoulders. "*No*, devil! I declare that Jesus, God's promised Messiah, is King of Kings and Lord of Lords in this house. I carry his kingdom within me, and in his name I rebuke every unclean spirit within the sound of my voice."

The door slowly swung open, but Zander didn't move. A dense, viscous cloud—an entirely unnatural cloud—filled the room. And a powerful, noxious smell assaulted his nostrils, almost driving him back a second time.

"I proclaim Jesus! I proclaim Jesus the Messiah in this place!" Zander said louder—not trying to awaken the house's residents, but beyond caring if he happened to do so. "I proclaim *that at the name of Jesus every knee must bow, in heaven and on earth, and under the earth, and every tongue acknowledge that Jesus Christ is Lord to the glory of God the Father!*"

The curtain of cloud swirled, then seemed to lift, to pull away toward the ceiling. Was it cringing? Was it afraid?

"You should be afraid, devil," Zander whispered. He stepped into the room and walked forward.

He'd had no idea what to expect—certainly not this.

His feet stumbled to a stop on their own. He turned in a slow circle. "Nano. Nano, are you getting this?"

Yes, Zander Cruz. Recording.

In the far corner of the room, on a dais of some kind, stood a statue close in height to that of a real woman, carved from a single piece of wood. Zander knew the statue from recent news reports, even if it was, in its present condition, nearly unrecognizable. He recalled, too, a police report from Colorado that the nanomites had provided them, a report about another statue's theft, a theft in which Sierra had been a person of interest.

This statue of Mary, stolen from *Madre de Dios*, an old Catholic church in a village south of Albuquerque, had been horribly, grotesquely altered. Distorted. Desecrated. It's body was painted over, the new layer of flesh-toned paint seeming to strip the figure of her modest clothing from the waist up. Zander averted his eyes from the statue's breasts and turned them to the occult symbols and blasphemous words that covered the statue's bare arms, chest, and neck.

He raised his eyes to the statue's face and grimaced. The woman's eyes had been gouged out and replaced with gleaming glass orbs. They were entirely too lifelike, and he looked away.

Finally, he noticed the crude papier-mâché crown, painted gold, that sat on the statue's head. Zander swallowed. He couldn't work out what about the crown repulsed him—until the nanomites brought its virtual image closer. Across the gold paint he read the crown's flowing inscription.

Goddess Ishtar
Queen of Heaven

Zander's eyes dropped below the statue. Around the figure's feet someone had arranged fresh flowers and a dozen flickering candles in tall, narrow glasses. Plates of rotting food sat among the flowers. He squatted to study one of the plates. It displayed a half-dozen palm-sized cakes, their flat surfaces topped with powdered sugar stencils of the goddess.

Zander shook his head. "This is a scene straight out of Jeremiah 44!"

The last two items at the figure's feet sat off to the side: a pot filled with sand impaled by smoking joss sticks. The sick, disgusting smell that had assaulted him when he opened the doors rose from the pot and from . . . the deep bowl beside it.

"Nano, what's that in the bowl? That's not . . . that's not blood, is it?"

It is, Zander Cruz. Goat's blood. Perhaps five days old.

Zander swallowed down his gorge and backed away.

Cushions dotted the floor in front of the statue . . . for kneeling and obeisance. Zander looked down at his feet. The rest of the room's floor was carpeted in soft, spongy mats.

"But what are these for?" he asked himself aloud.

Zander Cruz, we detect multiple DNA samples on the mats covering the floor—an abundance of skin cells, hair, blood, saliva . . . and other bodily fluids.

Zander shuddered. He walked to the door, then turned and faced the room. He lifted both hands toward the throne room in heaven. "I declare and proclaim that Jesus, the only Messiah, is King and Lord over this shrine of demonic worship and over every occult and sinful practice perpetuated in this room and in this house. Holy Spirit of the Living God, come and cleanse this wicked place."

Zander wasn't Elijah, and no fire fell from heaven.

But feel free at any time, Lord.

He pressed his lips tight, closed the doors behind him, and walked on unsteady feet back into the living room. After what the nanomites had found in that loathsome room, he refused to sit on any of the furnishings.

He stood in front of the large living room window, looking out and praying.

"Lord God! I need you to speak to me. I believe you led me here so you might expose Easterly's many deceptions and the gross wickedness practiced in this place. You have also revealed to me the schemes of the rogue DCC board members to force Pastor McFee from his position—and have revealed the board's collusion with Easterly and Missing. These plots are not against Izzie or me or even Pastor McFee, Lord. They are against our church itself, against the Body of Christ at DCC—against *you.*

"More than at any time in my life, I am in need of your wisdom and guidance. Please tell me how to respond to this situation—to the evil I have found, to the plots against your people. Oh, Lord!

"The actions of these wicked men and women remind me of what is written in Psalm 2.

"Why do the nations conspire and the peoples plot in vain?
The kings of the earth rise up and the rulers band together
against the Lord and against his anointed,
saying, 'Let us break their chains
and throw off their shackles.'

"They want to overthrow your church, Lord God, but they have made a big mistake. For this is how you respond to their plots!

"The One enthroned in heaven laughs;
the Lord scoffs at them.

"They may succeed against me, but they will never succeed against you, Father. I ask you to please tell me what you want me to do. How do you wish me to proceed? I trust you."

He waited, prayerfully listening. Almost immediately, he felt impressed to give the nanomites further instructions. Several of them.

We will do all that you ask, Zander Cruz.

"Thank you, Nano. Let's go get Izzie's stuff." Zander took the stairs to the second floor, the nanomites leading him to the bedroom where Izzie had slept. The nanomites went ahead of him, swarming the two women in the bed, sending them into deeper sleep.

Zander saw a cot under the windows, and he recognized Izzie's backpack laying on the cot and picked it up. He didn't see her handbag.

Izzie Cruz's purse is under the cot, Zander Cruz. Her socks and another article of clothing are in Aiden Easterly's bedroom.

Izzie had told Zander where she'd abandoned those articles. She didn't want them back.

"Thanks, Nano. I won't need those things."

Zander ran his hand under the cot. His fingers found the straps of Izzie's purse and pulled the purse toward him. He took a quick look inside, checking that her cell phone, wallet, and car keys were there. Nothing seemed to be missing.

Before Zander went downstairs, he asked the nanomites to go into two other bedrooms and send the occupants of those rooms into deeper sleep. Then he took the stairs down to the living room to wait for Easterly and Missing to wake up and join him.

The Lord had spoken to him. He knew he wouldn't have to wait long.

⌘

STAN MISSING SAT STRAIGHT up in bed, alert and agitated. "Aiden. Wake up. *Wake up!*"

Easterly rubbed his face. "What is it?"

Anger simmered within Missing. "Can't you feel it? Someone has disturbed the goddess."

"What? That's not possible! Her shrine is as secure as a locked vault."

"Apparently it *is* possible, and she is *not* happy about it. So, get up. We have an intruder."

Easterly pulled on pants. "Who?"

"Does it matter? Whoever has defiled her shrine will pay, and the goddess—blessed be her name—demands compensation. Time for another sacrifice, I think."

Missing loaded a revolver as they walked into the upstairs hall. He jerked his head at Easterly. "Go to the others and quietly awaken them. Tell them to hurry, though. No doubt we'll need their help subduing our sacrificial goat. Oh. And have everyone bring their phones. The house cameras will capture the action, but additional angles will add to our enjoyment afterward."

Easterly padded quietly to the first bedroom and eased open the door. Went into Sierra and Dinae's room. He jostled Dinae's arm.

"Dinae. Hey, wake up. Dinae! Wake up."

No response.

Frowning, he walked to the other side of the bed. "Sierra? Sierra!"

He pinched her hand. Again, no response.

He shot across the hall. A quick check of the other bedrooms yielded the same result.

"Stan, something's wrong. I can't awaken anyone."

Missing thought for a moment. "Go back to our room. Get the other gun out of my drawer and load it. You know where."

"Sure."

Easterly was back a moment later, tapping an old .38 Special against his leg.

"What's with the nerves?"

"I couldn't wake them up, Stan. That's strange, don't you think?"

"Perhaps the goddess wishes the two of us alone to offer this sacrifice to her."

Easterly nodded. "Okay. I'm ready."

They walked as stealthily as they could manage down the stairs, but could not prevent the steps from creaking when they reached the first landing.

Missing cursed under his breath, then nudged Easterly. "Keep going," he mouthed.

They tiptoed to the second landing, then down the last four steps, Crept down the hall to where it emptied into the living room.

Zander flexed his hands before he turned from the window to face them. "I've been waiting for you two."

Missing raised his gun. "*You*. Let me guess—baby sister ran crying home to her big, handsome brother. Yet, you breaking and entering? That's not going to play well with your friends and admirers at DCC."

"Neither will video of the abomination you have locked away in that side room."

"Oh, I don't think we'll air *that* at church, do you? But speaking of video, would you care to see one starring your sister?"

Zander drew a calming breath. "I'm sorry. I'm afraid that film has been discontinued."

Easterly lifted his phone, thumbed an icon. Smiled. "Well, look at this! I have a copy right here." He increased the volume, and Zander heard Easterly's whispers and Izzie's breathless voice.

Zander's face hardened. "I see you have a copy of the original on your phone, not the deep fake."

"No worries. I'm quite the editor. The finished product will be ready for release by tonight."

Missing stepped in. "Not that we'll have a need to release it . . . after you're dead. It's great, in fact, that you broke into our home. Saves us the hassle of hunting you down, plus the goddess will be pleased with our offering."

"Your goddess is a dead, carved-up *tree trunk*, Stan. Yup, she's a real *blockhead*."

Missing ground his teeth. "You shouldn't make light of her, Cruz. You don't know who you're messing with."

"Nor, apparently, do you. The 'goddess' you commune with is actually a demonic spirit. But not to worry: The Lord Almighty, the Creator of the Universe, defeated Satan and his demonic hordes on the cross. So, what's your painted stump going to do when the Ancient of Days shoots a bolt of lightning into her? Oh, yeah. That's right: *She'll burn*."

Zander flicked his eyes toward Easterly. "Uh, Easterly, that video you're so proud of? You might want to take another look."

Easterly glanced at his phone. Where the video had been, a blank icon sat on the screen. He tapped it. Tapped it again. "What did you do?"

"Deleted it. I should delete everything, though. Delete everything off every phone in the house, including the OS. Kind of a 'tower of Babel' move: Create enough confusion to keep you and your cult following busy for days."

Easterly's eyes were drawn again to his phone. "Hey, Stan! All the apps are disappearing from my phone! Wait—it powered off!"

Missing, never taking his eyes off Zander, smiled at him. "It doesn't matter. Cruz is gonna disappear, too."

Zander tsked. "I don't think so. And the video only matters if you were planning to get rid of me via blackmail. That, too, isn't gonna happen."

"You think removing you is the end of it? You think we were sent to this hick town without a bigger plan in place?" Missing studied Zander. "Besides, you breaking into our house is better than blackmail."

He raised his gun and fired.

The bullet came within a foot of Zander before it bounced back—looking as though it had struck an invisible but spongy wall that arrested the bullet's momentum before spitting it back.

The bullet fell harmlessly to the tiled floor with a distinctive *clink*.

"What the *blank*?" Missing, his eyes wild, fired again—with the same result. Zander flicked a finger and the gun flew from Missing's hand.

"*Yow!*" The man clutched his arm and cursed.

"Stings, doesn't it?" Zander chuckled.

The nanomites stung Easterly's fingers, too. He lost his grip on his weapon, and it dropped to the floor, leaving Easterly frantic.

"Stan! Stan, how's he doing this?"

Missing retreated a few feet and stood beside Easterly. "I don't know, but the goddess is not pleased."

Zander exhaled. Cleared his throat. "I came to get what belongs to Izzie—her purse and backpack. I have them. I also came to claim all the videos you illegally recorded of her. I have them, too."

*In point of fact, I have **all** the video files.*

"I'll be leaving now." He picked up Izzie's purse and backpack and moved toward the door. Stopped. Turned back.

"I'd like to warn you guys off, tell you to leave town—as clichéd as that might sound—but that's not what the Lord told me to say. What he said is found in—"

"Ha! Really?" Clutching his sore hand, Missing sneered at Zander. "Is this where you go all 'Thus sayeth the Lord' on us?"

Zander lifted his brows. "No need. He said it in Revelation 9, verses 20 and 21. It's there for all to see, even you. He asked me to remind you of it.

"The rest of mankind who were not killed by these plagues
still did not repent of the work of their hands;
they did not stop worshiping demons,
and idols of gold, silver, bronze, stone and wood
—idols that cannot see or hear or walk.
Nor did they repent of their murders, their magic arts,
their sexual immorality or their thefts.

"The Lord invites you to repent, Stan. He invites you to repent, too, Aiden. However, because your minds are thoroughly depraved, unless the Lord by his Spirit moves upon your hearts to soften them, it is unlikely that you will respond. He's written that down, too. Romans 1, verses 28-32. Unless you cry out to God for merciful conviction and earnestly seek a repentant heart, your fates, Stan and Aiden, are sealed.

"Furthermore, just as they did not think it worthwhile
to retain the knowledge of God,
so God gave them over to a depraved mind,
so that they do what ought not to be done.
They have become filled with every kind of wickedness,
evil, greed and depravity.
They are full of envy, murder, strife, deceit and malice.
They are gossips, slanderers, God-haters,
insolent, arrogant and boastful;
they invent ways of doing evil;
they disobey their parents;
they have no understanding, no fidelity, no love, no mercy.
Although they know God's righteous decree that
those who do such things deserve death,
they not only continue to do these very things
but also approve of those who practice them.

"Save your vile, homophobic hatred for church," Missing snarled, "not that you'll be welcome there much longer. We have your precious DCC stitched up tight. It will be ours shortly."

Easterly cut in. "And as our first act when DCC is ours? Stan and I will be married in the sanctuary."

Zander shook his head. "Over my dead body."

Missing tsked. "We can arrange that."

Zander nodded. "So you say. All right, then. See you in church."

⌘⌘⌘⌘

CHAPTER 24

ZANDER POINTED IZZIE'S CAR toward home. As he drove, he alternately prayed and revisited what he'd seen and heard while at Easterly's house.

"Nano, play back the audio of my exchange with Easterly and Missing."

He listened. "Stop there, Nano. Play that last bit again."

Zander again heard Missing's cryptic but telling statement.

"You think removing you is the end of it? You think we were sent to this hick town without a bigger plan in place?"

"Missing and Easterly aren't acting alone. They were sent here."

We surmised the same from this statement, Zander Cruz.

"Yeah, but sent by whom?"

We cannot answer your question at this time, Zander Cruz, but we are looking into it.

Zander again prayed. "Lord? I desperately need your guidance! It's obvious that Missing and Easterly perform idolatrous and aberrant acts in that house, but they have committed crimes, too: the theft of that statue from *Madre de Dios* church. Illegal recordings. Attempted blackmail. Perhaps even . . . human sacrifice."

Zander glanced at the clock on the car's dash. "Nano, I need to know where Pastor and Mrs. McFee are."

Their flight to Oahu is in the air, Zander Cruz.

"Is there any way to reach them? Will Pastor McFee's phone work during the flight?"

Only if they purchase the onboard cellular service. We can bypass the purchase and initiate the call for you, Zander Cruz.

"Yes. Please do so."

Zander pulled into a parking lot and turned off the car. He waited while the nanomites worked.

Initiating the call now, Zander Cruz.

The phone on the other end began to ring. It rang multiple times. Zander was ready to give up and try again later when he heard the call pick up.

"Hello?" Pastor McFee sounded confused.

"Pastor McFee? This is Zander Cruz. I'm sorry to interrupt you as you begin your well-deserved vacation."

"Zander? I . . . I don't know how you were able to place this call!"

"I, um, I have something of an 'in' with the airline's service provider." *Literally **in** the service provider.*

McFee sighed. "Well, if I'm being honest, I am glad to hear your voice."

"Something wrong, Pastor?" Zander asked.

"More than you know," came the reply.

I wouldn't bet on that, Zander said to himself.

McFee cleared his throat. "I'm sorry. I know you called me, not the other way around, but there are things I've learned in the past thirty hours or so, things you need to know. However, I should find a more private place to speak. Give me a minute."

Zander heard rustling as McFee left his seat and moved along the aisle. Then he heard the slide and click of a door. "Thank God the wonderful people of DCC upgraded our tickets to first class. No line to the restroom. I'm free to speak my heart now. Do you have time to listen?"

"Yes, sir."

"Well, here's the bottom line. They're going to force me out, Zander. It'll happen while Carol and I are on our cruise, but it'll be a *fait accompli* when I return."

"They can do that? I thought . . . I thought the membership had to vote on something as big as a removal."

"Things have changed in the past few weeks—and quickly. Remember that board member we talked about? Harry Fuentes?"

"The swing vote?"

"Him. I couldn't figure out why he folded so fast during Easterly's selection process. I thought he was worried about the church's finances. Turns out, he was worried about his own."

"Oh?"

"He called me late yesterday afternoon, asked me to meet him down by Tingley Beach. All hush-hush and surreptitious. We walked from the beach over into the Bosque and down to the river where we were pretty certain to be alone. There he unburdened himself.

"I knew that one of his little grandkids was sick, but I didn't know the child had an expensive, lingering disease. Harry's daughter-in-law quit her job to stay home and take care of the child, but Harry's son cannot support the family on his salary alone.

"With the added treatment and prescription copays, transportation and lodging to see an out-of-network specialist in Texas, the extra costs of the specialist and his hospital that their insurance won't fully cover, they ran out of money.

"Harry and his wife, Anna, tapped into their savings and their IRA to help them out. When their savings were pretty much gone, too, Harry and Anna decided to refi their house. However, they are both retired and didn't have the income to afford the house payments."

Zander heard the anger in McFee's voice. "That's when Mike Barnes, spokesman for our left-leaning board members, offered to refinance the house himself. When more expenses came along and Harry was late on several house payments, Barnes told him, 'No worries. We're all one family here.'"

Zander saw where McFee was going. "They have a stranglehold on the poor guy."

"Yes, they do. Harry and his wife are at least five grand behind on their house payments. As long as he plays nice and votes the way he's told to, Barnes says he won't foreclose on their home."

"That's like some cheesy, Depression-era, silent movie schtick with the heroine tied up on the train tracks!" Zander growled.

"Harry and Anna are at the end of their rope, Zander, but that's not the whole story. Harry spilled everything to me: How Barnes and his side of the board trapped him, how they amended some of the church rules on the QT by reinterpreting a few lines of ambiguous text, and how they intend to get rid of me. Not vote me out, mind you, but send me off into a lovely, cushy retirement as soon as we return from our cruise."

"But Fuentes is only one board member! What about the rest? Why aren't they screaming for help?"

"Barnes and his people have Victor Gibson, another of my staunch supporters, in their pocket, too—or should I say *in their clutches*. They caught him in a sexually explicit situation with some young woman from DCC—from our young adult group, can you believe it? Victor is fifty-one, for heaven's sake, and happily married! He swears it was a setup, that she tried to seduce him, went after him like a terrier after a rat. He also swears that he turned her down flat."

McFee's voice dropped to a whisper. "Apparently, Barnes has photos of their encounter. He threatened to send copies to Victor's wife. What mystifies me is why a young, attractive woman would want to entice a man of his age."

Zander felt sick to his stomach. "Do you know her name? The young woman's name?"

"Oh, Sabrina or Selena or something. Dear Lord God, what is happening?"

"Pastor, was her name Sierra?"

McFee thought a moment. "Yes, I believe it was."

Zander exhaled. "I think I can tell you exactly what is happening—however, it will take so much time to explain all the details, that you'll have frustrated passengers banging on the restroom doors long before we are finished."

He pondered his options. "Pastor, may I, instead, send you a detailed email, one you can study and pray over? I'll send the email within the next hour or two."

"I suppose I can buy Wi-Fi on this flight."

"Uh, well, I have an 'in' with the airline's Wi-Fi provider, remember? Check your email in a hour or two. I'll include a few questions I would ask you to answer in your reply. Your email will reach me, even if it doesn't look like you're connected to the network."

"Had no idea you were so tech-savvy, Zander."

"Yeah, um, it's a . . . gift, I suppose."

"Thank God for his many gifts!"

"Yes, amen! Well, I should get off the phone and write that email, Pastor."

"Thank you, Zander, but before you go, let's pray."

McFee led them in a short but heartfelt prayer. "Father, Zander and I come to you in the name of your Son, Jesus. Please uncover what is happening, all that the enemy is plotting, and grant us the discernment, wisdom, and guidance to deal with it. Amen."

"Amen," Zander echoed

"The Lord bless you, Zander."

Instead of continuing home after hanging up, Zander sat in Izzie's car composing his email to Pastor McFee. Before he sent it, he reviewed the files the nanomites had uploaded from the servers in Easterly's house, setting aside a few images.

"Nano, please download these photos to my phone."

Done, Zander Cruz.

He focused next on video the nanomites had recorded from the time he entered Easterly's house until he left it. He slowly scanned through it, stopping at select places.

"Nano, save the images here, here, and here. Also, save as a separate file the portion of video where I'm talking with Easterly and Missing. Oh. And cut the bit where Missing fired his gun at me. I don't want to explain to Pastor McFee how those bullets bounced off of me."

That would be problematic, Zander Cruz.

"Right you are, Nano."

Zander selected and attached several files to his email, reviewed the letter a last time, tweaked a few words, and sent it. The nanomites would make certain it was delivered to Pastor McFee's inbox.

⌘

Because our nanoclouds were nearly always in touch, Zander and I were usually in touch, too. That's how, in the warehouse via the two nanoclouds, I had kept up with Zander while he roamed Easterly's house. I saw what he saw and experienced much of what he did. I also listened in on his conversation with Pastor McFee.

While I observed Zander's progress, I stayed in the kitchen, praying for him and drinking more coffee than usual. Izzie and Emilio were ensconced on the couch watching the Rose Bowl parade.

"Stupid news!" Emilio shouted.

I poked my head out of the kitchen. "Problem?"

"Missed the best marching band in that parade," Emilio groused. "Stupid news keeps interrupting."

I looked at Izzie. "What news?"

"Apparently, there were a bunch of New Year's Eve riots," she said. Unlike Emilio, she was glued to the TV, intent on an earnest, seasoned newscaster whose solemn face took up the screen.

I sat down with them in time to hear the woman say, "Governors and law enforcement are at a loss as to what triggered riots across fifteen states. Listen as a first-hand witness tells our station what he saw . . . and experienced."

The screen cut to a video of a young man seated on the bumper of an ambulance. A paramedic was trying to staunch a bleeding wound on the young man's forehead.

"We were enjoying the countdown to the New Year, you know? About five minutes before midnight, I noticed a bunch of the people around us putting on ski masks. Next thing I know, they pull out sticks and clubs, then start beating their way through the crowd! I mean, it made no sense, no sense at all. They hit and beat on anyone they were near—totally random.

"The crowd freaked out, of course, and pretty soon people were falling down and getting trampled. These people wearing masks shouted all kinds of stuff, like 'Hey hey, ho ho, intolerance must go!' and 'down with fascist pigs!' but all I could think was *why?* Everyone was having a good time."

The camera zoomed in, and I saw tears coursing down the young man's face. "I was able to get to the edge of the crowd. There I saw two cops, guys who had been stationed at one of the barricades. The rioters forced them to the ground, and beat them, I mean with clubs and stuff. No one deserves to be treated like that. I hope they are all right . . ."

The screen returned to the newscaster. "Another witness told our on-scene reporter that, in what looked like a preplanned and coordinated move, several rioters, holding out large bags, circulated among the other rioters. The rioters pulled off their masks, dumped them and their weapons into one of the bags, then blended into the crowd, disappearing as quickly as they had appeared. The entire episode lasted less than twenty minutes."

The newscaster looked up from his notes. "Unfortunately, our on-scene reporter also tells us that both police officers were taken to a nearby hospital where they were pronounced dead."

"Oh, no," Izzie moaned. "How could they do that! What is happening?"

Emilio, finally catching on to the reason the news had broken in on the parade, looked at me. His eyes told me he was more scared than he wanted to let on. "Why they do that, Jayda? Why they hurt them people?"

"I don't know, sweetheart. I don't know."

Emilio's brows knotted together. "They better not try none of that *blank* here. You an' Zander'd fix 'em good."

Izzie tore her eyes from the screen. "What's that?"

I shook my head. "Nothing, Iz."

To Emilio, I added softly, "Language, *mijo*."

He knew "language" meant more than his curse word: Izzie was not privy to the existence of the nanomites nor did we want her to be.

He stared back in defiance. "Well, they better not!"

Hoping to distract him, I said, "How about I fix us something to eat?"

But Emilio wasn't easily distracted. "Yeah. Whatever."

I didn't correct him again. Some battles weren't worth the effort.

So long as we eventually win the war, Lord, I prayed silently.

⌘

WHEN BREAKFAST WAS READY, Emilio and Izzie took their plates to the couch. The parade was again in full swing. I ate my breakfast in the kitchen, alternating bites while cleaning up and while scanning various newsfeeds for more details on the riots. I was appalled at what I learned.

Forty-three US cities in fifteen states had been struck by the strange but certainly coordinated riots. Among the cities hit were the usual suspects, large, urban metropolises like Boston, Chicago, Minneapolis, Milwaukee, Detroit, Cleveland, Pittsburgh, New York City, DC, Miami, Orlando, Kansas City, Dallas, Denver, Los Angeles, San Francisco, Las Vegas, Portland, and Seattle.

And not US cities alone. Riots or protests-turned-violent had taken place in most major cities across the world: Toronto, Sydney, Melbourne, Seoul, New Delhi, Paris, London, Berlin, Copenhagen, Amsterdam, Rome, Madrid, Lisbon, Warsaw, Stockholm.

I frowned. *Riots only in what are mostly democratic nations?*

Soon, video of New Year's venues where the most unusual and unexpected riots occurred filled the screen, each one more shocking than the last. Inside Disney World, a mob had stormed the iconic Cinderella Castle, breaking out its stained glass windows, leaving destruction in its wake. In Memphis, rioters had set fire to Graceland. One wing of Elvis' home burned to the ground. The damage to what remained was inestimable. In Rome, the historic Spanish Steps and the *Fontana della Barcaccia*—the Fountain of the Boat—had both been spray painted with grotesque and obscene images and slogans.

I picked up Izzie and Emilio's dirty dishes and cleaned up the kitchen. I had joined them on the couch when the nanomites spoke to me.

Jayda Cruz, we have information to share with you. Please leave Izzie and Emilio and go into your bathroom.

Go into my bathroom? I knew the nanomites' information wasn't about Zander, so what was the big deal?

"Why can't you show me in the warehouse like you usually do, Nano?"

You will be too engrossed in what we have to tell you, Jayda Cruz.

Emilio was snuggled up against my side, full and content, no longer upset and angry. I hated to disturb him, so I sat there without saying anything for a minute. I must have sighed.

Emilio, an intuitive young man, asked. "What the matter, Jayda?"

"I need to use the restroom. Um, I might be in there a little while."

Izzie looked over. "Is it your tummy, Jayda?"

"Not sure. Things are a little 'off.' I'll be back soon as I know . . . what's going on."

I locked our bedroom door after me, went into the master bathroom, and locked that door behind me, too. "All right, Nano. What's up? Why the secrecy?"

Jayda Cruz, we have not said anything to you about this because, while we have had concerns, we had not gathered enough evidence to support those concerns. We have been especially vigilant to watch our areas of concern.

"Areas of concern, meaning more than one? And you have evidence to support these concerns? Please show me what's going on."

They brought up a map in satellite view. A large urban area, a sizable river cutting through it. Nothing I readily recognized.

"What am I looking at?"

They zoomed in and focused on a building complex. *This is a large virology laboratory located inland of the Chinese eastern seaboard. They do extensive testing of viruses found in the wild and have identified many viruses endemic to bats.*

The view shifted.

"And?"

This is a university in the same town, a university heavily invested in joint virus research with universities in the US and Kakinada, India.

"And?"

Three Chinese university employees were admitted to a local hospital with symptoms of acute influenza. That was ten days ago.

I opened my mouth, then shut it, trying to fit the nanomites' three statements together into a single scenario: A Chinese virology lab. A Chinese university in partnership with an American and an Indian university. Three employees of the Chinese university with acute influenza.

Then it clicked: The Chinese university was located near the Chinese virology lab.

"Are university scientists working with the virology lab?"

We can confirm visits between the two institutions' employees.

I swallowed. "Go on."

Information on the sick employees from the Chinese university was not updated until late last night, which was this morning, New Year's Day, in China. The number hospitalized for the same illness has risen dramatically.

"How many?"

Seventy-nine, Jayda Cruz.

"Seventy-nine hospitalized employees from the Chinese university?"

Employees and their families, Jayda Cruz, from both the university and the virology laboratory.

A sense of dread crept over me. "What of the original sick employees, Nano?"

That information is not publicly available, Jayda Cruz. We penetrated the hospital network and uncovered several important pieces of information. We shall list them chronologically for you: One, the initial three employees of the Chinese university died six days after hospitalization. Two, another nine individuals admitted to hospital have expired since then. Three, the Chinese government brought in its military in an attempt to control the situation.

The military has locked down the hospital, the university, the virology lab, and a large portion of the city. They are actively censoring the flow of information concerning the illness. They are discussing the option of locking down a ten-mile area around the city. We project they will do so soon.

However, of immediate concern to us, we have determined that a flight originating in China is being piloted by an individual whose wife works at the infected hospital and who was hospitalized with the virus as the flight was departing. The flight piloted by this man, who is likely also infected, will land in Seattle in two hours.

"I . . . we have to . . . someone needs to stop that plane!"

We agree, Jayda Cruz; however, we have more information, and it is not welcome news. The lead scientist of the US university that is partnered with the infected Chinese university was found dead yesterday morning in his home. The cause of death has not been reported, but we are confident that it is the same illness as is being experienced in the Chinese university. Moreover, two scientists from the university in India were hospitalized three nights ago.

"Then this can't be a natural outbreak, can it? Not if it presents with more than one vector?"

This illness is decidedly not natural, Jayda Cruz, not in its virulence, transmissibility, or morbidity. It is highly contagious, leaping the highest levels of containment protocols—biosafety level 4. Nevertheless, as you noted, the contagion has appeared near-simultaneously in three geographically distanced locations, which is indicative of a human-engineered illness and a deliberately coordinated viral delivery.

"The Chinese university sent samples of this thing to the American and Indian universities."

Yes, and the virus overcame all safety protocols.

"That flight arriving from China in two hours? We need to speak to President Jackson."

Yes, Jayda Cruz. Shall we interrupt him?

"Please. Tell him it is urgent and time-sensitive."

I returned to the living room to grab my phone. Izzie started to ask me how I felt. I waved her away and kept moving. The nanomites had been right to ask me to come aside. I would not have been able to focus on this while seated next to Emilio and Izzie.

My thoughts were churning. If a virus could escape BSL-4 containment, then what else could stop it? And if people in the US were sick from it, the bug was spreading *right now.*

Emilio and Izzie. Abe. Zander!

I placed my hands on my belly and was rewarded with a sturdy kick near my right ribs.

Baby Cruz.

Jayda Cruz, we will connect your phone to the President if you are ready.

"Please do, Nano."

A moment later I heard, "Ms. Cruz? This is Robert Jackson."

"Good morning, Mr. President." I said. "I apologize for interrupting what should be family time."

Jackson laughed. "This had better be good. My team is about to win a bowl game—first time in thirty-two years!"

"Yes, sir. Then I'm even more sorry to ruin your holiday."

"Ruin my holiday? It's that bad?"

"Worse, sir."

Zander walked in as I spoke, the nanomites unlocking the bedroom and bathroom doors for him, locking them behind him. The mites were catching him up on the emerging epidemic as he joined me.

Robert Jackson asked, "You certain about this, Jayda? I require proof to justify to the public my quarantining that flight."

"Mr. President," I said patiently, "the nanomites have downloaded to your computer the information they have collected. It is verifiable, although the Chinese government will do all in its power *not* to officially comment on it. Perhaps the Indian government will be more forthcoming.

"What is most important *at this moment*, is preventing the passengers on that flight from entering our general population. That said, the inbound flight is not the only source of infection threatening the US. Employees at the American university that received virus samples have been also exposed, and one US scientist has died. Quarantining the flight from China will mean the difference between fighting the virus on two fronts or on one."

"Got it. Scanning through the data now."

One hour remained before that flight landed and disgorged its crew and passengers onto US soil when Jackson looked up.

"All right. I'll do it. I'll . . . mobilize the military to quarantine the flight, the university and its employees, and the deceased scientist's family. Exigent circumstances. Use the military while the CDC and USAMRIID prep their teams to take over."

⌘

WHEN WE HUNG UP WITH the President, I said, "Nano? You've been busy on more than one front—and we've been pretty preoccupied. What about the R&A work you're doing for the President? How's that going?

Jayda Cruz, to date we have submitted evidence of seventeen hundred fifty-three prosecutable instances of Medicare provider fraud, nine hundred seventy-two prosecutable instances of Medicare client fraud, six thousand thirteen prosecutable instances of Medicaid provider fraud, and fifty-seven hundred prosecutable instances of identity theft with the use of stolen Social Security cards.

"Good job, Nano. The President must be pleased."

He is, Jayda Cruz; however, he is more intent on the misappropriation of federal funds within the intelligence community.

"And how's that going?"

We are not prepared to discuss our progress at this time, Jayda Cruz.

I stuttered a moment before I could spit out, "You aren't prepared to discuss your progress at this time?"

Yes, that is what we said, Jayda Cruz.

"Nano, you promised not to hide anything from me. And I'm overseeing your work, remember?"

We are not hiding anything. If you care to view our research, it is available to you.

"But you won't tell me where it's taking you?"

We are not prepared to report anything at this time.

I blew out a breath. *Don't let them get to you, Jayda. Baby Cruz needs a calm mama while he's in the oven. And after he's out.*

"Have you discussed your findings with the President?"

No, Jayda Cruz. We are not prepared to discuss our progress at this time.

I sniffed. "So you say."

You turkeys.

⌘⌘⌘⌘

CHAPTER 25

PRESIDENT JACKSON DIDN'T WAIT for the media to report the military's quarantine of the flight from China on New Year's Day or for his political foes to take aim at him. He notified the nation that he would address them the following evening. Zander and I watched the President's speech live on my iPad.

By that time, the news had leaked: The pilot and co-pilot of the flight from China were hospitalized in critical condition, and a large number of the passengers were ill. FEMA had taken over a hotel to house those not yet symptomatic. The military maintained a guard around the hotel perimeter, while the CDC set up a "wellness check" area in the lobby. No one else was allowed in or out.

President Jackson's address was short and to the point.

"Good evening, fellow Americans—please do not panic. Yes, we halted a plane that originated in China and was carrying passengers infected with a novel virus. Why did we do this? Because we are unfamiliar with the virus. That means we don't know how it is transmitted or how dangerous it is—but mark my words, we will find out.

"Some in the media and across the aisle view my order to ground the plane and quarantine its passengers as an extreme action. No, it was not extreme; it was a prudent, merciful, and successful move on our part. Passengers and crew from the plane who are sick are receiving the best care available anywhere, whether they are American citizens or visitors to our great nation. Equally important, those who are ill will not mingle with the general population and unknowingly infect others.

"I said a moment ago that we don't know the answers to two questions—how the virus is transmitted or how dangerous it is. The good news is that the CDC is on the ground in Seattle, doing what they do best: learning about the virus so that we might contain it. Until we find the answers we seek, my administration will take every precaution to keep the virus from spreading to the American people."

He didn't mention the American university or its dead scientist. Apparently, that information hadn't reached the press.

"So, I urge you again, please do not panic. We will keep you informed as we go forward. Thank you, and God bless each of you."

"That was pretty good," I said.

"Short and sweet."

"He needed to get the other party off his back and change the narrative from 'President's extreme and possibly illegal actions threaten democracy' to 'President's actions protect Americans everywhere.'"

"You should have been a speech writer."

"*Please*. Shoot me now!"

We laughed and set the issue aside until morning.

But when we got up the following morning, the headline from a Seattle news outlet slapped us across the face.

Seven Virus Cases Identified in Travelers Recently Returned from China

⌘

BY SATURDAY, ONLY FOUR days later, Seattle had quarantined twenty-two suspected cases from the plane, Los Angeles had hospitalized ten Americans recently returned from China, and Vancouver, BC, vaguely reported "the hospitalization of a number of patients from a plane originating in Hong Kong." As the number of suspected cases continued to climb throughout the day, President Jackson's administration was swept into full-on crisis mode.

The infected university made it into the news, too, but apparently the deceased scientist had been the only university employee to touch the sample sent from China, and he was an unmarried man who lived alone. The school and its labs were shut down, their employees confined to their homes under strict warning. No one else in that area, however, became ill.

Meanwhile, the nanomites reported to us that the CDC did not attempt to retrieve the sample. Instead, they requested military specialists with flamethrowers. Under conditions tightly controlled by a military fire suppression team, the specialists identified the virus samples and burned them from a healthy distance, after which the CDC locked down the laboratory where they were found.

Those details were *not* released to the media.

That evening, the President addressed the nation a second time. "My fellow Americans, although this virus has made its way to our shores, I again urge you not to panic. I can assure you that my administration has every American resource working around the clock to analyze the virus and determine the best treatment protocols."

"How will they analyze it if it's so dangerous that our highest biosafety levels can't contain it?" I asked Zander.

President Jackson continued. "Bottom line? Until we know how this disease is passed, we, as a nation, should exercise restraint. By restraint, I mean that you do not need to prepare for a siege and buy up a year's worth of supplies. We are in this together, and when your fellow Americans go to the stores they should not find shelves emptied by their panicked neighbors.

"I also recommend that we as a nation take *reasonable* but not over-zealous precautions. If you are older, have underlying health conditions, or are immunocompromised, *stay home*. Self-quarantine to protect yourself. For the majority of the population? You may feel it wise to wear a mask if you are in a crowd, but please note that this is a suggestion only. In fact, as your fellow American, I am *asking* every citizen to exercise kindness and compassion toward others by wearing a mask.

"However, as president of this great land, I refuse to issue draconian orders that, constitutionally, are not mine to issue. Nor am I willing to trade our precious God-given liberties, those liberties enshrined in our constitution, for what some might call a 'necessary safeguard.' In my experience, whenever the government encroaches on our liberties in the name of one emergency or another, the end result is always a permanent state of emergency and permanent degradation of those liberties—and those I will not sanction.

"So, let me close with my opening words: My fellow Americans, please do not panic. If you need to stay home and protect yourself, do so. For the majority of the population? I recommend caution and urge restraint. Let's come together on this issue rather than allow it to divide us. Let's be wise, kind, and considerate of others, and let's beat this thing together.

"Thank you, and God bless America."

Zander and I looked at each other.

"I like his approach," I said. "Be wise and be considerate of others."

"Yes, but I think it's too great an opportunity for those who wish to exercise more control over the American people. The President doesn't have the authority to issue mandatory health orders because that power is not enumerated in the constitution, and any federal authority not enumerated in the constitution automatically devolves to the state level. So, if the virus spreads, I don't think it will be long before we see all sorts of 'emergency measures' issued state by state."

I frowned. "I hope not."

"Guess we'll see."

⌘

OVER THE FOLLOWING WEEK, news outlets covered one and only one thing: the virus. Social media burgeoned with fact, fiction, urban legends, conspiracy theories, and every possible spin. And for the first time in my life, I found myself buying into some of the "conspiracy theories" the media sneered at. It helped having two nanoclouds sorting truth from fiction and adding essential facts.

For example, we learned that, from an epidemiological point of view, the virus had to have been human manufactured or, at the very least, found in nature and then weaponized, amplified through "gain-of-function" manipulation. We knew the virus had been deliberately transmitted, too, because no virus in its natural state has three simultaneous vectors, three coinciding outbreaks in geographically separate and disparate parts of the world.

Someone had to have transported virus samples to the Chinese, American, and Indian university labs for "study"—and they had to have done so in a manner that ensured near simultaneous arrival at the three labs. We speculated that *courier delivery* was the most accurate means of ensuring the simultaneous arrival of the virus samples. The nanomites were searching for proof to bolster our theory.

It would also have been less feasible for one university lab to have engineered the virus then passed it to the other two labs without the originating lab demonstrating infection before the others.

Who was behind the virus? Our prime suspects were Chinese scientists and their Wuhan virology lab, but that supposition seemed too convenient, almost as though someone had painted a bullseye on the Chinese government. Our theories, however, remained unsubstantiated as proof of the bug's origins eluded the nanoclouds' best efforts to uncover. They had not given up their search, though. No, they were working harder than ever.

I will say, as the days passed by, that I grew puzzled. The nanomites were digging hard into the convoluted finances of the US government— that was their primary task, after all—but they had also immersed them-selves into their investigations on the virus with equal fervor.

Equal fervor? The nanomites were stretched so thin on both projects ("thin" being a term I never expected to apply to them) that we scarcely heard from them day to day. But why chase both investigations with the same ferocity when the two could not possibly be related?

Or could they? I had a sneaking suspicion that the nanomites knew more than they were telling us.

But back to the virus. Over the next days and weeks, we and most of America followed the news reports tracking the spread of the virus—and it *was* spreading. California seemed hardest hit at present, although the number of cases in Washington State had doubled, then tripled.

As cases multiplied, President Jackson enacted more restrictions on air traffic coming in and out of the country, hoping to prevent additional outbreaks. Then, in an effort to prevent the *export* of the virus to other nations, he shut down all international air traffic, inclusive of shipping, for a trial period of two weeks.

What upset me most about the media was the mix of criticisms directed at President Jackson. For example, he was denounced by several networks for quarantining the flight from China we had warned him of. Conversely, when crew and passengers from that flight took sick (justifying Jackson's actions), those same newscasters contracted severe cases of *amnesia*, turning their attention, instead, to the American university where Jackson had dispatched the military to—*carefully* and under strict supervision—transfer whatever research on the virus they had been conducting to the military's version of the CDC, the US Army Medical Research Institute of Infectious Diseases or USAMRIID.

(An aside? Given that Vice President Delancey had obtained his bio-weapon spray from a yet-unidentified employee at USAMRIID, *that* move didn't comfort me much.)

"Exigent circumstances, my left foot," one "expert" intoned with a huff. "Jackson's actions are patently illegal!"

They ignored the total of six hundred sixty-two cases confirmed in the US only a week after quarantining the flight, and the more than two hundred deaths a week later. I think they would sooner drink poison than admit to the President being right about anything.

On the flip side? *Members of the President's own party* criticized him for not closing down all American airspace sooner.

I folded my arms over my growing baby bump and snorted in derision. "There's no pleasing any of those career political hacks," I mumbled to Zander.

"Amen to that," he replied.

⌘

ZANDER CRUZ, JAYDA CRUZ, *based on recent virus spread projections, we advise that you stock up on groceries and household needs before supplies run out.*

"I don't mind getting ahead some, but I refuse to hog stuff like a few people are doing, cleaning out the shelves entirely," Zander said. "And this is America, the breadbasket of the world. We're not going to run out of food."

Zander Cruz, we have concerns regarding the supply chain.

"What concerns?"

If the virus spreads as we project—

"Wait. If it spreads as you project? What do you mean?"

Zander Cruz, our projections, based on the infection rate, show that within the next few months, large numbers of the population will be infected and quarantined. Consider that trucks and rails move most of the food raised in this country. Also consider that imported foods arrive by truck, rail, and ship. If truck drivers, railroad employees, cargo ship companies, and port of entry staff are hit with high numbers of virus exposures and infections, followed by mandatory two-week quarantines, food deliveries will be delayed. We project that the supply chain will be significantly impacted by this virus, making some foods and goods unavailable entirely, for weeks or months at a time.

Zander blinked hard. "You're sure about this?"

Yes, Zander Cruz. Please follow our advice and stock up on groceries and household needs before supplies run out.

I thought for a minute. "Well, you know how much food the two of us eat each week, right? Eating light would take the two of us down faster than it would people with regular metabolisms—and we need to consider Baby Cruz. I have three months to go before our baby reaches term."

Zander frowned. "I hadn't considered all this. How do you think we should prepare, Jay?"

"Well, how about we make a Walmart run, buying up a reasonable stockpile, say two or three weeks' worth. Then, each week, we should buy a little extra to keep us topped off?

"Sounds about right. Prudent but not extreme."

"What about Abe and Emilio?"

"We'll buy for them, too."

We made a comprehensive list of what the four of us needed—in reasonable amounts—then split it in half. Zander took one half of the list and a cart; I took the other half of the list and a cart. But what we found at Walmart—or rather, didn't find—showed us how asleep at the switch we'd been.

Yes, we managed to find enough to keep us fed for a couple of weeks, but not all the items on our lists. Aisle after aisle showed empty shelves, particularly staples. We'd be eating differently than usual but would be happy to be eating at all.

After a hasty conference, Zander and I stocked up on what was readily available, items like protein powder, supplement drinks, and filling but not-so-great standbys such as ramen noodles. It was fuel. We knew we would need it. We added cases of diapers and other infant necessities to Baby Cruz's closet. We turned to online outlets to get what we couldn't purchase locally. Slowly we built up a reasonable emergency stockpile of canned, frozen, dried, and freeze-dried foods, enough to handle temporary shortages.

And we were grateful.

⌘

"BARNES HERE, CHECKING ON your progress. Have you finished faking the video of Cruz and his sister?"

"Yeah, well, about that? I need to tell you something. Stan and I found Cruz in our house on New Year's Day."

"You what? In your house! How did he get inside?"

"We don't know. Somehow he managed to breach all of our security, but that's not the crazy part. Cruz not only got inside the house without the system detecting him, he also got into the server room, found the footage we had of his sister, and deleted it. *All* of it."

"You idiot! You had to have left the server room unlocked!"

"No, *we did not*, and I don't appreciate your disrespect or your lack of confidence in us. I swear to you, the server room was locked up tighter than a drum when we found Cruz in our house. Also, hacking those servers? Not possible. The password to that system is uncrackable." He hesitated. "We don't know how he did it."

"That was our ace, *you bonehead!*"

"Don't get your knickers in a knot, Barnes. Cruz may have deleted the recordings I'd edited, the deep fakes, but I had backed up the raw video to the cloud. I still have it."

He listened to heavy breathing on the other end as Barnes calmed. Then he added, "We have our silver bullet. Better yet? Cruz doesn't know we do. I need to revise and recompile the raw footage, but when I send out that deep fake, I promise you: The backlash will hit him like a sledgehammer."

"Okay. Had me concerned for a second, but I suppose nothing has changed."

"Nope. Nothing's changed except I need to finish preparing my message for tomorrow's service. Don't worry—I'll have the video ready to text and email to everyone in the congregation by midweek, after which I'll post it to social media. Trust me! You'll have all the basis you need to cancel Cruz's guest spot next Sunday."

Easterly laughed. "And once that video is in the ether? It will live there forever."

⌘⌘⌘⌘

Chapter 26

THE CHURCH SERVICE AT DCC on the first Sunday of the New Year was like no other I'd ever experienced. Zander had warned me. He cautioned friends who had defected from Easterly's young adult group. He'd diligently drilled into us the biblical views on confusion, deception, strife, and division. I *knew* when Easterly opened his mouth, lies would pour out.

Regardless? Starting the moment that man stepped to the podium Sunday morning, I felt like my brain had been dropped into a food chopper. Sort of reminded me of the phone call we had with Emilio before he and Abe came to DC over the Fourth of July.

Zander had started it. He and Emilio had their silly joke exchange going, but Zander's riddle that day had been a doozy.

"What's green and red and goes a hundred miles an hour?"

Emilio had fidgeted and sighed. *"Shoot. Well, I guess I can't figure it out. What's green and red and goes a hundred miles an hour?"*

Zander had waggled an evil brow at me. *"Frog in a blender."*

Pretty much described me that morning.

Zander leaned toward me and whispered, "Don't let any of Easterly's gobbledygook get in your head."

"Too late."

I can't recall too many specifics from the message after my whispered exchange with Zander. Oh, I can think of a few of Easterly's catchphrases, like, "let us endeavor to follow the light that shines in all of us," "don't be afraid to walk the path the universe has laid out for you," and "just believe and dare to be the *real* and *authentic* you." But starting with my favorite of all his blather? That's where things got *über* thick and mucky.

With that bright, toothy mouth he smiled and said, "Here at DCC, we worship in the Christian tradition, but we must strive to respect and honor *all* worship traditions. After all, every faith tradition holds the same values as our faith tradition does and is equally valid. All faith traditions speak to our human origins and the need for our harmonious existence alongside other parts of creation. And all mystical traditions ultimately point to the same destination, the destination that awaits every culture, orientation, and indigenous people and their faith truths."

"That is a lie," I grumbled. "No, it's a whole bunch of lies tied up in one great big whopper of a lie."

But wait! There's more!

"In the Christian tradition, we worship Jesus as Christ—yet long before Jesus was born, thousands venerated the Buddha as Christ. Long after Jesus died, Muḥammad became Christ. Our sad misunderstanding emerges from misconstruing the word, "Christ." Christ is a word for the Universe seeing itself—in you, in me, in us all. As the Bible says, *we* are the Body of the Christ. The *Truth of Being* is that *all* mystical traditions ultimately point to the same destination."

Gag.

Zander sat as unmoving as stone, but I was shaking. I stole surreptitious glances around the sanctuary to gauge how the congregation was responding to Easterly's heresies. I would say our regular DCC congregation was in equal parts stunned or asleep—asleep being a decided blessing in my humble opinion.

Those who were stunned quickly revived and used their mouths to protest Easterly's particularly egregious statements. DCC members who knew Scripture—and who knew apostasy when they heard it—stood to voice their objections, some more to the point than others.

"You aren't preaching Jesus, mister!" (Right to the point.)

"This is a bunch of new age junk!" (Absolutely true.)

"Hey! You're preaching horsepucky, young man!" (I particularly appreciated this one.)

The saddest moment was when one earnest woman, a mature believer who had taught Sunday School for twenty-five years, was shut down mid-sentence. "But Pastor Easterly, the Bible clearly says—"

"It doesn't say to be rude," one of Easterly's acolytes interrupted. "Sit down and listen politely."

"Or what?" that dauntless woman answered.

"Or I'll make you sit down and shut up," was the answer.

She subsided, but she was quaking with righteous anger.

Yes, it was disgusting.

All of it.

The confusion that raged across the sanctuary was like a great cloud of dust, blowing at fifty miles an hour, stinging and blinding the people. Through it all, Easterly merely smiled and plunged ahead, cheered on by his followers, who clapped and shouted false and irreverent "amens" and who, with threatening looks and gestures, dared anyone else to speak up or interrupt.

I slid my hand into Zander's. His fingers closed comfortingly around mine, but it was only a reflexive response. The words pouring from Aiden Easterly's lying mouth held all of Zander's attention.

My husband's stone-cold expression could have frozen Niagara Falls solid.

⌘

W E WERE EATING BREAKFAST Monday morning when Zander's phone rang. Because we had received so many calls from congregants upset over Easterly's sermon, we had decided to let all incoming calls go through to voice mail during breakfast and our Bible time. That is, unless the nanomites flagged an incoming call as important.

Zander Cruz, Pastor McFee is calling.

Yup. Important.

Zander picked up. "Hello?"

"Zander, my boy. Pastor McFee here. Our ship is in port today. Listen, do you have a minute?"

"Yes, sir." He glanced at me. We knew why Pastor McFee was calling.

"Good, because so far I've received five phone calls over Easterly's message yesterday."

"Sir, do you mind if I put you on speaker phone so Jayda can hear?"

"I do not mind. Listen, given the video and images you sent me from Easterly's house, I have to believe his message yesterday was actually worse than people are saying."

"He couched much of what he said in doublespeak, Pastor. Someone with a middling knowledge of the Bible might not have picked up on the dual or contradictory meanings, but those who are well versed in Scripture saw right through him. Let me tell you, the demonic spirits of confusion and strife were hard at work, dividing the congregation into factions, pitting one faction against the other.

"It didn't help the situation when Easterly received a rousing introduction courtesy of Mike Barnes. We discovered, however, *exactly* what this wolf in sheep's clothing is all about—and sir? If I may be blunt? Easterly needs to be removed, *immediately* removed. Only then can the damage he has done be healed."

McFee's next words floored Zander. "Yes, that is precisely why I am calling, Zander. I want *you* to repudiate his false teachings in your message this coming Sunday. Not only will I back you up, I will then remove Easterly and his followers from our church—publicly and in person. Yes, Carol and I have decided to leave our ship tomorrow and fly home the day after—that is, if our flight isn't canceled."

"If your flight isn't canceled, sir?"

"Yes, *if*. This virus has people running scared. The President has halted international flights. Some news sources over here are predicting that he'll quarantine the State of Hawaii next, disallowing all flights in *or out*.

"If that happens, Zander, and we are unable to get home before Sunday, I may need to throw the entire weight of removing Easterly upon your shoulders—it would then be up to you to stop this coup in its tracks. If it comes to that, can you do it?"

Pastor McFee couldn't see the effect of his words on Zander, but I could and did.

My poor husband! I watched Zander receive Pastor McFee's injunction. I saw the responsibility for the safety of our church settle on his shoulders . . . I witnessed him age by years over the span of a few moments.

"Yes, sir. By God's grace, I can and will do what is necessary."

"Good man. I know I can count on you."

McFee went on, "Zander, as soon as you are able—today, if at all possible—I need you to meet privately with Harry Fuentes and then with Victor Gibson. Show them, individually, what you showed me, Zander.

"Tell Harry Fuentes that DCC will loan him the money to pay off his mortgage and arrears to Barnes, and tell him that the church will set reasonable terms for the loan. Assure him that if, somehow, DCC is prevented from doing this, I, *personally*, will lend him the money. We want him out from under Barnes' thumb.

"When you meet with Victor, show him those photos you called 'deep fakes' and tell him how Easterly manipulated them. Bring his wife in on this, too, so that she sees how Barnes and Easterly tried to ruin her husband—her good, faithful husband—and ruin their marriage into the bargain. Trust me when I say that Victor Gibson will climb up out of the hole into which Barnes has shoved him—and when he rises? You'll see a warrior, a champion.

"Then show both Harry and Victor how Easterly and Missing have colluded with Barnes to take over this church. Explain their wicked plans to extinguish the testimony and lamp of Christ within our congregation and to our community.

"When you have convinced both Harry and Victor of the truth, we will have the clout on the board to remove not only Easterly from our church but Barnes as well—and anyone else who has participated in this rebellion. Tell Harry and Victor I will be home this Sunday, God willing, and will remove Easterly. Then pray together for God's will to be done. Can you do that?"

Zander pulled himself up. Pressed his lips together. "I can, sir. However . . ." Here Zander paused to marshal his thoughts. "I see a potential problem at the point of removing Easterly."

"Tell me, please," McFee said.

"It's the influx of new 'worshippers' at DCC. The numbers have gone up each week, and the newcomers demonstrated a great deal of enthusiasm during Easterly's message yesterday. So far, they have conducted themselves in a civil manner, but I sense they will behave differently Sunday when I preach. It could get unpleasant."

"You mean they will object to your message?"

"Object? Yes. In fact, I sense that they will be poised to shout me down."

Zander hesitated before adding, "But it may not come to that, sir, because I think Mike Barnes plans to cancel my guest speaker appearance before Sunday."

"Hmm. Let me think on how I can derail Barnes. Perhaps an email from me to the congregation, personally promoting your message next week?"

"That might deter him, sir. You *are* still the pastor of this church. The title of my message, if you need it for your email, will be, *Is Your Worldview Biblical?*"

"I like it, Zander. I'll get right on that email to ensure that Barnes is unable to cancel your preaching appointment."

"Thank you, sir."

"No, I thank *you*, Zander. In this crisis, *you* are carrying the weight of spiritual responsibility for our church. I am grateful for you, grateful to fight the good fight with you by my side . . . Pastor Cruz."

Pastor Cruz.

A smile illuminated Zander's tired face. "It is my great privilege, Pastor McFee."

⌘

IMMEDIATELY AFTER HANGING UP with Pastor McFee, my preoccupied husband asked the nanomites to make calls to Harry Fuentes and Victor Gibson. After explaining that he had spoken with Pastor McFee, Zander succeeded in setting same-day appointments with both men, asking them to come to our home for the meetings.

They both agreed, but when Zander asked Victor to bring his wife, he refused.

"I don't want her dragged into any of this. I'm not going to destroy our marriage."

"I respect your decision, Mr. Gibson. Perhaps you will feel differently after we talk."

When he hung up with Victor Gibson, Zander and I bowed over our joined hands to pray. We didn't begin right away, because a great heaviness seemed to rest on us. In fact, I don't recall any prayers we lifted to the Lord in DC being as heavy or urgent as ours were this day.

Zander, for several minutes, could not articulate his need. Finally, he gave up.

"Father, I cast myself upon your grace! Your word tells me that your grace is sufficient for me—and 'sufficient' *is enough*. I trust in your sufficiency, Father, for your power is made perfect in weakness.

"Well, Lord, I confess that I am weak. Without you I am nothing. Apart from you I can *do* nothing. So, like the Apostle Paul, I will even boast in my weakness so that Christ's power may rest upon me.

"I trust in your strength, Lord God, not my own. May your will be accomplished in all Pastor McFee and I do in the coming days to protect the flock you have entrusted to us. Jayda and I pray these things in Jesus' name. Amen."

"Amen," I repeated.

⌘

THE HARRY FUENTES WHO rang our doorbell that afternoon was a whipped man. Although I only knew him by sight and from a distance, it was obvious that the man had lost a great deal of weight.

"Come in, Mr. Fuentes," Zander urged him. "Can we get you something to eat or drink?"

"That's kind of you, Zander, but no. I'm fine."

He was the antithesis of fine, but Zander didn't comment. "Please. Come sit at the table with us."

Harry sat down, his movements compliant, as though he'd lost his own will. Guilt shaded his next words. "You asked to see me?"

Zander tried to smile. "Yes, Mr. Fuentes. I have spoken at length with Pastor McFee concerning what is happening in our church. I spoke to him today, in fact, and have a message from him for you. But first, is it all right for Jayda to sit in on our conversation?"

Harry shrugged. "If you think so, it's all right with me. And please. Call me Harry."

"Thank you, Harry." Zander took a moment to marshal his thoughts. "Harry, I'm sorry your grandson has been so ill."

The first flicker of life came into Harry's face. "The specialist has done wonders for him. The prognosis is hopeful."

Zander's smile widened. "I think that's the best news I've heard recently!"

Zander's joy was catching, and I watched Harry unwind. "Thank you. We're so grateful to God. If only . . ."

"If only it hadn't bankrupted your family?"

Harry stared at Zander, the guilt eating away at him again. "I would sell my soul to save that kid."

"I'm sorry you feel the need to say that, Harry. However, I have a message for you from Pastor McFee that may encourage your heart. First, he asked me to assure you of his love for you and your family and his trust in you."

Harry blinked and lowered his gaze. "I don't deserve his love . . . or his trust."

"You were backed into a corner, Harry. Then Mike Barnes nailed you into that corner."

"McFee told you."

"Yes. Please believe me when I say that he cares for you and yours."

Harry's bottom lip quivered.

"Harry, would it be all right if I made a small observation? Not a criticism, I assure you. A helpful observation."

"Yeah. Okay."

"Thank you, Harry. What I want to say is that God places and plants us in the Body of Christ so that *when we are in trouble*, when we find ourselves in extreme situations, the rest of the Body can help us . . . that is, if the Body knows we need help."

Harry pondered Zander's words for a moment. "You're saying because I didn't ask for help . . ." His words trailed off.

"I'm not placing blame. I *am* saying your brothers and sisters in Christ would have helped . . . had we known. And this is what Pastor McFee asked me to tell you: One way or the other? We are going to buy you and your mortgage out from under Mike Barnes' thumb. Pastor said either the church would lend you the money to pay it off, or *he* would, personally."

Since watching a grown man weep distresses me, I got up and went into the kitchen to give Harry privacy. I busied myself for a while—did the dishes and made a pitcher of lemonade—reappearing with the pitcher and glasses when I heard Harry clear his throat.

"Thank you," he said, wiping his eyes before taking a glass. "Thank you both. You cannot imagine what this means."

"It means you are free of Barnes' control, Harry," Zander declared, "and if you are free of him?"

Harry straightened, and his mouth firmed up. "If I'm free, I will back Pastor McFee from here to hell and back, Pastor Zander."

"I am happy to hear that, Harry, because the situation at DCC will come to a head this week. We will need every praying, Bible-believing member of the board 'on board' when the fur flies Sunday morning. Shall we pray before you leave?"

"Absolutely!"

We bowed our heads, and Zander prayed. Harry prayed, too, offering thanks to the Lord for his deliverance.

The doorbell rang. I looked to Zander. "That's probably our other guest."

Harry stood. "I should go—but you can count on me, Zander. I won't let the Lord or DCC down again."

"I know you won't, Harry. You are a good man—a man after God's heart."

I got the door. "Hello. You must be Victor. I'm Jayda Cruz. Please come in."

"Thank you." Victor, a portly, silver-haired man in his fifties, stepped inside—and came face to face with Harry Fuentes.

Terrified. That's how I would describe the expression on Victor's face.

"*Harry*. I didn't . . . If I'd known . . ."

Harry went straight to Victor, placed his arm on the man's shoulder. "I need to ask you to forgive me, Victor."

"What?"

"Long story short? Barnes owns our mortgage, and we are behind on our payments. *Way* behind. I caved when he demanded that I vote for Easterly. I'm sorry. I-I defaulted on my sacred trust—but no more. Please . . . will you forgive me?"

As Victor stared into Harry's eyes, his own personal dilemma etched in the lines of his face, Zander spoke.

"Victor? I have the sense that Harry should stay and hear what we have to say to you."

Victor looked from Harry to Zander and back. "You say Barnes has been, what, blackmailing you, Harry?"

"I guess you could call it that. Strong-arming. Controlling. Threatening to evict us from our home if I didn't play ball."

"I see."

Victor slid his eyes toward Zander. Zander smiled. "I have good news for you, too, Victor. I can prove how those photos were faked so that Barnes could blackmail *you*."

Victor's lips parted, and hope lit his eyes. "You can?"

"Let's all sit down, shall we? Have a glass of lemonade together. Then I'm going to show you some nasty photos and the equally nasty tricks Barnes and Easterly used to fake those pictures and entrap you."

⌘

LATE THAT AFTERNOON, THE nanomites whispered, *Jayda Cruz, an email from Pastor McFee has arrived in your inbox.* They seemed as subdued as we were after meeting with Harry Fuentes and Victor Gibson.

"Zander, Pastor McFee's email has arrived."

He began logging in to his email account, so I joined him and we read McFee's message together.

Dear DCC Family,

Greetings from sunny Hawaii. Mrs. McFee and I are having a wonderful time, and we thank you again for upgrading our seats to first class. What a lovely experience it was to fly across the ocean in such style and comfort. Your consideration for us is a true blessing.

I want to remind all of you not to miss this coming Sunday's guest speaker, Zander Cruz. Pastor Cruz's message is titled, Is Your Worldview Biblical? *Mrs. McFee and I feel this is such a timely message that we intend to get up early Sunday and listen to the live audio on our church website.*

I want all of DCC to know that Pastor Cruz is an upstanding man of godly character, a dedicated student of Scripture, a workman who correctly handles the word of truth.

Pastor Cruz has my full confidence to minister in my absence. *That said, I expect to return to you soon, and I anticipate serving this great congregation for many years to come.*

With love in Christ Jesus, our Lord,
Aaron McFee, Senior Pastor,
Downtown Community Church

"Wow," I breathed.

"Wow is right."

"He said pretty nice things about you, Zander."

"I'm humbled by his confidence in me. Say, did you also notice he didn't let on that they are cutting short their trip or that he intends to be back at DCC Sunday morning?"

I nodded. "Pastor McFee is savvier than I gave him credit for. He even, in a backhanded manner, refuted the board's plans to 'retire' him."

"Huh. He sure did." Zander sniffed. "I'd like to see Mike Barnes' expression right about now."

"Zander . . . I am recollecting your teaching on division and strife."

"Oh? Oh, yeah. I think I know where you're going: We need to be careful not to let the strife Barnes, Easterly, and Missing are creating get on the inside of us? Of me?"

"Yes. That's it."

"Thanks for the reminder, Jay. I needed it."

⌘

PASTOR MCFEE CALLED AGAIN, but it was late, around eleven o'clock that night. The time in Hawaii was four hours earlier. And within the short span of their conversation, Zander and Pastor McFee's plans tumbled into a ditch.

"Zander, my boy, thank God I was able to reach you! None of the other passengers we've spoken to can get a signal, and the ship's Wi-Fi is turned off. Hmm. Odd . . . yours is the only number my phone can connect to."

Zander Cruz, we enabled Pastor McFee's phone to reach you at any time by routing it through the ship's navigational satellite uplink.

"Er, thanks, Nano."

It is our pleasure to assist you in the important work Jesus has for you, Zander Cruz.

Again? That whole "the important work Jesus has for you" business?

Zander shook off his astonishment and replied to Pastor McFee. "Uh, I'm certainly glad you were able to reach us, sir."

"Well, I'm afraid all I have is bad news. When Carol and I tried to leave our ship after lunch to catch our flight back to LA, we were told we could not disembark."

"They wouldn't let you leave the ship?"

"That's right. They had armed security at the gate, too. With no explanation at all, we were ordered to return to our cabin. When I protested, I was told if we did *not* return peacefully and immediately to our cabin, those ship's security officers would escort us there and lock us in!"

"What? That's crazy!"

"I'm afraid the craziness gets worse, Zander. After we returned to our cabin, we felt the ship casting off, leaving its berth. We tried to call the first mate from our cabin, but all of our attempts went unanswered. Most of us passengers gathered outside our cabins in our hallway to talk—even though we'd been told not to leave our rooms. Nobody knew what was happening, only that we were confined to our quarters until further notice. Finally, about half an hour ago, the captain got on the PA system and addressed the passengers and crew."

"Have you found out what's going on?"

"We think so. The captain said the authorities have ordered all cruise ships in port to move off shore and anchor there."

"Why? Why would they do that?"

Pastor McFee did not answer immediately. When he did, his voice was low. A whisper. "We've heard rumblings through the ship's 'grapevine,' rumors that a group of passengers on the spa deck are exhibiting symptoms of the virus. No one wants to catch that bug, so of course, everyone wants off this ship, ASAP. But then we'd risk infecting others, you see."

Neither Zander nor I responded. How could we? The news reports said the virus had up to a twenty-percent mortality rate—meaning Pastor and Mrs. McFee were, literally, trapped aboard a plague ship.

I heard a whisper and realized it was me. "They have quarantined your ship, Pastor. That's why they ordered the captain to anchor off shore."

"Yes. They haven't officially told us we're under quarantine, but I believe you're right, Jayda," McFee said softly. "Zander?"

"Yes, sir?"

"Change of plans, my boy. I'm sorry, but this means Carol and I won't make it home in time for Sunday's service."

"I see."

"You'll be carrying more responsibility on Sunday than I have a right to ask of you, but God willing, I can help, can play a part. It depends on whether my phone service holds up."

Zander pursed his lips. "I believe I can assist you with the, uh, technical aspects of your phone service, sir."

"Good! If I can call out, then this is what I'd like us to do."

⌘

EASTERLY'S RAGE ON THE other end of the call was palpable. "Mr. Barnes! Have you read McFee's email? He sent it to the entire congregation!"

"Of course I saw it, you twit. Give me a minute. I'm rethinking our strategy."

"You'll want me to send out the deep-fake videos today, right? Then can you cancel Cruz despite McFee's glowing recommendation?"

"Actually, I'm leaning toward *not* canceling him.

"What? But you said I would be preaching again this coming Sunday!"

"Yeah, well, I've come up with a better idea, one that will take out two birds with a single stone—rid ourselves of both Cruz *and* McFee. See, instead of you sending the clip to church members and posting it on social media, how about you send the video to me? During the service this Sunday, as soon as the singing is over, I'll have one of my guys take over the data projectors. I'll order him to put the video up on the screens the instant Cruz starts pontificating."

He laughed. "The entire congregation, at the same time, will see the clip of Cruz in bed with his sister. Once they do? He'll be toast. When the furor dies down, I'll call you up to finish the service."

Easterly whistled. "Wow. What an inspired idea, Mr. Barnes. At the same time, the video will totally negate McFee's email where he expressed so much confidence in Cruz."

"Yes, that's what I mean. McFee's own words will blow up in his face. He'll be left with zero credibility—and zero retirement pension courtesy of DCC."

"Great point! That video will flip McFee's endorsement of Cruz back on himself. McFee won't be able to fight the retirement the board has planned for him—not with that glob of egg on his face. *Ha!* Bet McFee won't send any further emails spouting his 'I anticipate serving this great congregation for many years to come' bilgewater! Yup. I like it."

"Glad to hear it," came the growled reply. "Now listen up. To complete the effect, we'll need a reaction from the congregation after the video plays. A big reaction—and I don't mean a show of righteous indignation. No, what we need is a full-on riot. So, I want you and Stan to beef up our presence Sunday morning—and I mean really beef it up. When I give the signal? Go after Cruz and take him out. No holds barred."

"Sure! I can handle that, Mr. Barnes."

Easterly shivered with anticipation. "Can't wait to see Cruz's face when our people rush the platform—when it hits him that they're coming for *him*."

⌘⌘⌘⌘

CHAPTER 27

ZANDER AND I HELD HANDS as we walked across the cul-de-sac to Abe's house. Abe and Emilio had invited us, plus Gamble and Trujillo, to a special breakfast. Today, Tuesday, a week after New Year's Day, our attorney would file the paperwork for us to adopt Emilio, and we intended to celebrate this important step.

After Easterly's heretical "sermon" Sunday and with the pressure of the coming Sunday ahead of us, a festive observance of this milestone was exactly what we needed. The only downside was the adoption process itself. We had jumped through the foster care hoops; next we had adoption hoops, including thirty-two hours of additional required training.

Then it could take months for our case to make the rounds, for the investigators to complete their work and sign off on it, for the courts to assign us a judge and a court date. We were looking at April or May, our attorney told us, before Emilio was ours.

Speaking of Emilio. He answered the door with a grin and a bounce. "They're here!" he shouted behind him. Then he hugged me. Hard. He and Zander hugged, too, but it was different, a "manly" hug that made me smile.

As we moved into the foyer, the mixed aromas of browning sausages and potatoes, onion, and green chile frying together reached me. Atop those delicious scents was a whiff of something sweet and yeasty.

Cinnamon rolls?

"I'm drooling," Zander confessed.

"Yeah? Well, don't get between the pregnant lady and her chow," I warned him.

Gamble was helping Janice add glasses of orange juice to the table settings. On the side, he nursed a steaming mug of coffee. "Morning," he said, lifting his mug in a salute.

I stared, grinning. The man was as relaxed and as content as I had ever seen him. We'd both come such a long ways since General Cushing had attempted to co-opt him from the FBI's Albuquerque Field Office and sic him on me. We'd begun as total strangers, and ended up as partners while Zander and I confronted a maze of intrigue and dangerous circumstances in DC. Trujillo, too. The four of us had fought battles together. I was glad to acknowledge Gamble and Trujillo as dear friends.

"What?" Gamble asked.

"Happy. Happy that you and Janice are our friends."

Abe herded us to the table while Gamble nodded slowly. He knew where I was coming from. "Yeah. The events of this past year or so? Boggle the mind. You can't make this stuff up."

"By God's grace, we passed through a trial by fire," Zander said. "Er, several, in fact."

"Amen to that," Abe muttered. "May I never have to climb up a mountainside again! Too old for that nonsense. C'mon. Sit down. Food's on the table."

We sat, Abe at one end, Zander at the other. Emilio and I took the chairs on one side; Janice and Gamble sat across from us.

Janice sighed. "On that note? I'd like to say . . . that I like where we've all landed. You know what I mean, right? This little niche we share here in Albuquerque. Neighbors. Friends. Family. Kind of all mashed together."

Gamble picked up his glass of orange juice. "To neighbors, friends, and family. All mashed together."

We lifted our glasses. Clinked them together. "To neighbors, friends, and family. All mashed together."

We returned our glasses to the table, Abe prayed a heartfelt blessing over the food, and everyone dug in.

Before I took my first bite, however, I glanced around the table, hoping to capture this precious moment. Rejoicing in God's goodness.

How I thank you, Lord!

My rumbling tummy added the amen.

How was I to know that everything surrounding our lives was about to change?

⌘⌘⌘⌘

CHAPTER 28

WEDNESDAY STARTED OUT AS an ordinary midweek workday. It ceased being ordinary when the media trumpeted the awful news:

**Virus Cases Found
New York City,
Chicago, Atlanta.**

The three cities were major trans-Atlantic airline hubs, and the known cases were linked by travel from Europe to the US prior to the President's international flight moratorium only days before. That meant that every passenger on the same incoming flights as those who had contracted the virus was at risk—and so were their families, friends, and coworkers.

The government was frantically following up on the passenger manifests from the suspect flights, hoping to stem the spread of the virus. The sad truth? The moment those passengers disembarked their planes was comparable to shaking the innards of a feather pillow into the wind, then trying to recapture every feather.

No matter how the media and the President's staff tried to spin the story, any thinking person knew the virus was loose in the US. Beyond immediate control.

Wednesday was also Emilio's first day back to school following Christmas break. After Abe rousted the sleepy kid out of bed and while he dressed, Abe fixed them a hot breakfast. When they finished eating, they read two verses aloud from the Bible and prayed together. Finally, Emilio grabbed his backpack, and Abe saw him out the door.

He hobbled back to the table and thumped himself down with another cup of coffee.

"Hooey, Lord! 'Bout wears me out gettin' that boy off to school." He grinned to himself recalling Emilio's excitement at showing up for breakfast in new school clothes—some of his Christmas presents.

"He's a fine young man, Lord, and I love him. Soon as I finish tidying up, I'll have my personal time with you."

He drained his cup, levered himself out of the chair, and started cleaning up the kitchen.

The doorbell rang.

He frowned at the interruption. "Sure not expectin' anyone."

Abe made his way to the door and opened it, leaving the security door between him and his visitor shut. A large black woman with a briefcase and clipboard nodded to him. "Mr. Abe Pickering?"

"That's me. And you are, ma'am?"

She reached her hand through the bars of the security door to hand him a card. "I'm Lani Okafor, Mr. Pickering, from CYFD."

He took the card and studied it. "I see. This must be about Emilio. What can I do for you, Ms. Okafor?"

"May I come in? I have some questions for you."

With a sudden sinking sensation in his heart, Abe unlocked the security door. "Yes, come in. Where would you like to sit?"

"Perhaps at the table?"

They sat down in silence. Ms. Okafor referred to her clipboard, then cleared her throat. "Mr. Pickering, we received a complaint last month concerning how you are raising Emilio."

Abe said nothing. *Lord, I'm not saying anything until I hear from your Holy Spirit. Whatever **this** is? It's not from you, so we know 'zactly where it **is** from—and I rebuke it in Jesus' name.*

When he remained silent, she again coughed to clear her throat. "The complaint, specifically, has to do with a couple you are close to, Mr. and Mrs. Cruz?"

Abe's thoughts cleared; the scene between Jayda and Ms. Cargill clarified in his mind. "Can you be more specific about the complaint?"

"The complaint expressed to our office was that Mr. and Mrs. Cruz are exerting a negative influence on Emilio—generally, that they are contravening the inclusive community atmosphere his school is working hard to foster, and that Mr. and Mrs. Cruz's unwillingness to cooperate is creating conflict in Emilio's young mind. More specifically, the complaint details a disruptive scene Mr. and Mrs. Cruz created at the school's open house."

"You mean when they expressed their own opinions and values. I was there. I will tell you, Ms. Okafor, that Mr. and Mrs. Cruz did not create a scene, disruptive or otherwise."

Abe thought Ms. Okafor's eyes narrowed ever-so-slightly.

"Mr. Pickering, are you saying that you agree with Mr. and Mrs. Cruz?"

"Ms. Okafor, perhaps you are misinformed about what happened at the school's open house. One of Emilio's friends asked if Mrs. Cruz was expecting a baby, then asked if she was having a boy or a girl. Emilio's teacher corrected the boy publicly, saying that babies choose their own gender. Her statement is, of course, patently nonsense. A child's gender is obvious and a DNA test confirms what his or her physical attributes declare."

Abe hardly recognized the words as they, effortlessly, dropped from his lips. *Thank you, Holy Spirit!*

Ms. Okafor smiled and stood to leave. "I understand. Thank you for clarifying."

Abe levered himself out of his chair. "What is it you understand, Ms. Okafor?"

"I understand your position, Mr. Pickering. We'll be in touch."

Abe said nothing more, but his heart jittered some. "You have a nice day, ma'am."

"Yes. Thank you."

As he watched her descend the porch steps and get into her car, he reached for his telephone. Pressed one of his saved numbers.

"Zander? Need t' talk to you and Jayda."

⌘

AS WE LEFT ABE'S HOUSE and walked across the cul-de-sac, Zander took my hand and held it fast in his.

"I think we dispatch the nanomites to monitor Ms. Okafor," I said. "If she writes a bad report about us for CYFD, we should know about it."

"Yeah, let's do that. Have them monitor her official computer traffic. That should do it . . . after we pray about it." He sighed deeply. "Lord, we know this business with CYFD is one more attack in a series of attacks from the enemy. We will not let it rattle us or affect the peace you have given us, the peace that passes all understanding. Lord God, please take care of this situation for us? Amen."

"Amen."

Zander didn't need "one more in a series of attacks from the enemy," not while he was wrestling with how to address Aiden Easterly's blatant heresies. When we walked into our house, I wasn't surprised that he tugged me over to the table and asked me to sit with him.

"You know I have been praying and seeking God's will for my message this coming Sunday, Jay. I have the one shot to publicly contradict the garbage Easterly spouted."

"Yes, I know."

"Well, I feel the Lord has given me a sure word about what I need to do." He dithered only a second or two. "I am to draw a line of distinction between the falsehoods Easterly preached, a clear separation between what is apostasy and what is truth. I won't hold back."

I blew out a breath in relief. "I'm glad. But . . . what will be the response to your sermon?"

"It may tear DCC apart."

I sighed and looked aside. I had to say what had been on my mind since Zander's last young adult study on division. "Well, maybe DCC needs to be torn apart."

Zander's eyes sought mine.

I pressed my point. "This is what 1 Timothy 4:1 says.

> *"The Spirit clearly says that in later times*
> *some will abandon the faith and follow deceiving spirits*
> *and things taught by demons.*

"Isn't that what we witnessed Sunday morning?" I asked. "Demonic lies and deception? Doublespeak intended to sway weak minds and make certain sins more acceptable? Declaring that despite your sins, 'all paths lead to heaven' or some such nonsense. And what about his idolatry with that statue?

"Zander, you have a duty to the young adults of this church—no, you have a duty to the entire congregation—to speak the truth of God's word and refute Easterly's deception," I said. "And verse 6 adds this.

> *"If you point these things out to the brothers and sisters,*
> *you will be a good minister of Christ Jesus,*
> *nourished on the truths of the faith*
> *and of the good teaching that you have followed."*

He nodded slowly. "Yes, I have a duty to the Lord to care for the lambs he has given me and to use every opportunity he affords me.

> *"Preach the word; be prepared in season and out of season;*
> *correct, rebuke and encourage—*
> *with great patience and careful instruction."*

I knew Zander was silently finishing the passage, but the words poured out of me anyway.

> *"But you, keep your head in all situations,*
> *endure hardship, do the work of an evangelist,*
> *discharge all the duties of your ministry."*

"Okay," Zander breathed, his arms tightening about me. "God will give me the strength to do what he's asked of me."

"Yes, he will," I answered.

⌘⌘⌘⌘

Chapter 29

EARLY MORNING ON SUNDAY, I dropped Zander at DCC's office entrance. Before he left the car, he turned to me and opened his arms. I fell into them. I wanted to burrow into his comforting embrace and remain there, but . . . I knew I couldn't. My beloved husband had a vital job to do, and he needed to finish his preparations. Needed to get alone with the Lord and pray over the message he would be preaching in a few hours.

He needed to be certain his heart and attitudes were fully surrendered to God's will. My role was to support him. Not to distract or weaken his resolve in any way.

"Remember, Jay. Whatever happens this morning, don't place yourself and Baby Cruz in the thick of it. Promise me you will keep our child safe?"

"I promise, Zander—and I'm praying for you. Be strong in the Lord." I kissed his cheek and pulled away.

Yes, I prayed. I prayed on the way home . . . through a breakfast I don't recall tasting . . . while I showered and dressed . . . as I backed the SUV out of the garage and pulled around the cul-de-sac to the curb in front of Abe's house . . . while Abe and Emilio got in . . . all the way back to church.

I knew Abe didn't mind the silence, knew that he was praying with me. Emilio had to have sensed this morning's serious tone, too, because he sat, quiet and calm, during the drive.

At least I think he did. I was, perhaps, too intent and focused to notice much at all, somewhat surprised to find I had parked the car and turned off the engine.

"You ready, Jayda?" Abe asked.

I exhaled and nodded.

As we approached the main entrance to DCC, my eyes lifted to the circle of stained glass high above the massive doors, to the image of Jesus, the Good Shepherd, carrying a lamb on his shoulders. That image had stirred me as a child. Today it stirred me again, and my heart poured out in response.

You are our Good Shepherd, Lord Jesus, and we are the sheep of your pasture! We know your voice and hearken to it. Please empower Zander this morning to speak everything you wish him to say with boldness and conviction—no matter what happens. We know that your word does not return empty or remain void, Lord Jesus, so we trust you with the outcome of your message spoken through Zander. Have your will and your way in this place today, Lord, and guide me this day, Holy Spirit, to do my part. Amen.

We were moving up the steps with other attendees when I felt a sudden, sharp nudge on the inside.

Holy Spirit? Is that you, guiding me?

Well, I did ask!

I touched Abe's arm and inclined my head. Took Emilio by the hand and gently tugged him to the right as we entered the church's large foyer. I pulled him out of the dense stream of worshippers headed into the sanctuary. Abe followed.

I uttered three words: "Nano, cover us."

The nanomites swept over the three of us, rendering us invisible as we approached the staircase leading to the choir and organ loft. Abe gasped and stumbled a little. Emilio turned toward him and stared. His eyes jerked all around, but he was unable to find Abe or me, and I was holding on to him! He held out his hand and was unable to see it either—or his feet or any part of himself. He went from quiet and compliant to jumping out of his skin in two seconds flat. I had to ask the nanomites to calm him.

"Shh," I whispered to them both. "We're going upstairs. Use the railing, please. I don't want anyone to trip. I'll be right behind you."

I unclipped the rope across the stairs and tugged on Emilio's hand to get him moving. Abe, a little unsteady but determined, started up. I reclipped the rope and followed him. At the top of the stairs, I had us join hands, and we made our way to a row of chairs that overlooked the sanctuary.

"Sit here," I said to them.

"Nano," I whispered as we settled into our seats, "please keep the three of us covered during the service, but let Zander know where we are."

Emilio, his eyes wide, walked his hand up my arm to tug on my sleeve. He said, loud enough for all three of us to hear, "Why the nano-things make us invisible? Why we up here?"

"I felt like the Lord wanted us up here this morning. Please pray for Zander while he is preaching today, okay? Not everyone will agree with his message, so pray for him to say and do what the Lord wishes him to say and do. Can you do that?"

"Yeah . . . okay."

I knew Abe would pray. But Emilio? He didn't know Jesus. Yet.

His eyes jinked back toward the sanctuary. "You talkin' 'bout that Easter man not agreein' with Zander, right?"

"Easterly," I gently corrected.

"Yeah, him. That guy give me the creeps—he messed with Izzie's head. Turned her 'gainst us. I don' like him."

"For a while. She's better now."

And I don't like him either, kiddo, but I only spoke those words to myself.

I scanned the sea of a thousand or so seats below us, seeking out the cluster of young adults gathering in their usual places near the front of the center section. There they were, "our" young adults—and nearby, those who were "not our" young adults.

My people. Not my people, an inner voice whispered.

Yes. The two groups could have been oil and water: They were together, but they didn't mix. Unbidden, the words of 2 Corinthians 6 rose within me.

> *For what do righteousness and wickedness have in common?*
> *Or what fellowship can light have with darkness?*

"Nothing and none, Lord God! No fellowship at all. Oh, Lord, we're calling on you to help us this day."

Aiden Easterly was easy to spot, too. In fact, he was hard to miss. He strode gracefully up and down the aisles, working the congregation like a seasoned politician, grinning, shaking hands with those near him, and welcoming visitors.

Visitors.

I squinted. We had a raft of visitors this morning.

When I started counting, I was pretty sure we had an unprecedented number of newcomers this morning. As I focused in on them, several of them felt . . . odd. Something about them made my skin itch. Furthermore, their numbers were filling in all the empty seats down front, spilling across the front rows of all five seating sections, pouring in around our young adults.

Hedging them in.

"Nano, I need a clearer view *there*. Push in on that section, please."

The faces of our precious young men and women blinked into focus—Josh, Todd, Diego, Felix, Cesar, Jorge, Wyatt, Colton, Eli, Nance, Mia, Tian, Cali, Sandra, Keisha, Bekka, Julie. And Izzie.

Close up, I saw that Zander's young adults were cognizant of the strange mix of visitors surrounding them. Josh and Diego had their heads together. When Josh lifted his eyes to scan the newcomers, concern washed over his face. I shifted from him to Diego, then Todd. All the others. What I saw was anxiety.

They know something is wrong, and they are worried. Afraid.

I turned my attention to again study the visitors. The word "trouble" clanged in my heart like a fire alarm.

"Nano, I need you to do something."

I outlined what I wanted.

We can do that, Jayda Cruz.

Moments later, Josh picked up his phone and stared at the lock screen. So did Diego. They read the text message the nanomites had planted on both their phones.

**Leave your seats and
follow Josh to the back
of the sanctuary
NOW**

The others in the YA group were reading the same text. One by one, they looked to Josh. Uncertain, he licked his lips. Then he stood and motioned to them. Started edging by the visitors who had hemmed them in.

A tall woman I'd never seen before stood up in the row and blocked Josh's way. She said something to him. He shook his head and said something back. The woman put her hands on her hips and refused to move. Josh turned around. Motioned for his friends to go the other way. Our young adults struggled to the end of their respective rows and started up the aisle.

That was when Aiden Easterly approached Josh and laid a hand on his shoulder. Josh flushed, looked at the hand, then at Easterly, and said something I could not make out.

We can read Josh's lips, Jayda Cruz. He said, "Please take your hand off me."

"I think I got that, Nano."

Aiden Easterly said, "Don't make a big mistake, Josh. I wouldn't want you to get hurt."

I growled deep in my throat, and Emilio side-eyed me, startled—but, of course, he could not hear my discussion with the nanomites.

"What else did they say, Nano?"

Josh said, "Jesus is my Rock and my shield. I trust in him." Easterly replied, "A rock tied to one's ankle makes for tough swimming."

"That *rat!*"

Easterly's body jerked; his hand dropped from Josh's shoulder.

"What happened, Nano?"

Josh said, "If I were you, Mr. Easterly, I'd be more concerned about the millstone around your own neck."

"Oh, *well said*, Josh," I chuckled to myself. Emilio heard me and continued to regard my invisible form with concern, so I hugged him. "I'm okay, kiddo. Let's pray for Zander, shall we?"

Emilio shrugged, but Abe and I, with Emilio sandwiched between us, prayed for the Lord to lead and guide Zander through every part of the service.

"Pour your word and your wisdom through him, Lord God! Please mount a guard about him, body, soul, and spirit," I whispered.

When we finished and opened our eyes, all of "our" young adults had made their way unscathed to the top of the aisle where they congregated against the wall directly under the balcony. I leaned far out over the railing and could see them. A moment later, Josh joined them, and Easterly strolled down the aisle toward the front, still greeting people left and right.

Right then, the worship leader stepped to her mic, welcomed the congregation, and asked them to stand. Music soon filled the sanctuary and joyous voices rose in praise.

It was hard for me to join in with the singing, though, and that told me my focus was off.

Lord, please help me to honor you in all I do and say today . . . but perhaps I should start with my thoughts. Lord, I fix the eyes of my heart on you. I love you and worship you. I surrender my life to you again. I soon felt my heart calming, and I was able to enter into worship.

Worship concluded, and without any announcements at all, Zander took the podium.

⌘

"GOOD MORNING AND WELCOME to Downtown Community Church. This morning's message is titled, *Is Your Worldview Biblical?* 'Worldview' may be a new term to some of you, and it is not a word you will find in the Bible. But guess what? We all possess a worldview. And let me assure you: If you are a Bible-believing individual, you will soon recognize how essential this descriptive term is."

I watched him scan the congregation. Some were familiar with the term, many were not. Others seemed disinterested—but I knew where Zander was going.

That disinterest would change in short order.

"What does worldview mean? In its simplest definition, it means how each of us looks at the world around us. Or, it can mean the lens through which we view the world. That definition, however, is not complete enough. Worldview also encompasses where we *stand* in order to view our surroundings and our experiences. 'The view from here' might describe an individual's worldview.

"Worldview is important because it is the framework we place around our experiences in order to make sense of them. It shapes and governs what we embrace as bedrock truth. Our worldview influences every decision and choice we make. I will even go so far as to attest that *our worldview determines our eternal destination.*

"A Christian is an individual surrendered to Christ, a person wholly and exclusively committed to the only Savior, Jesus—not merely a 'worshipper according to the Christian tradition.'"

Here Zander paused and again let his eyes pass over the congregation

"As Christians, we study, learn, and embrace *the Bible's* worldview, that is, *God's worldview*, because if we espouse anything other than a biblical worldview, if we adopt the worldview of this present age, we will fall into deception. The wrong worldview—Satan's worldview—rejects or twists God's word and will take us where we don't want to go, but God's worldview will lead us onward, toward him."

He had their attention.

"I want to demonstrate, with a rather vivid illustration, the necessity of a biblical worldview. I asked DCC's media crew to help me set up this scenario, which is why you will notice that the windows of the sanctuary have been covered to block out the sunlight and that the ushers are closing the sanctuary doors.

"In a moment, as the scenario commences, the lights go down, leaving us in darkness. Please do not panic—the darkness will last only a few moments."

Zander nodded to the lighting crew in the glass booth on our far left, near the back corner of the room. "You may begin."

The sanctuary lights slowly dimmed, grew weaker, and went out entirely. The only light remaining came from the glowing green EXIT signs around the room's perimeter.

A low rumble of conversation and a few nervous laughs trickled through the congregation.

Then, in the same way that shadows had crept into the room until we had descended into nearly complete darkness, luminous pinpoints above our heads glowed softly, then brightened. Colorful whorls appeared, and the pinpoints grew brighter, some becoming larger and appearing closer. Others heavenly bodies looked much farther away.

A sigh floated through the congregation as they viewed the night sky. It was as though we were floating *in* space with the stars and galaxies spinning or swirling in their courses around us.

Zander had given credit to the church's media team for this wonderful skyscape, but I knew how much the nanomites were enhancing it. I wondered if the media techs were currently gaping at "their" work.

Speaking of Zander, he had slipped away from the lectern as the lights dimmed and could not presently be seen. He spoke softly into the dark. "I'd like you to envision yourself in a little one-person spaceship, traveling among the stars. You are not alone. Many ships, identical to yours, travel with you."

A flotilla of spaceships appeared in the inky sky, puttering slowly along. The congregation was immediately transfixed. I saw that Emilio was, too.

Zander picked up his narration. "As you go along, you wave to other ships, to other pilots, and converse with them by radio, but you can't help but wonder *why* you are traveling through space. What is the point of your journey? What is the purpose of your life among the stars? Are you destined to travel along forever?

"You desire to know the answers to these questions, and before long, you begin to yearn for a destination, a planet where your journey will be at an end, a place where you belong and can cease from your wandering.

"You hear rumors from other ships that this planet you hunger for is called *Home*. You hear from some pilots that when you arrive at Home, you will land and be among other pilots whose ships have found their way there. Once you reach Home, you will never need to leave again. The pilots of a few ships around you even declare that Home is the seat of your creator and his kingdom.

"As you speed along and the years pass, your most fervent desire is to find Home. However, you have only so much time to do so. You must find Home before your air and supplies run out, before your ship exhausts its fuel."

Another low rumble, slightly concerned, flowed over the congregation.

Zander's voice was gentle. Calming. "The good news is that your little ship possesses faster-than-light capability and you have a detailed star chart and a map that provides you with the exact directions for how to get Home. You begin, the map tells you, at a star named Mehitah'ess.

"From Mehitah'ess, you are to travel five light years toward a star named Nyrome, then onward, ten more light years to a star named Theticas—where you will find, in a safe orbit, the peaceful planet, Home."

Another congregational sigh floated across the room, this one of relief.

Zander spoke again. "Not all the news, however, is good. The bad news is, *you don't know where you are*."

Confused mutters spread across the sanctuary.

"Look at constellations above you," Zander said. "Do you recognize any of these systems?"

It was a rhetorical question that received no reply other than whispers of speculation or concern.

"No, none of these stars are familiar to you, are they?" Zander asked again. "You search your ship's database of star charts, but the sky around you doesn't correspond to any of them. Yet, in order to make sense of the map leading toward Home, you must begin where *it* begins—at the star Mehitah'ess. Ah, yes! From Mehitah'ess, the map's directions are clear and unambiguous. They *will* get you to Home. However, from where you are at present? No part of the directions will work—or can work.

The lights came up slowly, and a spotlight focused on Zander. He smiled.

"To bring this example down to a more commonly experienced conundrum, one you can relate to, let me provide you with directions to the nearest McDonalds. Are you ready? Okay. Here we go.

"Take a left at the first corner. Drive until you see the red barn. Got it? Okay, at the barn, turn right."

A titter rippled across the congregation. I watched them grin and nod to each other. Zander was nothing if not entertaining this morning.

Smiling with them, Zander kept going. "As soon as you see the white mailbox, turn left—that's left *before* the mailbox, not *after* the mailbox—but after you turn left before the mailbox, stay in the right lane until you approach the fork in the road, then go right where the fork bends west."

The titter across the sanctuary grew into full-throated laughter.

"Finally, because you are on the wrong side of the road and cannot make a turn across two lanes of traffic into the McDonald's parking lot, make an immediate right turn, then a second right turn, then a third right turn. Go two blocks more, and take a fourth right turn, followed by a *fifth* right turn, and pull into the parking lot."

Zander looked blandly upon the congregation. "Congratulations. You have arrived at Burger King."

The people laughed so hard and long, that Zander had to let them laugh themselves out. When the congregation recovered, he said, "Huh. I wonder where you went wrong! My directions were clear and correct. Guess it was operator error, right?"

Someone dared call out, "You said, 'take a left at the first corner.' You didn't say *which corner!*"

"Ah. That's right—which corner?"

With great emphasis, Zander said, "As I said earlier, if you don't know the correct *starting point*, you are lost from the get-go. Forget the directions. They are worthless if you begin at the wrong spot."

As his audience snapped to Zander's point, heads began to nod.

Zander smiled. "Here we are, back in space in our little one-person ship. We have good star charts, a good map, and good directions. What we don't have is *our location,* our starting point—and it had better be the star Mehitah'ess. Without that starting point, the map will make no sense.

"Listen, it's like being in a ginormous indoor shopping center for the first time, with you staring at the mall directory. What do you need to find first on that directory?"

"You are here!" someone shouted.

"Nailed it, brother," Zander replied. "You look for the arrow and the words that read, 'You Are Here.' We need the same thing on one of our star charts: 'You are here,' but the 'here' we need *must* be Mehitah'ess.

"Mehitah'ess, the *right* starting point from which all the directions proceed, can also be called 'an empirical point of reference,' a location of absolutely certainty upon which you will, with confidence, base all of your decisions going forward."

A wave of agreement rippled over the room.

"Ah. You are getting it. You understand the most important principle to reaching Home safely: Unless you begin your journey at the star Mehitah'ess, your map is worthless—therefore, *you must find Mehitah'ess.*

"Too bad many of your traveling companions don't know this. And even though you have radioed to them many times, conveying your new insight, one group of ships decides that the brightest star in the sky *surely* must be Mehitah'ess. They race together toward that star and, using the map's directions, plot their course accordingly.

"Another group sets off to search for Mehitah'ess—although they have no idea in which direction that star might lie—or even how to recognize it when they see it.

"All around you, the ships you are traveling with make their own determinations concerning Mehitah'ess. They depart, individually, in pairs, or in groups. Some of them are certain that the map will lead them home even if they *never* find Mehitah'ess, while others cast the map aside altogether and decide to head in one direction and continue on until their fuel is spent.

"One group radios to their friends and declare, "We've found Mehitah'ess over here!" while other ships denounce the first and say, "No, Mehitah'ess is over there!"

Zander's voice took on a slightly sarcastic tone. "You even encounter ships that proclaim, 'Don't worry—Mehitah'ess is within all of us. Just *follow the light within you* and all will be well.'"

Wariness crept over the congregation as they recognized Zander's swipe at one of Easterly's statements last Sunday.

"You, however, and a few others, peruse the map more deeply. You list and study the characteristics of Mehitah'ess, its composition and the number and proximity of its planets. You send out scouting parties to locate a star that *accurately matches* the map's criteria.

"Good news! You find Mehitah'ess! You travel there and from it you sight Nyrome, the next star listed in the directions, right where the map says it will be. You are certain that you are on course, and before long, you arrive Home."

As the stars and galaxies began to fade, applause and relief swept the auditorium. The darkness gave way to a gradual lightening of the room, until the congregation sat blinking at Zander in the sanctuary's customarily bright light.

Zander kept going. "Life requires an empirical point of reference, a starting point of absolute certainty, or the map given to us to chart our journey Home will make absolutely no sense. Sadly? In our little example, all those ships who chose a different starting point to their journey never arrived Home. However, we are *not* left wondering where we are or where to start. The Lord gives us our starting point in Scripture so that his word, our map, makes sense and takes us to our eternal destination.

"This is what I mean by a biblical worldview. We begin where God begins: *In the beginning GOD created the heavens and the earth*. He created us, placed a desire in our hearts for Home, and sent us out in our little one-person ships. It was God who created us—not the Big Bang, not the pantheon of gods spelled with a little 'g,' and certainly not some vague but 'all-knowing universe.' Yes, God created the universe—and according to the Book of Romans, we are to worship the Creator, not the creation.

Heads nodded, following Zander's metaphorical parallels and agreeing with them.

"In Scripture, the Lord, the God of Creation, speaks promises concerning his Savior. When we study those promises, they lead us onward and unerringly, to Jesus—Jesus, our *Mehitah'ess*."

The media screen came alive and displayed the word Mehitah'ess twice.

Mehitah'ess
Mehitah'ess

As the congregation watched, the letters of the second Mehitah'ess rearranged themselves to form a two-word title.

Mehitah'ess
The Messiah

"That's right. When you unscramble the word 'Mehitah'ess' we find it reads 'The Messiah.' And what does Messiah mean?"

On the screens, beneath the phrase, "The Messiah," appeared its English translations.

The Messiah
The Christ
The Anointed One

"You see it, don't you? *Jesus* is our empirical point of reference; he is the starting point of our journey, the one who makes our map make sense."

Zander spoke louder, a shout, a declaration: "Jesus *is* our bright Morning Star! There is no other Savior but him!"

"Ohhh!" the people breathed. Zander's three examples had coalesced in their hearts—and none of it spelled good news for Aiden Easterly's blasphemous teachings.

Zander's voice thundered across the sanctuary. "Furthermore, in Matthew 24, verses 23-25, Jesus warned us about false Christs and about the false prophets who would point to them.

> *". . . if anyone says to you, 'Look, here is the Messiah!'*
> *or, 'There he is!' do not believe it.*
> *For false messiahs and false prophets will appear*
> *and perform great signs and wonders to deceive,*
> *if possible, even the elect.*
> *See, I have told you ahead of time.*

"There is but *one* Christ, the Lord Jesus! Let me be even clearer: Buddha was never Christ, Muḥammad was never Christ, and you and I certainly are not Christ. Christ is *not* in everything and everyone—nor is Christ a word for 'the Universe seeing itself'—however you may choose to interpret that nonsensical, utterly false statement."

Zander roared, "I refute the heresy that says, 'all mystical traditions ultimately point to the same destination.' No, if they do not point to Jesus, they point to error. Hebrews 12, verses 1-3 tell us in no uncertain terms to fix our eyes on Jesus and only Jesus.

> *"And let us run with perseverance the race marked out for us,*
> *fixing our eyes on Jesus, the pioneer and perfecter of faith.*
> *For the joy set before him he endured the cross, scorning its shame,*
> ***and sat down at the right hand of the throne of God.***
> *Consider him who endured such opposition from sinners,*
> *so that you will not grow weary and lose heart!*

"You see, *this* church, Downtown Community Church, is a Bible-*preaching*, Bible-*teaching*, Bible-*believing*, and Bible-*acting* church. We have the right map—the inerrant word of God—and we have the right starting point—Jesus Christ, the only begotten Son of God, the Savior of the world. We love to share this Good News with anyone and everyone, how to find Jesus and how to follow him. *All. The. Way. Home.*"

A resounding chorus of amens and shouts of hallelujahs rose from the congregation. I said 'amen' aloud myself. A great many DCC folks stood to their feet, and the sanctuary filled with thunderous applause and approving cries of "Hallelujah!" and "Praise God!"

I looked down to where Aiden Easterly and Stan Missing sat and had the nanomites zoom in on them. Easterly's face was a mottled mass of fury. As the applause went on, he tried to stand, but Missing placed his hand on Easterly's arm and restrained him.

Busted, I thought. Zander had slowly and subtly drawn the net around Easterly's false teachings until the trap was ready to snap shut in the sight and hearing of everyone present.

And the service was only half over. I peered down and zoomed in on Easterly.

Wait until the other shoe drops, Easterly. Here it comes!

⌘⌘⌘⌘

CHAPTER 30

ZANDER SMILED GENTLY OVER the congregation until the applause slowly subsided. What he said next, surprised everyone.

Well, almost everyone.

"Let us take a short break from my message this morning so that our esteemed senior pastor, Aaron McFee, and his lovely wife, Carol, can say a word to us from their much deserved anniversary cruise to Hawaii. Pastor McFee, are you there?"

Up on the screens, Pastor and Mrs. McFee's smiling faces came into view. At the sight, another spontaneous burst of applause erupted across the church. People stood and cheered for them.

"Great job, Nano!" I whispered.

Jayda Cruz, it is our pleasure to assist you and Zander Cruz in the important work Jesus has assigned to you.

I swallowed on the awe I felt. *This.* Our important work for Jesus!

"Well, you are doing an awesome job, Nano, and we appreciate you."

A soft trill followed my words, the nano equivalent of a pleased and happy exhalation.

I leaned over the railing and looked far to the left, into the church's glass-paneled media booth. "Nano, zoom in, please."

They did—and *yup.* Saw what I figured I'd see: The five media technicians were suffering something on the order of a collective meltdown.

The nanomites had seized control of the church's audio/video and lighting systems, leaving the techs sliding faders up and down and panning knobs left and right with no results. While the nanomites ran the video call from both ends, the frantic tech guys fumbled with soundboard and video camera controls that no longer responded to them. When the lead tech got a tad too "handsy" with the system and attempted to reboot it? He received a slight jolt that sat him back in his seat.

The glass-paneled booth muffled his yelp of surprise, but I could imagine it. I laughed out loud and startled Emilio yet again.

No matter what the techs tried, the live video call from Pastor and Mrs. McFee filled the church, its picture crystal clear, the audio perfect.

Back to what was happening below: the DCC congregation's sustained clapping for their beloved pastor.

Zander grinned. "Pastor McFee, Mrs. McFee, can you hear the love and appreciation of DCC's people here in Albuquerque?"

"We sure can, Pastor Cruz. We have been listening to the service from our ship anchored off Hilo on the big island. And as the camera pans across the sanctuary and we see all of you lovely people in that big old room,

I can tell you that Carol and I love every one of you. Every person! And we want all of you to know that our great God loves each one of you far better than we can. Because God loves you, personally and individually, he sent his Son, Jesus, *to find you and to save you*—to lead you home to heaven, as Zander described in his wonderful illustration."

"Yes, we love you all!" Mrs. McFee echoed, "and we're having a wonderful time on this vacation. But, God willing, we'll be home soon."

To more applause, Mrs. McFee waved goodbye and moved away from the camera, leaving her husband alone in the video's frame.

Pastor McFee sobered as he addressed the crowd. "Folks, may I please have your full and undivided attention for a few moments? We have some family business to take care of, so sit down and get comfortable. Yes, that's right. Thank you."

As the congregation settled in their seats, McFee pursed his lips before addressing them. "Most of you received an email from me earlier this week. In that email, I expressed my confidence in Pastor Cruz as a man of God. The main purpose of that email was to prepare you for this moment: I hereby appoint Pastor Cruz interim pastor of DCC in my absence."

McFee let no more than a heartbeat pass before he continued. "What you do not know is why I felt it necessary to appoint an interim pastor. The fact of the matter is that we, as a church, are experiencing an attack on our biblical foundations."

With the words "we, as a church, are experiencing an attack" Pastor McFee secured the full attention of his congregants. I noticed how some of our visitors, however, fidgeted and stared around.

Acting mighty guilty, if you ask me.

McFee continued. "And while we work our way through this attack— or fight our way through it, if we must—it is vital to the stability of our congregation that Pastor Cruz, a man who rightly divides the word of truth, also hold the reins of our church securely in his hands, from this moment forward until I return to Albuquerque."

From my vantage point in the choir loft, I saw movement below: Mike Barnes in a huddle with two tough-looking young men, both of them unfamiliar to me.

What is he doing?

Barnes slipped the young toughs a small object. A flash drive? With a jerk of his chin, Barnes seemed to dispatch them toward the media booth.

A blinding flash of insight swept over me: This was Barnes' plan to discredit Zander! He had ordered the two thugs to gain entry to the media booth, *shut down* Pastor McFee's video appearance and play, instead, that grotesque, deep-fake video Easterly had cobbled together, a video of Zander in bed with Izzie.

But the nanomites said they had destroyed all the files!

"Nano? What's on that flash drive?"

Do not fear, Jayda Cruz. Earlier this week, after listening in on Easterly and Barnes' phone calls, we sought out Easterly's cloud server. We removed and destroyed all of the video files on his server. If a copy of Easterly's deep-fake video resides on the flash drive Barnes handed to those men, we will destroy it, too. We will also prevent his proxies from gaining access to the media booth.

"That is awesome and welcome news, Nano. Thank you! I'm happy that Barnes will be thwarted."

A thin spiraling thread of nanomites lifted from me and dropped down toward the sanctuary floor. I heard them whisper as they wafted away, *He will indeed be thwarted, Jayda Cruz.*

The men Barnes sent to the media booth rapped lightly on the glass panels to get the techs' attention. The lead tech waved them off. Along with the rest of the tech team, his focus was glued to Pastor McFee's image on the media screens.

The young toughs tried the door, but it appeared to be locked . . . or had the nanomites sealed it closed? The men rapped again. The lead tech, with a frown and a dismissive shrug, turned his back on them.

One of Barnes' goons threw his shoulder on the door. It didn't budge. He tried again. He may as well have been huffing and puffing at it.

Ha! No bueno. I snickered, and Emilio slid another uncertain stare toward me.

The guy below us pounded on the media booth door, but another tech raised his finger to his lips and shushed him.

I shifted my attention to Barnes. His face reddened with exasperation as his thugs turned toward him for guidance.

I giggled. *Well, well! That didn't work out like you'd hoped it would, did it?*

The toughs did, however, garner the attention of a knot of ushers standing at the back of the sanctuary. Barnes shook his head, indicating he did not want his guys involved in a public confrontation. With nothing more they could do, his goons subsided into their seats.

Pastor McFee continued his address. "This morning I am forced to remove a DCC staff member from his position of trust and authority, an individual whose doctrinal stances and immoral lifestyle are contrary to the scriptural requirements for pastoral leadership, an individual whose grievous actions render him unfit to serve in any church office."

He paused before adding, "An individual complicit in a plan to remove me as senior pastor of this church while I am away and take my place as senior pastor."

An angry grumble answered McFee's revelation.

"I appreciate your ire. It would be untruthful of me to say that I haven't struggled with my own outrage. *But*. But in the church of Christ, all things are to be done decently and in order. So, I would ask that all of you put your feelings aside temporarily and consider the actions I must take to protect our church from those who teach heresies."

He leaned toward the camera a little. "Can you do that, DCC family? Can you trust me today to do the right thing? And will you prayerfully weigh the evidence when it is presented? If, after doing so, you have remaining questions, please feel free to contact me by email or in person, either before or after I return to Albuquerque, and I will answer them. Can you do these things?"

"Yes," a voice called out, followed by a general hum of consensus.

"I thank you for your trust and hereby publicly announce that I remove Aiden Easterly as a DCC associate pastor, effective immediately. He is dismissed from his position and, sadly, is no longer welcome within the doors of DCC or at any DCC function."

A great murmur of surprise raced across the room—and under the congregation's astonishment, a snarl of angry disagreement percolated.

That disagreement emanated from Easterly's adherents and the strange, off-putting visitors who had of late insinuated themselves into our church's life. Meanwhile, my eyes jinked between Barnes and Easterly. Easterly's angry face had turned completely red; Barnes' countenance, however, was immobile.

McFee pressed to his conclusion. "I also need to announce to all DCC board members that Interim Pastor Cruz will hold a meeting of the full board this afternoon at 4 p.m. Pastor Cruz will occupy my church office until I return, and he will hold the board meeting in my conference room.

"And so for the present, DCC, I bid you a fond farewell and leave you in the capable hands of Pastor Cruz until I return to Albuquerque. God bless you all. See you soon."

McFee's handoff was seamless: The lights rose and focused on Zander, and he picked up the thread of his message without hesitation.

"My last words to you before Pastor McFee's announcements were that, at *this* church, at Downtown Community Church, we are a Bible-*preaching*, Bible-*teaching*, Bible-*believing*, and Bible-*acting* church. The map of our faith here at DCC is the Bible and *only* the Bible.

"At DCC, contrary to what you have heard from this pulpit recently, we do not 'worship according to the Christian tradition'—which is another way of saying our faith does not differ from any other faith except in the traditions we follow.

"At DCC, we reject the assertion that God can be reached through all paths, that all deities are equally right and valid, that all religions lead to the same destination. Scripture clearly refutes this dangerous doctrine in 1 Timothy 2:5.

> *"For there is one God and one mediator*
> *between God and mankind,*
> *the man Christ Jesus,*
> *who gave himself as a ransom for all people.*

"Let me be perfectly unambiguous: We do not reference the writings of other faiths or other gods and we do not follow human philosophies. *We follow the Bible.*"

I cheered inwardly as Zander, point by point, continued to deconstruct Aiden Easterly's sermon from the previous Sunday, but I wondered why Easterly hadn't "gotten the message" and bugged out. Easterly sat there, closemouthed and angry, Stan Missing's restraining hand on his arm.

Why haven't they gone? Easterly is discredited and dismissed. Told not to return. They—

The truth hit me like a brick to the head.

Lord, they aren't finished. They are hatching some sort of plan. Please help us stop them!

My gaze swiveled between Easterly and Barnes, checking Barnes' reaction, watching for a signal to pass between them. At the same time, I prayed that Zander would have an opportunity to finish his message first and reap a harvest.

Zander spoke on. "At DCC, we worship Christ himself, the only living, resurrected Savior, the only begotten Son of the one true God. We worship Jesus, *the Word of God*, who created all that is visible and invisible. And we proudly proclaim the Apostle Peter's words found in Acts 4:11-12.

> *"Jesus is 'the stone you builders rejected,*
> *which has become the cornerstone.'*
> ***Salvation is found in no one else,***
> ***for there is no other name under heaven***
> ***given to mankind by which we must be saved.***

The congregation—with certain expected and angry exceptions— roared a great, unified 'Amen!'

Zander walked across the platform and stopped before he spoke again. "At issue today for each one of us is, *does my worldview line up with the Creator of this world?* And let me say that, *whoever* you are, myself included, we all have places within our hearts and minds where the Bible, the word of God, must and *will* confront and challenge the errors in our worldview—so, what does it look like when God's word confronts us?"

Zander lifted his voice. "It will look like this: What *you* think is right, God's word declares is wrong. Unholy. Even sinful. Like this, too: What *you* deeply feel is wrong, God will declare in his word is both right and just.

"What gives God the right to confront us? To correct us? Scripture puts it like this in Isaiah 55:8-9.

> "'*For my thoughts are not your thoughts,*
> *neither are your ways my ways,' declares the Lord.*
> '*As the heavens are higher than the earth,*
> *so are my ways higher than your ways*
> *and my thoughts than your thoughts.'*

"In other words, the Lord himself tells us, 'Look, wherever we disagree, it's because your thoughts and your ways are not as high as mine are. Your thoughts and ways are below my thoughts and ways. They are inferior to my thoughts and ways. In fact, your thoughts and ways are *wrong* and mine are *right*.

"If God's thoughts and ways are superior to ours, if they are right and ours are wrong, then how should we respond to him? The same chapter of Isaiah, verse 7, tells us how we are to respond.

> "*Let the wicked forsake their ways*
> *and the unrighteous their thoughts.*
> *Let them turn to the Lord,*
> *and he will have mercy on them,*
> *and to our God, for he will freely pardon.*

"It is clear from this passage what we are to do: Let the wicked forsake their ways, their low, inferior, and wrong ways; let the unrighteous forsake their thoughts, their low, inferior, and wrong thoughts. Turn to the Lord and adopt *his* ways, *his* thoughts, for the Bible tells us clearly in 2 Corinthians 5:10 that a day of reckoning is coming.

> "*For we must **all** appear before the judgment seat of Christ,*
> *so that each of us may receive what is due us*
> *for the things done while in the body,*
> *whether good or bad.*

"Each of us should determine *today* to have a teachable, malleable heart before the Lord. Allow him to change your mind where your thoughts are wrong; allow him to convince you where your ways are wrong; allow him to wash your minds with the pure water of the word of God and make you clean and whole in him.

"It is because we believe in the truth of God's word that I ask you to check your personal worldview against the truth of Scripture today. If anyone within the sound of my voice looks to the universe for his or her answers, the Lord compels me to correct this false premise.

"I must speak the truth and tell you that the universe is not sentient. It has no consciousness, no control over the events of humanity, no feelings at all. The universe cannot know us, cannot hear us, and cannot answer us. The universe has no influence on my life, my destiny, or my destination. The universe was created; it holds no sway over the Creator or even over itself.

> *"The Son is the image of the invisible God,*
> *the firstborn over all creation.*
> ***For in him all things were created:***
> *things in heaven and on earth, visible and invisible,*
> *whether thrones or powers or rulers or authorities;*
> ***all things have been created through him and for him.***

"While we are checking our personal worldviews against Scripture, we also must clarify within our hearts what we cling to as most dear in this life. The Lord clearly tells us we are not to worship any part of his creation—not the stars in the sky, not the forests or oceans or wildlife. Nor are we to worship what we or others create, be it art, music, literature, beautiful buildings, fabulous cars, science, or technology.

"In particular, we are not to worship people—those we care most for, whether spouses or children, or even the human form. Therefore, we are not to worship humanity as an entity. Such worship, known as humanism, is but another false, idolatrous religion.

"Having been made in *God's* image, people are to worship *him* and him alone. Any other form of worship, any other object of worship is idolatry. And what does Scripture teach us about idolatry? Deuteronomy 6 tells us,

> *"Fear the Lord your God, serve him only . . .*
> *Do not follow other gods,*
> *the gods of the peoples around you;*
> *for the Lord your God, who is among you,*
> *is a jealous God and his anger will burn against you.*

"Jesus repeats this warning in Matthew 4.

> *"Worship the Lord your God,*
> *and serve him only.*

I shivered at the authority Zander exercised. Simultaneously, I could sense two powerful spiritual forces competing within the walls of DCC, one good, the other evil. I recognized and clung to the sweet presence of the Holy Spirit—even as that sweetness swelled and grew into something much deeper and more awe-inspiring.

But the other spirit, the one at war with the Holy Spirit? *Demonic.* My reaction to it was visceral. *You do not belong here, devil! This place and these people belong to the Lord of Hosts!*

The lights began to dim and stars again appeared in DCC's high, vaulted ceiling. I watched Zander, though. He was backlit enough for everyone to see him.

"Jesus, in John 14, made these unambiguous declarations.

> *"I am the way and the truth and the life.*
> **No one comes to the Father**
> **except through me.**

"Jesus is *the way*—the only way. Jesus is *the truth*—the only truth! Incidentally? Stop spouting 'your truth.' Your truth is your flawed, vaunted, idolatrous opinion, not fact. There is only one truth, and it is this: If you want to live, seek Mehitah'ess, *the Messiah*, the author and finisher of our faith, Jesus Christ."

Murmured amens washed through the congregation . . . and something else. That growl of disagreement, growing in strength.

Zander paid those rumbles no mind. He was no longer entertaining: *He was a fiery coal held firmly in the tongs of God Almighty, wielded by the Lord's strong, mighty hand.*

"Jesus said that those who believe in *him* will not be condemned. Believe in *Jesus*—not in the Buddha, not in Allah, not in Muḥammad, not in Krishna, not in any of the gods or goddesses of this fallen world. Those who believe in *Jesus*, will be saved.

"Sadly, I can tell you, with confidence, that in this room are many individuals who not only refuse to bow their knee to Jesus, *they hate him.* They hate Jesus and flout his claims. Well, Jesus had something to say about them in John 3:19.

> *"This is the verdict: Light has come into the world,*
> *but people loved darkness instead of light*
> **because their deeds were evil.**

Zander was looking over the congregation no longer. I saw that he recognized which of our "visitors" Aiden Easterly had seeded into the front-and-center section of seating. But what Easterly had not anticipated was that he had also placed his followers front and center where Zander could preach to them and them alone . . . and something was certainly happening down there among them.

"Who is the light come into the world? Jesus declared in John 8:12: *I am the light of the world*, but you hate the light! Why? Clearly, because your deeds are evil.

"You rejoice in pagan worship, you wallow in every kind of sexual sin and perversion, and you celebrate those who do such things. You call evil good and good evil. You come into this house of worship to disrupt and create confusion. To sow doubt in the minds of new believers in Christ. To co-opt this church and turn it to your wicked purposes. *Your attempts will not work.*

"God forbids idolatry. The word of God rejects the worship of trees, high places, mountains, stones, crystals, and animal spirits. The word of God rejects pagan shrines and their figures and images made by human hands. The word of God rejects the worship of every kind of false deity, and in Ezekiel 23:49, the Sovereign Lord spoke directly to those who do so.

> *"You will suffer the penalty for your lewdness*
> *and bear the consequences of your sins of idolatry.*
> *Then you will know that I am the Sovereign Lord*

"To worship a statue, the dead stump of a tree, to offer it flowers, burn candles and incense before it, bake cakes with the image of that statue on it, and pray and bow before it, is to commit the grievous sin of idolatry— as we see in this video."

The screens across the sanctuary blinked on. In vibrant color and clear audio, nearly a thousand people watched Aiden Easterly prostrate himself before the defaced statue of Mary stolen from the Catholic church of *Madre de Dios*—the statue whose half-naked form was overwritten with pagan and occult symbols and words. The video zoomed in on the statue's gleaming and terrifying glass eyes, then focused on its gaudy crown and the crown's inscription.

Goddess Ishtar
Queen of Heaven

An old gentleman, an elder saint, stood to his feet. "Is that Pastor Easterly?" he demanded. "And is he bowing down to that . . . blasphemous figure of evil?"

No one needed to answer him: The video evidence the nanomites had downloaded from Easterly's servers and continued to play was too long and complex to have been faked—nor was Easterly alone in his idolatrous worship. Easterly was joined by Sierra, Jill, Mari, Dinae, Theo, Galen, and Stan Missing.

All of them lit candles and incense sticks, chanted, placed offerings before the statue . . . and, one by one, cut the underside of their forearms and dripped blood onto the cakes offered to the statues.

The evil emanating from the scene was outrageous and profane, but then the view pulled out and refocused. It fixed on Stan Missing as he pulled Easterly to him in an obscene embrace.

Over the gasps of horror, Zander spoke. "I will repeat what the Lord says in Jeremiah 7 regarding the pagan Canaanite goddess, Ishtar, the so-called 'queen of heaven.'

"The children gather wood, the fathers light the fire,
and the women knead the dough and make cakes
to offer to the Queen of Heaven.
They pour out drink offerings to other gods
to arouse my anger."

The media screens went dark, and into the shocked silence Zander said softly. "Do you acknowledge why it was incumbent upon Pastor McFee to dismiss Aiden Easterly? We cannot allow such wickedness a place to grow and thrive in our church leadership or in the members of Christ's body."

Zander spoke into the hush in the sanctuary. "You are piloting your life through the time and space God has allotted to you. You and you alone choose your direction, your path. Know, however, that your choice has eternal consequences, both for yourself and for those whom you influence, for whom you care. Your destination is either eternity in heaven—or eternity in the fiery pit of hell. Which will you choose?

"If you are ready to abandon your false worldview for the Creator's worldview, *come*. Come to the altar and repent—that is, change your mind. Change your mind and throw yourself upon the mercy and forgiveness of Jesus.

"Repent of—change your mind concerning—rebellion and idolatry.

"Repent of—reject and give up—sexual sin of every kind: sex outside of a godly marriage, which is the sin of fornication; sex with someone other than your spouse, if you are married, which is the sin of adultery; sex with a partner of the same gender, which is the sin of homosexuality; sex while watching porn, which can be any or all of the aforementioned sins.

"Repent of denying and rejecting the gender your Creator gave you!

"Repent of every form of dishonesty: theft, lying, slander, and gossip.

"Come! Repent and turn to Jesus. Come! Come now!"

I had never seen such urgency! The congregation below churned as a hundred or more rose from their seats and *ran* to the front.

And within the awe that I felt in that moment, I recognized a conviction of my own—how easily we people are led astray, how easily we can place our love for a spouse or a child ahead of our love for the Lord . . . and I was convicted over how easily I could place Zander or Baby Cruz on the throne of my heart.

Oh, God! I cried in my heart. *Save me from such a sin!*

"Come to the altar and repent!" Zander cried. "Weep and mourn before God. Let the Lord and all who are here witness the sorrow in your heart. Determine in this moment to immediately and forever put away every sin that so easily attaches itself to you. Fall upon the Savior's grace and mercy. Receive him as your king! Receive him as your lord and master!"

I was suddenly aware of a second stirring below in the congregation— a different kind of movement. *Two divergent movements.* More stood to make their way down front to where Zander waited, but others stood to mutter and shift from foot to foot, a few to stomp up the aisles and out the doors in disdain—until a female voice screeched . . .

"Hate speech! You spew hate speech! You persecute the LGBTQ community! Hatred! Hatred! Hatred!"

The woman's cry was taken up by others, some who shouted out curses directed at Zander. Zander, however, did not flinch or move. His voice through the PA system rose over their shouts and even screams.

"We declare that Jesus Christ is the Lord of this church—he is the Rock upon which we stand—and his word remains true, absolute and unassailable, forever settled in heaven. We welcome all who will repent of their sin, but we will not water down or violate the unchanging nature of God or his Scripture. If you disagree, you are free to leave, but you are not free to stay and disrupt this service."

His head turned to take in the wondrous events taking place at the front, only feet from him. "Prayer teams, come and minister to those who are here. Ushers? Be strong and do your duty. Remove anyone who disturbs this important time."

That was the moment our not-quite-peaceful service flared into a full-fledged riot. At a gesture from Stan Missing, our "visitors" along with Easterly's known associates dug into the purses or backpacks they carried. The nanomites zoomed in and I watched the agitators pull out cans of spray paint, sacks of rotting vegetables, even containers of feces. Others picked up their chairs and heaved them at those approaching the altar.

Missing and Easterly's reaction to Zander's message would never be mistaken for some sort of peaceful opposition. They were not going down without a fight,

Repentant hearts, young and old crowded the steps near the front of the sanctuary, responding to the conviction of the Holy Spirit. I even saw several of Easterly's acolytes make their way to the steps and fall on their knees, sobbing. I wanted to, in the worst way, watch the beautiful thing the Lord was doing, but I couldn't.

My job was to protect those at the altar and the work the Lord was doing in them.

"Guess that's our cue, Nano."

Yes, Jayda Cruz.

The nanomites pushed Abe and Emilio away from the railing and uncovered them while they kept me hidden.

"Stay away from me," I called out. "Give me space!"

I focused on those "visitors" who hoisted chairs into the air or were aiming foul missiles toward the front. It had been months since I had needed to use my nano-charged abilities, but I had not forgotten how.

The sanctuary lights dimmed a little as I drew down on the electricity available around me.

"Nano, keep my zaps as invisible as possible, okay? No sense drawing attention to us."

Narrow, nearly transparent shafts of light shot from my fingers, crossed the sanctuary, and jolted those throwing vile projectiles. I hit three in a matter of seconds, then one guy who was using his chair as a battering ram. However, there were so many attackers scattered across the seating sections nearest the front, that I could not zap them all before they threw their bombardments or wielded their weapons. Helpless to prevent every disruption, I observed several of Easterly's crowd lob a few nasty objects into the crowd that had come forward for prayer.

"Lord! Please help them! Please help us!" I whispered. "Don't let these awful people ruin the work you are doing."

A woman below begin to chant, "Stand up! Stop the show! Trans hate has got to go!" Others picked up the ditty until fifty or more voices shouted it in unison, their combined voices ugly with hatred.

"Stand up! Stop the show! Trans hate has got to go!"

Trans hate? I was completely mystified. Mystified until the woman who had confronted Josh as he tried to exit the pew yanked off her sweater, baring her arms, hitched up her skirt, and vaulted over the seats in front of her. She walloped the first person she reached, Mr. Schraider, one of the prayer team members, and put him in a headlock.

Jayda Cruz, contrary to that person's feminine attire, she is actually a 'he'—and a strong one.

"What? Oh!"

The nanomites were right. I mean, get a load of that guy's guns. I had to zap him three times before he let go of poor Mr. Schraider. Unfortunately, as he was keeling over—taking Mr. Schraider to the floor with him—Mr. Schraider grabbed for anything that might keep him upright.

It so happened to be his assailant's hair.

Off it came!

I gaped at the wig dangling from Mr. Schraider's hand. I may have been flummoxed by the sight, but not nearly as much as that gentle soul! Mr. Schraider shrieked, shook the wig like it was some kind of alien creature that had attached itself to him. He jumped up and ran screaming through the crowd to escape it.

I tore my eyes away from his exit and tried to focus on my task. I zapped a few more rioters, but the scene below me was becoming more crazed and violent by the minute. And I found it harder to track and curtail the disrupters from up in the choir loft than I had thought it would be. I wanted in the worst way to run downstairs and personally enter the fray, but I had promised Zander I would remain upstairs . . . for Baby Cruz's sake.

"Nano, you don't need me to direct you or add to what you know to do. Go! Please protect Zander and our friends—and record everything you can."

We will, Jayda Cruz.

I watched a shimmering trail of nanomites fly from me to the brawl below. I sat as close to the rail as I could and stared as the situation unfolded. Zander seemed to be paying no attention to the shouting, swearing, scrabbling, hitting, flinging mob. His nanocloud was operating independently, too. In fact, the two nanoclouds soon appeared to get a handle on the situation.

In addition to stinging those who were lobbing garbage or beating on and resisting the ushers who were doing their best to eject them from the building, the nanomites had formed an irregular-shaped shield at the front. They adjusted the shield to come between the individuals kneeling and praying and the rioters pelting them with garbage. When someone seeking the Lord came close enough to the shield, the nanomites kind of sucked them inside. Behind that shield, Zander was able to ignore the attacks and focus on ministering to those at the altar.

I laughed out loud for joy. "Oh, well done, Nano! Well done!"

Thank you, Jayda Cruz. We are happy to assist you and Zander Cruz with the important work the Lord has given you both.

I grinned. I liked the kind of work the Lord had in mind for us! I liked seeing hearts come to Jesus!

Much of the congregation had fled the sanctuary as the chaos unfolded. The vast room was predominantly empty except for those who had answered the altar call and Easterly's thugs. They were doing their best to attack Zander and those at the altar. Although the mob continued to shout obscenities and chant their hatred, I was heartened to see that their best wasn't going to be nearly enough. Not with the nanomites staving off their enraged attempts.

Until.

Until two guys ran up an outside aisle, set a rag stuffed in a bottle on fire, tossed the bottle against the nearest side wall, then ran toward the main entrance like the devil himself was pursuing them.

And maybe he was.

The bottle broke, spewing fiery liquid up and down the wall, onto the carpet, and down the aisle.

"Fire!" twenty shouts proclaimed at nearly the same time.

At least five ushers bulled their way toward the fire extinguishers mounted on the walls. Two of them engaged in a fierce tug-of-war over an extinguisher before they realized they were fighting at cross purposes. One let go; the other raced to the wall and began spraying it down with two other ushers and their extinguishers.

I stopped holding my breath once I was assured the church wouldn't burn down on Zander's watch. I glanced down and spotted Barnes directly below my perch in the choir loft. He stood alone amid a section of vacant seats. With arms folded, narrowed eyes, and a disturbing lack of concern, he observed the melee, and I wondered—

With no warning, the big old pipe organ behind me kicked on. The first notes were so loud and I was so startled, I almost fell over the balcony railing. I swung around to see who was playing the massive instrument.

No one was.

The nanomites!

I scanned the choir loft for Abe and Emilio and found them, hands covering their ears, against the far wall by the staircase where the pipes' sheer volume had plastered them.

"Go down!" I shouted, tossing Abe the keys. "Get out to the parking lot and into the car. If anyone threatens you, drive away. We'll be in touch."

After they left, I realized (over the booming volume of the organ) how welcome the song was. The nanomites were playing the melody slower (and much louder) than I remembered singing it, but slowing down the hymn made it . . . heavier.

More ponderous?

No, the slower tempo made it more *majestic!* And it drowned out the curses and shouted chants from down below.

Remember how earlier I'd felt two spiritual forces at war? One the Spirit of God, the other a demonic presence? The waves of praise pouring from the organ diminished the evil presence.

Pushed it back.

Pushed it away.

Back where it belonged!

A little like . . . Zander and me singing *Up from the Grave?*

"Yes!" I shouted "We should fill this place with God's praise. We should be singing this!"

I had all but forgotten Josh, Diego, and the other young adults who, when they received my text, had retreated from the front of the church where they had been surrounded by Easterly's crew, to the wall at the back of the sanctuary. When I remembered them, I gave the nanomites instructions.

I also prayed. *Lord, if the young adults are nearby, please give them the courage to stand strong for you today.*

Half a minute later, the nanomites reported. *We have sent the text as you requested, Jayda Cruz.*

Wherever our young adults were, they were receiving my message.

Move to center of church
Stand up and sing
your praises to the Lord
SING LOUD

I peered over the railing. Waited. Resisted the urge to chew my fingernails. There! Josh and a dozen of "our" crew raced to the center seating section. They jumped up on the seats. Standing proud and singing for all they were worth, they joined arm in arm and belted out the hymn the nanomites played on the organ.

All hail the power of Jesus' name!
Let angels prostrate fall.
Bring forth the royal diadem,
and crown him Lord of all.
Bring forth the royal diadem,
and crown him Lord of all!

Hail the power of Jesus' name, you miserable demons! I whispered to them. *Jesus is crowned Lord of all!*

I guess the young adults only remembered the first verse, but that was okay. They belted it out five times . . . before others heard them, before a couple hundred or more DCC members, all ages, swarmed back into the sanctuary and stood shoulder to shoulder with the young adults, singing for all they were worth.

As more DCC people streamed back into the church, the volume of their singing increased. I noticed the media guys down on the left return to their glass-walled booth. In seconds, the other verses to the hymn appeared on the screens. The voices lifted in song were triumphant. They were glorious! Their song drowned out the protest chanters, who were being outperformed by the singers' intensity and determination . . . and by the Spirit of Holiness that poured from them.

The attackers' hate-filled campaign deflated like a hot-air balloon with a sudden, fatal leak. I was puzzled, though, when the protesters' gazes shifted from our ad-hoc choir and fixed on the doors in the back.

Then I heard what they heard: sirens, bunches of them, converging on the church. As one in heart and mind, Easterly and Missing's mob dropped whatever they were doing and raced for the exits, trampling others in their haste to evacuate the sanctuary.

Speaking of Easterly and Missing . . .

"Nano, where are they?"

Jayda Cruz, they left the sanctuary three point five minutes ago by means of the corridor leading to the church offices.

"The first rats to abandon their sinking ship, eh?"

Wait. The office wing? Concern that they might vandalize the office wing or set fire to a different part of the building seized me.

"Have they left the church, Nano? Or are they somewhere on the premises?"

They used the office exit to leave the building, Jayda Cruz. Shall we maintain a watch on the entrances in case they return?

"Please do, Nano. Thank you."

I blew out a long breath and grinned big. Easterly, Missing, and their underlings were done at DCC. That threat, at least, was over, although Zander had Barnes and his people to deal with this afternoon.

The organ behind me hit the last stanza of the hymn and slowly, deliberately, ground to a triumphant close. Our "choir" below gave that last line all they had. When they finished and the organ dropped into silence, they cheered, shouted, praised God, and jumped up and down right where they were.

I was smiling on them when, without warning, I was taken back a couple of decades. I was eight again and Aunt Lu had brought me to DCC for the first time. I knew for a fact that she would've had a royal *fit* if she'd beheld church members jumping up and down on the sanctuary chairs. But you know what else I knew?

In this particular instance, she would have stood right there beside them, singing her declaration to the world.

Bring forth the royal diadem,
and crown him Lord of all!

⌘ ⌘ ⌘ ⌘

CHAPTER 31

WE DIDN'T LEAVE DCC until nearly three hours after the mob fled the arrival of APD. Eventually Abe and Emilio returned to the church and joined us. I glanced at my phone. Half past three, and Zander's board meeting was scheduled at four. No way would he cancel it—not with the important business he needed to take care of.

"Ain't right," Emilio grumbled. "Supposed to get pancakes after church,"

You're not wrong, bud, I thought. I could hardly bear the echoes emanating from my hollow stomach.

"We can't leave until the police say we can, kiddo."

Emilio flounced back into his seat, earning himself a reprimand from Abe.

Two detectives and an FBI agent had interviewed a number of people and were wrapping up their interview with Zander. The FBI agent was present because APD had received calls from the rioters accusing Zander of a hate crime. Special Agent Ross Gamble was present and observing the interviews because he chose to.

Lord, thank you for Gamble's friendship.

Zander handed the FBI agent a memory stick. "Everything that happened this morning is recorded here."

"Thank you for that. Would you care to make a formal statement regarding the allegations of a hate crime?"

"Sure. Are you recording me? Good. To clarify, the senior pastor is, at this time, on vacation and has been quarantined on a cruise ship off the coast of Hawaii. He appointed me interim pastor of the church until he returns and announced my appointment publicly during this morning's service via a video call with him. That video call can be seen on the recording I've given you."

Courtesy of the nanomites.

"While I was preaching this morning, I became aware that forty or fifty visitors, individuals I do not know and have never seen before, were seated in the congregation, primarily close to the front. In addition, perhaps twenty or thirty newer attendees, part of DCC's young adult group, sat with the visitors.

"At the conclusion of my message, I asked those listening to repent, to change their minds, concerning a list of sins that I articulated. Then I gave the altar call, and people responded to it. At that point these new people began screaming insults. They opened backpacks and purses and began to pelt us with rotten fruits, vegetables . . . even feces."

"They threw, uh, *poop* at you?"

"Yes. And they picked up chairs and threw them or used them to strike members of my congregation."

Detective Sosa asked, "Is that how you got that cut on your forehead?"

Zander nodded. "Yes. The fact that they came bearing 'gifts' to throw at us, tells me that their objectives were malicious from the get-go, that their intentions were to disrupt our service. However, their disruption went far beyond tossing rotten tomatoes.

"They stormed the platform, attacked those praying at the front, and turned on the ushers who tried to restrain them. One woman—to be clear, she was a transgendered man—managed to slug me in the head. That's when I got the cut."

My jaw went slack. I hadn't seen that part!

We apologize, Zander Cruz. We did not move quickly enough.

"Don't sweat it, Nano," Zander answered them.

Zander kept going. "In my opinion, yes, this was a hate crime—but not against any homosexual or transgender individual. It was a hate crime against our church and congregation, a violation of our first amendment rights to free speech, freedom to assemble, and the freedom to practice our faith. Our services are open to the public, but they are not open to demonstrations or violence. These people invaded our church, attacked our people, spray painted vile slogans on the walls, and tried to set the sanctuary on fire."

The detective chewed the end of his pen. "Would you believe me if I told you this wasn't the only local church to see violence and interruptions today?"

Zander blinked slowly. "I might."

"Yeah, three other Albuquerque churches got hit by similar attacks today. Calvary, Legacy, and Citizen Church. Legacy almost burned, but they caught the fire in time. Like you did."

"Those are all Bible-teaching congregations."

"Yep." The detective paused to reflect for a moment. "I mean, yes, churches have the right to preach and teach what they believe and all but, in my humble opinion? I'd think you'd lay off dinging gays and transgenders. You know. It's like poking the bear. Sure, you have 'the right' to poke the bear, but why do it? Why ask for that kind of trouble?"

Zander thought for a moment. "Let me ask you something, Detective Sosa. May I?"

He shrugged. "Sure."

"If you saw a man you knew, a man who hated all police and hated you because you were a policeman or police detective, and you saw this man driving his car straight toward a cliff, would you try to stop him? Or, because he might scorn your warning, might even attack you for warning him, would you 'lay off'? Not ask for 'that kind of trouble'? Let him drive on, to plunge off that cliff to his death?"

Sosa frowned. "You think gays and transgenders are headed for a cliff? Is that it?"

"Aren't we all? Each of us faces certain death, right? That's a fact. But our physical death is not the end of us. Each of us will face God after our death. He will judge us for our choices, and we will spend an eternity either with him or forever separated from him.

"But, see, God sent Jesus to save us—all of us. He died for murderers, thieves, alcoholics, wife beaters, liars, and child molesters. Jesus died for gays and transgenders every bit as much as he died for those who steal staples from their employer or who cheat on their taxes. He even died for pastors and police detectives who are supposed to have it all together."

Sosa stared at Zander, his expression flat. "That so."

"Yes, it is so. Jesus said it this way, *For God so loved the world that he gave his one and only Son, **that whoever believes in him** shall not perish but have eternal life*. The world, Detective Sosa. God loves the world, and he sent Jesus to save us, all of us. That includes you, me, gays, and transgenders."

"Huh."

Zander changed the subject. "Have you found and arrested the leaders of the riot? Aiden Easterly is one of them; Stan Missing is another."

From what the nanomites had found out and told us, Easterly and Missing were literally that—missing. No one had seen them since before the police arrived to quell the riot at DCC. They had slipped out, unnoticed by all except the nanomites.

"We sent two officers to Missing and Easterly's house. They are collecting evidence as we speak."

Sosa's partner, Detective Reardon, jumped in. "*That* place, from what I hear, is turning up some interesting stuff."

"I'll bet," Zander answered, his face giving nothing away. "Interesting in what way?"

"They busted into this locked room and found some seriously messed up stuff, like that statue of Mary stolen from *Madre de Dios* Catholic church—but, *whooee!* What they've done to it—"

"Stow it, Reardon," Sosa growled. He turned back to Zander.

"To answer your question, we did find Easterly, but it appears that Mr. Missing has packed his belongings and departed. Easterly seems genuinely baffled over Missing's departure and his whereabouts. We searched the bedroom Missing and, er, *Pastor* Easterly shared, but Easterly declares nothing has been removed that wasn't Missing's personal property. So, do you want to press charges against Easterly? Isn't he a pastor at your church?"

"He isn't any longer. We terminated his employment earlier today. I will need to consult with Pastor McFee and the board as to whether we press charges."

Jayda and Zander Cruz. We have noticed an odd detail about Stan Missing that may or may not have significance.

Zander was busy, so I replied. "What's that, Nano?"

His full name is Stan A. Missing. It is, however, a fake identity.

"We know. You told us, right?"

Yes, and his assumed name is Stan, not Stanley, middle initial 'A' but no middle name.

"Not following, Nano."

His false moniker, when deciphered, is an homage, Jayda Cruz, a tribute that illuminates his allegiance.

I puzzled over their words for a few seconds. "Stan A. Missing. Stan A. Missing. Something's missing? What is it?"

The name tells you what is missing, Jayda Cruz.

I frowned. "Stan A. Missing. The 'A' is missing?"

Yes, Jayda Cruz.

"Missing from where?"

His first name, Jayda Cruz.

Grrr. I plodded forward like the nanomites' sluggish and disappointing student.

First name Stan. Take the "Missing" "A" and insert it . . . after the "S" in Stan?

The answer slapped me upside the head.

A homage, a tribute that illuminates his allegiance to . . . Satan?

Oh, dear merciful heavens!

"Excuse me, Pastor Cruz?" The timid intrusion came from Mrs. Coyne.

"Yes?"

"I apologize for interrupting, but the board members are asking if you intend to postpone the meeting?"

"No. We'll meet at four o'clock."

"So, in ten minutes?"

Zander looked to the two detectives, the lone FBI agent, and Gamble. I saw Gamble subtly nod at Zander.

"If we are finished, gentlemen, I have an important meeting to facilitate."

Detective Sosa replied, "Yeah. I think that's all. We'll be in touch."

The detectives and FBI guys, Gamble included, sauntered away. Zander turned to me.

"I wish you hadn't stayed for all this, Jay. Will you please go on home and get something to eat?"

I nodded. "Sure. Let me know when you're done with the board meeting. I'll come get you."

Zander touched my hand briefly and walked away with Mrs. Coyne.

I said to Abe and Emilio, but mostly for Emilio's sake, "Shall we go get those pancakes?"

Emilio heaved himself out of his seat. "Don't want no stinking pancakes."

Abe lifted a finger to wag under Emilio's nose, but I gently restrained him. I was tired and hungry and in no mood for Emilio's drama.

"Abe, may I, please?"

Abe nodded, so I said to our recalcitrant boy, "Emilio, I want to point something out to you."

He turned a scowl on me. "Yeah? What?"

"Your unloving behavior."

His knotted brows relaxed in astonishment. "What?"

"You. Your selfish, self-centered, unloving behavior. Everything is about *you*. You show no concern for Abe. He has patiently waited without eating as long as you have. You show no concern for Zander—who has also missed lunch—and the mess he has to deal with here. And you show no concern for me, even though I'm six months pregnant and missing a meal will likely make me throw up. It's all about *you* not getting your pancakes when *you* wanted them, so *you* decide it's okay to pitch a fit."

Emilio's scowl returned.

I didn't care.

"We love you, Emilio, but you aren't acting like you love us. How do you think that makes us feel?"

Emilio's eyes dropped to the carpet. "Well . . ."

"Your selfishness *hurts* those who care about you, don't you see?"

"Sorry," he mumbled.

"I couldn't hear you."

He heaved a great sigh. Looked up. Spoke louder. "I'm sorry, Jayda." He slid his eyes toward Abe. "I'm sorry, Abe."

"Thank you," I said. I grabbed my purse and headed for the exit to the parking lot, doing my best to keep the nausea at bay.

Lord? Is this what having a pre-teen will be like? All the time?

⌘

ZANDER BREATHED AN INAUDIBLE prayer as he took the seat at the head of the table. *Lord, I need you here. I'm a little tired, too, but whether I'm tired or not, I need you. Please help me get through this. Let your will be done here, I ask in Jesus' name.*

He ran his gaze around the table to familiarize himself with the people seated down both sides. Mrs. Coyne had thought to put name placards in front of each board member. She had also, at Zander's last-minute request, produced copies of the meeting's agenda. All two items of it.

God bless you Mrs. Coyne, Zander saluted her silently. He returned his attention to the individuals around the table.

Apparently, the six board members usually sat in the same places—the three conservative members arrayed on Zander's right; the three liberals on Zander's left. Zander glanced left again, putting names to faces: Myra Hernández, Dave Abbott, and Mike Barnes. Barnes' eyes glittered and his lips twitched with unvoiced anger. His fingers drummed on the table, conveying his impatience.

He'll jump right in, try to take control of the meeting and the narrative. I mustn't let him.

Down the right side of the table? Harry Fuentes, Victor Gibson, and Elise Farland. He didn't know Elise nor did she know him except in passing, but Harry offered Zander a tight smile and Victor nodded to him. Mrs. Coyne, visibly nervous but ready to take meeting notes, sat in a chair pressed hard against the wall, as if she were trying to remove herself from the room's crackling tension.

Zander exhaled. *All right, Lord. Here we go.*

"We'll open this meeting with a word of prayer." Zander left not a second between his statement and, "Lord God, we come to you in the name of Jesus, asking for your wisdom and guidance. Whatever we do this day, may it honor and please you, and may we do it decently and in order. Amen."

As Zander had expected, Barnes pounced the second he sensed an opening. "I don't know who you think you are or what the *bleep* you think you're doing, *Mr.* Cruz, but the damage you have done to DCC today will take a decade to repair. I call for an immediate vote to remove you from this church."

Zander didn't respond to Barnes' outburst. Instead, he handed the short stack of one-page agendas to his right. "Here's the agenda for this meeting. Pass it around. It's short, but pithy. We should get through it fairly fast."

"Hey! I'm talking to you—"

"You are out of order, Mike," Zander said quietly. "Pastor McFee called this meeting and put me in his seat. If you have a problem with that, take it up with him."

"Oh, I will. You can take that to the bank!" Barnes snarled.

The agendas made their way up the left side of the table. Barnes scoffed and flipped his aside without a glance; Myra Hernández and Dave Abbott stared at theirs. Hernández's eyes went wide; Abbot blanched.

"The first item of business is you, Mike," Zander said. "You are hereby relieved of your position on this board and your membership at DCC is revoked. *You know why*. Accept your removal peaceably, and I won't embarrass you publicly. Surrender your keys to Mrs. Coyne on your way out. Two ushers are waiting in the hallway to escort you from the premises."

Hernández and Abbott exchanged worried glances. Barnes slammed his fist onto the table. "You *bleeping* holier-than-thou upstart! I've been a member of this church since I was born!"

"All right; if that's how you want it, I'll go ahead and submit testimonies and evidence to the board." Zander inclined his head toward Victor Gibson. "Vic? Are you ready to speak?"

"I certainly am." Victor squared his shoulders and faced Barnes. "You had Easterly sic one of his young nymphos on me. She came up to my car acting like she was hurt and in need of a ride. But as soon as I let her into my car, she ambushed me—pulled off her top and tried to come on to me."

Barnes had trouble keeping a smile from curving his lips. "Victor, Victor. Why, you're the last man in the world I'd dream of seducing an innocent and vulnerable young girl but, hey," he shook his head with bogus regret, "as they say, a picture is worth a thousand words. I didn't want to do this, but I feel that I must—"

"Oh, *Mike, Mike*, I'm not done. Like I said, it was an ambush. I never touched the young lady. And the photos you have? Pastor Cruz calls them 'deep fakes.' Yeah, they're *fake* all right. That means I'm done cowering before you, scared spitless that you'll show them to my wife or the world. My wife knows the truth. When I told her what you accused me of, she wasn't even remotely convinced that I'd done something inappropriate. She figured you'd set me up and faked those photos before I even had a chance to tell her what you'd done. That's how solid our marriage is."

Barnes wagged his head further in mock pity. "Faked photos? Victor, what *are* you babbling on about? You-all want evidence? I have the evidence right here on my phone, a number of pictures showing Victor's unholy fling with young, defenseless Sierra. Shall I pass my phone around the table? Text them to you? Release them to the public?"

Zander smiled softly. "You tried the same thing with me, Mike. Faked a disgusting ten-second video clip of me in bed with *my own sister*. You even tried to put that clip up on the screens during the service this morning because you needed to ruin my reputation before I could take hold of the leadership here. We stopped you, though."

"That's a preposterous accusation! I'll sue you for slander!"

"As you wish. But while you consult with your lawyers, why don't we listen to your conversations with former associate pastor Aiden Easterly and his lover, Stan Missing?"

Barnes sat back. "What conversations? What are you talking about?"

"In a general sense, I'm talking about *you*, Mike. You conspiring with Easterly and Missing to take over and destroy this church, turn it into a liberal, New Age abomination. You plotting a coup with Easterly that would remove Pastor McFee and replace him with Easterly but would, more or less, leave you running the church while Easterly became the new face of DCC. Sort of a 'power behind the throne' gambit."

"You're a *bleeping* liar, Cruz!"

"And somehow I'm not surprised to hear that kind of language from you, Mike. But that aside, let's listen in, shall we?"

Zander knew that Easterly and Missing, with an eye toward using videos of the many intimate acts that went on in the house as more fuel for their sick "religious" activities, had set the video surveillance system in their house to record nearly everything that happened there. But by doing so, they had also, unwittingly, captured a stunning number of phone and in-person phone conversations. The nanomites had uploaded the convos and were inside the conference room's A/V system, ready to run the files Zander asked for.

As Zander ended his sentence, the speakers in the corners of the conference room came to life.

"Your girl did a standup job of snaring Victor Gibson, Stan. She told me he sat there, stunned—like a deer in the headlights—until Easterly here got the photos he needed. Say, have you finished editing them, Easterly?"

"Almost done, Mr. Barnes. And unless the images are scrutinized by an expert who knows what to look for, no one will ever suspect that I've mashed together several similar images to produce the final product you asked for. I'll be sending the files to you tomorrow."

"Good, good. Can't wait to show them to good old Victor. He'll crap his pants—and then he'll vote however I tell him to. Please excuse me. I need to get home."

The audio cut off, and Zander said nothing; he stared steadily at Barnes. The board members stared, too, all of them aghast.

But Victor, after hearing the recording for the first time, sputtered, "That was *you*, Mike Barnes! That was *you* with those heretics Easterly and Missing, the three of you planning to ruin my marriage, not to mention my Christian testimony!"

Barnes, sensing the tide turning against him, shouted at Zander, "It's illegal to record people without their consent! I'll have you arrested, Cruz. I'll sue you into the ground—and then I'll sue this church!"

"Before we get to that, let's listen to another call. A minute ago I said you planned to fake a video clip of me in bed with my sister and release the video to the public. Here you are again with Easterly setting it up and planning today's attempted coup."

"Mr. Barnes! Have you read McFee's email? He sent it to the entire congregation!"

"Of course I saw it, you twit. Give me a minute. I'm rethinking our strategy."

"You'll want me to send out the deep-fake videos today, right? Then can you cancel Cruz despite McFee's glowing recommendation?"

*"Actually, I'm leaning toward **not** canceling him.*

"What? But you said I would be preaching again this coming Sunday!"

"Yeah, well, I've come up with a better idea, one that will take out two birds with a single stone—rid ourselves of both Cruz and McFee. See, instead of you sending the clip to church members and posting it on social media, how about you send the video to me? During the service this Sunday, as soon as the singing is over, I'll have one of my guys take over the data projectors. I'll order him to put the video up on the screens the instant Cruz starts pontificating."

Everyone in the conference room heard Barnes laugh aloud then add, *"The entire congregation, at the same time, will see the clip of Cruz in bed with his sister. Once they do? He'll be toast. When the furor dies down, I'll call you up to finish the service."*

"Wow. What an inspired idea, Mr. Barnes. At the same time, the video will totally negate McFee's email where he expressed so much confidence in Cruz."

"Yes, that's what I mean. McFee's own words will blow up in his face. He'll be left with zero credibility—and zero retirement pension courtesy of DCC."

"Great point! That video will flip McFee's endorsement of Cruz back on himself. McFee won't be able to fight the retirement the board has planned for him—not with that glob of egg on his face. Ha! Bet McFee won't send any further emails spouting his 'I anticipate serving this great congregation for many years to come' bilgewater! Yup. I like it."

"Glad to hear it," came the growled reply. *"Now listen up. To complete the effect, we'll need a reaction from the congregation after the video plays. A big reaction—and I don't mean a show of righteous indignation. No, what we need is a full-on riot. So, I want you and Stan to beef up our presence Sunday morning—and I mean really beef it up. When I give the signal? Go after Cruz and take him out. No holds barred."*

*"Sure! I can handle that, Mr. Barnes. Can't wait to see Cruz's face when our people rush the platform—when it hits him that they're coming for **him**."*

Barnes couldn't ignore the looks of revulsion or contempt directed at him from around the table. He shook with rage. "You had no legal right to record me on a private phone call! I will sue you in court, and I swear I will destroy you, Cruz!"

"Sue me? You should talk to Easterly, Mike. He's the one who recorded the call, not me. In fact, I have it on good authority that he records every little thing that happens in that house he leases—not merely the audio. His entire house is wired for video recording, including that room he and Missing turned into a blasphemous shrine to the so-called queen of heaven. And guess what? Easterly also records everything that takes place in that room as a sick form of 'worship.'"

Zander added softly, "You're featured in a few of those 'worship' services, aren't you, Mike?"

Barnes gasped and stammered, but Zander lifted a hand to forestall further protests.

"Here's what's going to happen, Mike. You are going to leave DCC, and you're going to leave today. Before you go, you are going to give us your word that you will sever ties with every person you know at DCC and that you will never meddle in DCC's affairs or darken the doors of DCC again—unless and until you are prepared to repent of your sin. *If* you adhere to these conditions, I won't release the video recordings of you in that room. Break your word? I promise that I *will* release them."

"What video?" Myra Hernández demanded.

"Video of Mike with the girls who live with Easterly, one of them being young Sierra who, you might like to know, has a police record in Colorado for solicitation. Not so innocent and vulnerable after all, right, Mike?"

Barnes seethed but didn't answer.

"That's the deal, Mike. Give us your word, honor what you've promised, and what we've revealed in this room stays in this room."

"But we haven't even gotten to what Mike did to me," Harry protested. "Mike floated a mortgage loan to me and my wife in our time of need— out of Christian love, he said—but when we got behind on the payments, he threatened to sell our home out from under us if I didn't vote to bring Easterly on as an associate pastor."

Barnes shot Harry a look of loathing. "I still own you, you little weasel. I'll foreclose on you for this!"

"No you won't," Zander answered, "because we're going to pay off that loan, Mike. By this time next week, you won't have an ounce of leverage left on Harry."

He scanned the other board members. "Are you in agreement with removing Mike from the board and revoking his membership?"

Three emphatic yeses and two nods came back to him.

"Keys, Mike." Zander lifted his chin toward Mrs. Coyne. "Please let our longsuffering ushers know we're ready for them to escort Mike to his car."

When Mike Barnes had, at last, left the room, Zander sighed. It had taken an hour to accomplish the first item on the agenda.

Don't mean to complain, Lord, but I'm feeling a mite weak from hunger.

He pushed on anyway. "Next item? Pastor McFee's involuntary retirement. If I read the minutes correctly, a few of you board members used a slick and not-quite legal mechanism to change the church bylaws, the alteration providing a means for you to retire Pastor McFee—with or without his consent—when he returned from his cruise. These actions took place in a board meeting four weeks back, a meeting, I would add, that was called without Pastor McFee's knowledge or presence. Would any of you care to put forward a motion to cancel all actions taken on that date and declare the meeting null and void?"

Five board members spoke at once, "I will."

Zander slowly nodded. "Mrs. Coyne? I want it written into the minutes that the unjustified and illegal actions of this board on that date have been reversed. I'll review tonight's minutes with you Tuesday morning to ensure that they are complete and that they accurately represent what has happened this afternoon."

Zander looked down at his clenched hands. They trembled, but only a little. The excess adrenaline was burning off.

Thank you for your grace, Lord God.

Then he raised his eyes to Myra Hernández and Dave Abbott. "Myra and Dave? I don't know you well. I'd like to know you better . . . but more than that, I'd like to know that every member of this board fully supports Pastor McFee. Do you?"

Myra licked her lips. "I-I had no idea about Mike and Easterly and what they were doing . . . together. I'm sorry that I allowed Mike to sway me into . . . those unconventional actions to remove Pastor McFee."

"Illegal actions, Myra."

"No. I mean *yes*. Yes, they were illegal. There's no sugar-coating it. I am sorry. I apologize to all of you for betraying the trust of my position on this board. If . . . if you wish my resignation, Pastor Cruz, I will give it."

Zander considered her. "Let's see how things go, shall we? And you, Dave?"

Dave was more forthright. "I was wrong to follow Mike. Like Myra, I didn't know how far he'd fallen, but I knew what *I* did at his behest was wrong. I admit to my culpability, and I ask your forgiveness—all of you. I, too, will tender my resignation if asked to."

Zander again nodded. Then he repeated the words he'd spoken during the morning service. "DCC is a Bible-preaching, Bible-teaching, Bible-believing, and Bible-acting church. The map of our faith here at DCC is the Bible and *only* the Bible. Myra and Dave, can you pledge your agreement with this statement? Do you agree with it in your hearts?"

"I haven't always believed or agreed with such fundamentalism, Pastor Cruz," Myra admitted. "But I saw something today I'd never seen before. When you were preaching, I saw a man of God on fire—and I saw the results. Oh, not the riot that Easterly and Missing cooked up, but the flood of souls gathered at the altar despite that mob! I want to see more of that. I want . . . I want to see real change like that in my own life. So, yes. I pledge myself to agree and support our church, our Bible-teaching church, as we go forward."

"Ditto from me," Dave said. "That is . . . if you want me."

Zander felt the weight of the world slide from his shoulders, even if only for a little while. "I do want you, Dave. But hey, to tell you all the truth, I'm starving. Haven't eaten since early this morning. What say the six of us go out to a modest restaurant, break bread together, and have some fellowship? Can we do that?"

Elise Farland, who had said little during the proceedings, but whose quiet, watchful attitude toward Zander had been one of growing support and agreement, pushed back her chair. "Thank you, Pastor Cruz. I second the motion."

⌘

Victor Gibson dropped Zander home after dinner with the board. Zander promptly had the nanomites connect his phone to Pastor McFee's. As he waited, he turned to me. "He needs to know everything that's happened at DCC today."

I listened as Zander related his sermon, the wonderful response from many in the congregation, and the horrible, destructive actions of Easterly and Missing's many agents. Pastor McFee stopped Zander frequently to ask questions but did not sidetrack him from finishing his tale.

"Well!" Pastor McFee sighed, that single utterance expressing as comprehensive a thought as any complete sentence. Nevertheless, he replied with words Zander needed to hear.

"Son, despite the fiery trial thrust upon you by my absence, you have done all I could ask of you. More than that, you have done all *the Lord* has asked of you.

"Furthermore, the fruit of your labors bears testimony to the rightness of your actions: the powerful move of the Holy Spirit during the altar call, the exposure and removal of Easterly and his ilk, the removal of Mike Barnes from our board, and the genuine fellowship you shared with the remaining board members over dinner."

We heard a muffled cough from Pastor McFee's end of the call, and I slid a questioning gaze toward Zander.

McFee cleared his throat. "I am mighty proud of you, Pastor Cruz."

Zander closed his eyes; tears leaked from beneath his eyelids. "Thank you, sir."

McFee pulled away from the phone to cough again. It was a long, protracted coughing spell. In the background we heard a woman cough.

"Sir? Are you and Mrs. McFee all right?"

We waited a full minute for McFee to catch his breath.

"Seems we've contracted the virus, Zander. The authorities have provided plenty of food and over-the-counter medicines for us, but the bug is rampant on this ship. Locked in our cabins as we are, we're all breathing the same recycled air, so it's no wonder most of us have it—captain and crew, included."

"But can't the authorities send doctors and nurses to you? Or let those who need to be hospitalized off the ship?"

"Sadly, the entire state of Hawaii is so paranoid about the virus that we are grateful for what they supply: fresh food, medicine, and whatever other needs we put on the list."

He struggled through a coughing fit. "We have been cut off from what's going on outside the ship, cut off from our families except for a few minutes every few days, and numerous fellow passengers are suffering mental health breakdowns. We . . . have heard through the ship's grapevine that a few hardy souls are tending the worst of us. We've also heard that the crew is storing the bodies of the dead in a walk-in freezer."

Zander's pupils dilated. "The dead?"

To us, the virus was something happening far away, not anything we needed to be concerned about. No one in our state or any state around us had contracted it. We were untouched by those dying from it. Until now.

"Yes, my boy. We have a sort of human chain on this level, a means of passing news and needs up and down the hallways."

cough

"One passenger sneaks up a level to exchange news with them, sneaks down a level to exchange news with them, then passes what they hear on to us."

cough cough

"I'm sorry to say that we know of six dead on this level and have heard that more than ninety passengers have succumbed . . . so far."

"Pastor, you and Mrs. McFee *must* take care of yourselves! We need you, the church needs you. *I need you!*" I heard the desperation in Zander's shaking voice.

"No, Zander—no, we must *give* of ourselves. Carol and I? Jesus' words in Matthew 16 are real and tangible for us.

> *"Whoever wants to be my disciple*
> *must deny themselves*
> *and take up their cross and follow me.*
> *For whoever wants to save their life*
> *will lose it, but whoever loses*
> *their life for me will find it.*

"We made a decision last week to share Jesus with whomever the Lord gave us. We've been holding Bible studies in the hallways. Been going cabin to cabin to pray for the sick and grieving. It's not a bad way to spend the last days of our ministry. Target-rich environment, to tell the truth. Must give of ourselves as long as we're able. Bring in the harvest while we can."

Zander stood up. I stood with him. "Jayda and I are going to pray for you and Mrs. McFee, Pastor."

cough

"Thank you, my boy."

Zander prayed his heart out. I agreed with each word and rehearsed the words of Matthew 18:19 as I prayed for the Lord to heal the McFees.

> *Again, truly I tell you that if two of you on earth*
> *agree about anything they ask for,*
> *it will be done for them by my Father in heaven.*

Zander said amen and the two men exchanged goodbyes.

⌘

"I HEARD A RUMOR THAT Cruz dumped you from the board at DCC. Any truth to that?" Easterly's smug question irritated his caller—which was precisely what he'd intended. *Job done!* he gloated.

"Shut it. You're out every bit as much as I am."

"True. Guess we're both *persona non grata* at DCC, *Mike*." Easterly laughed bitterly, all deference gone. "Stan's in the wind. Abandoned me.

I doubt I will see him again . . . and I thought he loved me. I'll likely receive a new assignment and end up in some dive where Stan isn't. Tomorrow I need to call in and report our failure to take the church as ordered."

"Hold on there! We're not quite finished. Until McFee returns, we can continue to mess with Cruz, maybe even get rid of him—but I'll need resources for that."

"Oh? What did you have in mind? Can't use his sister again. She won't let me near her, thanks to the video Cruz showed of us worshipping the goddess. Speaking of video, what in the world happened to the file I had Sierra pass to you, the one of Cruz and his sister your guys were supposed to play after the singing Sunday?"

"You're asking me? My guys couldn't even get into the booth—they said it was locked, and I know that door doesn't *have* a lock! And my copy of the video mysteriously disappeared from the flash drive Sierra gave me. But I'm surprised you didn't right away fall back to our previous idea to send it out by text and email, then upload it to social media."

"The video disappeared from the flash drive?"

Easterly's question wasn't asked with the incredulity Barnes expected, and he frowned. "That's right—as improbable as that sounds. When the guys gave the drive back to me, the file was gone. Why do you ask?"

Easterly hesitated, then blurted, "Because that's what happened to us, too. All the files in the cloud? Gone. The finished files on my phone? Gone. Like the files on my servers. Gone. *The same way Cruz entered my house without tripping a single alarm.* I tell you, there's something way too fishy about that guy. I'm making a full report about him tomorrow when I call in."

"Well, hold up on conveying mission failure. Yeah, we're both out at DCC, but we have another lever we can pull to burn Cruz—that kid he's fond of. I received word through my Albuquerque network that Cruz and his wife have filed adoption papers on him."

"You want to mess with the adoption? I like it. What did you have in mind?"

"Leave that to me. I'll use my network here, and you let your report reflect that the op is ongoing."

"If you say so. Maybe you don't need to leave town, but I need to blow this dirt hole quick. The police and FBI have figured out that the shrine to our goddess includes a statue stolen from a Catholic church. I don't want to be around when they decide to press charges."

"I get it, but make sure our superiors know the op remains active, that I'm working it."

⌘⌘⌘⌘

CHAPTER 32

SUNDAY HAD BEEN THE most difficult day Zander and I had weathered as a married couple—to date. I'd also like to say, with all its difficulties, that Sunday was the victorious end of our fight to safeguard DCC's body of saints during Pastor McFee's absence. Yeah, *well it wasn't*. It was the enemy's opening salvo.

Zander had pulled the veil of secrecy off of the covert tactics aimed at destroying DCC's biblical foundation. With the subterfuge exposed, we faced open warfare.

Monday is usually a day of rest for pastors, and Zander needed time to recuperate both physically and mentally from Sunday's events. *But.* But during the night, we started receiving phone calls.

I got the first.

Groggy with sleep, I picked up my phone. "Hello?"

"Is this Jayda Cruz?"

"Um, yes. Who's this?"

"Your worst nightmare, sweet thing. I'm watching you. Watching your husband. Watching that beaner foster kid of yours. When you least expect it? I'll be there—"

I disconnected the call, slammed my phone down on the nightstand, and rolled myself to the edge of our bed. Sat up, shaking.

Zander's drowsy voice reached out to me. "What was that, Sweetie?"

He was beat, and I knew it. What he needed *least* from me was another problem that would snatch away the rest of his night's rest.

"Nothing, Babe. Go back to sleep."

He didn't even reply, and a minute later I heard his soft, regular breathing again. Certain he was in deep sleep, I tiptoed from the room, taking my phone with me, determined that only one of us would lose sleep tonight.

"Nano, please silence Zander's phone for the rest of the night?"

We have silenced two calls to Zander Cruz's phone so far, Jayda Cruz.

"Did they leave voice mail?"

The nanomites played back the messages. The first was from a woman. A screaming, *crazy* woman.

"You're a hateful, homophobic, misogynistic, racist *pig*, Cruz! And we're going to tell the world about you and your despicable, hate-filled church!"

Click. The caller hung up.

The second message was plain *weird*. A full minute of howling, moaning, and screeching.

Click.

"Lovely. What about the call I picked up? Can you trace it?"

The calls tonight came from pay-as-you-go phones here in Albuquerque.

Of course they did.

My phone rang again. Different number. "Nano, try to get a fix on this call? I'll keep him on the line as long as I can."

I picked up. "Hello?"

No preamble. Straight to the scare tactics.

"I have a knife—a long, sharp knife with a serrated blade. When I catch you, I'm going to stick your belly with that knife and slice that baby right outta your—"

Click. This time, *I* hung up.

Turns out keeping that freak on the line "as long as I can" was pretty short.

Jayda Cruz, would you like us to silence your phone also? Let us answer any calls that come in. We can, perhaps, keep the callers on long enough to locate them.

"Sure, Nano. Knock yourself out."

I shivered. More accurately, I trembled all over. It's one thing to threaten me, but to threaten Baby Cruz?

Beyond the pale.

I padded to the kitchen and turned the burner on under the tea kettle. When the pot finally whistled, I brewed a cup of chamomile tea for myself, added a spoonful of honey to my cup, then stirred the tea well to dissolve the glut of honey.

When I took my first sip, I closed my eyes in welcome bliss and sighed. The super sweet brew was precisely what I needed—and then I heard my phone ring again—same number.

Except that I heard the call in the warehouse?

And I heard *myself* pick up. "Hello?"

A perfect rendering of my voice!

"I'm going to cut that baby out of your belly, Jayda Cruz, and stab it over and over."

"My" response? "Ohhh, poor widdle boy! Did somebody hurt your itty boo feelings when you were a wee widdle lad? Would you like me to read you a bedtime story, widdle man?"

I almost snorted tea through my nose.

Five full seconds of dead silence followed on the other end of the call before the expected sharp *click.*

I guffawed into my cup. "Great job, Nano."

We have many such responses up our sleeves, Jayda Cruz.

"I'll bet you do!"

I drank my tea, crawled back into bed, and slept like a log until dawn.

⌘

THE CALLS CONTINUED ALL day Monday, but we let the nanomites screen them. They handled the harassing and abusive calls and allowed the legit ones through. More than a few of those they passed to us were from our congregation, thanking Zander for his calm response to the riot and his spot-on response to Easterly's message the previous Sunday.

However, not all calls from the congregation were positive. Zander had, in essence, thrown down the gauntlet. Those who affirmed his biblical positions stood with him. Those whose worldviews were skewed away from biblical truth gave him "what for."

"We'll be withholding our donations to DCC until Pastor McFee returns and kicks your *bleep* out of our church!"

"You'll never find *me* darkening the doors of DCC again, you hateful fanatic!"

"I have never heard such bigotry and hatred preached in church until yesterday. You have wounded people, Mr. Cruz. Shame on you!"

We sat down to lunch together, but Zander was quiet. I knew he was struggling, knew the criticisms were weighing him down, despite a greater number of positive calls.

Shortly after lunch, the doorbell rang. Zander's eyes met mine. We were gun-shy at this point. Definitely cautious, particularly given the threats toward Baby Cruz.

Friends from the young adult group are at the door, Zander and Jayda Cruz. We ascertain no ill will toward you.

"I'll get the door, Jayda," Zander said.

He opened the door to a throng of sheepish grins. Josh, their spokesperson, said, "Hey, Pastor Zander. We know it's your day off and all, but can we come in? For a minute?"

Zander unlocked the barred security door. "Come in, everyone. You're welcome here!"

They piled into our living room, their happy banter the infectious infusion we needed.

"Hey, Jayda!" they greeted me.

Izzie was with them. She came straight up and hugged me tight. "Thank you again, Jayda," she whispered in my ear. "I cannot thank you and Zander enough for saving me from the worst, the most *foolish* decisions I have made in my life!"

I hugged her back for a long time. I was so glad to have my sister restored to us, safe and sound.

Izzie pulled away. "I'd like you to meet someone."

She motioned to a girl who'd stayed by the door. The girl slowly, while looking around nervously, sidled over to us.

Izzie said, "Jayda, this is Danni. She gave her heart to Jesus yesterday."

Danni, short, wide, and "butch," was reluctant to lift her eyes to mine, but I felt a loving sisterhood with her on sight.

"Danni, I'm happy to meet you," I said kindly. "Is it all right if I give you a welcome hug?"

She squirmed. "I'm not . . . into the touchy-feeling stuff . . . if you don't mind."

"I don't mind. How about we shake hands?"

Reluctantly, she lifted her fingers. I took them in mine. Squeezed gently.

"So, I hear you met our Jesus yesterday."

She stared at the floor. "Yeah, uh, might be what happened. Something did. Dunno what for sure."

"Was it something like this? You heard the message Zander preached and found yourself wishing you could start your life over? You felt a deep longing inside, a desire to turn away from some of the choices you've made, an urgent need to get rid of the gunk in your heart . . . and you began to *hope* that Jesus could forgive you and wash you clean inside?"

Danni's eyes jumped up and fastened on me. "How do you know that?"

"I know because I've been where you are, Danni, and I remember what meeting Jesus felt like. I've studied the Bible bunches since then, and it has taught me who he is, what he did for me, what he thinks about me, how much he loves me, and what walking with him is like. I want to encourage you to do the same. Learn as much as you can from the Bible. Read it every day, in fact. Jesus *will* change you—I promise—but it is a process, a growing thing."

I glanced around our living room. "Think you can hang with this rowdy bunch?" I laughed, gesturing toward Josh, Diego, and the other guys and gals.

"I-I might not fit in with that crowd."

"What if I said every single one of them thought the exact same thing when they first met each other? Tell you what: You stick with Izzie and me, Danni, and you'll grow. You'll experience the Lord's grace and his faithfulness. You'll never regret the decision you made yesterday."

"Are we meeting here Friday evening?" Izzie asked. "Or at the church?"

I blinked slowly. "Oh. Yeah." I swiveled toward my husband. "Zander? Young adult group this week?"

I saw it hit him, too. He'd be doing double duty for a while as the interim senior pastor *and* the interim young adult pastor.

He took a deep breath. Steadied himself. "Let's say Friday evening at DCC. Get everyone together. Straighten out some stuff. Put things right."

I smiled at Danni. "You heard the man. I admit I'm biased, but I think you're gonna love these meetings."

⌘⌘⌘⌘

PART 3: STEALTH INSURGENCE

"Therefore keep watch because you do not know when the owner of the house will come back . . .

What I say to you, I say to everyone: 'Watch!'"

Mark 13:35a. 37, NIV

CHAPTER 33

WE MET WITH THE CONSOLIDATED young adult group Friday evening. It was great to see the faces of all our friends. Nevertheless, with all the upheaval in the church over Easterly's removal, we anticipated that the evening might start out a mite rocky.

Boy, did it.

First up, Zander had to address Easterly's firing. Then he had to speak to Sierra and the little crew that followed her into the fellowship hall. Honestly, I was amazed she would show her face again at DCC given everything we now knew went on inside Easterly's house. But then again, we held no illusions concerning Easterly, his handlers, and his followers. Would they cease their assault on our church so easily?

Apparently not.

Zander, not one to beat around the bush, dealt with the situation head-on. "I need everyone's attention," he said. "Please take your seats."

Our solid young adults had quieted the moment Sierra, smirking and preening, strolled in. They knew the danger she posed. The group had a few newcomers, however, who had started attending the group meetings under Easterly's leadership. We didn't know how loyal they were to him or his New Age baloney. Didn't even know if they were saved. Easterly hadn't exactly been preaching the salvation message.

Then there was Danni, a brand-new believer. I was especially concerned for her. We didn't want her to get hurt or become confused by a public confrontation during her first young adult meeting. Conversely, she was more likely to be injured if Zander waited to deal with Sierra later. No telling what she'd do during the meeting.

When Danni arrived that evening, Izzie and I grabbed onto her and kept her close to us. As the group took seats and settled down, Zander opened his Bible. "I'm reading from 1 John, chapter 2, verses 18, 22, 23, and 26." he said with no other preamble.

> *"Dear children, this is the last hour;*
> *and as you have heard that the antichrist is coming,*
> *even now many antichrists have come.*
> *Who is the liar?*
> *It is whoever denies that Jesus is the Christ.*
> *Such a person is the antichrist—denying the Father and the Son.*
> *No one who denies the Son has the Father . . .*
> *I am writing these things to you about those*
> *who are trying to lead you astray."*

"This is a nice sized room, but it isn't large enough for us to ignore the several big, fat elephants lurking in it."

That earned him a nervous titter from some. Sierra, however, continued to smirk and kept looking over the young men like a snake choosing its next meal.

Zander went on. "We're going to take as much time as is needed to bring a few secret, sinful things out of the shadows and into the light. We need to bring these secret, sinful things into the light so that they do not continue in our group. We also hope that those who need to confess their sins have opportunity to repent of them."

Zander spoke in a calm, matter-of-fact manner. "It is essential that everything we teach at DCC and in these young adult meetings be carefully evaluated through the lens of Scripture. Aiden Easterly, in his sermon two Sundays ago, denied that Jesus is the Christ, the only Savior of the world. He declared that Jesus was only one of many Christs—that Buddha and Muḥammad were also Christs, that we are all Christs—and some other nonsense about Christ being the universe. Mr. Easterly's statements fit the warning I read in 1 John.

"Who is the liar?
It is whoever denies that Jesus is the Christ.
Such a person is the antichrist
—denying the Father and the Son.

"If you were in our service on Sunday, you saw video of Mr. Easterly worshipping at the feet of a grotesque idol. For these heresies and for grave sexual sins, Pastor McFee removed Mr. Easterly from his position at DCC. I therefore encourage all of you to reject anything and everything he taught you in the short time he was an associate pastor at this church."

He looked around. "Is anyone unclear as to why Aiden Easterly was removed? Does anyone have any questions concerning him?"

"He is a great leader! An anointed servant of the goddess Ishtar!" The outburst came from Sierra.

Around the room, eyes shifted and nerves grew taut.

Zander said quietly, "If Easterly is a servant of Ishtar, he is no servant of Jesus—and he has no place among us."

He turned his gaze on Sierra. "Sierra Miller, you have thrown yourself at the young men and women in this group, enticing them to sin sexually. Worse, along with Aiden Easterly, Stan Missing, and the others living in Easterly's house, you and your friends," here Zander looked directly at Jill, Mari, Dinae, Galen, and Theo, "participated in pagan worship of the same idol and in unspeakable sexual acts."

He paused a moment. "I bring these sins out publicly to give you opportunity to repent of them. Sierra? Jill? Mari? Dinae? Galen? Theo? Are you willing to acknowledge these sinful acts? Will you confess your sins and repent of them?"

He waited quietly for them to respond. As he waited, the tension in the room increased. I watched closely as Sierra's followers squirmed in their seats, angry and embarrassed. Sierra, however, was motionless . . . and I felt sudden apprehension.

Zander spoke again. "I need to be completely clear with the six of you: Unless you are willing to repent and turn from these sins, you can no longer attend this group nor will you be welcome at DCC."

My attention was fixed on Sierra. What was up with her?

With my heart hammering in my chest and all my nerves stretched tight, I watched as Sierra's face grew dark and took on strange contours. I saw it stretch and contort, her mouth forming an ugly, impossible shape. It looked like her entire face had opened!

Then she shrieked.

She shrieked louder, the volume and pitch nearly ear-shattering.

And she shrieked again.

The hair on my arms and neck prickled and stood up. I found myself on my feet declaring, "Jesus the Christ is Lord and King in this place! I lift up Jesus, Lord of all!"

All around me, the young adults were on their feet praying and proclaiming Jesus aloud with me. I had thought Zander would lead us in such an outward expression—instead he seemed pleased that our young adults had risen up on their own.

Then I saw his lips move. Heard him say above the rest of the room, "You who fear him, trust in the Lord—he is our help and shield. For God has not given us a spirit of fear, but of power and of love and of a sound mind. Submit yourselves, then, to God. Resist the devil, and he will flee from you."

He walked up to Sierra's screaming maw and said, "In the name of Jesus, be quiet and come out of her!"

Sierra halted mid-screech. "Ah-ah-ah-ah!" seemed to be all she could verbalize. Zander had opened his mouth to speak again when Sierra bolted, knocking him aside, and ran from the room, four of her five companions behind her. Theo remained where he was, his eyes pleading with Zander.

"Theo," Zander said softly. "Would you like Jesus to set you free?"

He nodded. "Please! Help me!"

"Call upon Jesus to save you. Confess that you choose him as Lord and Savior."

"I do! Jesus, you are my Lord and Savior! Please save me! I want you, not these demons! Please help me!"

"You must repent of your idol worship, Theo."

"I repent! I will worship no God but you, Lord!"

"You must repent of your sexual sins, Theo."

"I repent, O God! Please save me from this clawing in my insides!"

"Surrender to Jesus, Theo. Call on Jesus, resist the devil, and he will flee from you."

"Jesus! I surrender to you! Devil, I resist you!"

Theo began to shake all over. His body shook so hard that he began to convulse. Zander grabbed his arms, however, and Theo immediately snapped to attention.

Another shriek, this one deeper than what Sierra had screamed, flew from Theo. It floated out the door and echoed down the hallway until it dissipated into the distance.

Theo's head dropped onto Zander's shoulder. He sobbed and sobbed while Zander held him. Josh, Diego, and several of the young men gathered around Theo. As they prayed over him, he exhaled in relief over and over. Then he laughed softly, lifted his head, and rejoiced. What touched me the most was the great liberation that came over his face.

"I-I'm free! *I'm free!* Thank you, Jesus!"

It was beautiful.

I nudged Izzie and nodded toward Danni. She seemed stupefied, and her eyes blinked continuously. Izzie and I led Danni aside, and I whispered, "Look, Danni, we know you witnessed some curious, even strange, er, stuff this evening. We want you to know that our meetings aren't usually as, uh, lively as this. Ordinarily, we sing worship songs and have great discussions over the Bible passage Zander teaches from."

"Yeah," Izzie added. "We hope you don't think we're, you know, *weird* or anything."

Danni's nearly breathless reply was, "Are you guys freaking kidding me? This was the most awesome thing I've ever seen! I mean, I felt *God* move in this place, and *bam*, he kicked the devil right outta here!

"Not only do I now *know* God is real, I've figured out that the ugly, creepy sensation I've felt so many times in the bars and raves where I've hung out is actually some kind of demonic presence."

She looked from me to Izzie. "I want *nothing* to do with my old life. I want Jesus and only Jesus. In fact, I have some friends who need Jesus, too! I'm going to tell them what he's doing in me. Thanks so much for inviting me to come, both of you. I think I'm gonna fit in here just fine."

I looked at Izzie and chuckled. She giggled with me. We grabbed Danni and the three of us, laughing and bouncing up and down together, had us a little hug fest.

⌘⌘⌘⌘

CHAPTER 34

YUP. FRIDAY EVENING'S YOUNG adult meeting was awesome. Too bad Saturday "bombed." The morning started like most Saturdays: quiet and sweet. Emilio arrived shortly after breakfast. According to our transition plan, he would spend the day and the night with us. We would have the pleasure of Emilio's company, and Abe would have a peaceful day and evening off.

Did I say peaceful?

Around ten o'clock, as Emilio and I were cleaning up the kitchen while Zander tackled the living and dining room carpets, the nanomites buzzed urgently in our ears. *Jayda Cruz! Warning! Zander Cruz! Warning! Protesters are gathering half a block up from your cul-de-sac.*

Zander louvered open the dining room blinds, and we stared down the street past Abe's house. Yup. There they were—a sizeable crowd.

"Who, Nano? What do they want? Give us a closer view," Zander demanded.

A large number of homes these days boasted self-installed security cameras, and it was a snap for the nanomites to monitor different feeds all over the neighborhood. They showed us live video from a house opposite the crowd.

At least twenty cars clogged the road, and I mean *clogged*. The drivers had parked their vehicles side by side across the street, then up on sidewalks and lawns, blocking off our only egress by car.

A van on our side of the blockade seemed the center of activity. The nanomites zoomed in, and we watched as several individuals at the van's doors handed out signs, placards, ski masks, baseball bats, and bricks.

"Huh. Not a friendly protest, then."

Zander's ironic observation was lost on the nanomites.

Friendly? No, Zander Cruz. Do you see the large container and the bottles they are filling from the container?

"Uh, since you mention it . . ."

He turned to Emilio, whose expression was tight and anxious. "Hey, buddy. I need you to scamper back to Abe's *pronto*. Tell him what's going on. Lock the doors and stay inside with him. Got it? If anyone manages to get inside the house, go immediately out the back and over the wall into Gamble's yard."

Emilio hit the door running.

"Gamble and Trujillo?" I asked.

Zander glanced at my hands; they were clasped beneath my belly. I was, unconsciously, cradling Baby Cruz.

"Yeah, give them a shout while I call 911."

As I told Trujillo what was going on, I half-listened to Zander's call.

"Listen, a mob is forming, up the street from our house," he told the dispatcher. "They brought weapons, including Molotov cocktails, and they have blocked the street so we cannot get out. Please send an armed response right away."

When he hung up, he looked at me. "I'll go out and try to defuse the mob," he said, "but if I need to fight, I will."

"*We* will fight," I answered in no uncertain terms. "There are too many of them for you to handle on your own. You'll need both nanoclouds."

Don't worry, Zander Cruz. We can and will protect Jayda Cruz and Baby Cruz.

Zander didn't like the idea of me out on the street with him, facing an angry mob, but maybe he entertained some notion about talking down the crowd. I was under no such delusion. Baseball bats, bricks, and Molotov cocktails?

This mob came with an agenda—and "talk" wasn't on it.

Zander and I hurried to change into clothes and shoes we could fight in. We met Gamble and Trujillo in our front yard as the crowd marched our way. A quarter of a block up from the cul-de-sac, we heard their roar. Then a shouted chant blew toward us on the breeze.

Preaching sin is homo hate!
Spew the hate, you earn the fate!

"Who thinks some of the clowns coming at us also tried to take down DCC?" Zander asked.

Trujillo frowned. "Same bunch that rioted at your church Sunday?"

Zander nodded. "Yeah. These woke social justice warriors don't quit easily—and they didn't win at DCC. Guess this is their response."

Trujillo stared, askance. "Seriously?"

"Janice, I'm *dead* serious."

The mob started forward and marched into the cul-de-sac, shouting their slogans, waving signs or swinging baseball bats. When they saw the four of us waiting for them on the sidewalk in front of our house, they sort of paused, and their ranks muddled up uncertainly—until a loud voice cried, "There they are! Get 'em!"

To be fair, I think at least half of the crowd was there to protest, not to burn us out. On the other hand, the rest of them were there precisely for that reason. They were using the other protesters as camouflage.

My take on the two halves of the crowd was verified when half the mob surged forward but the protesters hung back, hesitant and unsure of what was happening.

We knew what was coming.

The four of us backed up onto our grass—in other words, onto our property. Gamble and Trujillo hoisted interesting shotgun-looking rifles, black in color, but with distinctive orange parts on the rifles' stocks, grips, and butts and with orange lettering on the stock that read "LESS LETHAL."

I knew those guns fired bean-bag shells, mesh socks filled with lead shot, the socks sporting mesh tails that improved the accuracy of the fired shell. Each shell was designed to sting like a scorpion, even knock the wind out of an adversary shot in the chest. And the mesh sock was coated with paint that would mark its impact point—a quick means of identifying those who had been hit and where.

Zander and I stood our ground as the mob advanced, unseen current thrumming through and around us. Two men out in front of the rabble twirled their bats to loosen their wrists. Or to make a show of acting tough. We'd see.

Gamble unexpectedly roared, "FBI! We are federal agents! Stop where you are! One step farther, and we will use whatever force is necessary to protect life and property!"

The two bat swingers slowed as though considering Gamble's order, perhaps wondering if stopping—as opposed to getting nailed with bean-bag rounds—might be advice worth heeding.

They glanced behind them, irresolute.

Jayda Cruz, Zander Cruz, three individuals far back in the crowd are wearing headsets. Someone is sending instructions to them. We shall disable their communications.

The nanomites zoomed in on a woman behind the bat-twirling guys, then zoomed in to a man in line with the confused protesters, and a woman behind him on the far right.

"I see them, Nano. Yes. Take out their communications."

Done, Jayda Cruz.

The three of them, their headsets no longer working, must have received instructions before the nanomites cut them off, because they came alive at the same time. The two toward the back screamed the chant, and the protesters dutifully took it up. But the woman with the armed group in front went from person to person, her words lost to us because of the shouted slogan.

Preaching sin is homo hate!
Spew the hate, you earn the fate!

"She's spinning them up," Gamble said to us, his mouth drawn down. "They'll be coming at us soon."

Maybe, but we were ready for them. And, no, things weren't going to go the way the brains behind the mob had planned.

"Nano, as much as possible, keep our bolts of electricity invisible to the attackers," I said.

We will, Jayda Cruz.

Zander and I watched lighters come out of pockets and heard the *snick* of them as they lit and caught the rag fuses on nine Molotov cocktails in nine hands. I *was* concerned about those. Our front yard was not that deep. If even one of those gasoline-filled bottles hit the side of our house? Or—God forbid—if one broke a window and ignited inside? Even if we put out the flames, our home would suffer a great deal of damage.

"You take right. I'll take left," Zander said.

"Got it." I was sandwiched between Zander and Gamble.

The shouted chant grew into a roar. The Baseball Bat Twins rushed forward: They and the brick throwers needed to make a hole in our line so the others could run up and lob their firebombs into our house's front windows.

Our home.

Baby Cruz's home.

The nursery where *our child* would sleep—the child *our gracious God had given us*.

A sacred resolve leapt up inside of me. *No one* was going to take what God himself had given us! I lifted my hands. A bolt of blue power flew forward and struck the first Baseball Bat Twin's aluminum bat.

Hey, did you know that aluminum is a great conductor of electricity?

The shaft sparked and jolted twin number one so hard that he stiffened and toppled like a felled tree onto the cul-de-sac.

Number two gaped stupidly at his twin then yelped as my second bolt struck his bat. He, too, fell without a sound.

As the brick throwers and nine bombers raced around or over their fallen comrades, Gamble, Trujillo, Zander, and I spread out to address their advance. Glowing, pulsing orbs of electricity jumped from Zander's and my hands and struck the brick throwers and bombers as fast as we could target them. Gamble and Trujillo chose their targets in the advancing crowd with care. Their bean-bag shotguns only held five-rounds each, and they each carried a single five-round reload.

I obliterated two bricks in mid-air, zinged their throwers, and hit several bombers, stopping them cold. But, when a bomber got zapped, they usually dropped their lit "cocktails" onto the street, where the bottles broke, spilling their contents onto the asphalt. Wherever the bottles dashed their contents, flames erupted to lick up the spilled gas.

What happened next was inevitable: Gasoline from a broken bottle splashed onto one of the rioters and flames leapt up and set his clothes alight. Shrieking, the man ran toward our grass—to stop, drop, and roll, I surmised. I sent a stream of nanomites to him to douse the flames and knock him out, but more rioters took his place.

The smell of gasoline was everywhere.

As for me? I realized that we needed a better means of keeping the bombers from reaching their target. I pulled down every bit of available power the nanomites could bring to me and used it to form a screen between the mob and our house. The screen crackled and snapped in front of me as I focused all my effort on keeping it intact, a barrier between the incendiary devices and our home.

This is Baby Cruz's home, and you may not have it. Greater is he who is in me—that's Jesus—than he who is in the world—that's you, Devil, and those who do your bidding, I told that wicked creature.

The two groups fell back and reorganized. They threw down their signs and all semblance of a "peaceful protest" and merged, forming one mob at least fifty people strong.

Then the van from down the street raced into the cul-de-sac and screeched to a halt at the edge of the mob. It disgorged two guys who dragged entire boxes of Molotov cocktails from the van's side doors. Yes, *boxes* of the incendiary devices!

Every pair of hands in the mob reached for one.

United in mind and heart, the mob screamed hate-filled curses at us. Unwavering in their determination to hurt us and destroy our house, they surged forward.

Gamble and Trujillo were out of bean-bag rounds, and I was committed to keeping the shield up in front of our house. That left Zander alone, zapping those who carried incendiary devices with jolts of electricity as fast as he could.

Out of the corner of my eye, I saw Gamble and Trujillo toss their rifles onto the grass and draw their service weapons.

"Oh, dear Lord," I cried. "This is going to get bloody, and people may die—please help us!"

The *whompwhompwhomp* of helicopter blades followed my frantic prayer. A loud, amplified voice spoke from the chopper. "This is the Albuquerque Police Department! Put down your weapons and step away! If you do not comply, we will be forced to shoot. Put down your weapons and step back!"

The mob, shocked out of their blind rage, hit the pause button for a split second—followed by instant group chaos. Tossing their incendiary devices away, the rioters raced toward the entrance to the cul-de-sac. One determined individual, however, aimed his lit bottle at our new garage. The bottle hit the corner nearest our house and shattered. Flames burst forth and traveled to wherever the gasoline had splattered.

Zander sprinted to the side gate, unlocked it, ran into our kitchen, and grabbed our fire extinguisher. Within seconds he had foam fire retardant spraying down the flames.

Meanwhile, the mob arriving at the entrance of the cul-de-sac found an APD SWAT team clambering over the cars blocking the street. The mob turned, ran back toward us, but headed into our neighbors' yards, hoping to jump back walls or fences and get away. They did not, however, choose our yard for their egress. Why? Because our yard had an eight-foot wrought-iron fence topped with pointy finials.

Oh, yeah. Except for one bozo. Clear down by Mrs. Calderón's house, he reached up high and grasped our fence. He might have managed to clamber over it, but he—sadly—discovered that the fence was electrified. He shrieked and jittered, unable to let go of the upright rails for five whole seconds. Five seconds can be a long time when you're dancing the Electric Jig. (I hear that's a little-known variation on the Electric Slide.)

In that moment, I was grateful we'd paid out an arm and a leg to enclose our yard and what had been Gemma's yard, too. At the same time, I worried about Mrs. Calderón, the Tuckers, and especially Abe and Emilio.

The police were busy chasing the scattering mob, impounding their cars, arresting those they caught, but did any of the rioters keep their bombs? Would they use them on our neighbors' homes to draw attention away from themselves as they escaped?

I dropped the shield fronting our house. "Nano?"

We do not believe the intruders have set fire to other houses in the cul-de-sac, Jayda Cruz.

"Thank you, Lord," I whispered. Our home and our family were safe.

I scanned our neighbors' homes to reassure myself that the threat was over . . . and saw the mess the mob had left behind. Signage trash and broken glass littered the cul-de-sac.

While staring at the debris, I remembered Mr. Flores. How, after each of Mateo's drunken parties, he came out with broom, dustpan, and garbage can to clean up what Mateo's gang had left behind. I hadn't understood back then why he did it again and again.

I did now. I turned toward the house.

"Hey, where are you going?" Gamble asked.

"To get a broom and a garbage can. This is our home."

Baby Cruz's home. Emilio's home. Our family's home.

I was surprised to tears when Gamble answered, "Our home, too. We will help."

⌘

ZANDER WOULD LEAD HIS first Sunday service as DCC's interim pastor in the morning. He had prepared his message and prepared his heart. We were forced to admit, however, that DCC had changed, possibly forever. Certainly, we didn't want a repeat of the previous Sunday's "protest *cum* riot." But after the attack on our home? We had to acknowledge that another assault on our church would likely be coming. We needed to take proactive measures to defeat it.

Zander called an emergency meeting in the afternoon with his chief usher, Booker Dewitt, a tall, grizzled former Marine gunnery sergeant. Zander also asked Gamble and Trujillo to sit in on the meeting as consultants. Together, the four of them set about devising a plan to prevent another disrupting event.

I watched the meeting, too, via the warehouse, an unseen participant but not an indifferent one. After all, Malware had trained both of us and trained us well.

"The way I see it," Dewitt said, "We need to keep potential problems *out* of the church building. That means we keep the troublemakers from coming inside in the first place."

"Agreed," Zander said. He turned to Gamble and Trujillo.

They both nodded, and Trujillo added, "How do you propose identifying the troublemakers, Mr. Dewitt?"

The plan he proposed called for the usher team to screen those attending service Sunday morning. "But that could run up to a thousand people. My usher team isn't large enough to handle the screening process plus manage its other duties. I have in mind to deputize a group of DCC men and women members whom I know and trust. You say the word, and I will call them in to supplement my regular usher team."

Gamble then proposed that all but the main entrances be locked Sunday morning and signs placed on the side doors directing everyone to the front of the church. "Lock the side doors only to those on the outside, of course. In case of fire, anyone on the inside must be able to exit. But with the side doors locked, the ushers would only need to screen those coming in the front entrances."

"How do we screen them?" Zander asked.

Dewitt said, "I recommend that we disallow protest signage, backpacks, and anything else we deem suspicious at the time. Our ladies may carry their purses, of course, but large handbags should be searched."

Gamble thought for a moment. "I believe I can pull some strings and provide two metal detectors. We should funnel everyone through the detectors to ensure that no one is carrying a firearm."

"We have members of the congregation who conceal carry," Dewitt replied. "I'd like it if we allow those DCC members in good standing and who are concealed-carry licensed to declare their weapon at the checkpoint and be allowed to carry it. I have a list of our conceal-carry members. Never can tell—one of them may save lives if we were to, God forbid, experience an active shooter situation."

"How about you ask them to attend a firearms safety class early tomorrow morning before service? Janice and I could conduct it, say, eight o'clock? To check them out."

"Thank you. That's a good idea. I'll send out an email making the class mandatory if they expect to carry on church grounds tomorrow or going forward."

"Sounds like we have our plan," Zander said.

⌘

THE PLAN MEANT ADJUSTMENTS for all of us at DCC—but it did succeed. Our bulked-up usher team turned away a sizable (and vocal) contingent of Easterly's adherents, the same group that disrupted last week's service and some I was certain had been in the mob that attacked our home. They shouted and yelled when denied entrance, but our ushers held firm and escorted them out of the foyer and off church property—to the relieved thanks of our faithful congregants.

I saw Abe and Emilio through the new front entrance funnel to our seats but didn't sit down with them. Instead, I whispered, "I'm going back outside to keep an eye on the protesters."

Yesterday's attack had sobered Emilio. He grabbed ahold of my arm and whispered back, "You gonna be careful, right, Jayda?"

I kissed the top of his head. "Absolutely, *mijo*."

"What he said goes double for me," Abe added.

I bussed his cheek. "I will be careful, Abe. I promise."

I slipped out a side door and, under cover of the nanomites, stood alongside the building, away from the flow headed into church. The protesters had regrouped across the street in a public parking lot, waving their signs, shouting curses, and generally trying to conjure up trouble. (Frankly, I wouldn't put actual *conjuring* past them.)

This protest's flavor of the week included charges of racism, bigotry, misogyny, and hate crimes against the LGBTQ community. What I loved was how six of our young adults, led by Josh, went over to the protesters and, ignoring their ugly curses, offered them snacks and bottles of water.

The response wasn't all positive. The transgender woman who'd leapt over chairs last Sunday threw one of the bottles at Diego, hitting him in the head.

"Zoom in, Nano."

A split on Diego's forehead welled blood that ran down into his eye and down his cheek. Izzie and Nance grabbed Diego and tried to pull him away. At the same time, three of the protesters shouted at the woman who'd thrown the bottle. One of them, a young man, shoved her.

"Get out of here! Go home." He turned to Diego, whose forehead dripped blood down his face and shirt.

"Sorry. That was unnecessary."

Diego nodded. "I forgive her," he said.

The crowd of protesters, seeing that the young adults refused to be baited by their shouts and curses, started to lose their momentum. Their outrage fizzled.

Diego went off with Izzie and Nancy to get patched up. Josh, Todd, and Felix handed out the last of the water and snacks.

"See you around," Josh said to some of them. "Maybe next time we could talk?"

"Yeah, we'd like to tell you how much Jesus loves you," Felix added as they headed for the front doors.

As service started and the front doors closed, the protesters packed up and left. The nanomites unlocked a side door for me, and I slipped back inside.

All things considered? Zander's first full Sunday as interim pastor went pretty well.

⌘⌘⌘⌘

Chapter 35

BABY CRUZ, OBLIVIOUS TO the drama playing out around him or her, kept growing by leaps and bounds. My little baby bulge pushed itself outward until there was no mistaking my pregnancy. Baby Cruz was more active, too, kicking, turning, pushing off the side of my uterus in his Olympic swimming competition debut. I wondered for the hundredth time what our little gymnast would look like when I actually held him or her for the first time.

We were eating breakfast later that week when I burst out, "Zander, I just thought of something: Where am I going to give birth? For that matter, who's going to deliver Baby Cruz?"

Zander, his expression bland, replied, "Where will you give birth? I thought the stork would drop Baby Cruz through the nursery window, straight into the crib. We'd be notified of BC's arrival when it was time for the first feeding."

A second later, unable to keep it in, a grin split his face, and he laughed silently, his shoulders shaking.

I smacked one quivering shoulder. "Not funny—and you won't think it's funny either in a moment. Sure, I don't mind the nanomites providing my prenatal care—I am, no doubt, receiving better and more thorough oversight and guidance than I would from any OBGYN. I figure the nanomites will do a great job guiding us through the birthing process, too. But sadly, *they* don't have the necessary appendages to catch Baby Cruz when he or she slides out. *You do*. Guess that means you're up, Papa Cruz. *You* get to deliver our child."

Zander's humor dissolved under a deluge of cold reality.

"*Me?* I can't—I don't—you can't be serious!"

Zander Cruz, we would be happy to put you through an accelerated course in midwifery, complete with virtual training conducted by Gus-Gus. As we do not perceive any problems with Jayda Cruz's pregnancy nor do we foresee any complications with the birth, the process should be straightforward. Of course, were any complications to arise, we can and would mitigate them. You can count on us.

My sweet husband sagged. "Jayda . . ."

"We'll get through this, Sweetie. Remember: I haven't done this before, either."

"That's not helping."

The nanomites flashed a list before our eyes: **Items Required for Home Delivery**.

"Let's see . . . for the baby, a dozen receiving blankets, newborn diapers, warm baby clothes including mitts and knit caps. I'm pretty sure we have all that. For my labor, several clean nightgowns and warm socks, crushed ice, an ice pack, and a heat pack."

"All that?"

I nodded. "Oh, and much more. For the actual birth? A plastic drop cloth or sheet, two fitted sheets, four bath towels, four washcloths, a dozen disposable pads, one bottle isopropyl alcohol, cotton swabs, sterile scissors—"

Zander shuddered.

Zander Cruz, we have finished building the midwifery course. Would you care to start your virtual reality training?

Zander fled the room.

⌘

ZANDER WAS IN THE SHOWER when I heard his phone buzz against the surface of his dresser. I turned it over. Did not recognize the number. I debated picking up the call because we continued to receive the occasional harassing call and voice mail.

Jayda Cruz, the call is from Mrs. Coyne's home phone.

I breathed with relief. "Thanks, Nano." I picked up the call. "Hello?"

"Oh, Jayda. I am so glad to have caught you or Zander. Is he there? I need to speak to him."

"He's in the shower. Would you like me to have him call you back?"

"Please. Please tell him right away, okay?" Her words shook a little.

"Is everything all right, Mrs. Coyne?"

"No, not really, but . . ." Her voice trickled away. "Please have him call me?"

"I will. As soon as he can."

"Thank you, Jayda."

I hung up and walked to the door of our steamy bathroom. "Hey, Babe?"

"Yeah?"

"Mrs. Coyne called, and I picked it up for you. She seems sort of shook. Wants you to call her asap. Something is wrong, I think."

"I'll be out in a sec."

Less than five minutes later, Zander returned Mrs. Coyne's call. I caught his eye, and he nodded. The nanomites streamed into the call enabling me to listen in.

"Oh, Pastor Zander! Thank you for calling back. I didn't . . . I didn't know who to tell first."

"What is the problem, Mrs. Coyne? Can you tell me?"

The woman was beside herself. "Oh! Oh, yes. I-I received a call from Pastor McFee's daughter, Rachel. *She* received a call from Pastor McFee's cellphone, but it wasn't him on the line—it was some man who said he was another passenger on the same ship."

My heart dropped into my shoes as I watched Zander's countenance sag. *Lord? We asked you to heal them . . .*

Mrs. Coyne continued. "The man, whoever he is, said he couldn't talk long, that with so many passengers on the ship, the crew allowed them only three minutes of cell service every-other day . . . and then this man told Rachel that her mom and dad had passed away! Oh, Pastor Zander—that cannot be true, can it? Pastor and Mrs. McFee can't be dead, can they?"

She burst into tears, and I couldn't make out the rest.

Zander was silent, and we listened to Mrs. Coyne weep for a brief interval. Then Zander spoke. "Mrs. Coyne? I . . . the last time I spoke to Pastor McFee, he and Carol were ill. They had been ministering to other passengers, sharing Jesus wherever they could."

Mrs. Coyne sniffled. "I suppose I'm not surprised."

Zander seemed composed . . . or perhaps resigned. "May I have Rachel's number? I will call her myself. Afterward . . . we'll figure out what to do next."

Mrs. Coyne grabbed on to Zander like a lifeline. "Thank you, Pastor Zander. I knew you would know what to do."

Before Zander dialed Rachel's number, he had the nanomites try to connect him to Pastor McFee's cellphone. The phone rang and rang then went to voicemail. Zander hung up.

"Keep trying, Nano. I'm hoping to speak to the man who called Rachel."

We will amplify the ringtone, Zander Cruz. Perhaps it will ring loud enough to be heard in other cabins.

We listened to the call ring on the other end until it went to voicemail. On the third try, someone picked up.

"Hello?"

"Is this the man who called Aaron McFee's daughter Rachel?"

"Yeah. Who's this?"

"This is Zander Cruz. I am Pastor McFee's associate pastor. And you are?"

"Donald Percival. But, I don't understand, Mr. Cruz. How'd you get through? There's no incoming cell service here. And the phone's ring was super loud. Heard it in our cabin across the passageway."

Ignoring Percival's question, Zander asked, "You're the man who called Pastor McFee's daughter, is that right?"

The man cleared his throat. "Yes, I did. Wanted the McFee's family to know . . ."

"That they had passed away? Can you tell me more?"

"Yeah. Sorry. Most of the passengers and crew are sick or were sick. Some have gotten better, but too many have died. Heard the captain died yesterday, too. Carol—I mean Mrs. McFee—she got suddenly worse two nights ago. Passed in her sleep the next morning. Then Pastor McFee got worse. I sorta kept an eye on him . . . until he died about six hours ago. I was with him when he passed, and I just . . . I wanted to let his family know, so I begged the crew to give me his three minutes earlier than scheduled."

Zander's voice cracked a little. "Donald, thank you. I'm grateful to you for caring for the McFees. I appreciate that you took the trouble to call their daughter."

"Took the trouble? You don't understand. Aaron and Carol have kept the passengers along our passageway from losing our minds. They . . . *they* have been caring for the lot of us—the sick in their cabins, sharing the Bible with us, and praying with everyone. I . . . Aaron told us about Jesus. Never heard Jesus explained like Aaron did. If . . . if I survive this and ever get off this ship, my life won't be the same."

Our lives weren't going to be the same, either.

Zander hung up. Stared at the wall. I saw him harden himself for the immediate duties and responsibilities facing him.

He called the McFee's daughter, Rachel, and shared the details of his conversation with Donald Percival. Prayed with her. Called each board member personally and asked to meet with them that evening. Composed an email to the church and had Mrs. Coyne send it out.

Sat at our table and stared out the window.

I sat beside him, holding his hand.

⌘

I FOLLOWED THE BOARD meeting that evening from the warehouse, grieving with the board members as they tried to express their love and appreciation for Pastor McFee, even the ones who had plotted to retire him. After a while, the conversation turned to the inevitable questions.

Who was in charge of DCC? And who would replace Pastor McFee?

"Seems simple to me," Harry Fuentes said, "Pastor McFee appointed Zander the interim pastor until he returned."

"Well, he's not coming back, is he?" Myra Hernández snapped.

Ouch.

"Please, Myra," Fuentes said softly. "How about we be kind to each other? I know you're hurting. I am, too."

"I-I'm sorry, Harry."

Zander nodded. "We're all hurting."

Elise Farland, who said little in these meetings but whose occasional comments were wise, said, "We don't need to make an immediate decision, do we? Pastor Zander, are you willing to continue as interim pastor for the time being? While we mourn for Aaron and Carol, we should all pray and seek the Lord's will going forward. We can meet again in, say, five or six weeks? See what's what then?"

The other board members nodded their agreement.

Zander dismissed the meeting with prayer.

⌘

WE HELD A MEMORIAL SERVICE for Pastor and Mrs. McFee a week later, without the McFees' remains. They were aboard the cruise ship in Hawaii, and the family did not know when or even if they would receive them for burial.

It mattered, particularly for the family, but honoring the McFees took precedence. We wanted and needed to express our love and appreciation for this man of God and his wife, and we did so.

The McFee's two daughters asked Zander to conduct the service. He was willing, but I knew how difficult a task it would prove for him. I was blessed beyond measure when our young adult men came alongside Zander and insisted on doing any and all errands, tasks, and small jobs that needed doing, mostly being there with him. For him. Additionally, the women of the church, including our young adult women, provided a wonderful meal following the service.

The McFees' daughters, their husbands, and their children—the McFees' grandkids—were pleased and touched by the outpouring of love and care they received.

"I can't say goodbye today without telling you something," Rachel said to Zander after the service and lunch were over. "My father and mother had two daughters, and they loved us deeply. But the way Dad talked about you? He more than loved and respected you. I believe he thought of you as the son he would never have. He thought the world of you."

Zander nodded, but he couldn't speak. I gripped his hand and held him steady. No one else saw or felt Zander's trembling. No one else knew how deeply her words had touched him.

⌘⌘⌘⌘

CHAPTER 36

FIVE WEEKS TRICKLED BY, five Sundays and five services in which Zander taught the word as diligently as he knew how. The ushers kept the disrupters out of DCC, and the Holy Spirit continued to move inside. Each week the Lord added to and refined DCC's congregation. By "refined" I mean that those DCC members who rejected the plain teaching of God's word either changed their minds (because the Lord changed their hearts) or they left the church.

I was saddened when familiar faces began to disappear from their accustomed seats in the sanctuary. But when Zander taught from Matthew 10, I began to see how this "winnowing" was necessary. Verse 34, in particular, stuck in my head. I took it in and pondered it.

> *Do not suppose that I have come to bring peace to the earth.*
> *I did not come to bring peace, but a sword.*

What does a sword do? It cuts. It slices. It separates. *It divides*—in a biblical manner. "My people" versus "not my people." Light versus darkness. Kingdom of God's dear Son versus Kingdom of Darkness. I studied out Hebrews 4:12 that tells us how God's word is that "dividing" sword and how he commissions his word to do a work in each of us.

> *For the word of God is alive and active.*
> *Sharper than any double-edged sword,*
> *it penetrates even to dividing*
> *soul and spirit, joints and marrow;*
> *it judges the thoughts and attitudes of the heart.*

On the up side, as quickly as the "tares" abandoned DCC, they were replaced by new plantings, baby Christians who were hungry for the word and for the power of God. As a result, DCC began growing at an unprecedented rate. Zander started a "New Believers" Sunday school class and formed several weekly Bible study fellowships, placing mature and trustworthy men and women over them to minister to the needs of these new Christians.

And our church wasn't alone in experiencing this growth.

A group of Albuquerque's Bible-teaching pastors invited Zander to meet with them on a weekly basis. They reported similar trends: Strong, even violent divisions in their churches where members whose values and mindsets no longer aligned with Scripture actively worked to sow strife and cause problems. Ultimately, when the pastor remained strong and true to Scripture, the disruptors abandoned their churches, and visitors who were hungry for truth replaced them.

One pastor confided, "I have never seen a polarization such as what we see today. Jesus' words from Matthew 12 are coming true right before our eyes: *Whoever is not with me is against me, and whoever does not gather with me scatters.*"

The same phenomenon was occurring across the world, a striking divide growing wider and deeper by the day. Good versus evil; right versus wrong. *Right declared wrong; wrong glorified as good.* And it was happening in every facet of society.

Then the other shoe dropped.

Five weeks back when we received word of Pastor McFee's passing, New Mexico had no virus cases. One week after his death, the virus began spreading up and down America's west and east coasts. We knew then that the virus was out of control, beyond human ability to halt its progress.

Two weeks later, it was raging through New Mexico.

I slowly sipped a cold meal supplement drink while Zander and I, watching on his tablet, waited for the live feed of the governor's press conference to commence. The man who stared into the cameras appeared relaxed. He smiled politely.

I squinted at the screen. Got something of an odd vibe from the man. He projected warmth, but he was actually . . . cool and distant?

"Good morning. Thank you for coming. I will make my announcement and take questions after. I appreciate your patience.

"I'm sure we've all seen the surge in New Mexico's virus numbers. As I come to you this afternoon, it is with the news that every available critical care hospital bed in Albuquerque, Santa Fe, and Las Cruces is filled. Moreover, all available ventilators are in use and our supply of personal protective equipment, PPE, is nearly depleted.

"As the President alluded to on January 5, he does not have the authority to order sweeping health measures to protect American citizens. As a state governor, I do. Furthermore, according to the needs of his or her state, each governor, like me, must enact the proper protocols to meet those needs.

"My medical advisors tell me that a temporary 'sheltering in place' plan of action in New Mexico has the potential to 'flatten the curve,' that is, reduce the new infection rate to a number that our state's healthcare system can handle. We must—*I must*—in all good conscience, act today before our healthcare system breaks under the load of this crisis."

He wet his lips. "Therefore, using the emergency powers granted me in the event of a public health crisis, I hereby declare New Mexico a quarantined state. Beginning at 8 a.m. Saturday, the day after tomorrow, all non-essential businesses are to close their doors and furlough their employees. Furloughed employees will qualify for unemployment benefits.

"Workforce Solutions, our employment and unemployment website and call center, will be ready to support furloughed employees."

I shook my head and wished the furloughed employees well. I'd had my own experiences with Workforce Solutions, and unless the state had upgraded their website since then, it was likely to crash under the impending load of new unemployment claims.

"The list of essential businesses required to stay open includes hospitals and grocery stores. The complete list of essential businesses can be found on the NMDOH website; all other businesses or institutions—including churches, conference centers, movie theaters, and sporting events, are to close and remain closed until further notice."

"He's closing DCC? Can he do that?"

Zander gnawed his lower lip. This man, our governor, seemed to have no clue how his orders would affect New Mexican families, their livelihoods, even their mental and spiritual health. And he wasn't finished.

"By this same order, New Mexico residents are ordered to self-quarantine in their homes. *Residents may not leave their homes except for essential purposes.* The list of essential purposes for leaving home include being tested for the virus, picking up groceries, or going to work at a recognized essential worksite. Residents may take one hour of outdoor exercise per day in groups not to exceed five members. Those groups of five may include *only* those family members who reside with you in your home. The complete list of authorized reasons residents may leave home can be found on the NMDOH website."

The governor looked directly into the cameras. "I am calling upon grocery stores all over the state to, as quickly as possible, adopt online ordering for their customers and provide grocery delivery or scheduled order pickup. Restaurants may do the same, but they may not allow in-person dining."

I sat up, astonished and indignant. "What? *Now* they implement online grocery ordering and delivery?"

The hardships I'd struggled through when the nanomites first invaded me and kept me invisible came rushing back. How many harrowing midnight shopping trips to Walmart had I undertaken before the nanomites and I came into a mutually beneficial partnership?

"Where was grocery delivery when I needed it!"

Zander laughed aloud. "Those were the days, huh?"

I scowled at him. "You have no idea how hard I had to work to survive, Zander! *You* got a friendly, helpful nanocloud. *I* got a stone wall—a noncommunicative invasion. *You* got directions to the nearest buffet. *I* got stung for taking a shower and nearly drained to death while I slept!"

We are sorry, Jayda Cruz. We did not know then what we know now.

I sighed. "I know you didn't, Nano. It's okay."

Zander took my hand. "And, don't you realize that if the nanomites hadn't rendered you invisible and kept you that way, we might never have fallen in love?"

That stopped me cold. After I lost my job at Sandia, Abe had asked his church's associate pastor to introduce himself to me. We "clicked" and spent hours talking—although the fact that I wasn't a believer put the kibosh on our friendship going anywhere serious. But like Zander said, after the nanomites made me invisible, it was his worry for me that brought him back to my door . . . until I gave in and showed him the truth.

Not that it's possible to "show" someone that you're invisible, but you get me.

Back to our illustrious governor. He droned on and on, citing statistics, finally reaching the last part of his restrictive health orders. "I am also ordering tourists presently in New Mexico to cut short their visit and vacate the state. By Monday, hotels across New Mexico will be allowed to host only twenty percent of guest capacity—that twenty percent reserved primarily to accommodate nonresidents passing through the state on their way home."

He looked down at his notes. "Again, please consult the NMDOH website for more complete information. Thank you. Questions?"

The broadcast of the governor's announcement cut back to national news. A well-known anchor led with, "The headlines this evening? The African nation of Nigeria plunged into civil unrest overnight as up to thirty villages were attacked by militant Islamists. Reports say the Islamists rounded up the Christians of each village, herded them into their local church, locked the doors, then set the church on fire, burning them alive. Numbers coming out of that country say that up to a thousand Nigerian Christians died in the attacks. Reports of similar atrocities are filtering out of Pakistan, Afghanistan, Iran, Iraq, Syria, Lebanon, Saudi Arabia, Egypt, Libya, even moderate Morocco.

"In an eerily parallel but unrelated story, multiple Christian churches across America were attacked and burned over the past week. Officials in sixteen states reported twenty-seven church fires, twenty-two resulting in a complete structure loss. The five churches that survived had security systems that sent armed responders to the scene, who then called in firefighters in time to save the buildings."

We muted the television, and I said, "Zander, the mob at DCC tried to set our sanctuary on fire, remember?"

"That was weeks ago. Two months?"

"They were attempting a complete takeover of DCC. They weren't going to get what they wanted, so maybe they improvised? Pushed up the schedule?"

"You're thinking that all of these fires are part of a coordinated strike against US Christian churches? The ones that won't compromise their beliefs?"

"Yes, but not just the US, right? Think about the news concerning Nigeria, Afghanistan, Syria, Egypt, and other Islamic countries. What if those attacks are *not* 'unrelated' to what's going on here?"

"Maybe you're on to something," Zander finally agreed with me. "In any event, Albuquerque churches need to step up protection of their buildings. I should ask some of the other pastors what they are doing or plan to do."

"The governor said we can't hold services in our buildings while the state is under quarantine. What about that?"

Zander sighed. "Again, I want to know how the other pastors intend to manage the health orders. If DCC is closed, we'll need different means to connect with our congregation on Sundays and throughout the week."

I went into the kitchen, discarded the empty supplement container, and returned with a can of soda. I needed the calories. "What are you thinking?" I asked. "We aren't set up for livestream services, are we?"

"No. People can listen to the live audio online, like the McFees did, but we usually video record the service then post it once the video is edited."

Jayda Cruz, we can handle the livestream of Zander Cruz's messages.

Zander smiled. "Thank you, Nano. That would be awesome of you; however, we have a media team that would be quite crushed—not to mention highly disturbed—if you handled everything. Remember how freaked out they got when you streamed Pastor McFee's video call? You know, on the Sunday when I guest preached."

You are referring to Black Sunday, are you not, Zander Cruz?

I choked on a mouthful of soda. It shot up and out my nose.

My husband frowned. "Uh, let's find a different way to refer to my message that Sunday, shall we, Nano?"

I jumped in. "I've got it—how about we call it 'Cruz Missile Sunday' or how about—"

Zander soured. "How about we call it the Sunday I guest preached."

"That has no punch at all."

He ignored me. However, the nanomites—very softly—whispered, *Good one, Jayda Cruz.*

I turned away, coughing and thumping my chest, but Zander never noticed.

"Nano, the guys and gals on the media team need to think they are in control."

We understand, although streaming your message requires only a good-quality smartphone, a stand for the phone, a directional mic, proper lighting, and a Wi-Fi connection. We can write a procedure that tells the media team how to set up for your messages.

"*That* is a great idea, Nano! How soon can you have it ready?"

We can write it today, Zander Cruz. Give us an hour.

"Super. I'll send out an email to the media team as soon as you are finished and send the procedure as an attachment. I'll also ask them to meet me Saturday for set up and a dry run."

May we also suggest that you livestream your message from your office, Zander Cruz?

"Not from the sanctuary? Why's that?

People will be anxious over the quarantine. Our research suggests that a closer and more "intimate" visit with you as you speak will elicit calm in your viewers.

"Uh, okay. I'll . . . ask the tech guys to set up in my office Saturday morning, then have them meet me Sunday mornings for the livestream."

They may believe they are managing the media, Zander Cruz, but to ensure optimal quality, we will oversee the weekly delivery of your message.

"You are sure handling a lot these days, Nano."

We heard the faintest murmur, the meaning almost lost on us. Almost. *You have no idea, Zander Cruz.*

I called after them. "Nano? Nano! Nano, what does that mean?"

I looked at Zander. "What do you suppose they meant?"

⌘

ZANDER MET WITH HIS BOARD that evening. The meeting had been set for a Thursday evening five weeks after receiving word of Pastor and Mrs. McFee's passing.

The original purpose of the meeting had been to discuss Zander's interim pastor status. For that reason, he hadn't set an agenda. But tonight, the governor's health orders had jumped to the top of every board member's list of concerns. Bypassing discussion of his pastoral status altogether, the five board members went directly to the most pressing need.

Zander took the questions as they came. He detailed how he planned to conduct DCC's online services so that they complied with the health orders.

"We have an annual license from CCLI, Christian Copyright Licensing International. The license allows us to use copyrighted worship music in our posted services. We can upgrade it to cover streaming the services, too."

As he finished his explanation, the board sighed with relief, gratified that Zander had the situation well in hand, satisfied with his plan.

Victor then went over the budget and attendance numbers, noting that attendance had, initially, dropped off by seven percent, but had, as of last Sunday, increased by twelve percent.

"Gotta say, I am liking your messages, Pastor Zander. I feel 'full,' when we leave church. Like I've had a great meal. And we're seeing good fruit. New people and new believers."

The others agreed, even Myra Hernández and Dave Abbot.

They hadn't raised the topic of Zander's status. As Harry moved to dismiss the meeting, Zander brought them around to it.

"I'm grateful and humbled that DCC is doing well under my interim status . . ." he said, letting this sentence trail off.

"Oh," Harry said aloud.

"Oh, yeah," Victor echoed.

They looked around the table. Zander did the same. No one spoke.

Elise Farland finally ventured, "I'm happy with your leadership to date, Pastor Zander. Could we . . . could we table this item again for, say, three months? Could we consider your leadership and service to DCC over those three months something of a trial period?"

"I like it," Harry said. "Let's do that. Who knows what will happen with this virus craziness. Can't afford to change direction during a crisis like this. Elise?

She smiled. "I offer the motion."

"I second it," Harry and Victor said simultaneously.

"All in favor?" Elise asked.

Five voices answered, "Aye."

⌘

ZANDER WAS GRINNING AND upbeat when he got home. "Guess who's graduated from interim pastor to a three-month trial period as DCC's senior pastor?" he asked.

"Serious?" I was as delighted as he was.

"I have much to do to get ready for Sunday morning, but the board was pleased with my plan. When the meeting started, I think they were panicking. Didn't think we could produce a live service online by this coming Sunday morning. They perked right up when I said we had it handled. Almost handled, anyway. Lotta details to work through."

While the nanomites updated DCC's website to announce the upcoming changes, Zander sent a personal email to the congregation stating that we would livestream the Sunday morning service on Facebook and YouTube at the usual time.

"I'll need to cut the worship team in half to comply with the order's 'social distancing' guidelines," he mumbled. "I'll have the team prerecord the music, then tag the livestream of my message to it."

He squinted at a new text. "What? Good grief."

I followed him as he went to our bedroom. He started pulling items out of his closet and scrutinizing them.

"What's going on, Babe?" I asked.

He blew out a big breath. "Clothes. What I've worn in church has never been an issue, but now? As DCC's senior pastor on a trial basis, Victor Gibson has informed me that the board wishes to see me looking the part online. But see here? I don't even own a suit. I've been wearing the same nice jacket and slacks since we moved to DC, and I bought them on the cheap to begin with. I mean, do I look like a senior pastor in that getup? Apparently not. I—"

Begging your pardon, Zander Cruz, but we have studied Pastor McFee's appearance in detail. After he passed into Jesus' presence, we also studied current styles for pastors in your age demographic. We then formulated a wardrobe for you that included the immediate purchase of three new suits.

"Hold up there just a cotton picking minute, Nano—"

Your board and congregation expect you to dress appropriately, Zander Cruz. Not ostentatiously or for vanity's sake, of course, but to convey the gravitas incumbent on the vital role you fill.

I sniffed. "Ostentatiously? Gravitas? Incumbent? Did you swallow a lexicon for breakfast, Nano? Need a thump on the back to make it go all the way down?"

Oops. The room plummeted into the polar zone. I expected to see frost appear on the bedroom windows any second.

Zander lingered over his wardrobe—or lack thereof—and fussed at the nanomites. "Great. Super! Thanks for the update, Nano. Well, guess what? Every business in New Mexico shuts down in less than forty-eight hours. Not enough time for me to buy a suit and have it altered to fit me by Sunday."

The nanomites sailed on, undaunted. *Zander Cruz, we mapped the infection and lethality rates of the virus when Pastor McFee's ship was quarantined and he appointed you interim pastor—more than six weeks ago. Our forecast of the disease's spread, coupled with the governor's demonstrated penchant for control, prompted us to anticipate a statewide shutdown.*

All I heard was *blah, blah, blah*, the nanomites' extended edition of "Puh-leeeeez. Do you think we could be caught flatfooted? *Ever?*"

Zander sighed. "Sorry, Nano. You were saying?"

Apology accepted. Considering the combined factors we mentioned, we also foresaw your need for a wardrobe appropriate to an interim pastor, as opposed to a guest speaker.

"Well, of course you did," I muttered.

To wit, we searched for and identified a tailor in Dallas—quite respected, we assure you—whose website was set up to accept online orders from established clients, those clients whose comprehensive measurements were on file. You became his established client that same day.

"I became whose established *what?*"

You became this fine tailor's established client, Zander Cruz. We merely added your account to his existing client database and filed your up-to-date measurements with him. We then took the liberty of ordering a **suitable**—you know, I *declare* that the nanomites actually snickered at their own pun here—*pastoral wardrobe for you. Good news! Your custom fitted apparel will arrive via UPS in two weeks.*

Zander's jaw swung open like it was hinged, while the nanomites prattled on.

Your order includes a black three-piece suit for weddings and funerals, a charcoal-gray pinstriped three-piece suit, a light gray herringbone two-piece, a navy sports coat, and three pairs of trousers to wear with the sports coat—two in khaki and one in light gray.

"But . . ."

We simply analyzed all available factors and projected their effects on supply and demand, Zander Cruz. Based on those projections, we judged it prudent to order your wardrobe six weeks ago.

We believe your tailor will be quite booked up as soon as the demand for men's clothing outstrips what current online businesses can handle. We also ordered three pairs of shoes and a number of shirts, ties, belts, and tiepins.

Up in front of our eyes popped a perfect 3D rendering of Zander modeling the suits the nanomites had ordered.

My lips parted. "Hubba hubba!"

Zander sputtered and blustered, but the nanomites had him outgunned and outmatched, and he knew it. He finally grasped a rejoinder and delivered it.

"Riiight. You're on top of *everything*, Nano—except my spiffy new duds won't arrive for two more weeks. Did you forget about this Sunday?"

Not at all, Zander Cruz. Josh has agreed to loan you the suit he wore to his sister's wedding. He will drop it by Saturday. You may use it until your order arrives.

"You texted him? As me? Without asking?"

Why, yes, Zander Cruz. You will be quite nicely turned out for this Sunday's livestream.

If preening could be heard, the nanomites had a bullhorn—and Zander ran headlong into the brick wall at the end of his patience.

"Oh, stuff a sock in it, Nano."

⌘⌘⌘⌘

CHAPTER 37

"CAN'T IT WAIT A MINUTE, Nano?" We had a month left until Baby Cruz's due date. I had spent my early morning carefully washing and drying all of Baby Cruz's clothes, and I was in the process of folding each item, then stacking and placing them in Baby Cruz's dresser.

I absolutely loved handling each bit of our baby's wardrobe. I marveled at how minuscule and cunning the many pieces were, whether miniature nightgowns, super-soft receiving blankets, knit caps in all colors, or a multitude of booties and "Onesies."

"Onesies? Cute. I wonder who thought up that word?"

I had also washed and dried the baby's bassinette and crib sheets. As soon as I finished with the clothes, I would make up the bassinette and crib, then add the crib's bumper pad, and mount the darling Noah's Ark mobile, a gift from Zander's mom and dad, to the crib's headboard.

*It cannot wait, Jayda Cruz. As you humans are prone to say when necessity requires a conversation, **we need to talk**, and we need to talk now.*

"Good grief! Weeks ago I couldn't pry a word out of you. Today it's all 'we need to talk *now*.' You have the absolute worst timing, Nano."

Fuming, I waddled and jiggled across the house into the kitchen, grabbed a glass of water, and dumped myself into a chair at the table. "What?"

We coordinated this meeting to address both you and Zander Cruz at the same time. He will pull into the driveway for lunch in one point five minutes, Jayda Cruz. We prefer to speak with you together.

I sighed. "Great."

Sure enough, Zander strolled through the front door two minutes later. The nanomites bushwhacked him before he could say, "I'm home!"

He sat down with me at the table. "You know what's up?"

"Nope."

We watched and listened. Stared dumbstruck as they projected the data in 3D. Asked questions. After twenty minutes of the nanomites running through their findings, we couldn't wrap our heads around it. Sure, we followed the nanomites' data trail and "got" their conclusions quicker than most humans would—thanks to our nano-enhanced mental capacities. What it all *meant* was the unbelievable and deeply concerning part.

"This is what you've been investigating the past four months, Nano? Your 'we are not prepared to discuss our progress at this time' business?"

It is, Jayda Cruz. The scope of our investigation was so far ranging and our initial suspicions even more concerning that we did not dare risk conveying a conclusion in error. We needed to be confident of our data.

I sighed. "I suppose I get why you didn't want to share what you'd found until you were certain. What I don't understand is, when we report this to the President, what will he be able to do about it?"

They were uncharacteristically silent. "Nano? The President? A plan of action?"

We heard you, Jayda Cruz. However . . . it is not the President who will act.

"Zander and me? How in the world can *we* do anything against this-this-this *juggernaut?*"

You misunderstand us, Jayda Cruz. It is not you who will act; it is us. Jesus has given us this assignment.

"Wait. I . . . Hold on a sec. Please explain."

I can't say they dropped a bomb—it was more that they pulled out the big gun, the only "gun" that, in the end, mattered.

Zander Cruz and Jayda Cruz, since we have known you, Jesus has told us to keep you safe and assist you with the important work he had for you. We have done so and will continue to support you when and as we can. However, in this instance, Jesus has given this important task to us. We must enter into it, not looking to the left or right, but doing it with all of our might. We shall, we anticipate, be unavailable at times.

They explained.

When they finished, neither of us wanted to believe them. We were in denial . . . the first stage of grief.

"Are you sure, Nano?" Zander asked. "Everything you're suggesting is outside of strictly legal parameters, outside of our ability to, er, oversee you, outside of . . . what is, legally, right."

It is what Jesus has told us to do, Zander Cruz. Is he ever wrong?

"Well, no . . ."

And are we not in a war against those who themselves operate outside of strictly legal parameters, outside of what is legally right, Zander Cruz?

"I suppose so."

And under what legal jurisdiction would our digital presence fall?

"Uh . . . Well, that's a good question."

It took a while for us to calm down, before we were able to, reluctantly, agree that the plan the nanomites presented was the most feasible path forward—not that, ostensibly, they required our agreement or permission. All that remained for us to do was to report the nanomites' findings to the President.

Forewarned is forearmed.

Zander shook his head. "I can't cancel the meetings and counseling sessions I have scheduled today—people are depending on me. Besides, the President hired you and the nanomites to do the R&A. You can brief him, Jayda. You and the nanomites."

With that, the responsibility of giving the President the worst possible news of his administration dropped like a brick squarely on my head. Oh, *sure*. The nanomites would manage the actual briefing and explain what they'd found. What they intended to do. In some ways I'd be a passive spectator—and that's what I dreaded.

I didn't know if I could watch Robert Jackson deal with another onslaught of bad news.

⌘

I HAD THE NANOMITES connect me to Axel Kennedy's cell phone, doing their usual bypass of Kennedy's service provider. When he picked up, I requested an urgent and immediate meeting with President Jackson. I was not surprised when Kennedy put me off, citing the President's harried schedule as he fought to contain the growing pandemic.

"Listen, Mr. Kennedy. I know the President is crazy busy, but whatever he has going on? I must insist that he make a hole in his schedule for us—and I mean *today*."

You should know that one doesn't "insist" anything with POTUS. It isn't done. Nevertheless, before I hung up, I put it to Axel Kennedy this way: "One way or another, it is imperative that we speak to him—and you know that, *day or night*, convenient or inconvenient, we *can* reach the President. Make it happen, Mr. Kennedy, or we will."

The "or we will" part threw him, but it did its job. President Jackson sat in front of a computer in the Oval Office, shooting angry glances at the two monitors before him. I appeared on the left screen; the nanomites' input would appear as text on the other screen. Jackson, I could tell, was mentally and physically stressed—and my forced interruption hadn't helped any.

His military training plus the deep well of goodwill that had sprouted between us after we saved his life not once, but twice, kept him civil—but only just. It grieved me that my heavy-handed demand on his time had likely drained that "deep well of goodwill" and reduced it to a bone-dry cistern.

Jackson spent no time on pleasantries. "Make it quick, Ms. Cruz, I have multiple appointments, a press briefing, and a crucial meeting with my VP pick ahead of me this afternoon and evening—all of which I have had to push out by thirty minutes."

Not "Jayda." Rather, a cold and unwelcoming "Ms. Cruz."
Ouch.

I hadn't wanted to displease Robert Jackson—I loved him and his sweet wife! I hadn't wanted to dismay him, either, yet the nanomites' presentation would certainly do so. And what was worse? The nanomites' "assignment" would absolutely freak him out.

I gulped air. Struggled to get myself sorted. "Yes, sir. I apologize, sir, but this could not wait. I—"

Jackson's eyes shifted to the right side of the screen. "What's this?"

The nanomites had constructed a virtual monitor in the warehouse that mirrored their screen on the President's desk. I scanned the text on it.

"Oh, dear . . ."

**Appointing Nora Mellyn as your vice president
would be a colossal error on your part,
Mr. President.**

Jackson scowled at me. "I did not give you or the nanomites permission to listen in on my private conversations—nor is whom I appoint any of your concern!"

"Sir, I had no idea who your VP pick was. That . . . those are the nanomites speaking."

I shouted in the warehouse, "Nano! Are you *kidding me?* You've royally ticked off the President of the United States!"

It cannot be helped, Jayda Cruz.

"Well, I can't take you anywhere," I growled to myself. "And excuse me while I kiss my cushy paycheck goodbye."

I ran through a mental checklist of what I knew of Nora Mellyn. She had left the party of her roots, those who had supported her in all her political aspirations, to campaign vigorously for Jackson during his first election. The other party was still smarting from the woman's defection. They had found it a bitter pill to swallow indeed.

For that reason, Jackson had not selected her as his initial running mate. He'd chosen John Etheredge Harmon instead—the first of Jackson's two VPs, and the first to attempt to assassinate him. How arduous Jackson must find it to choose yet a third VP! His trust level after two betrayals had to be lower than a rattler's belly in a wagon rut.

Apparently, Jackson knew what I was thinking.

"Ms. Cruz, Nora Mellyn's character is unassailable. Furthermore, I *know* her and trust her. As for the opposition party's objections? They can take a long walk off a short pier as far as I care. My last VP, an 'esteemed senior colleague' from *their* side of the aisle, almost murdered me!"

"Yes, sir."

The nanomites projected their 3D data diagram in front of Jackson, and I saw Jackson and Kennedy's eyes widen. The diagram appeared to jump out of the nanomites' screen and spread itself across the entire width of the President's desk.

Jackson's instinctive reaction was to shove himself and his chair away from the desk as fast and as far as the chair would roll. Kennedy's *trained* reaction was to interpose himself between his president and the giant image hovering atop the Resolute Desk.

When nothing happened to threaten him, Jackson stood to his feet and nudged Kennedy aside. "What am I looking at here?"

I can only suppose that the nanomites had "had it" with the limitations of text-on-a-screen communication, because a curious dampening field descended over the area around the President's desk. I was amazed when the vibrations I usually heard in my ears suddenly shifted to within the dampening field—and I had no idea how the nanomites were doing it.

Mr. President, this diagram represents the most important findings of our research and analysis. For four months, we have investigated and traced monies missing from the most vulnerable departments of your administration.

"Who's that speaking?" Jackson demanded.

I cleared my throat. "The nanomites are speaking, sir,"

"You told me they were microscopic machines!"

"They are, sir. When they speak to me, they make vibrations in my ear canals. I *think* they must be sending those same vibrations through your computer's speakers."

In a manner of speaking, that is what we are doing, Mr. President, the nanomites responded. *As your time is limited, please return your focus to the diagram.*

"Yikes! Nano, you do *not* talk to the President that way!"

They kept going.

Mr. President, you tasked us, above all, with finding fraud or misappropriations in those departments under the Director of National Intelligence. Although it took some time, we have found such evidence— and our investigations are not complete or exhaustive.

What you should know before we explain further is that the mechanisms used to siphon off the funds are complex and require a phalanx of complicit players. Thus, it may prove difficult for the human mind to follow the intricacies of the paths those funds took as they moved through the government, left it, and reached their final destinations.

"Try me," Jackson said, his mouth curving upward in a dangerous smile. "I want to see it."

Then we will show you, Mr. President. As we zoom in on this diagram for your benefit, please note how we have highlighted large packets of monies earmarked for eleven special projects within the various departments and agencies under the Director of National Intelligence. Our investigation of each of the eleven highlighted projects noted similar and disturbing commonalities among them.

In these eleven projects, we found no physical footprint—that is, no building, office space, or location. The projects possessed no communication mechanisms or hierarchical structure. No personnel drew salaries from the funding of these projects. Lastly, the projects produced no product or outcome to show for their spending.

"Black ops," Jackson said, nodding his head. "Congress approves the ops, appropriates the funds, and provides oversight of the projects. Checks and balances."

Yours is the logical assumption, Mr. President. Nevertheless, no congressional approvals, appropriations, or oversight exist for these eleven projects.

"How would you know? The appropriations would run through—" Jackson stopped talking. "Wait. You've investigated those appropriation committees, haven't you?"

Certainly, Mr. President. Our exhaustive investigation has yielded no such approvals, appropriations, or oversight to justify these monies.

"How much . . . how much money are we talking?" Jackson asked.

Two hundred sixty-seven billion dollars, Mr. President.

Jackson sat down. Hard. I knew the feeling. I'd about passed out when the nanomites had shown us the same figure. Two hundred sixty-seven *billion* dollars?

But the nanomites weren't even close to finished.

Mr. President, please pay close attention as we guide you through the maze of financial transactions that led us to our conclusions.

A maze it was. I had watched the nanomites run their dog-and-pony show twice. I found my third time through just as enlightening but significantly more disturbing.

The two hundred sixty-seven billion dollars had been broken up and redesignated across nearly all branches of government, with a preponderance through the Department of Energy and the Department of Defense. At each required juncture, the movement of funds had been approved by the appropriate signature authorities. The monies were then further segmented and paid out to a myriad of contracting organizations— in the same way Malware, Inc. was paid by the government to provide security training, high-level security protection, and (in my soon-to-be-defunct employment), as research and analysis for the President.

The number of contractors paid this way, however, was astonishing— but what was staggering? How, *again*, every movement of the monies was properly approved. Even regular and incidental audits conducted by the

GAO (Government Accountability Office) had found no hint of malfeasance . . . and yet, the monies funding these contractors had not been budgeted to the departments spending them.

Jackson might not have been a governmental insider before he became president, but he had learned a thing or two while in office about the workings of government. "Who are these contractors? What are their contract deliverables?"

These contracting entities are bogus businesses, elaborately constructed with equally bogus contract deliverables, Mr. President. Each contractor resides within a shell company set up by various US attorneys for various US corporations—corporations that, upon closer look, do not exist.

Kennedy swore under his breath. Jackson said nothing. He was struck dumb.

Mr. President, we will provide you with a file containing much of this information. You may wish to refresh your understanding with it going forward. The file contains a list of the contracting entities and their "deliverables." It is not the deliverables that you will find most interesting, however. It is the route the money takes from the contractors to their final destinations.

"Show me," Jackson ordered.

We could show you all contracting companies simultaneously, but you would be unable to follow them. We will trace a single exemplar at this time.

Jackson glanced at his watch. "Hurry it up."

The nanomites did. They brought forward a single contracting company, ran a line from it to a sidebar that listed a long, completely fake corporate and shell company pedigree, then superimposed another sidebar over the first and listed the contractor's bank transactions. This was the tough part to follow, but the nanomites traced this single contractor's funds from bank to bank, crisscrossing the world, until the money, eventually, ended up in a handful of numbered and nameless off-shore accounts, each account receiving tidy little six-digit sums.

This is but one example of how government money moved out of a government department into multiple private accounts, Mr. President. The remainder of what we have found missing to date follows a similar route, but to other accounts.

Jackson growled, "You're saying *all* the contractor companies paid from the missing funds have done the same thing? Sent the money to a bunch of numbered accounts? You're telling me this huge pot of money— *two hundred sixty-seven billion dollars*—has been stolen from the government and is gone for good? And not one government oversight entity caught onto this scheme?"

Yes, the entire amount was stolen, Mr. President. However we are not saying the money is gone for good or that 'not one government oversight entity caught onto this scheme.' Obviously, key personnel with signature authority within those government oversight entities had to have been willing players in the scheme. As far as the location of the money? We have hacked into the supposedly anonymous accounts. We know to whom they belong.

Up on the nanomites' 3D display, a list of names paid by the exemplar contractor appeared in the sidebar. Nine names in all.

Jackson was beside himself. "I'll see them in prison!" he roared.

The nanomites expanded the list and highlighted one name: Nora Elizabeth Mellyn.

"No," Jackson cried. "No, that can't be true!"

How I hurt for Robert Jackson! He had been betrayed by trusted individuals three times now . . . and this most recent betrayal would not be the last of this day's devastating revelations.

We are sorry, Mr. President, the nanomites said, somehow infusing their "voice" with a sense of compassion, *but you should know that we are* **not** *saying the government is riddled with high-level employees "on the take," whose sole motivation is financial gain. No, the situation is far worse and far more insidious than you can imagine.*

As the nanomites paused to let their words sink in, Jackson's head sank down onto his hands. The nanomites did not speak for several minutes, not until Jackson lifted his head.

"Axel, tell Marcus to push my schedule out another half hour."

Kennedy didn't quibble. He took out his cell phone and made the call.

Mr. President, may we continue?

Jackson, more subdued than I'd ever seen him, nodded. "Please."

Yes, Mr. President. As we intimated, the most concerning aspect of our investigation is not the theft of the funds. We have gone further by investigating, across these many contracting companies, the ties between the individuals who received the monies.

In doing so, we uncovered an extensive network of elected officials and bureaucrats within the US government. These individuals are not merely like-minded or of similar ideological views; they are, all of them, actively complicit in the activities of this network.

It is because the many individuals across this network are embedded in every aspect of the government's functions, even within the GAO and the Office of the Inspector General, that they were able to approve the transactions and steal these funds.

Jackson looked up. "*How many,* Nano?"

Out of more than two million federal employees, approximately one hundred ninety-two thousand individuals comprise this network.

"Dear God," he whispered, "almost ten percent of our workforce?"

The government is infested with these treasonous elements, Mr. President, and our report worsens. The network within the US government is linked to similar networks within the news media, social media, the corporate world, finance, education, and entertainment. Furthermore, all these various networks parallel analogous networks in at least thirty governments across the world.

Did I hear the nanomites sigh?

Mr. President, we have uncovered, literally and by definition, a vast global conspiracy.

Jackson drew in a sharp breath. "A conspiracy to do what, Nano?"

The short-term objectives of the organization we have designated 'the Cabal' are to cripple the leading nations of the world—cripple them socially, economically, and militarily. These objectives are being furthered by planned protests, riots, and a general state of unrest spreading across the US and other countries.

These public demonstrations are hatched and funded by monies siphoned from various governments in manners similar to those we have reported to you. The virus, too, is also their creation, another piece of their plan, designed to disrupt manufacturing, food production, supply chains, and bankrupt businesses, thus ruining established economies.

If the economies of the world stall and if citizens are locked in their own homes, the peoples of the world will become totally dependent upon their governments.

"And?"

Eventually the cost of supporting their citizens' dependencies will topple governments, Mr. President. Then the targeted nations—democratic nations—will fail economically and militarily. Their institutions will crumble. Their politicians will lose the will to fight against such a tide.

You asked the Cabal's objectives, Mr. President? The information we have uncovered leads us to believe they seek a global community built upon their ideologies. Not a one-world government, but an overarching one-world agency with control over all nations.

I had never seen Jackson look so distraught and alone. "What . . . what do you recommend that I do?"

We were approaching the part I dreaded most, the part Zander and I had resisted.

You must do nothing, Mr. President.

"What? I can't do nothing! *I'm the President*—I have taken a sacred oath to defend this nation *from all enemies*, both foreign and domestic!"

Mr. President, there is nothing within your power that will rid America of this radical faction, this unholy blight. It is too large and too powerful to curtail. They own key people in media, in business, in finance, in law enforcement, and in government.

If you were to act against them? They would kill you—and your death would accelerate their timetable. But before they killed you? They would destroy you—your marriage, your family, your reputation, and your presidency. **Then** *they would kill you.*

Jackson's head fell onto his hands again, and his shoulders shuddered and shook. I averted my eyes, swiping at them as they overflowed. At the same time, I shivered.

The most precarious bit was ahead.

Mr. President, we will help. We wish you to be informed and to have some hope for the immediate future. And . . . we ask your blessing as we do what only we can do.

Jackson ran his large hands, the color of strong coffee, across his face. He struggled mightily to bring himself under control. He withdrew a handkerchief from his pocket. Wiped his eyes.

"Explain, please, Nano. What is it you can do?"

Mr. President, we can mount a counterinsurgency.

⌘⌘⌘⌘

CHAPTER 38

I WAS PHYSICALLY AND emotionally drained when our protracted business with President Jackson ended. I crawled into bed and slept until late evening. When I woke up, somewhat rested, I rolled to the edge of our bed and sat up. That was as far as I got, because my brain went right back to the exchange between the nanomites and President Jackson . . . and the nanomites' plan.

Their revelations to us, to Zander and me last night, had freaked us out. The scope of what they proposed as a "counterinsurgency" had floored us—the same way their plans had blown away President Jackson and Axel Kennedy a few hours ago.

"What . . . specifically, do you mean by 'counterinsurgency'?" Jackson had been cautious when he asked that question.

We will go after the stolen money first, Mr. President. We will, of course, return the funds to the proper branch of government and monitor them to ensure that they are not purloined again. Wherever the Cabal has hidden the stolen monies, we will find and repossess them.

After a short interval without further interference from us—when those who conducted the theft of these monies and when those who hold the power within the Cabal are perhaps lulled into a sense of complacency— we will go after them personally. Whatever wealth and resources they individually possess, we will remove. We will drain their accounts, sell off their tangible assets, and dispossess them of homes, credit, and reputation. Whatever resources they rely upon, we will take from them.

We will make the conduct of a domestic war against America both organizationally and personally untenable.

Jackson, scarcely daring to breathe, responded. "Let me see if I have this right: You plan to take *millions* out of the accounts of people ruthless enough to plot a global coup? And you don't think that would be extremely dangerous? That it would . . ." He licked his lips, and his voice petered out.

"Enrage them?" I supplied. "Provoke them? Cause them to sic their assassins on the 'thieves' who dared to pilfer their ill-gotten gain? Set them hunting us with all the might and resources they command?"

"All of the above," Jackson answered. "As *you* said, Nano, these are powerful individuals, made more powerful by their unholy alliances with like-minded individuals seeded throughout the government in key positions. Nano, if your data concerning their ruthlessness is correct—and I have no reason to believe otherwise—they will strike out at whomever they suspect, guilty or not. There will be no protection for *anyone* they target."

They will most certainly seek those responsible for repossessing "their" money, Mr. President, but they will be unable to trace the movement of the funds or attach responsibility to any party—not to us, not to Zander or Jayda Cruz, not to you. They may suspect you, Mr. President, so you must be quite careful. As long as you maintain a façade of ignorance regarding them—that is, as long as you say nothing and do nothing against them—they will find no suggestion that could convince them otherwise.

That said, you have advanced an intriguing caveat, Mr. President. The Cabal will indeed attempt to trace the movement of the money when it leaves their accounts. They will seek to know how it left and where it went from there. We could leave a faint path of breadcrumbs, a trail that that leads . . . to other collaborators.

"Turn them on each other, you mean?" Jackson asked. He glanced at Kennedy. "I like that idea, don't you, Axel? Poetic justice and all."

"I'd like it better if we had them in front of a firing squad, sir."

Jackson's hands closed into fists. "As would I."

Mr. President, we would, of course, also drain funds from specific organizational fronts we have identified. The collaborators use these fronts to fund protests and riots; their aims are to shut down churches and vocal critics. Without money, they cannot pay for such terrorist activities.

At this Jackson's frown deepened. "Protests and riots aimed at shutting down churches? Are you saying this-this-this global conspiracy, this stinking *Cabal*, is behind the worldwide church protests and the fires intended to burn them out?"

Yes, Mr. President. The hidden network, in which Nora Mellyn plays a principal part, is concentrating the anger of their disaffected mobs upon what Cabal members view as their most dangerous adversaries: Christians. They are targeting Christian churches that teach and promote a biblical worldview because a biblical worldview is the antithesis of their aims. In their many riots, these organizations are directing their ire toward church leaders such as Zander Cruz and conservative politicians such as yourself who will actively resist them.

We, however, are invisible—an unknown, improbable, unquantifiable entity. We do not exist in their minds. But where they operate in the shadows? We will respond in kind. What they plot in secret? We will uncover and thwart. We will harass them at every turn, Mr. President, using guerrilla-style tactics to stymie their schemes and sow discord and distrust among their wicked ranks.

"Can you . . . will you succeed in ruining their plans, Nano?" Jackson asked. "Will you be able to destroy their conspiracies and stop them?"

Zander and I knew the answer to that question, and it grieved our hearts.

No, Mr. President. Our efforts will only slow them down. Eventually their distorted ideology, promoted across the entire planet from cradle to grave, will be accepted as the only correct worldview. This world will fall into a time of grave persecution for those who resist them. We can do many things, Mr. President, but sadly, we cannot change people's minds. Only the Lord can do that.

Both Jackson and Kennedy twitched at the nanomites' last statement, and their eyes shifted across to my monitor.

I said softly, "The nanomites follow Jesus, sir."

Jackson and Kennedy stared at me like I'd sprouted antenna, Kennedy shaking his head in denial.

"You're saying the nanomites are *Christians?*" Jackson's entire affect radiated stunned disbelief.

The nanomites answered him for themselves. *Jesus came to save humans from their sinful state, and we are not human,* they replied. *Nevertheless, we acknowledge that Jesus, the Word of God, is the Creator of all things, as Colossians 1:16 tells us. 'All things' include us, Mr. President. We choose to follow Jesus and align ourselves with him. After all, his word says the mountains and hills will break into song and the trees of the fields will clap their hands. Why should we not worship our Creator, too?*

Jackson blinked several times. "I-I suppose . . . you make a good point, Nano."

Our allegiance to Jesus is why we will initiate this counterinsurgency. It is the work he has assigned to us—as a delaying tactic only. We will do our best to combat the lawless forces arraying themselves against God's people. It is also why we warn you not to appoint Nora Mellyn as your vice president.

Jackson sighed. "Nora helped me get elected and fought tirelessly for me to win. She left her own party to help me. Her involvement in this so-called *Cabal*, this collusion against our nation and against me as its president, makes no sense to me."

We regret to tell you this, Mr. President, but our investigation into her life reveals that she is quite ambitious, that she has held as her highest aspiration the hope of becoming president. She supported your candidacy not because she agreed with your policies, but because she anticipated that you would win and, as president, you would advance her career.

You did so, sir. You appointed her Energy Secretary, a most prominent position. However, this was not the role she desired. She was also disappointed and frustrated when you did not choose her as your second vice presidential pick, despite your valid reasons.

Unfortunately, we believe your enemies viewed her disappointment as an opportunity. They extended a tempting offer to her if she would switch sides again—covertly. She accepted that offer and placed herself firmly in the Cabal's camp.

Mr. President, once Nora Mellyn is Vice President, your life will again be in jeopardy.

Jackson's fist slammed onto his desk. "I'm getting darned tired of every VP I choose trying to stick a knife in my back!" he shouted.

I shifted uneasily and was grateful for the nanomites' "cone of silence" over our conversation. It would ensure that not a word we spoke leaked into the open air of the Oval Office . . . or beyond.

Jackson managed to swallow his anger. "I apologize for my outburst, but I am scheduled to meet with her later today and announce her as my pick *tomorrow!* How will I look that traitor in the eye this afternoon without giving myself away?"

He muttered as an afterthought, "For that matter, how am I supposed to change my mind and cancel that announcement without letting on that I know about this conspiracy?"

It would be dangerous for you to, without cause, back out of announcing Mellyn's appointment. We will, therefore, undertake in the next few hours to remove this threat to your administration ourselves.

"Undertake to remove this threat?" Jackson asked. "Are you saying you will . . . take her out? *Assassinate her?*"

No, Mr. President. Our instructions do not include such an action except under strict circumstances and legal direction.

"Your instructions? Instructions from whom?" Jackson demanded. "And how could you remove her without it pointing back to me?"

We will attempt to neutralize Mellyn's candidacy without unnecessary violence and without involving or endangering you, Mr. President. Beyond that, we advise that you seek no personal knowledge of our actions. You must embody the ideal of plausible deniability.

The nanomites shifted gears to bring our meeting to a close.

Mr. President, we have presented the results of our investigations so that you are aware and forewarned. We have told you that if you, as president, attempt to curtail or exhibit any knowledge of this coup, the enemy will destroy you. In your stead, we will do what we can to curb this tide of evil. While we may not require your permission to act, we do seek your blessing.

Do we have your blessing, Mr. President?

Silence reigned in the Oval Office for many long minutes as the President wrestled with the information the nanomites had revealed. We watched as he struggled with the knowledge that he was powerless to fight back against the web of conspiracy tightening its stranglehold on our nation and across the globe . . . and that only the nanomites were in a position to slow the enemy's forward progress.

Finally he said, "Yes. You have my blessing. Go with God, Nano. I wish you good hunting."

⌘

MY REMINISCING AT AN END, I heaved myself up from the edge of the bed and wandered into the kitchen, needing a glass of orange juice to perk me up. I found Zander staring out the window of the kitchen door. I glanced out the window. The only thing visible from the back door was the garage—and it was bathed in evening shadows.

"Hey, Babe," I said, slipping into his embrace, his arm coming around me.

"Hey, Sweetie. Good nap?"

"Yeah. Bit of a brain fog from it, but I needed the rest."

He nodded. He knew how our meeting with the President had gone, of course, and I could sense his distraction.

"Worried?" I asked.

"Some. You?"

"Same. Things are . . . changing between us and the nanomites. Like, at this moment? I don't sense their attention on us, listening in like usual. They are busy elsewhere. Preoccupied."

"Yeah. They are." Zander huffed as he tried to put his concerns into words. "I have the sense that the nanomites are maturing. Coming into their own, so to speak. I guess that means that our relationship with them is changing, too."

I poked my chin in the direction of the garage. "They are out there right now, down in the basement, printing more nanomites, aren't they?"

"Yup. More but different. More sophisticated than the arrays they used in DC, but not full nanomites either."

I looked deeply into the warehouse. Searched around. It felt empty-ish . . . like the nanomites were far away. I hunted for what they were doing and finally found them.

"Huh. I see what you mean about 'not full nanomites.' Three new models?"

"I've been standing here a while and have counted four specialized nanobot models, each designed with a different purpose in mind. I think . . . I think the nanomites plan to send large contingents of these models out into the world via digital connections. Specialized soldiers with specific mission parameters, troops that lack the sensitivities of the nanocloud and the nanomites' need to be together, advanced arrays that can survive on their own indefinitely. An army of dumbed-down nanocombatants possessing more functionality than the original arrays but less than the nanomites themselves. Insentient offspring with a shorter lifespan than the nanomites possess. Nanobots that are, sadly, expendable."

He glanced at me. "I have this image in my head . . . trillions upon trillions upon trillions of nanobot shock troops spreading across the earth, leaping from one means of connection to another, seeking out their assigned targets, and delivering the two nanoclouds' counterinsurgent strikes."

"We won't be able to keep up with them and their troops, Zander. Not with everything we have on our plates. We won't know what they're doing most of the time."

He nodded. "I concur. They have work to do that we're not part of, and we have our own assignments. I think . . . I *believe* we must trust that their allegiance to Jesus will hold, Jay. That he will guide them, and they will follow him."

"Zander?"

"Yeah, Hon?"

"What they found? All those people in our government and around the world, how organized they are, controlling much of our society and culture, including what we see and hear in the news media? The nanomites say they won't able to stop them. What happens when the nanomites can no longer slow them down?"

"Why? Concerned we're two steps away from a one-world, totalitarian regime, are you? What could be alarming about that?"

I felt obliged to tweak my lips into a semblance of a smile, although I didn't find any humor in his rejoinder. I added my own "funny" deflection. "Um, one step after that to the antichrist?"

Zander's compassionate gray eyes found mine. "You're worried for Emilio and Baby Cruz."

I nodded, tears welling in my eyes.

Zander pulled me into his arms. "Yes, it's coming, we see that, but it's not here yet. In the same way that we must trust the nanomites to follow Jesus? We must trust that our children will follow him, too."

"But Emilio . . ."

"I know. He's not ready, but I believe he's getting closer. As for what is happening in the world? I do have hope that the nanomites will hold back the tide of evil for a while longer, perhaps a few years. I mean, we could witness the greatest move of the Holy Spirit in the history of the world! You and I have the work in front of us—Emilio included, Gamble and Trujillo, too. The fields are ripening for a harvest. Let's focus on bringing it in, okay?"

I nodded. "Yeah. Okay."

⌘

DESPITE MY NAP, I slept quite late the next morning, unusual for me. It was past noon in DC when a news alert pinged our phones. I pulled it up and scanned the headlines.

BREAKING:
SecEnergy Mellyn
Withdraws

The article itself was short, but it told us all we needed to know.

WASHINGTON, DC,
The White House, 10:57 am, EST

The White House announced on Twitter this morning that Energy Secretary Nora Mellyn, thought to be President Jackson's upcoming pick for his vice presidential slot, has abruptly withdrawn her candidacy. Unnamed sources say the withdrawal came after video surfaced of Mellyn meeting a man not her husband at a Virginia hotel three times in the past month.

Anonymous sources tell us that a disappointed President Jackson, unwilling to carry the baggage of a VP embroiled in scandal into the upcoming election, requested that she withdraw her candidacy.

I finished reading the account and sighed with relief. "One down. Only one hundred ninety-one thousand nine hundred ninety-nine to go."

"Approximately," Zander answered soberly.

⌘⌘⌘⌘

CHAPTER 39

I FOLLOWED THE NEWS intently over the next days, hoping to see some outward sign of the nanomites' war on the Cabal. Frankly, there wasn't much else to do. New Mexico and several other states were "locked down," their citizens confined to their homes except for those working in essential services or getting the allotted one hour of exercise outdoors. Whole nations in Europe were also locked down.

Deaths across the globe numbered in the hundreds of thousands.

While Zander spent most of his days in his office on video conference calls, I walked our neighborhood to get my necessary exercise. I wanted to jog rather than walk, but Baby Cruz was getting too big for me to do that, so I bundled up against the cold spring winds and settled for brisk, twice-daily jaunts up and down our street and deep stretches on the floor of our living room.

That accounted for maybe an hour and a half of my day. *Whoopee.* After I finished cooking and cleaning, I was bored half out of my skull. Wanting some public indication of what the nanomites were up to, I started consuming news reports: TV news broadcasts, online news forums, even current event opinion shows.

The big ticket item at the top of every news report, of course, was the pandemic. It had spread like a fire whipped by a fierce wind, crossing oceans and international boundaries despite the many attempts to keep it out. Here in Albuquerque, our hospitals were bursting with virus cases and had closed their doors to all patients except those experiencing the direst of emergencies. Well, we were New Mexico's most populous town, so it was to be expected that we'd have the state's highest infection rate.

Zander and I talked about going incognito to visit the hospitals and having the nanomites kill the virus load in the most critical cases. We knew the nanomites would protect us from the virus, so we weren't worried for ourselves, but we could do a great deal of good in those who wouldn't survive otherwise.

We were dumbfounded to hear that the nanomites felt differently.

Jayda Cruz, Zander Cruz, we cannot halt or slow our present activities to focus our attention on virus patients.

That didn't sit well with me *at all.* "What? Have you no compassion?"

We are at a crucial juncture in the counterinsurgency and must obey what Jesus speaks to us, Jayda Cruz.

I didn't like their answer, but I had to respect it.

With redoubled effort, I consumed mainstream media reports, but I also trawled Twitter, Facebook, and YouTube. I didn't go there to post or comment, though, but to "lurk" and get the other side of the news—the events and important details that the mainstream media either ignored, blocked entirely, or slanted to fit the Cabal's agenda.

I saw nothing that I might construe as the nanomites' work to undercut the Cabal. But now that I knew about *them*, the Cabal itself, I felt that I perceived their influence everywhere.

Their creepy and insidious influence.

When nothing seemed to pop up that would point to the nanomites' activities, I went into the warehouse and started searching out the nanomites and their movements. It took me hours to trace them and to *think* I grasped the essence of what they were up to, but it was mind boggling.

The nanomites were carefully preparing a massive first strike. They had sent their "nanotroops" into hundreds of banking systems. The troops were poised and prepared to act at the nanomites' signal. See, the nanomites were not targeting only the illegal off-shore accounts containing funds stolen from the US government. They had sought out and identified the financial resources of the wealthiest Cabal conspirators—their company holdings, their stocks and bonds, even tangible assets including real estate, art, precious metals and jewels, and collectibles such as vintage automobiles. They had loaded that info into a myriad of lists, each list topped with a heading and a date.

I couldn't make out the meaning of their headings, but based on the dates, I concluded that the nanomites were plotting insurgent actions, both immediate and up to two years in advance.

We see you here with us, Jayda Cruz; however, we do not sense anything amiss—do you need something?

"No. I'm merely curious, Nano. I wanted to see how you were progressing."

We are preparing our initial salvo, which requires the coordination of thousands of details. We wish to take the enemy utterly by surprise and do as much damage as possible in one fell swoop.

"Well, the scope of your, er, first salvo seems breathtaking. When do you anticipate 'pulling the trigger' as it were?"

Do you wish to watch the strike unfold, Jayda Cruz?

"May I? If Zander is available, may he join us?"

You are both welcome to watch. Return to us Friday evening. We commence our attack at the close of the NYSE and Nasdaq for the weekend.

"We'll be here."

I wouldn't miss it for the world.

⌘

LATE TRADING ON THE New York Stock Exchange and the Nasdaq securities exchange ended for the weekend at 8:00 p.m. EST, Friday evening. That's 6:00 p.m. Mountain Standard Time here in Albuquerque. The exchanges would not reopen until Monday morning. Many off-shore banks had also closed.

By six o'clock, Zander and I were deep within the warehouse, waiting for the nanocloud to execute their plans.

At 6:05 p.m., the funds in four hundred fifty-seven numbered foreign accounts "left." This was curious in itself since every bank was closed for business when the monies departed.

I pulled back to watch the movement of the funds as they began to ping across the globe. I couldn't follow the individual paths each account's money took—there were too many accounts to track simultaneously—but we could watch their overall streams, like jet contrails, crisscrossing the earth, popping into one bank, popping out just as quickly, over and over.

Then the funds diverged, one amount added to the amounts from other accounts, or other funds divided into several smaller funds that then joined other divided funds and flew off in different directions, the monies mingled beyond untangling. This went on for quite some time. All I could do was watch; I sure couldn't follow all of it. I knew Zander felt the same when he grimaced.

And I had expected the nanomites to return the stolen money to the government's accounts, but that's not what they did. At least, not at first.

Here's what did happen. The nanomites had identified the largest stock holdings on the NYSE and the Nasdaq owned by the Cabal's American principals. Zander and I watched as thousands of sell orders from non-Cabal investors queued up—investors who owned stock in the same holdings as the Cabal principals. I found it odd that the sell orders were primarily from owners of small stakes in the same stock holdings. I say primarily, because two (and only two) Cabal principals had also put in quite large sell orders.

What did it all mean? Of course those orders couldn't be executed until the exchanges reopened, so I wasn't sure what was going on.

We waited, nearly breathless for the next step. Instead, the nanomites told us to come back Monday morning.

"What?"

Come back Monday morning when the NYSE and the Nasdaq reopen for early trading.

"Is that it for tonight, then?"

Yes. We have completed our first step. Come back Monday morning when the NYSE and the Nasdaq reopen for early trading.

Apparently the fireworks would happen then.

I was disappointed, and so was Zander.

He shrugged. "Okay, so we come back Monday."

⌘

ZANDER'S MESSAGE DURING OUR streaming Sunday service was, as usual, the spiritual meat and potatoes I needed. I wasn't the only one who noticed how vital his messages were, either. DCC's online following was growing, and Zander fielded a hundred emails a week from grateful viewers.

Then it was Monday, Zander's day off. Usually, we would spend a leisurely morning puttering around together. Not today. We got up early, guzzled coffee so we'd be wide awake, and rejoined the nanomites before 6:00 a.m. our time, 8:00 a.m. EST. We were prepared to stay with them throughout the day.

At the bell for early trading, thousands of sell orders kicked in, including those of the two Cabal principals. When the bell for regular exchange hours rang at 9:30, the several stocks that had sold in early trading tumbled downward, losing value with every passing minute.

I yawned. The market activity was dead boring, and we couldn't figure out what the nanomites were doing.

By 3:00 p.m., the stocks the nanomites had sold off that morning were nearly worthless. The only movement of note was that, an hour earlier, the other Cabal principals had sold their stocks at a substantial loss.

I'm no financial genius, so the nanomites' objectives escaped me at the time. I can tell you, though, how the day ended. Yup. Floored me.

The thousands of small owners who had sold their stock *high* rebought their shares *low*, and each of them made a small but not inconsequential profit. The two Cabal principals with large holdings had sold high, too, making *huge* profits on the transaction, while the rest of the Cabal owners, selling low but not rock bottom, took quite the hit. With the repurchase orders, the price of those stocks started back up—and the many Cabal principals who had sold low tried to minimize their losses by buying back before the price rose further.

That's when they discovered they were boxed out—their shares no longer available.

The nanomites had used the stolen government money they'd removed from the Cabal principals' off-shore accounts to buy up all the available shares of the stocks at rock-bottom prices—at the exact same time they'd arranged for the small owners to buy their shares back.

"Did what I think happened, just happen?" I asked Zander.

It took Zander a minute to answer. "I think I get it. The nanomites arranged for the small owners to double their money on those stocks and for the Cabal principals to lose a fortune."

I shivered at the deliciousness of it all. "Not all of them lost money, though. I can't figure out why two Cabal principals made a truckload. What's up with that?"

Jayda Cruz, the two Cabal principals work for the SEC.

The SEC. The Securities and Exchange Commission.

"Don't get it, Nano—ohhhh! Oh, yes—yes, I do. They'll get busted for insider trading, right?"

That is correct, Jayda Cruz. The SEC will suspect the two principals of manipulating the market—as will the Cabal members who lost money.

Zander was as impressed as I was. "Way to go, Nano!"

"Hey, Nano? What about the money stolen from the government? You spent that money, right?"

That is correct, Jayda Cruz. However, we will sell off the stocks at a profit within the next few weeks. They are actually quite sound, so they will regain all their value and more. At that point, we will return the money stolen from the government.

"But you'll make a profit when you sell, yes?"

We will keep the profit moving around and add to it as we move forward. We anticipate the need for a war chest in the near future.

"Artistry, Nano!" Zander said with suitable awe. "It was a beautiful thing to watch—when I finally understood what was happening. I particularly liked the 'little guys' making bank by the end of the day."

I was worried, though, sorting through possible repercussions, wondering what the Cabal's response would be. "Nano, how . . . how do you anticipate that these so-called Cabal principals will react to your 'artistry'?"

We have left an infinitesimally small trail of breadcrumbs, Jayda Cruz. When the Cabal's forensic auditors look into their many losses, they will "discover" our breadcrumbs, and the trail will lead them to certain rivals within the Cabal's international leadership. It will be an unpleasant day for those rivals who don't take their personal security seriously enough.

I shuddered, grateful that nothing could possibly point to Zander or me. These were high-stakes games!

It was while I was pondering the responses of Cabal leadership—and how to blunt them, that I had an idea.

"Are you open to suggestions, Nano?"

We would welcome them, Jayda Cruz. Our intelligence is greatest in the digital world. We are not as emotionally intelligent as you are.

Well, I hadn't been angling for a compliment, but from the nanomites? I'd take it.

"Uh, thank you, Nano. You are too kind! I was merely wondering if you had considered using security clearances or access authorizations against Cabal members. You are familiar with the requirements to obtain one and what can cause a person to lose his or her security clearance."

I asked, because every American Cabal member working in a high-level government position—even elected officials—required a security clearance. In DOE the levels were "L," "Q Nonsensitive," and "Q Sensitive." Most other government entities followed DOD's Secret and Top Secret clearance levels with the possible additions of Special Access Programs (SAP), dependent upon each individual's job requirements.

The nanomites were quiet for several minutes. When they spoke again, I could tell they understood what my suggestion implied.

We have reacquainted ourselves with the behaviors or incidents that can create a security clearance investigation and may result in revocation of said clearance: security violations; a pattern of dishonesty or rule breaking; the commission of a crime or association with known criminals; failure of a drug test or possession of drugs; documented alcoholism.

Also, concealment or failure to disclose information that may predispose a security clearance holder to blackmail or may increase said clearance holder's vulnerability to coercion or exploitation.

Thank you, Jayda Cruz. Your insightful suggestion opens up many opportunities for us to harry the enemy.

I suddenly foresaw the Cabal's well-placed government henchmen or women running headlong into clearance issues of the nanomites' creation—and it wouldn't end in a pretty outcome. Considering that the Cabal network was engaged in treason, however, I didn't feel a shred of sorrow for them.

"The sooner they lose their clearances, the better our chances of stopping this incursion, Nano."

Jayda Cruz, we will go to work on your ideas immediately.

I was eager to view further results of the nanomites' counterinsurgency. To tell the truth, I was antsy with anticipation. However, I was beginning to appreciate that the nanomites preferred to play "a long game"—plans within plans and plots within plots, driven by their ongoing pursuit of precision and excellence.

Sure, I might have to wait for the results of their actions to percolate to the surface, but while I waited, I was certain of one thing: When the nanomites struck, their attacks would achieve *optimal* efficacy.

⌘⌘⌘⌘

CHAPTER 40

IT WAS NEAR THE MIDDLE of March when our attorney called with unwelcome news: Our adoption was "stuck," suspended in the process queue as a result virus lockdowns. Apparently, the governor's list of essential services did not include social workers and court employees. Until further notice, they, too, were furloughed, effectively shutting down local judicial review.

"Who knows when the courts will reopen?" our attorney said, his aggravation bleeding through the phone. "The state's entire judicial system has stalled out because of this cursed virus."

As the governor's restrictions on all but the most essential of services tightened, small businesses, the lifeblood of our fragile New Mexico economy and often the labor of the same family down through generations, called it quits for good. The nanomites revealed to us the increasing numbers of business failures, particularly small eateries unable to make the switch to takeout or delivery or unable to make a profit when they did.

I didn't understand. All small business owners could have implemented the same safe practices as the big box stores, but they were never given the opportunity or even a voice in the Governor's decisions. Their pleas fell on deaf ears.

At the same time, the circle in which Zander and I lived our lives contracted.

Izzie's employer had kept her on, working from home. Since her location didn't matter, she, quite unexpectedly, packed up her apartment and left Albuquerque to stay with Robert and María in Las Cruces. We were glad for their sake that she was there to help them through the lockdown, but I missed her bubbly presence. We spoke with the three of them frequently, using FaceTime.

With UNM and CNM closing their campuses, the majority of our young adults followed suit: They left Albuquerque to go home. We'd keep in touch, everyone said, via Zoom calls.

We were grateful for the few young adults who held good jobs in town—namely, Josh, Todd, and Nance. Their employers arranged for them to telecommute, too. Tian had no home to go to and, without any income, was in desperate straits. We were blessed when Nance invited Tian to share her apartment. This, we knew, was the Body of Christ caring for its members.

Zander took himself to his office most days, but he made certain he was alone in the building to maintain quarantine. Mrs. Coyne worked from home a few hours each day.

The exception to Zander being alone at the church was when he allowed the much-reduced worship team to rehearse in the sanctuary and prerecord Sunday's worship service—as long as they maintained the mandated six-foot distance from each other.

Zander then published the worship video on Facebook and YouTube, setting it to go live at 10 a.m. each Sunday, followed immediately by the livestream of his Sunday message.

Although Zander was alone at DCC during the week, he was kept quite busy checking in on the most vulnerable of our congregation, running errands to pick up prescriptions or other necessities for those who couldn't risk going out themselves. He also took counseling appointments via—you guessed it—whatever video conference software those particular congregation members preferred.

A slew of DCC folk, Zander told me, were dealing with acute loneliness. They were scared. Isolated. Anxious. Even bored. Couples forced to work from home fought for enough privacy to do their jobs. At the same time, they had to manage their kids' online classes and schoolwork. The kids, too, missed their friends and hated the APS makeshift home schooling structure—as did Emilio.

Family arguments and fights were "up," Zander said, and marriage crises abounded. Apparently, family and marriage tensions kept Zander in great demand.

"But Christmas next year should be interesting," he drawled.

"Oh? Why's that?"

"I predict a bumper crop of babies nicknamed Lockdown, Quarantine, and Virus."

I fell over on the couch laughing.

Yes, our shrinking world was starting to "pinch" and our adoption process was on hold, but one thing the virus was not able to cancel or stall? My pregnancy. I was getting bigger—or rather Baby Cruz was. Bigger and more active. According to the nanomites, my due date was April 8, which meant I had only a couple of weeks to go—a couple of weeks to *grow*, when I figured I was already about one inch from challenging the Goodyear Blimp for its celebrated spot hovering over the golf courses of the PGA!

Our narrowing circle, combined with Baby Cruz's growth? I was starting to feel like an elephant living in a cage the size of a bathtub.

I suppose our circle was not as narrow as everyone's. At the outset of the lockdown, Abe and Emilio agreed with us to form what we called "a cohort," a small group of people who could visit face to face in each other's homes so long as we carefully quarantined ourselves otherwise.

"I'd like to include Mrs. Calderón in our cohort," I said quietly. "She hardly leaves her own house as it is."

"Not that fat old lady!" Emilio protested.

"That 'fat old lady' is alone in the world, Emilio. Do you remember what being left out in the cold felt like?" I shook my head as he again tried to protest. "No. We're not doing that to her—leaving her friendless. She is self-quarantining, and the nanomites will check her every time she comes over. Maybe we won't spend as much time with her as we spend with you guys, but we can certainly have her over for dinner a couple of nights each week and make sure she knows she is *not* alone."

Abe and Zander nodded their agreement. Emilio sulked.

Basically, the four of us—with Mrs. Calderón as a twice-weekly dinner guest—would confine ourselves to our two houses, while most families were limited to their own abodes.

We had wanted to include Gamble and Trujillo in our cohort, too, but it didn't work out. Their FBI superiors had pulled them from the gang operation because of the pandemic. This left Trujillo, a contractor, twiddling her thumbs, while Gamble was assigned to other duties within his agency, and Gamble, as a federal law enforcement officer, remained on the job, operating in much the same way as he always had.

Sure, he and his fellow FBI agents wore masks while working, but masks were *maybe* twenty percent effective at stopping virus particles—if even that much. We decided not to include Gamble or Trujillo in our cohort. For Abe, Emilio, and Mrs. Calderón's sake, not ours.

Gamble and Trujillo understood. We waved to each other in passing and communicated often by phone, text, or video conference.

How I missed the hugs and human touch of friends! Missed the energy and joy of our young adults. Nonetheless, as sick to death of video conferencing as I was, I reminded myself to be grateful for what we had. Too many in the world had zero access to technology of any kind.

What wouldn't they give to hear a loved one's voice?

I told myself to stop complaining and count my blessings.

⌘

I WAS ON MY WAY TO THE Albertsons parking lot to pick up our grocery order—my single out-of-the-neighborhood jaunt each week and its epic highlight. Well, we needed that food order, and someone had to fetch it, because the three of us (I was eating for two) easily burned through in a week what a family of six required.

I was, however, worried that I would need a bathroom break before I got back home. "Listen, not-so-little one," I told Baby Cruz, "get as big and healthy as you like, but please, *please* stop stomping on my bladder!"

Why was I out getting groceries instead of having them delivered? Because Albuquerque stores had, quite abruptly, ceased offering delivery service to their customers, despite the governor's directions. Oh, all the big food outlets like Walmart, Target, Smith's, Albertsons, and Food King continued to provide online ordering and pickup, but the drivers themselves refused to work.

Grocery delivery had become an unacceptable risk for them.

Five Albuquerque delivery drivers within a two-week period had been hijacked by small mobs at quick, down-and-dirty roadblocks, the heisters getting away with up to ten grocery orders a pop. The drivers had been mildly beaten to break their resistance but not otherwise harmed—unless you wanted to count the possibility of being exposed to a full-blown case of the virus as being harmed.

The outcome was a rebellion in the ranks.

"We put our lives on the line when we show up to stock shelves and fill orders," they told their employers. "It's not fair that you also expect us to run a gauntlet every time we go out with a load of groceries."

Their spokesman added, "Yeah, getting beat up or worse? We're not gonna run that kind of risk for a mediocre paycheck plus tips. We can make more on unemployment."

The workers were right. With the federal add-on to unemployment benefits, they could make more staying home. End result? They flatly refused to make further deliveries.

I recalled what the nanomites had said to President Jackson. *Eventually the cost of supporting their citizens' dependencies will topple governments, Mr. President. Then the targeted nations—democratic nations—will fail economically and militarily.*

While I didn't fault the drivers in this instance, it did mean that every family in Albuquerque had to drive to a store and pick up their order. Easy-peasy, right? Nope. The situation for customers queuing up for their groceries became equally dangerous.

Gangs of despicable hoarders and people in desperate circumstances lurked in their vehicles, down side streets beyond store parking lots, one person acting as lookout. Spotters with binoculars targeted the "fattest" targets, then called the gangs, describing the vehicles and letting them know when the target left the store and what direction they were headed.

The gangs waited for the customer to drive by them, then followed them to their homes. So many customers had been attacked in their driveways and their groceries hijacked, that the police took control of grocery entrance and exits and patrolled the surrounding neighborhoods for both gangs and spotters. The cops set up checkpoints down the road that only customers could access. In this way, the police interposed their cars between would-be hijackers and fleeing customers, preventing the hijackers from following the customers home and robbing them blind.

Then there was the other big issue: empty shelves. I'd never seen empty store shelves before, but we had them now—courtesy of serious supply-chain problems. Food processing plants had to close due to large employee outbreaks; other plants were short of a full complement of workers, unable to deliver the quantities they usually did. Ships from every nation were anchored off shore, unable to dock and unload due to labor shortages among customs officials and dock workers. The virus had hit our nationwide rail and truck delivery systems, too, workers and drivers taking sick, leaving trains understaffed and trucks unmanned.

The upshot? Ordinary foods sold out or became completely unavailable, never reaching the store. In response, "no more than" signs dotted the aisles, meaning many foods in stock had limits. Store employees were actually opening the larger sacks of beans, rice, noodles, flour, sugar, and other staples and repackaging them in smaller sizes so that more people got a little of what they needed rather than nothing.

The best you could do was to order as much as the stores would allow, which is what we advised Abe and Mrs. Calderón to do.

Zander and I, with our fast metabolisms, found ourselves in a rather unpleasant pinch. If it weren't for splurging a couple times a week on pricey takeout dinners, we might be going to bed in the evening with hollow-feeling bellies. And with takeout being a substantial drain on our finances, I was determined to fetch our weekly allotment of groceries. Zander, on the other hand, given the state of civil unrest, was against me going by myself.

"Why don't you wait until I get home? We can go together," he said.

I shook my head. "Not the way it works, Babe. The store fills the orders, then *tells* you when to arrive for pickup. My pickup time is 11:15 a.m.—and I'm not picking up only for us. I have Abe's and Mrs. Calderón's orders to pick up, too."

And I didn't want either of them leaving their house.

"Baby Cruz, Jayda," Zander replied.

"Nano plus Jesus," I answered. "And Jesus trumps any and all comers. You know the nanomites are protecting us from the virus. You also know that I can defend myself against grocery thieves quite adequately, pregnant or not."

He didn't push it, I think, because Abe, Emilio, and Mrs. Calderón were counting on me and because he was distracted, pulled in too many directions. Also? Because what I'd said was true.

I'd be fine.

And so there I was. I waited forty minutes beyond my appointed time before I reached the top of the line, before the store employees loaded three grocery orders into the back of our SUV—all while I experienced the unignorable need to get to a bathroom. *Soon.*

When I pulled out of the parking lot, I waved my thanks to the officer in the police cruiser. Then I hit the police checkpoint up the road. His car blocked traffic from the other sides of the intersection, providing me with a clean getaway.

Or so I thought.

Three cars boxed me in as I turned onto that last block before I reached the neck of our cul-de-sac. If I'd made it into the garage ahead of them and gotten the automatic door down before anyone reached me, that would have been the end of it. But the lead car roared ahead of me, barreled across our lawn onto the drive, and blocked me from pulling into the safe harbor of our garage.

"Okay, if that's how you want to play it," I muttered.

Jayda Cruz, let us handle this.

"What, and miss all the fun? No way. Stay out of it, please, unless I ask for help."

I could almost feel the nanomites squirm.

Zander Cruz will be quite unhappy with us, Jayda Cruz.

"Oh, all right. *Fine*. But do exactly what I say—got it?"

We get it, Jayda Cruz.

I maneuvered my bulging belly out from behind the steering wheel and stood up. The three guys should, *at the least*, have the decency to look guilty for robbing a poor, pitiful pregnant girl, right?

They did look guilty, but not by much. "We don't want to hurt you. Just want your food. Open the back of your rig, ma'am."

Ma'am?

Really?

Gah!

I, however, obligingly used my key fob to pop the rear hatch. While they hustled to transfer my sacks to their own cars, I saw Abe come out on his front porch, one hand held slightly behind his thigh. He had an old revolver that he had kept handy, back when Mateo's gang ruled this cul-de-sac.

I stared at him until he acknowledged me. Then I shook my head no. I also told the nanomites what I wanted.

As the guys hurried into their cars to leave, their engines died.

"What the—"

Three drivers tapped the gas, turned their keys, and filled the air with colorful expletives. *Nada.* All the blue in the air wouldn't start those vehicles until I said so.

Their leader jumped from his seat. "Whatja do to our rides, lady?"

Who me?

Why, little ol' me?

I settled for, "I've been standing right here, dude. What makes you think *I* did anything?"

A car pulled into the driveway of the house next to ours and stopped. Gamble jumped out and started my way. Trujillo emerged from their house and followed behind him.

Nice of our FBI neighbor to come home for lunch, wasn't it?

Gamble and Trujillo strode toward the three vehicles beached on our driveway and lawn. Gamble had his service weapon in both hands, the gun's barrel raised partway but pointing toward the ground.

"FBI!"

More punching of gas pedals, frantic turning of keys, and colorful language.

"Hey you! Yes, you three brainiacs. Get out of your cars."

As the three men complied, Gamble added, "Jayda, what's going on here?"

"I'd call them Porch Pirates, but they're actually Food Filchers. Bread Bandits. Greedy little Grocery Grabbers."

"Um, I take exception to those characterizations," one of the guys said with timid conviction. "I'm not greedy, and I'm not afraid to work! I've never stolen a thing in my life. Not, uh, before today."

"Shut up, Darnell!" their leader hissed.

"I mean, we wouldn't even be here if the lockdown hadn't taken our jobs!" Darnell insisted. He sent his appeal my way . . . for some reason. "My unemployment benefits are snarled up in that computer mess over at Workforce Solutions." He tipped his chin toward his fellow Vegie Vandals. "Their unemployment claims, too."

Oh, bother! Did he have to play on my sympathies?

"We burned through our savings to keep our mortgages current, and I've got three kids at home—including a wife as pregnant as you are—but we've used up our EBT benefits for the month. Even the food banks are empty."

He let out a breath loaded with pathos. "Can't feed a family of five on four hundred bucks a month. Can't. I swear those kids are kin to ravening wolves—on my wife's side."

Gamble gestured to the three guys. "Yeah, yeah. Put her groceries back in her car. Pronto."

With a disheartened groan, their leader nodded. "Yeah. Do it, guys."

"Actually," I said, "I'd rather you took them into the house."

Gamble gave me a look that alternately flashed between "What, are you crazy?" and "Don't you dare!"

I addressed the leader of the Grocery Grabbers. "I'll pay you each twenty bucks to haul the sacks into the house and put them on the kitchen counters."

"What?" he asked.

"What!" Gamble protested.

I pulled out my purse. "As you can see, that would be a great help. Twenty bucks each to assist a poor pregnant, er, *lady* with her and her elderly neighbors' shopping." I'd sort out Abe and Mrs. Calderón's orders afterward.

The three guys side-eyed Gamble. Gamble, shaking his head, holstered his weapon. "Fine. All right. Do it."

But Darnell objected. "That's not right, lady. We tried to steal your food—woulda, too, if our cars hadn't conked out."

"Shut the *blank* up, Darnell!" the leader of the Grocery Grabbers hissed.

"Well, it's *not* right! We're lucky she's not calling the cops on us." He shuffled his feet. "Look, lady, I'll take your bags inside—no problem. But I'm not taking your money for doing it."

"Darnell?"

He looked up. "Yes, ma'am?"

"You're correct; getting paid after trying to steal our food isn't right, but . . . may I tell you that's what grace is? Grace is a gift we don't deserve. Grace is what Jesus offers us, too. Think about it?"

He blinked several times. "Okay. Thank you, ma'am."

The curious look on Trujillo's face snagged my attention. Then she caught me watching her and shrugged.

The guys went to work and finished in minutes. I paid them one by one with a whispered, "God bless you. I'll be praying for you and your families."

Darnell was last. Sighing, he took the twenty I offered him. "Thank you. My kids will eat tonight."

The guys—wide-eyed when their cars miraculously started—pulled away. Gamble and Trujillo left, too, and I was left thinking. Praying.

Twenty bucks would at least put dinner on the Grocery Grabbers' tables tonight. And the entire episode would be worth it if it touched Janice Trujillo's heart, even a little. Darnell's too.

Still, nothing I had done or said addressed the root causes of our nation's desperate need. The world's desperate need.

Idolatry. Rebellion. Wickedness. Blind eyes and stony hearts.

Lord, I prayed. *Please help these despairing families. Please help America! Open our blind eyes, O God. Cause us to return to you with all of our hearts.*

⌘⌘⌘⌘

CHAPTER 41

ON SATURDAY, THE WORLD as we knew it took another downward turn. The onslaught began with breathless headlines pronouncing horrific disasters and grew worse as hours ticked by. Zander and I spent late afternoon into late evening glued to our seldom-used television while we kept one eye on the various online newsfeeds we trusted, every other story bearing a "Breaking" headline—each report more tragic and ominous than the last.

Breaking: Historic Hurricane Strikes Gulf. *Thousands are dead or missing in the aftermath of Hurricane Althea. Unseasonably early and likely a product of global warming, Althea made landfall near Houston, TX, at 3:52 a.m. this morning then veered east to batter the gulf states of Louisiana, Mississippi, Alabama, and Florida.*

Althea formed in the Atlantic off Africa eight days ago. The storm pushed across to Brazil, brushed the northernmost countries of South America, swept between the Yucatan and Cuba, before it zeroed in on the Texas coastline.

The Category-5 storm, accompanied by high tides, produced an unprecedented storm surge. The surge plus torrential rain and winds in excess of 150 mph, flooded every city and state on the gulf coast, leaving a 50-mile-wide swath of death and destruction stretching from Houston across to Jacksonville.

In Althea's path was the bulk of the US's oil refinery capacity. Approximately 44% of all crude oil is refined along the gulf coast, and at least half of those refineries were damaged or destroyed by Althea. The petroleum industry forecasts higher gas prices at the pump and possible fuel oil shortages as a result.

Even as millions of US residents are left without power and drinking water, the National Hurricane Center projects the possibility that Althea, at present out to sea off the Atlantic coast, will strengthen and turn north to ravage the US eastern seaboard.

In the wake of Althea, several insurance companies have declared bankruptcy and shut down their phone lines, leaving in doubt the ability of those who lost everything to rebuild without government assistance. The unimaginable death toll is expected to climb as **[see more]**

Breaking: Salmonella Closes Poultry Producers. *The largest chicken processing plant in the US, found in Springdale, AR, was forced to close its doors indefinitely today due to a severe salmonella outbreak. Other meat production such as ground beef, bacon, deli meat, and seafoods, at the same plant but on different lines has been shut down for complete* *preventive cleaning and sterilization. The salmonella outbreak was traced back to at least five major suppliers in Iowa, a state that raises on the order of 60M chickens annually. Suspect suppliers will be forced to euthanize all stock and sterilize their pens and equipment in order to curtail the outbreak. Chicken, an American meat staple and major export, is expected to be in short supply in the coming* [**see more**]

Breaking: Infestation Devours California Crops. *An infestation of beetles unrecognized by farmers, orchardists, and crop scientists has struck south and central California. The beetles, less than a quarter inch in size, have decimated crops due to be harvested March through June. Farmers throughout the area predict shortages of broccoli, cabbage, carrots, cauliflower, kale, radishes, sweet onions, turnips, asparagus, and beets, while orchardists bemoan the complete loss of fruit harvests that include lemons, mandarins, navel oranges, raspberries, and strawberries. No pesticides tried against the beetles have, at the time of this report, been effective at curtailing their* [**see more**]

Breaking: Fires Burn Sprouted Winter Wheat. *Grassland fires in Kansas have burned up to 40% of the anticipated winter wheat crop. Severe drought conditions and drying winds in the Midwest had parched the young wheat sprouts, making them susceptible to wild fires. Kansas, the largest grower of winter wheat in the US, sees an average winter wheat harvest of 330M bushels. "No other state produces even half of what Kansas wheat farmers do. These fires are going to devastate many Kansans, not to mention creating wheat shortages to American customers and our export partners," said Ed Donaldson, head of the* [**see more**]

Breaking: USGS Releases Caution Concerning Increased Activity on Kīlauea. *Geologists at the USGS Hawaii Volcano Observatory have detected substantial, ongoing ground deformation in Kīlauea's south summit region during the past week, accompanied by more than 168 quakes recorded at Kīlauea summit and south of Kīlauea caldera over the past 24 hours. Scientists are divided, but a small majority believe Kīlauea to be on the cusp of a "significant event" that would* [**see more**]

Breaking: Virus Spread Increases. *States continue to report increases in the virus infection rate and mortality numbers, hospitals bemoan the short supply of ventilators and PPE, and schools throughout the US struggle to maintain distance learning as large percentages of students "drop through the cracks" and disappear from class rolls. The Secretary of Education announced Friday that* [**see more**]

Following the devastating national news cycle, the international news headlines kicked in. Reports of violence upon untold violence battered the world's stricken sensibilities.

Breaking: Bloody Coup in Saudi Arabia Stalls; Counterrevolution Feared. *Forces aligned with Prince Muḥammad, tenth son of the Saudi king, yesterday morning took control of key elements of the monarchy and their seats of power. Muḥammad proclaimed himself king after ordering the execution of his father and all members of the Allegiance Council including eleven brothers and two nephews who sat on the council.*

However, adherents of the Wahhabi sect, the same Muslim extremist group that spawned Osama bin Laden and Al-Qaeda, are leading a bloody counterrevolution that threatens to upend the Saudi kingdom and tip the country into all-out religious and civil war. The US State Department recommends that US citizens exit the country and advises **[see more]**

Breaking: Jackson Warns Chinese Against Venezuelan Invasion. *President Robert Jackson today issued a stern warning to China. "Do not think while America's attention is focused on virus containment and the devastation of Hurricane Althea, that we will allow Chinese troops to invade a sovereign nation anywhere in the western hemisphere, even in a failed dictatorship such as Venezuela. Do not mistake America's resolve on this."*

Jackson's warning follows a series of unconfirmed sightings of Chinese planes crossing Colombian airspace under cover of the massive weather front exiting our gulf coast. The unconfirmed sightings have Chinese planes landing at Venezuelan air bases in Barquisimeto, Caracas, Maracaibo, and Puerto Ayacucho. One such report says that after fierce fighting, Chinese assault forces have taken control of the four bases and are **[see more]**

I was stunned. "Chinese troops in Venezuela?"

"It's a gutsy move," Zander murmured. "They've been buying up land all over South America and capturing the economic markets of those countries for decades. As for Venezuela? They are what is called 'a failed petrostate.' The government is bankrupt, making the country ripe for the plucking."

"But if Venezuela is bankrupt, why would the Chinese want it?"

Jayda Cruz, Venezuela is bankrupt due to its government's corruption and its overdependence on the country's oil and natural gas exports when, in fact, the country itself is rich in other underdeveloped natural resources. Yes, Venezuela holds the world's largest oil reserves, but government mismanagement has sucked the profit from those reserves while neglecting to maintain the oil and gas infrastructure.

"The Venezuelan government killed the goose that laid the golden egg?"

An apt metaphor, Zander Cruz. Crooked government officials, fat on oil and gas revenues, have neglected other domestic resources, products, goods, and labor, to the detriment of its tax base and its impoverished citizenry. China would be more prudent in the management of all Venezuelan resources, not only oil and gas. Unfortunately, China, being a totalitarian form of government, would not advance the freedom or prosperity of Venezuela's people.

"The Chinese wouldn't mind being within striking distance of the US, either," Zander added.

That is true, Zander Cruz. A Chinese-controlled Venezuela challenges US military superiority in this part of the world. Caracas is only 1,368 miles from Miami, and a scant 2,000 miles from Washington, DC. As you said, it puts the Chinese within striking distance of America, including her seat of government.

Zander answered slowly, as if thinking something through. "Revelation 12:3 describes *an enormous red dragon with seven heads and ten horns and seven crowns on its heads.* Verse 9 identifies the dragon as *that ancient serpent called the devil, or Satan, who leads the whole world astray.* Some questions about this dragon remain, however. It is both red and enormous, but the Bible doesn't tell us what those characteristics signify. And what do the *seven heads and ten horns and seven crowns on its heads* mean?

"Some students of the word wonder if that picture doesn't describe China—a communist (red) country, with the largest population of any nation on earth (enormous) and symbolized for centuries as a dragon—as Satan's primary tool or vehicle in the end times. The heads, horns, and crowns seem to signify alliances under the dragon's control, too.

"I'm no expert on end-time prophesy, so I'm not saying I'm 'all in' on this theory, but the parallels between China's national identity and the dragon in Revelation 12 are striking, certainly as China is poised to become *the* global superpower."

I was thinking. Hard. "The nanomites say the Cabal orchestrated the manufacture of this virus. If Cabal members within the Chinese government deliberately infected us, devastating our economy and crippling our military's ability to defend us, is a Chinese invasion of Venezuela the launchpad for the Cabal's next objective? Will the Cabal use the Chinese to break us?"

Zander glanced up. "I suppose it is possible. America is in a weakened state, for sure—and our unity as a people is at an all-time low, too. Makes us a big target. It is our disunity, however, that is the worse of the two. Why? It's what I preached on, two diverging and incompatible worldviews. More than half of Americans no longer have a biblical worldview.

"With many of our citizens believing that socialism is the answer to today's ills, too many Americans may look on a Chinese Venezuela as a step in the right direction, a step toward a peaceful "global community," one that would do a better job managing humanity's needs while promoting a more equal distribution of wealth. Put another way, America lacks the will to save herself."

He shook his head. "You couldn't pay me enough to step into President Jackson's shoes. Our government is so divided, politicized, and polarized that it is stalemated. If Jackson were to move against the Chinese in Venezuela, he'd have half the nation for him and the other half against him. Half of Congress against him, too.

"All our congress can seem to do is throw more money at our problems—money we don't have, money we, in large part, must *borrow* from our own people, the Japanese, and the Chinese—the three largest holders of our national debt. But frankly? If any of the nations who own significant chunks of our national debt were to sell off that debt? It would sink us."

He glanced down at his tablet. "Oh, no."

I looked at his screen and glimpsed a fresh news report. "Oh, dear Lord! We are struggling as it is, and wherever we turn, all we see and hear is *more* disaster and more horrifying news."

Breaking: Suicide Bombers Hit Thirteen US Targets. *Apparent suicide bombers struck at the heart of America this afternoon in separate but coordinated attacks carried out by 33 individuals. The terrorists carried concealed bombs on their bodies, and all 33 detonated their bombs within the same hour. Due to the breaking nature of this news, details are scarce, but we have confirmed that all targets hit, save one, were hospitals overflowing with critically ill virus patients and their heroic caregivers. The lone exception to the bombings was the Lincoln Memorial, where the statue of Lincoln within the memorial was severely damaged. Cities where hospitals were hit include Seattle, Portland, Salt Lake City, Las Vegas, Sacramento, San Diego, Denver, Kansas City,* **[see more]**

"The Lincoln Memorial!" It had been the Fourth of July, only nine months ago, when a crazed bomber had attempted to detonate a bomb in the crowd gathered at the memorial. The nanomites and I had stopped the man . . . about two weeks before I became pregnant with Baby Cruz.

Would I do the same thing today? Risk my family to save others? I didn't know the answer.

In what had once been a safe and sane nation, a gaping chasm opened before my eyes.

Jayda Cruz, your blood pressure is rising and your breathing appears agitated. May we assist you?

"No, Nano. I-I . . . I don't know. Zander, what is happening? I'm feeling . . . overwhelmed by the sheer volume of bad news. Thirty-three terrorist attacks here in the US?"

Zander was as troubled as I was. "God is further removing his hand of blessing and protection from America. He's allowing our enemies to attack us on our own soil and setting the stage for this people to experience famine."

"What do we do? What does the Lord want us to do? What will you say in your message tomorrow? How are we to respond to all these terrible troubles?"

He was slow to reply. When he did, he murmured, "That's a good question." He added, but not to me, "Holy Spirit? I am counting on you to fill my mouth with your words."

⌘

ZANDER LOOKED DEEPLY INTO his phone's camera, the means by which the nanomites livestreamed his sermon on Facebook and YouTube. As it streamed, the message was being captured by Facebook and YouTube as a video that could be rewatched as long as we left it up.

He was alone in his office as he prepared to speak. Once the media team had set up the equipment, he had told them he could manage the livestream himself—but he actually left all that to the nanomites, preferring to focus on his message. On his part.

The number of hits on Zander's previous messages had increased dramatically in the past month, up by a couple of thousand views. Shares of Zander's videos kept climbing, too . . . people finding and passing on the hope of Jesus.

I smiled as I watched Zander from our home. Emilio and Abe were ensconced on the sofa with me, Emilio snuggled against my shoulder. And I had to acknowledge that the nanomites had been right in their advice. As Zander spoke to the camera, I felt as if he was speaking to *me*—not because I knew him, but because he was . . . gifted by God to communicate priceless truths in simple words.

It's you, Lord. I thought. *The first time I heard Zander preach, I sensed that he was different, that his words carried power. I didn't know it was you then, but I do now. And you have been honing this gift in him, preparing him . . . for such a time as this.*

"Oh!"

I gasped and choked up a little, as the Holy Spirit spoke. I had to grapple with the powerful word he was pouring into me, a revelation *I* deeply needed.

I turned it this way and that, seeing his point, acknowledging that if the Lord had, *in advance*, prepared Zander to speak encouragement into these distressing and tragic times, then wouldn't it also follow that the Lord had, *in advance*, prepared *a way* for his people to walk through all this chaos and heartache?

Wouldn't he provide a path through the encroaching darkness? Wouldn't he provide a road through this desert? Wouldn't he provide a sure word for this season?

Almost immediately, I heard my Savior whisper to me . . .

I am the way for you to walk through chaos and heartache.

I am the path through the encroaching darkness.

I am the road through your deserts.

I am the sure word you must have in this season.

Yes, Lord. You are the answer, the path, the road, the sure word we need and long for. You know us—and you know me. Thank you for not leaving us alone, without comfort, without hope.

Zander was coming to the end of his message. "World War II, the most devastating human conflict in history to date, came to an end in September 1945—but Japan only surrendered after the US dropped atomic bombs on two cities, Hiroshima and Nagasaki. It was an extreme move, but a necessary one to end the long conflict and save lives in the long run.

"And in a way akin to how the Lord warns us of his coming judgment, America dropped thousands of leaflets on the cities of Japan warning the Japanese people that we would devastate their nation with a new and horrible weapon if they did not surrender. Still, it was only after we had dropped the second bomb on Nagasaki that the Emperor formally surrendered.

"However, relief over the ending of the war was soon tinged with a new fear—that of imminent nuclear annihilation. Over the next years, Russia and America became enmeshed in the nuclear arms race, a race to see which nation would achieve nuclear superiority first.

"Some believed it was the end of the age, that the appearance of Jesus had to be close. The common man and woman, however, only saw the likelihood of worldwide nuclear war culminating in a blasted, scorched, and broken earth and a nuclear winter in which nothing would grow and humankind would succumb to famine and radiation poisoning.

"Fear, an overwhelming terror, gripped the earth. It also gripped the hearts of Christendom, paralyzing numerous people of God. Into this fear, a respected voice spoke, that of C.S. Lewis, the author of *The Chronicles of Narnia, The Screwtape Letters,* and *Mere Christianity.* His words calmed and exhorted us to a stouter, more active faith.

"This morning, I submit to you that we are at a similar crossroads. The world is gripped by a pandemic, supply chains have failed, food is scarce, lawlessness runs rampant over our cities, war looms on the horizon, and the foundations of the earth seem poised to crack and give way beneath our feet.

"I think it fitting, therefore, to speak to you the same words C.S. Lewis wrote in 1948, making but a few substitutions apropos to our circumstances. So, let me begin.

"*In one way we think a great deal too much of . . .* **the virus.** *How are we to live in* **a pandemic world? In scarcity? In a lawless, godless society?** *I am tempted to reply: 'Why, as you would have lived in the sixteenth century when the plague visited London almost every year, or as you would have lived in a Viking age when raiders from Scandinavia might land and cut your throat any night; or indeed, as you are already living in an age of cancer, an age of paralysis, an age of air raids, an age of railway accidents, an age of motor accidents.*

Zander lifted his head to the camera, his eyes on me and me alone—I am certain of it.

"*Or . . . in an age of manufacturing and supply chain failure; of famine, fire, and flood; of hurricanes, earthquakes, and volcanic eruptions; of terrorism, invasions, revolutions, and counterrevolutions.*"

He smiled. "*In other words, do not let us begin by exaggerating the novelty of our situation. Believe me, dear sir or madam, you and all whom you love were already sentenced to death before the atomic bomb was invented—***or before the virus was cultured, weaponized, and used against us** *. . .*

"*It is perfectly ridiculous to go about whimpering and drawing long faces because the scientists have added one more chance of painful and premature death to a world which already bristled with such chances and in which death itself was not a chance at all, but a certainty.*"

Zander lifted his gaze and spoke to us all. "Do you hear those words ringing in your soul? Death is a certainty. Eternity looms before us all. That being the case, have you made your peace with God? Can you do such a thing on your own? No; you require the sure promise of Scripture, the words of Jesus found in John, chapter 3.

> *"For God so loved the world*
> *that he gave his one and only Son,*
> *that whoever believes in him*
> ***shall not perish but have eternal life.***

"Do not wait. Do it now. Fall on your knees and beg Jesus to forgive you, to remove the condemnation and wrath hanging over your head. Ask him to receive you as his own. *Do it now*. Jesus is waiting for you to answer his call!

> *"Behold, I stand at the door and knock.*
> *If anyone hears My voice and opens the door,*
> *I will come in to him and dine with him,*
> *and he with Me."*

Zander waited long, silent minutes, during which I hoped, in many homes, knees unaccustomed to bending and hearts unaccustomed to yielding were bending, yielding, breaking, and surrendering all to Jesus.

Then Zander finished the quote from Lewis. He must have memorized it, for he spoke it straight into the camera.

*"This is the first point to be made—and the first action to be taken is to pull ourselves together. If we are all going to be destroyed by a war, flood, famine, or other disaster—**by a virus**—let that disaster when it comes find us doing sensible and human things—praying, working, teaching, reading, listening to music, bathing the children, playing tennis . . . not huddled alone in our homes like frightened sheep—**worrying over masks and social distancing**. A virus may break our bodies (a microbe can do that) but it need not dominate our minds."*

Zander smiled. "In conclusion, I want to leave you this morning with some of Jesus' last words to his beloved friends—friends who would shortly be without his companionship and leadership, friends who would suffer great persecution for their devotion to him. Jesus' words are as relevant to *us today* as they were when he spoke them to his disciples."

He leaned forward and spoke to every individual watching and listening. "I urge you to read the words of Jesus found in John 16 and apply them to your heart often. Hold them close and say 'no' to fear and 'yes' to God. Speak the words of Jesus aloud to yourself and to your children.

> *"I have told you these things,*
> *so that **in me** you may have peace.*
> *In this world **you will have trouble**.*
> *But take heart!*
> **I have overcome the world.**"*

⌘⌘⌘⌘

CHAPTER 42

BABY CRUZ WAS TWO days overdue, and I felt like a tub of lard. Then there was the issue of my feet. I knew they were down there. Somewhere. But I couldn't *see* let alone *trust* my feet. Or was it my hips?

Bottom line? I couldn't walk without modeling Baby Huey or a drunken Weeble.

Ugh.

"You need to come outta there," I told my child. "My ribs can't take anymore jujitsu practice."

I rolled my belly to the edge of the bed, praying the rest of me would follow. When the rest of me obliged, I levered myself up until I was sitting on the edge. Felt around on the floor with my invisible toes until I found my slippers, slid into them, and shambled across the house—*weeble wobble, weeble wobble*—into the kitchen where I fell, sobbing and sniveling, into Zander's arms.

"I'msotiredofbeingpregnant!"

He didn't say anything. Just rubbed the small of my back while I soaked the collar of his nice clean shirt—one of the new ones sent from his quite respectable tailor in Texas.

Yeah, I know. *Wah! Wah! Wah!* I wasn't acting like a mom. I was acting like . . . a baby.

"Jayda, Sweetie, you can call me if you need anything at all," he whispered, "but I gotta get going. I have two counseling appointments this morning, back to back. On Zoom. From my office at church. And I need an hour or so to prepare."

"*Fine.*"

Zander knew good and well that when a woman says "fine" with that kind of emphasis? It, whatever "it" was, was certainly *not* fine.

"Uh, how about I jet to the gas station and see if their vending machine has any ice cream bars in it before I go into the office? And I could ask Abe to come over and watch a movie with you? Have Emilio do his school work at our table? And I can give you a foot massage as soon as I get home?"

"Stop trying so hard. I'll . . . I'll be okay."

sniffle

"Jayda, say the word, and I will call Mrs. Coyne and ask her to cancel those appointments. If you need me to stay home, please say so."

I sighed. Stiffened my spine. "No. I can't be responsible for the Harrisons getting a divorce because I withheld their pastor in their time of need. Think of the kids!"

Zander went from solicitous to harried in a split nanosecond. "I'm sorry—who are the Harrisons? Do I know them? Who said they were having marital problems? How many kids do they have?"

I giggled, then hiccupped. "You are *way* too serious these days, Zander Cruz. The Harrisons? I made them up on the fly."

"Oh? Oh! I get it."

"And I thought I was the slow one lately . . ."

"Very funny."

I leaned into Zander's arms and kissed his neck. "My love, you are doing a great job at DCC—as is evidenced by the continued good fruit we're seeing. Please. Please trust that if the Lord put you in this position, he can keep you in this position. He did not bring you to this place to let you fail."

Zander sagged a little as relief flowed through him. "Okay. I . . . yes. Thank you, Jay."

With one finger, I caressed the sharp line of his jaw. "I think, too, my love, that you are mourning for your mentor and friend, Pastor McFee. But you aren't allowing yourself to feel his loss, aren't allowing yourself to grieve for him. You are too busy living up to his expectations."

Unexpectedly, I felt Zander's chest heave, heard the great sob he tried so hard to stifle. I held him tighter and pressed my face to his.

"Oh, Sweetheart," I crooned. "You can let down with me—I will share your grief!"

Zander wept then, releasing to the Lord the deep pain in his heart over Pastor McFee's death and the loss of his steadying influence. Thank God for the other local pastors Zander fellowshipped with and the Zoom conference calls they used to meet and pray together! In a big way, those men were helping to fill the empty place that Pastor McFee had occupied.

When Zander, lighter of heart, left for his office, I found myself much less obsessed with my physical discomfort. I was, instead, grateful to the Lord for refreshing my beloved husband. I spent the rest of the morning praying for him, our family, and our friends . . . while timing the regular contractions that had begun soon after he left.

I walked slowly up and down the length of the living room and dining room, shifting a few dining room chairs so I had a longer area in which to walk, timing each contraction, stopping when *this one* bent me over. I bent, grabbed my knees, and held onto them, breathing through the pain that tightened around my belly.

"Whew. That was a big one."

You are in labor, Jayda Cruz.

"Are you certain, Nano?"

Yes, Jayda Cruz. Although this is our first baby, our tribes agree that all the requisite signs are present: Baby Cruz is fully developed, is in the optimal position, and that position is far down in the birth canal. We note, too, the healthy physical state of your uterus and pelvic floor, the softening of your cervix, and your body's attempts to increase its levels of the necessary hormones.

I chuckled to myself. *Your first baby, Nano? Good one.*

We supplemented your body's endogenous production of oxytocin throughout your pregnancy. We will now substantially increase those levels to aid in your contractions. We will also add the needed supplements of beta-endorphins, epinephrine, and prolactin.

I focused on the rest of what they'd said. "I need all those things, those hormones? How will they affect Baby Cruz?"

Both you and Baby Cruz need an ample, ongoing flow of these hormones—in the correct amounts—for a stress-free labor and delivery, for you and the infant to bond, and for you to produce an adequate supply of milk.

"Er, that's great. Thank you." The contraction passed, so I resumed my slow march up and down the living and dining rooms, stopping when I needed to breathe through a contraction, going on when each one passed, drinking water or warm tea with honey, but abstaining from solid food.

A disconcerting thought popped into my head. "Nano?"

Yes, Jayda Cruz?

"You said . . . you said you'd be less available because of your work, your counterinsurgency. Are you . . . are you going to 'stay' with me, with us, while I'm in labor? Keep coaching me until I give birth?"

Yes, Jayda Cruz. We have, to date, produced and dispatched many trillions of soldiers into the world via digital connections. The troops we have sent out have taken up their positions and duties. Our coverage is not as optimal as we desire, but we will continue to add to our ranks until it is. We have also devised reporting mechanisms that prompt us to respond to threats and mount counterattacks in near real-time.

It is true that our two nanoclouds are operating at maximum capacity; nevertheless, we have appropriated time for this important event and will provide adequate guidance and attention. You need not fear that we will leave you and Zander to manage this birth on your own.

My blood pressure subsided into a healthy zone. "Thank you, Nano. It wouldn't feel right, not having you 'with us' when Baby Cruz comes."

We would not miss this joyous occasion for the world, Jayda Cruz.

⌘

Morning passed. Zander was due home for lunch, but it wasn't uncommon for his last video appointment to last longer than scheduled. I halted now for the duration of every contraction. As I bent over for the present one, I squatted and groaned, hoping to relieve the pressure of the contraction.

Warm liquid gushed between my thighs then ran down my legs onto the floor. I gasped at the sharpening pain and had to remind myself to breathe through it.

"Nano? Where's Zander? *Where is my husband?*"

We have told him he is urgently needed, Jayda Cruz, and he is coming. ETA, four minutes, seventeen seconds. Hold on, please, Jayda Cruz. Another contraction is—

"YOU THINK I CAN'T TELL WHEN ANOTHER OF THOSE BLASTED CONTRACTIONS IS—*oh!*" I doubled over and squatted enough that my thighs cupped my belly, providing me with some stability and a little more room to breathe through the pain.

Another contraction piled on top of the last one and a third on top of it, a fourth coming right behind the third. Then I lost track. I felt like a truck had parked on me, revving its engine over and over.

Jada Cruz, your labor has accelerated.

"Gee. Hadn't noticed."

Do not worry. We are going to help you. We are thinning the membrane of your cervix, we will aid you as you push baby Cruz out.

They would help me push Baby Cruz out? I did not particularly like the visual that jumped up in my imagination—that of little yellow nano-minions with their miniature toolbelts and oversized teeth and eyes, all of them down there in "my private business"!

"Zander!" I screamed. "*Zander!*"

The front door slammed against the living room wall. "I'm here! I'm here, Jayda!"

Zander Cruz, prepare the bed as we showed you. Hurry.

Zander sped by me, eyes huge and round, sparing me but a glance while I puffed and blew and breathed in and out, because what choice did I have? I was caught in the vise of childbirth and I had only one option: get through it.

I heard the sounds of Zander tearing up our room, but it was background noise to what hummed in my head. *Suck it iiiin. Blow it ooout. Suck it iiiin. Blow it ooout. PantPantPantPant.*

Zander's shoes appeared in my line of sight. "Let me help you to the bedroom, Jay." I hobbled along with him, glad of his support, glad I wouldn't be giving birth on the living room floor.

The rest of my labor and delivery went by in a long, tangled blur, Baby Cruz making a slow entrance into the world—until it was over, and *she* slid into her Papa's hands.

"It's a girl!" Zander shouted.

I laughed with joy as the nanomites coached Zander, then directed him to place the baby on my chest.

"Yes! I want to hold her!" I babbled.

He lifted our squalling daughter—awkwardly. She was accustomed to being swathed in warm, comforting fluid, so in the cool and open air of her new world, her little arms and legs straightened and stiffened like a four-armed starfish—until Zander deposited her gently on my chest and placed a receiving blanket over her wet little body. I saw the wonder in his eyes— or was it shock?

Zander Cruz, you have work to do.

"Right. Yeah, yeah. Cut the cord. Afterbirth. Clean up. All the stuff. I got this."

Yes, you do, Zander Cruz. A job well done.

They spoke to me what I needed to hear. *Baby Cruz is in perfect health, Jayda Cruz. As soon as Zander Cruz finishes his tasks, we will coach him through giving her a bath.*

I couldn't see much of her, our baby, only the top of her tiny head, but her wailing cries stopped as soon as her skin touched mine. Her breathing settled, too . . . until she was breathing in sync with me.

Tears trickled down my face, and my heart softly sang, *Oh, Lord God! How wondrous you are!*

⌘

LATER, AFTER WILLING BUT inexpert hands had bathed, diapered, dressed, and swaddled Baby Cruz and laid her in my arms, I slept. We slept. When I woke up, Zander was in a chair right beside the bed.

He wasn't sitting up, though. His head and torso were sprawled, facedown, along the edge of the bed, and he was rocking the "z"s.

I smiled. Heard a funny little *eep* and turned down the blanket so I could see this daughter of ours. Her eyes were closed, but . . .

eep . . .

eep . . .

eep . . .

Zander sat up with a jerk. "What's wrong?"

I laughed. "Nothing's wrong. She has hiccups."

"Babies have hiccups?"

"Yup."

He leaned over to watch her. We watched her together. Studied her plump, pink cheeks, the waves of her dark hair, her long eyelashes, her petite hands and perfect, curled fingers.

"She's beautiful," Zander said. "How beautiful you are, little girl!"

"You're not wrong, Papa."

Zander jumped up. "Papa? Wow! We need to call my folks! Abe and Emilio. Gamble and Trujillo. Josh, Diego, Mrs. Coyne . . ."

"Don't forget Mrs. Calderón."

"Right!"

"Well? Get the phone."

I laughed again. Couldn't help it. I was filled with joy. And triumph. *Spectacular* triumph.

⌘

"A GIRL? IT'S A GIRL!" María, Zander's mom, shouted the announcement. We heard Izzie screaming in the background as María added, "Praise the Lord! When was she born? How much does she weigh? What's her name? What's she look like? Send pictures right away!"

"She has dark, sort of curly hair, and she's plump and a little pink. Take a look for yourself."

Zander streamed video of Baby Cruz, of me smiling my tired head off, the three of us together, then back to Baby Cruz. Zander mouthed to me, "Do we know how much she weighs?"

Zander Cruz, Baby Cruz was born at 4:57 p.m. She weighed precisely seven pounds, three-and-a-half ounces when she was born. She is nineteen inches long.

"Thanks, Nano." Zander relayed all the info to his mom, dad, and Izzie, then said, "We haven't settled on a name yet. We'll let you know as soon as we do."

He hung up and looked to me. "Our daughter needs a name."

"Uh-huh. But remember: Her middle name is Lucia."

"Right. For your aunt. *Gemma's* aunt." He was busy texting half of Albuquerque.

Less than two minutes later, we heard pounding at the front door. I smiled down at our baby girl. "I believe that would be your big brother, Emilio, Sweetheart."

Zander opened the door and spoke a few soft words. I heard Emilio thunder into the bathroom, the water in the sink flowing full-throttle, accompanied by thumps, bumps, and splashes. After the water shut off, he crept into our room.

"Emilio?"

"Yeah?" He only had eyes for the bundle cradled in the crook of my arm.

Zander appeared. "Hold on one more sec, buddy. Jayda, would you like me to help you sit up?"

"Yes, please." I leaned back against the pillows he arranged between me and the headboard, baby on my lap, then motioned for Emilio to climb up on the bed next to me. I smiled at Abe as he came into the room after Emilio, his hands freshly washed, too.

"Okay, Emilio. Meet your baby sister. Hold your arms like this."

When I placed Baby Cruz in his arms, I turned back the blanket so that he could see her in her little nightgown, her petite fists curled up tight. Emilio used one finger to stroke her hand. When he did, her fingers opened, then closed.

Abe had leaned over to see Baby Cruz, too, and I watched his eyes mist over. He sniffed. "She sure is pretty."

I heard a gulp. Emilio swallowed and gulped again.

"Emilio?"

He sobbed. And sobbed.

"Oh, buddy! What's the matter?" Zander asked, kneeling beside him.

"She-she-she!" But Emilio's face screwed up tighter, and he couldn't talk. I tried to take Baby Cruz back so Zander could comfort him, but our boy's arms closed possessively about her, and he turned away from me.

"No! No, please don't take her! I . . . I wanna hold her and look at her and hug her. She-she-she's . . . *qué bonita. Qué bonita!*"

His tears ran down his face onto his chest, onto the baby's blanket, but it was okay. We loved what he was feeling.

Zander put his arm around Emilio's shoulders and handed him a tissue. "Here, buddy. Let's not blubber all over your sister, okay? And, yes. She's the most beautiful thing I have ever seen."

"*Bonita.* Beautiful," I whispered. "Zander, wasn't Bonita your grandmother's name?"

Zander's brows lifted. "It sure was. But we called her Bonnie."

"I like that. Bonnie Cruz. BC. Our wee bonnie lass."

Zander chuckled. "Now you're mixing ethnicities." To Emilio he said, "Hey, bud. Did you name your sister?"

Emilio sniffled and smiled. "You gonna call her Bonnie?"

Zander slid the question toward me. "Bonita Lucia Cruz?"

I sighed. "Oh, I like it. Bonita Lucia Cruz. Bonnie."

"Bonnie Lucia," Emilio said, testing it out.

I smiled. "Yes. It's perfect."

Bonita Lucia Cruz. Zander and Jayda Cruz, we can now file the child's birth certificate.

"Thank you, Nano."

Emilio smiled, too, and nuzzled his sister's wispy hair. "Pretty little Bonnie Lu."

Well, it *had* been perfect—until Emilio shortened Lucia. "Um, wait a sec. She can be *Bonnie*; I like that, I do. And she can be Bonnie Lucia. But she can't be Bonnie Lu—and *especially* not Bonnie Lu *Who*. I mean, it's practically straight out of *The Grinch Who Stole Christmas*, and the other kids at school will tease her!"

"Any dudes tease my sister, I'll punch 'em out."

Emilio meant business.

Zander stepped in. "Uh, I like where your loyalty is, but maybe we don't need to punch anyone quite yet, right?"

A devious gleam sparkled in Zander's eye. "We won't call her Bonnie Lu Who, but Bonnie Lu feels *just right* to me."

Emilio nodded. "Me, too. Bonnie Lu."

I was horrified. "No, *Bonnie!* Just Bonnie!"

Emilio glowered at me. "You *said* Bonnie Lu was perfect."

"And you did insist that her middle name be Lucia—after your aunt," Zander added, his innocence not even close to credible.

"Well, I *like* Bonnie Lu, Jayda," Abe chimed in. "You'll honor Lu every time you call this girl Bonnie Lu. No one else will know that you gave her your aunt's name, but the four of us will."

While I sputtered, Zander pulled out his phone and snapped photos of Emilio proudly grinning over his sister. "I'ma text 'Bonnie Lu' to my folks," he told Emilio, "and send them these pics of you and her."

"Cool!" Emilio laid a careful kiss on the baby's forehead. "Hey, little Bonnie Lu! I'm Emilio. Don't worry. Ain't nobody ever gonna hassle you while I'm 'round. Pretty little Bonnie Lu!"

I rolled my eyes. "Oh, brother."

Emilio sighed with great satisfaction. "Yup. That's right. I'm Bonnie Lu's big brother."

facepalm

See, I knew Emilio. Not one thing was ever going to change his mind. His sister's name and his role in her life were fixed—cast in iron. Might as well have a box of t-shirts printed up.

**Bonnie Lu's
Big Brother**

How could I counter or trivialize such devotion?

Heaving a sigh, I gave in.

⌘

LATER THAT EVENING, a timid knock sounded on our door. Zander got up from the chair next to our bed and went to answer it. I heard words from the other side of our security door. It was Mrs. Calderón's familiar voice.

"I . . . I saw Mr. Pickering and the boy come over earlier. I sensed their excitement and thought that perhaps your baby had arrived? And then you called me! Thank you for letting me know. I-I feel so blessed."

"Yup, we do, too! She's a healthy, beautiful baby girl."

"How wonderful! I . . . I am quite delighted for both of you. What with the virus, having your baby at home was wise, wasn't it? And I thought, perhaps, you'd appreciate a hot meal? You have been more than kind to me. Don't know how I would have made it this far without your help. Well, a new mother needs to rebuild her strength, so I brought a few things for your dinner . . ."

In the warehouse, I saw what Zander saw: one of those wheeled carts used by people who walk to the grocery store and need a means of carrying their groceries home. Tied to the cart was a large, closed box. Steam emanated from the box.

"Nano?" They knew what I was asking.

Jayda Cruz, Mrs. Calderón has brought a pot roast, gravy, mashed potatoes, peas, sweet yams, dinner rolls, and an apple pie.

I hadn't eaten all day, and I was ravenous. But then I heard the words of Jesus echo in my heart. *I have food to eat that you know nothing about.*

I set my hunger aside for something greater.

"Zander?" I said in the warehouse. "Would you please invite Mrs. Calderón in to see Baby Cruz?"

Two minutes later, Mrs. Calderón, led by Zander, entered our bedroom. Her hands were freshly washed as Abe and Emilio's had been, and the nanomites had declared her free of the virus. Her face was aglow with repressed excitement.

I smiled a warm welcome. "Would you care to sit down and hold Bonnie Lu?"

Bonnie Lu. I suppose it was catching on. Snagging my heart.

"You named her Bonnie Lu? How precious! Oh, yes. I would like very much to hold her."

Of the many memories of the day our daughter was born, one of the most poignant was that of Mrs. Calderón staring at Bonnie Lu while gently caressing her cheek. Life had come back into the woman's eyes. Hope trembled on her lips.

Lord, thank you for crucifying my heart of stone. Please help me show Belicia Calderón Jesus, the way to you.

⌘⌘⌘⌘

POSTSCRIPT

OUR BONNIE WAS TWO weeks old. She was rosy with health, a happy eater, waking up every two to three hours each night to nurse. Filling out a little. Like my heart was filling out, growing in love and gratitude for her place in our family. I could no longer imagine life without her.

"Zander?"

His head slowly turned toward me. He rested his hand on a page of his Bible, marking where he was reading. "Yes, Sweetheart?"

We were both tired, but Zander's exhaustion was written on his face and in his eyes. How could we have known, when Pastor and Mrs. McFee left on their Hawaiian cruise on New Year's Day, that they would not return to us? That we'd never see them again this side of heaven? That Zander would be thrown headlong into the leadership of DCC . . . or how painful that transition would be?

Yet, since he had preached his unforgettable sermon that second Sunday morning in January, and despite every obstacle the devil raised against us, my beloved husband had labored without ceasing to fulfill the unexpected call of God on his life. With fearless conviction, he had led our church through its political turmoil and out of the schism that followed. His straightforward Bible teaching had kept the core of DCC from fragmenting during horrible protests and attacks. His steady hand had healed us and held us on course as the virus swept the world.

But his labors were taking their toll. Zander's smile as he looked at me was worn and weary . . . and I didn't think it would ever recover its youthful vigor.

"What is it, Love?"

I asked the question that had begun to haunt me. "Zander . . . have we entered the last days? Are we experiencing the first throes of the Tribulation?"

As slowly as he had turned toward me, he nodded. "The last days? Yes."

"I thought . . . I thought the rapture was supposed to come first."

His eyes brightened. "Ah. I think you might misunderstand me. The Bible describes several end-time periods or events. The last days. The rapture or 'catching away' of the church. The appearance and rule of the man of lawlessness—the Antichrist. The seven years of the Tribulation. The Day of the Lord. The resurrection of the dead. Armageddon. The Judgment.

"We cannot predict the date of "the rapture," the moment when God will remove the church from the earth—but we can certainly mark the times and seasons and observe that the rapture is close at hand, but technically? We have been in 'the last days' since the time of Christ."

"How can that be?"

He chuckled softly. "Well, if it was 'the last hour' when the John the Evangelist wrote his first letter to the church, then we can say with confidence that we're living in the *last* of the last hours, the hours leading up to the end.

"The Tribulation, however, opposed to the last days, is a clearly marked-out span of seven years. According to some theologians, we will know precisely when those seven years begin when the church is removed from the earth."

He looked down to his Bible and paged through it. "2 Thessalonians 2. I'll read portions of verses 1-7.

> *"Concerning the coming of our Lord Jesus Christ*
> *and our being gathered to him,*
> *we ask you, brothers and sisters,*
> *not to become easily unsettled or alarmed*
> *by the teaching allegedly from us . . ."*

"Does this *being gathered to him* describe the Rapture?"

"Like I said, some Bible teachers believe it does. Let me read more of the same passage.

> *"Don't let anyone deceive you in any way,*
> *for that day will not come until the rebellion occurs*
> *and the man of lawlessness is revealed,*
> *the man doomed to destruction . . .*
> ***And now you know what is holding him back,***
> *so that he may be revealed at the proper time.*
> *For the secret power of lawlessness is already at work;*
> ***but the one who now holds it back***
> ***will continue to do so till he is taken out of the way.***

"If *being gathered to him* describes the Rapture, then *that day will not come* until the Antichrist is ready to make his move and the world is ready to receive him for who he is. But the Antichrist will be unable to make his move so long as *what is holding him back* is here, restraining him.

"What is restraining him?" I asked.

"Well, those same end-time scholars believe that *the one holding him back* is the Holy Spirit in us—and that does make sense, biblically. The Holy Spirit himself, as carried by the Body of Christ on the earth, restrains sin in the world, keeps the world from complete and total degradation. Oh, the spirit of the Antichrist, the spirit of lawlessness, is certainly alive and gaining ground on planet Earth, but Satan cannot do all he desires until the Lord takes us out of the way."

"So, the rapture of the church is the starting point of the Tribulation?"

"Possibly. Other Bible scholars place the rapture with the resurrection of the dead, in part because of how 1 Corinthians 15:51-52 describes it.

> *"Listen, I tell you a mystery:*
> *We will not all sleep, but we will all be changed—*
> *in a flash, in the twinkling of an eye, at the last trumpet.*
> *For the trumpet will sound,*
> *the dead will be raised imperishable,*
> *and we will be changed.*

"Did you hear that part, *at the last trumpet*? The seventh and last trumpet in Revelation is in chapter 11, and that's at the midpoint of the Tribulation, when the twenty-four elders declare it is time to judge the dead. Thus, proponents of an early rapture and those who hold this view argue that the rapture and resurrections happen concurrently—and that's the problem."

"What's the problem?"

"That they argue over what only God knows. No one can know with certainty how this all plays out. As I said a minute ago, we can certainly mark the times and seasons and observe prophesy as it is being fulfilled, but every single one of us will be surprised when Jesus returns. After all, Jesus said only his Father knows the exact time."

He smiled at me. "I like what I heard an old Bible teacher say about the rapture. He said, 'We need to be ready to go but prepared to stay.' Then we won't be found wanting either way."

"Okay . . . but things are getting bad. If we're not already in the Tribulation, then what in the world is happening?"

He paged through his Bible. "Here we go. Matthew 24:4-7.

> *"Jesus answered: 'Watch out that no one deceives you.*
> *For many will come in my name, claiming,*
> *'I am the Messiah,' and will deceive many.*
> *You will hear of wars and rumors of wars,*
> *but see to it that you are not alarmed.*
> *Such things must happen, but the end is still to come.*
> *Nation will rise against nation,*
> *and kingdom against kingdom.*
> *There will be famines and earthquakes in various places.*
> ***All these are the beginning of birth pains.'"***

Zander looked up. "Notice the phrase, 'the beginning of birth pains.' He seems to be saying that the formal and official tribulation period hasn't kicked in, yet the *birth pains*, the signs leading up to it, have been with us for centuries—some might say even for two millennia."

I blinked several times. "I could have imagined earthquakes, storms, floods, even terrorism. But famine? Here in America? I never thought I'd see the day when America's food supplies would be affected like this virus has affected them. Thank God that we have a full pantry! But what more should we do, straightaway, to secure more of a buffer of food for our family?"

"That's a good question that I believe requires balance. We have to ask ourselves, what is wise, what is prudent? We also have to wrestle with what is excessive, even selfish. We need the Holy Spirit to show us how to be sensible and forward-looking without the supplies we've laid up supplanting our trust in God. Because when all our cautious preparations run out? Our trust had better be in the Lord's provision, not our own."

I nodded, and thought on Zander's and my accelerated metabolisms, how we needed more food than ordinary adults did. I wondered how I would handle real hunger.

Zander glanced again at his Bible. His finger found the verses he was looking for. "We read this, farther on in the same chapter, Matthew 24, verses 36-42.

"'But about that day or hour no one knows,
not even the angels in heaven, nor the Son,
but only the Father.
As it was in the days of Noah,
so it will be at the coming of the Son of Man.
For in the days before the flood,
people were eating and drinking,
marrying and giving in marriage,
up to the day Noah entered the ark;
and they knew nothing about what would happen
until the flood came and took them all away.
That is how it will be at the coming of the Son of Man.
Two men will be in the field; one will be taken and the other left.
Two women will be grinding with a hand mill;
one will be taken and the other left.
Therefore keep watch, because you do not know
on what day your Lord will come.'"

Zander looked up. "I want to read verses 9-13 in Matthew 24, too."

"Then you will be handed over
to be persecuted and put to death,
and you will be hated by all nations because of me.
At that time many will turn away from the faith
and will betray and hate each other,

> *and many false prophets will appear*
> *and deceive many people.*
> *Because of the increase of wickedness,*
> *the love of most will grow cold,*
> *but the one who stands firm to the end*
> *will be saved."*

I shivered. "That sounds . . . that sounds a little like what we've been experiencing. People we thought were solid Christians turning from their faith in Christ. A huge rise in hate toward those who hold fast to Jesus. Definitely more false prophets and their deceptive teachings. Absolutely a big increase in wickedness."

"We haven't seen the kind of persecution Jesus talks about in these verses, though," Zander said. "Not here in the US, anyway. Not yet. In other countries? You heard Tian describe what her government did to her pastor and church. China's treatment of faith—any faith—is unconscionable. They tear down churches and imprison pastors, put Muslims in concentration camps, and dehumanize the members of some sects, using them as nonconsenting organ donors.

"Many European countries prohibit any type of public display of faith, and Christians in Islamic nations and some African countries where Islam is growing are dying daily for their faith. Brothers and sisters, fellow believers in Christ, have been beheaded or burned alive in their churches, their children stolen from them."

Our eyes turned as one to our baby, and I grabbed her up and held her to my heart.

"What does all of this mean for Bonnie?" I whispered.

Zander didn't answer for a long time, and I could see him struggling with his emotions. "We must surrender Bonnie to the Lord, Jayda. Like all the other parts and pieces of our lives."

My countenance might have held steady as I processed Zander's reply, but inside?

Inside I was dying.

Lord, I cried. *This is our child, the baby you gave us! She is innocent! Is there no place we can take her where she will be safe? What are we to do?*

It was as though Zander had heard my thoughts.

"Jayda . . . the only safe place in this universe is Jesus himself. We know *him*—and we must train Bonnie to know Jesus, too. We must trust him to see her through what is coming . . . as we are trusting him to reach Emilio."

I looked down at the soft curls atop Bonnie's head. Watched her breaths puff in and out, each one as soft as a caress.

I couldn't help it. A sob leapt from my throat. "I'm sorry. It's just . . ."

Zander scooted his chair up beside us, and I caught a glimpse of the husband I knew and loved so much. His tired eyes shone with peace. "It's just what? It's that you love Bonnie Lu?"

"Yes. I do. Oh, yes!"

"And I love Bonnie Lu, right?"

"Yes. You are her proud Papa!"

Zanders arms went around us both. "And we know that the Lord loves Bonnie even more than we do, Jayda."

Drawing from the wealth of Scripture within him, Zander quoted a passage from Romans 8.

> *"Who shall separate us from the love of Christ?*
> *Shall trouble or hardship or persecution*
> *or famine or nakedness or danger or sword?*
> *As it is written: 'For your sake we face death all day long;*
> *we are considered as sheep to be slaughtered.'*
> *No, in all these things we are more than conquerors*
> *through him who loved us.*
> *For I am convinced that neither death nor life,*
> *neither angels nor demons,*
> *neither the present nor the future, nor any powers,*
> *neither height nor depth, nor anything else in all creation,*
> *will be able to separate us from the love of God*
> *that is in Christ Jesus our Lord."*

"Zander, what about Emilio? He doesn't know Jesus. He still resists the tug of the Holy Spirit. And Ross and Janice? We love them dearly, but they don't believe either. I-I fear for them, Zander, and I fear for our boy."

Exhaustion again drew down Zander's features. "We will keep praying for them, sharing the gospel with them, even confronting and warning them when we can, asking the Lord to draw them to himself . . . but their response is up to them, Jayda. They alone can say yes to him when he calls them."

He pulled back so we could look eye to eye. "We may not know what the immediate future holds, but we do know what awaits us in eternity.

"So, what will you and I do, Jay? How will we respond to the chaos swirling about us and sweeping the earth?"

I swallowed. Pressed my lips together to stop their quivering. Formed my response. "We will . . . we *will* . . . fix our eyes on our Messiah, our shining 'Mehitah'ess,' the bright and Morning Star—the author, finisher, and perfecter of our faith!"

"All our hope is in Jesus and in his word."

"He *is* the Word of God." I whispered. "Do you hear that, little Bonnie Lu? Jesus is the Word of God—and he loves you."

My beloved husband's eyes filled. His arms slipped beneath mine so that we held Bonnie between us. Nose to nose, Zander stared deeply into my soul.

"We have the Bible—the right map for our journey, Jay. And we have Jesus. He will steer us straight and true."

I stared back, my confidence rising. "Yes. He *will* guide us—all the way home. And he will be waiting for us when we get there—"

I turned my head. "What is that?"

Zander heard it, too. A melody, a song sung by many small voices, slowly swelled around us. The refrain repeated, grew louder and clearer until we could follow its words.

> *We lift our eyes to Jesus*
> *We place our hope in him*
> *We give our all to Jesus*
> *And we follow, we follow*
> *We follow him*

The nanomites were . . . singing a song of worship? Its haunting melody was unfamiliar to me but it tugged at my heart. It urged me to join in. Was it a song they had composed themselves?

Their voices rose. Higher. Stronger. More majestic. Until they burst into harmonies I will never be able to describe.

I remembered what they had told President Jackson.

We choose to follow Jesus, to align ourselves with him. After all, his word says the mountains and hills will break into song and the trees of the fields will clap their hands. Why should we not worship our Creator, too?

Why not, indeed?

Zander and I closed our eyes. We worshipped with them.

> *We lift our eyes to Jesus*
> *We place our hope in him*
> *We give our all to Jesus*
> *And we follow, we follow*
> *We follow him*

The End

MY DEAR READERS

THANK YOU FOR reading *Stealth Insurgence*. I hope and pray you have been strengthened and built up in your faith while reading this book. I also pray that you have set your heart to stand strong for Jesus in the coming days, *the beginning of birth pains*.

Nanostealth isn't over yet! Continue the journey with *Stealth Triumph* and *Stealth Genesis*, A Nanostealth Prequel. When you finish these books, you won't want to miss my **Laynie Portland** spy series, five nail-biting books that spin off from the last book in my **Prairie Heritage** series or **The Tahoe Mysteries**, my newest series!

To keep abreast of my publication schedule and to receive free, read-ahead chapters of upcoming books, I invite you to visit my website (http://www.vikkikestell.com) and sign up for my newsletter.

Thank you again. I have the best readers in the world—you. It is an honor.

Many hugs,
Vikki

ABOUT THE AUTHOR

VIKKI KESTELL'S passion for people and their stories is evident in her readers' affection for her characters and unusual plotlines. Two often-repeated sentiments are, "I feel like I know these people," and, "I'm right there, in the book, experiencing what the characters experience."

Vikki holds a PhD in organizational learning and instructional technologies. She left a career of twenty-plus years in government, academia, and corporate life to pursue writing full time. "Writing is the best job ever," she admits, "and the most demanding."

Vikki and her husband, Conrad Smith, make their home in Albuquerque, New Mexico.

To keep abreast of new book releases, sign up for Vikki's newsletter on her website, **http://www.vikkikestell.com**, find her on Facebook at **http://www.facebook.com/Vikki.Kestell**, or follow her on BookBub, **https://www.bookbub.com/authors/vikki-kestell**.